THE
Honeymoon
COTTAGE

MATTHEW TYNDALE

WESTBOW
PRESS®
A DIVISION OF THOMAS NELSON
& ZONDERVAN

WestBow Press books may be ordered through booksellers or by contacting:

WestBow Press
A Division of Thomas Nelson & Zondervan
1663 Liberty Drive
Bloomington, IN 47403
www.westbowpress.com
1 (866) 928-1240

ISBN: 978-1-9736-9688-9 (sc)
ISBN: 978-1-9736-9687-2 (e)

Library of Congress Control Number: 2020912854

Print information available on the last page.

WestBow Press rev. date: 8/6/2020

Prologue

I SAT STARING at the City from the rear deck of my boat anchored on The Brisbane River. This was a sheltered spot not more than thirty metres from The Botanical Gardens situated on the river bank. It was Friday evening and through the canyons of the city buildings I could see office workers as they scurried home for the weekend. Others, whose laughter bounced across the water, were dashing to their favourite nightspot. The late storm I had been expecting, moved steadily up the river from Pelican Bay. Large drops of rain began to splatter on the cabin top, increasing in intensity until nothing could be heard above the roar of the tropical downpour. The reflection of the city lights on the water around me, was splintered into sparkling foam by the pounding rain. I reluctantly moved into the cabin and closed the door behind me.

The storm had ushered in the night and I sat in the darkness enjoying the solitude with a cigar and Single Malt. The boat was a 1979 built 37ft beauty, which was finished in white with plenty of varnished timber trim. Earlier today I had purchased this craft from it's original owner who lived in the upper reaches of the river. Tomorrow morning I would continue my passage downstream into the Bay, then up the coast to Redcliffe and home. The weather report had promised a fine day and I knew it would be a wonderful cruise.

I switched on the television which I could hardly hear above the storm and one of those genealogy shows flickered across the screen. Some celebrity was digging through dusty archives in a search for their family history and showed photographs and documents from the past. As the storm eased I took more notice of the program and it set me thinking of my own past. Who were my ancestors? What had brought me here to this boat on this river, in Queensland Australia, on January the 20th 2018? I gave my memory free reign, took out my laptop and began to write.

Introduction

IT WAS SPRING 2018 and as I drove across the new bridge to the town of Redcliffe my face was gently caressed by the cool sea breeze. Childhood memories flooded through my mind like the tide beneath me.

Redcliffe in the 1960's was a small holiday and fishing village north of Brisbane. The Redcliffe Peninsula was reached by driving across the old Redcliffe Viaduct, which was the name of the bridge connecting Redcliffe with Woodgate. Two huge concrete spans have long ago replaced the wobbly old wooden bridge.

For the toll of one shilling visitors used to make the trip across the shallow water of Cod Inlet and enjoy a time of rest and recreation on one of Redcliffe's fine beaches. Small price to pay to enjoy a holiday in the genuine Queensland paradise we called our home. Holiday houses were common and the foreshores would be filled with happy campers, who would pitch their tents for weeks or longer at the many beach camping areas. Fishing and family fun were the names of the game in the Queensland sun. One was never far from the sparkling blue waters of Pelican Bay, with the dazzling white sand hills of the Islands in the distance to the East.

In my mind these days were indeed the good old days. When I refer to the Redcliffe Peninsula as being a paradise, I'm probably thinking of the time period in Australia during the 50s and 60s.

To me, this period was a paradise no matter where one lived in the world. The times in which we now live, seem miserable confused and mercenary by comparison.

I realise we tend to look through rose coloured glasses whenever we reminisce but some look through dark glasses and miss the truth. It was a time of great freedom and prosperity after the Second World War and yet it was a period which saw the growth of a great and sustained fall in morals. I see this now with the benefit of hindsight but back then I would have seen the change and called it progress along with everyone else. We now know that progress at any cost is not progress at all but just the opposite. Situational ethics and a kind of self–righteousness became the benchmark of behaviour for much of this New World. Morals and good manners took the last train for the coast and were never seen again. Bible based standards of righteousness were gradually seen by some as outmoded and by many as old fashioned.

However, this was not to be the case with Quinny whose whole family held views on every subject, which were black and white all the time. Quinny was a mate of mine back in the late 50's and early 60's. I learned later that his family would be seen as left–wingers, while mine would be seen as right-wingers. This information wasn't necessary or pertinent to our lives at that time. One either believed in God and the Queen or one didn't. In this political climate it's a wonder we became mates at all. Our backgrounds were totally different. I was born in County Darnley England, while Quinny had entered this world in Brisbane, Queensland Australia. We were both born in the year 1948, which for both countries was a time of rebuilding after the war. It was a bustling time plenty of jobs and prosperity just around the corner.

Dad was a builder in England with a very good business. His brother ran the family farm. Even at my tender age I knew we were fairly well off, not rich but better off than most financially.

The other kids in the village called my younger brother and me the 'posho' kids. Maybe because we went to school and Sunday school on a regular basis and didn't live in a Council house.

Maybe it was because Mum wouldn't allow us to join the Boy-scouts with those 'other' boys down the lane.

I don't think Mum's attitude was quite in keeping with Lord Baden Powell's vision for the Scouting movement in our region and the rest of the known world. Come to think of it, we weren't allowed to join the cricket club or the football club either but we always had plenty to do at home. We played together, with the dog, in the field and stream behind our house, even when it was cold and snowing. We played in Dad's building yard practising our bricklaying skills with his expensive unmarked new bricks, turning most of them into common bricks before being chased off into the house by 'the men'. I remember Sunday drives and holidays at the seaside.

The weather in the North of England can make life very difficult for those who work in the building trades and I know Dad found this a real problem. Constant battles with snow, rain and frost must have driven him to distraction. This is the main reason Mum and Dad decided to pack up the family and take us all to Australia where the sun is constantly shining.

The Sun is a wonderful star but it's constant shining can make the building game fairly average sometimes. Too much sun, too much snow. What are you going to do? I know Dad suffered as a 'new chum' when he first started working in the Queensland sunshine but we were happy in our house at Seaside Avenue Garborough. What a huge change it was for my parents to move to the other side of the world with a young family and settle in to a completely new lifestyle. What a great adventure it was for all of us. However, even the most epic adventures have their downside as we will discover. The move from a green and pleasant land to a brown and boisterous one, would not be easy for some.

Chapter 1

"WOULD YOU BOYS like a lolly?" asked Aunty May, our short Maltese Aunty, who was calling to my younger brother and me from the top step at the rear of her house. Her house was situated in Langford, a suburb north of Brisbane. The year was 1958.

"Yes please," we answered in unison.

She threw down two of what we called sweets. We hid our disappointment on this hot day. We were confused and not for the first or last time since arriving in Australia a short time ago. The word lollie to us meant an iced lollie, or ice block. A small disappointment you might say but a relevant one to us considering the hot weather. We ate our lollies and marvelled at the number of ants on the ground and just about every other surface in this country. How to avoid walking on them, or having them walk on us? It was just one more burning question.

We stayed with Aunty May and Uncle Clarry for a few days. They had met and married when Clarry was a Digger during the war. He was a typical Aussie. I remember being enthralled while watching him roll his daily ration of cigarettes while sitting at the kitchen table with his cup of steaming black tea. I remember his brown wrinkled face, his big ears and big smile. He would wink at me across the table, when Aunty May voiced her disapproval of his smoking. I could tell he idolised her. She always wore black clothing. I hadn't seen this before and asked uncle about it. He told me that a lot of Continental women dressed like this.

I asked him in my broad little 'Geordie' accent "Is that why she talks funny?"

He replied "Yes lad. She's French you know. She left the convent to marry me." He winked.

That night as I lay in bed in the sleep-out at the front of the house I listened to the trams rattling along Langford Road.

I wondered why everyone except those from the North of England spoke with a strange accent. This was a very exciting time. The next day I learned that we would soon be moving to Aunty May and Uncle Clarrie's holiday house in Garborough, while Mum and Dad looked for a house to buy. Dad would also be looking for work. As I say, a very exciting time.

I hadn't given it any thought but my brother and I were told we would then be able to go to school. Garborough State school would be the school of choice.

I think it was Uncle Paul's Australian Holden car. which took us over to Garborough. It had very impressive red leather upholstery. From memory, he was the husband of Aunty May and Uncle Clarrie's daughter. I think their house was next door in Langford Road. The relationship of family members wasn't very important to me at that age but cars had always been and still are. As we bounced our way across the Redcliffe Viaduct, it seemed that the sparkling blue water of Pelican Bay was welcoming us to our new home. Trawlers and pleasure craft criss-crossed the bay in lines of white foam. We were all amazed at the colour of the red soil. Even Dad, who had been born into farm life, had never seen the like of it before.

We arrived at the holiday house to be greeted by more red soil and more ants. After a childhood of listening to wee birds whistling tunefully, the raucous screeching Australian birds with their brightly coloured plumage and odd names, made quite a change for me. I'm sure we were all in the same boat with that experience. What a beautiful place Garborough was in the late 50's.

We were in paradise at last and it had been a very long journey. In this part of the world not many people wore hats, or even shoes. While Mum made sure we started each day wearing shiny shoes, I quickly learned to take them off as soon as I was out of sight. At school I did as the other children and removed my shoes, putting them in my school 'port' until the day was over.

I remember my first day of school in Australia as if it were yesterday. Funnily enough, my brother who is only eleven months younger than I am, doesn't remember it being a traumatic experience at all. He remembers very little of our early days in England, or the trip to Australia. When we discuss these event now, we come to the conclusion that a ten year old boy sees the world very differently to a nine year old.

We were packed off to school in our best clothes, new crew-cuts (and shoes) and were taken to our classrooms to be introduced to the class and stared at. My school teacher Mr Cuthbert, urged the other children to be kind to me and help me through this difficult time. I don't remember what my brother's experience was on his first day. I hope it was better than mine. More humiliation was to come however. While sitting in class wondering what I had done to deserve this fate, a bell rang somewhere and everyone filed outside and into the playground. What's going on? Is school finished at this hour of the morning? Joy of joys, oh happy days. But wait, Mr Cuthbert is saying something.

"Aren't you going out for your little lunch Matty?"

"My little what?" I replied, 'Sir' I added succinctly. I was in no mood for communication of any kind, unless it was someone in authority telling me I could go home.

"Your little lunch. Don't you have any? This is when we have our morning break."

Somewhere deep inside I heard a penny drop "Do you mean morning tea?" I asked quietly.

I realised we weren't going to be fed and watered like in our English schools and began to feel hungry, stupid and lonely. I'm sure I had tears in my eyes, well almost. Dear Mr Cuthbert placed his arm around me which was a great comfort and halted any crying urges I may have had. We shared his own 'little lunch'. Another bell sounded, the other kids filed back into the room and we all sat down at our desks. Mr. Cuthbert gave me a wink. I knew he wasn't going to mention my little lunch faux pas to the rest of the class.

When it was time for big lunch I was more prepared for it but not with sustenance. Once again my teacher shared the tea from his Thermos with me, and talked about his new Ford Prefect 100E. It was pale blue with red interior and parked in pride of place under a shady tree in the playground. I was feeling much more at ease now in my surroundings.

"Would you keep your eye on it for me during play time Matthew? I don't want it getting damaged by any of the rough children with their cricket balls and such."

"I'll watch it. Can I go close and have a look?" I asked.

"Yes Matthew but no one else."

I thought it was one of the most beautiful cars I had ever seen. Dad had always had Prefects in England, but earlier models. Later on in the year one of the head teachers did show up with a better car. He bought a black and grey Ford Customline V8. He called it Blackbird but he never parked it under Mr Cuthbert's tree. After that day, my mother always packed us an embarrassingly large, almost picnic standard meal, for our little lunch and big lunch.

Our early trips to school on the Green bus were interesting, to say the least. Neither of us had ever been on a bus before, so in a sense it was a great adventure buying a weekly ticket and having the conductor punch it for every trip. The conductor was the only one allowed to stand while the bus was moving. I was impressed by his nimbleness and the tools of his trade which were carried around his waist in aged leather pouches. I particularly liked the shiny alloy ticket machine with which he dispensed the relevant ticket, with the punch of some buttons and the flick of a lever. The driver drove the bus and the conductor looked after the passengers. He kept the other kids in line when they poked fun at us with our fresh crew-cuts, strange accent and shiny shoes.

"Hey you kids, leave the new chums alone!"

We weren't the 'posho' kids any more, we were the baldies. Fair dinkum, sometimes you just can't win. The conductor would wink at those whom he considered his regulars. The whole system made the trip enjoyable for me.

My brother and I quickly learned the pecking order among the boys at school and the way to establish ones self was through fighting. These fights were totally unavoidable and usually took place during the lunch break or after school. The inevitability of them amazed me. I didn't realise ten year old boys could be so territorial. It was like living Lord Of The Flies.

We were both strong boys and a good size and we stuck up for each other. Before I decided to test myself I watched a few of these fights. They were more like wrestling scuffles with one ending up sitting on the other's chest while on the ground and preventing the opponent from getting up. The loser's arms and hands would be pinned thus preventing any retaliation and bringing about the end of the 'fight'.

As kid's fights normally do they quite often lead to more fights until a sort of mutual truce is agreed with a grudging admiration achieved usually followed by friendship. I didn't do too badly in these scuffles once I learned the art of leverage and counterweight. I had a plan and it worked. Of course, once I began to win I was everyone's friend and included in all activities, even some activities which weren't allowed.

Success with girls in England must have come through who you were. The class system I suppose. In early Queensland it was more about where one stood in the local order. Isn't this a sort of class system, with the onus on the individual having to prove who they are amongst the other roosters and chickens? I found that girls were more interested in being around me after my social position had been established. This was very important to me at that time but that, as they say in the classics, is another story.

Chapter 2

MY FATHER JOHN Tyndale, was a gentleman in the true sense. I never heard him curse or swear and I never heard him utter a bad word about anyone. He didn't hang around Pubs or gamble. He was always quick to listen, slow to speak and ready to help those in need. He wasn't proud, loud or brash. He loved Mum and the rest of us and until he became ill, was always interested in our lives. One can't ask for more than that from his father. Having said that, I don't remember having sat on his knee or received a hug. He used to send me on a strange errand occasionally. Chip was the nickname Simon and I shared.

He'd say, "Chip, run to the shed and get me a sheet of sandpaper lad, if you would."

Dad used the sandpaper to trim his toe nails which were as hard as iron. I do remember him coming to my sickbed when I was young, on more than one occasion when I was suffering a bad cold. He would bring his own special recipe for such an occasion. A mixture of butter, chest rub, sugar and honey formed into cubes designed to sit on the tongue, melt and be swallowed. This was wonderful Doctoring.

I remember Dad hitting me on only one occasion. I was being cheeky to Mum and I didn't notice him enter the room. The resulting backhander sent me rolling through the door and into the other room. No words were exchanged but a lesson learned. I knew why I had a sore head and I wasn't cheeky to my mother any more. This did not result in me hating my father and the world in general, like in the modern movies. It resulted in me being chastised for my bad behaviour, no more, no less. It was called discipline back in the day but in this undisciplined world it would be called assault. Go figure.

He was always one for fixing things. He seemed to have a gift for building or fixing anything, any time, anywhere. I used to watch him working through these projects he would undertake, whether in the shed or on the building site and I strove to be like him.

I found out later on that all Dads were not like mine, in more ways than one. As it turned out, I inherited his gift of building and fixing, which is probably why I ended up taking a trade rather than being a teacher as Mum wanted. All of the siblings were encouraged to be confident and self sufficient by our parents but I think this training alone is not quite enough to get us through our lives. Having confidence in our own abilities is very important and more than that, being confident in who we are. Mum was the type of mother who would always stress that we must remember 'who we are' whenever we went somewhere even slightly important. There was a certain manner of appearance and behaviour which was expected of us all. I didn't fully understand it when I was young but found myself teaching my own children the same.

Being brave and honest was important in our household as well. These are two traits I noticed missing in many other families as I grew up. This phenomenon could have been a sign of later times more than anything else or even a lack of personal discipline in some families. I know Dad was a disciplined and steady character. Among the medals he won during the Second World War was the George Medal for bravery which he earned during his time in Bomb Disposal. In Normandy he was one of the hundreds of troops evacuated from the beach, while under heavy air and artillery attack at Dunkirk. He also carried the King's commendation for bravery with an Oak leaf on his War medal. Dad was heroic but more than that, he was my hero and still is, even though he passed away many years ago. I know nothing of his dreams or fears. He obviously believed in working hard to support his family, because that's what he did.

Mum and Dad were a couple of the original house renovators who bought, lived in and sold houses. This was profitable for them. Who knows? They may have been better staying in England and continuing rather than coming to Australia. Hindsight really is a luxury.

We were one of the first families on the Peninsula to have a television set. My brother and I couldn't remember a time when we didn't have one. I don't know whether it was the same for my older brother and sister who lived through the war years. One of the first programs I remember watching was the tied Cricket Test in Brisbane between Australia and The West Indies. I was barracking for Australia. My favourite player was a West Indian pace bowler. When we moved into our own house in Australia, the Ice-man was still travelling around the streets selling blocks of ice for the many ice chests in which people kept their perishable groceries. The average ice chest looked something like a small refrigerator. Refrigeration came later when Dad purchased a brand new Silent Knight Refrigerator with a built-in ice cube tray. Apparently they were fairly expensive to run because the motor wasn't controlled by a solenoid switch and ran all of the time. This was later replaced by a Westinghouse refrigerator, with built in freezer compartment.

The Fruit man, the Bread man, the Milk man and the Rawleighs man all plied their businesses around the suburban streets but the most obvious of them all, was the 'Dunny' man. Most houses in Queensland at that time, if they didn't have a septic for their waste, had an outside toilet usually down the back garden. Inside this small structure was a wooden cabinet, which contained a large can, to which access was gained through a small wooden door at the front. This can, for the purpose of cleanliness and germ control was coated with a creosote mixture. A box of sawdust stood beside the cabinet. A couple of handsful of sawdust were added to the can after each visit, to cover up the last deposit. The lid was then supposed to be dropped to keep the flies out. Some folks forgot to close the lid in their haste to vacate the premises. The smell inside the outside dunny, particularly during a long Queensland summer, was interesting to say the least. It is firmly etched into my memory. Dunny was the slang word used for these toilets because they were usually as dark as a dungeon inside and presumably as smelly.

Spare a thought for the people who had the job of driving around the streets in their trucks with the lidded receptacles on the back. The men would have to run into each property with a clean can on their shoulder, in which they would carry the fresh sawdust to dump into the sawdust box. The full and sometimes overflowing can was then slid from the cabinet and the new clean can installed. The full can was then heaved onto his shoulder after a badly fitting lid was added. The brave man then ran out of the property with various indescribable substances splashing down his back. He then deposited the full can into it's place on the truck. He and his mate, who looked after the dunnies on the other side of the street, would then drive a bit further up the road followed by a swarm of groupie-like flies to repeat the process ad-nauseum. We all assumed they must be very well paid for doing this work. They and the garbage men, who also came running into the yard to empty the bin, were always cheerful and friendly to the householders. If we didn't do well at school, we were advised by the teachers that we would end up with a job like these if we didn't study harder. Some kids thought this would be an excellent outcome and played up like second- hand washing machines.

I found school work easy and can honestly say I liked school. Looking back, I don't know why I didn't get more involved with sport. Until I went to High School this was to be the way it turned out. I almost hate to say this but I think I was more interested in girls. I was certainly intrigued by these wonderful people. Of course, I now see that this attitude was probably a kink in the hose pipe of priorities.

At the age of twelve I became a rebellious teenager and my behaviour at school suffered. In my Scholarship year, which was Grade 8. the year before High School, I too played up like a second-hand washing machine. It was suggested, in no uncertain terms by the school masters, that I take my desk and chair onto the verandah, where my unruly behaviour wouldn't upset the plebs. That was my classroom until we all went to High school. Ho hum.

My report cards always said things like, 'Matthew isn't trying hard enough,' or 'Matthew would achieve much more if he applied himself to his work.' I think they really meant 'We're glad he's going to High School soon.' My heart goes out to my big brother. He was enjoying his first posting as a young teacher at Garborough School this same year. I wonder if he ever admitted to anyone that I was his little brother. He had his own car of course and he would drive me to school sometimes. I thought this was really cool. The school- work was quite easy though, and I was able to hear the lessons from my perch outside. During this time when I was enjoying the freedom of the school to go wherever and whenever I pleased, as long as I didn't upset the other students, I met Quinny. Ronald Owen Quinn was his name, and we were to become mates.

I was walking back to class from the toilet block. He was carrying a rubbish bin and picking up paper scraps and other rubbish in the playground. A teacher stood nearby keeping an eye on his progress. I paused for a while and watched his progress for a moment also. It was obvious from his spiky demeanour that he wasn't performing this service on a voluntary basis.

I said "G'day mate".

He replied quietly, "Is the weacher totching?"

After saying this, he became more agitated. I glanced at the teacher, who was standing with his back toward us and said, "No he's not."

He stopped what he was doing for a moment and said, "Sorry about that. When I get nervous I talk in...."

"Spoonerisms?" I ventured a guess.

"Yeah, how did you know?" He asked me with a frown.

"Quinn! get back to work. You,....Tyndale get back to class or you'll be up to the office."

The supervising teacher had turned around and was advancing on us with a thunderous scowl on his face. I headed back to the relative safety of my verandah. The teacher continued berating Quinny until the boy was so tongue-tied he didn't even attempt answering. I knew some teachers could be pretty callous but this was really bad behaviour on his behalf. This was bullying and I hated bullies. As I settled at my desk I knew this teacher was deliberately trying to demean Quinny and I wouldn't forget the incident in a hurry.

Most Queensland schools were high-set in those days to catch the breeze and provide shade for the students to sit and rest, or take part in outside activities in the heat of the day. There were no air conditioners or water coolers in our day. However, we did get a free drink of milk every day. If the milkman had placed the crates of small milk bottles in the shade we would have a drink of cool milk. If not, then our drink could be anything from tepid to quite warm.

It was a Government initiative to help children get sufficient calcium in their diet. I think it was also designed to make sure some of the kids had something to eat at school.

It wasn't until I attended Garborough School that I became aware of certain children who seemed to lack what the rest of us took for granted. A situation developed in which a young English migrant girl was found scrounging through the playground rubbish bins for food scraps to eat. She had only been at the school for a few days and some of the children had already begun to make fun of her behaviour and her dirty, scruffy appearance. This upset me. I had never been aware of poverty before and never been exposed to it at school, that's for sure.

My teacher interrupted an argument between some of us outside the classroom one morning. A couple of us were denouncing others who had been teasing this poor girl. Fortunately she wasn't present to hear this discussion. I knew she must have been going through a very difficult time in this new country, without adding all of this.

This teacher was our Grade 7A teacher. He was a young man and perhaps fairly inexperienced in dealing with these situations. Even as a young child I was adversely impressed by the clumsiness of his attempt to remedy the situation. As we sat in class that morning awaiting our first lesson he asked this unfortunate girl to leave the room for a moment or two.

She left the room and stood against the wall just outside the door. Whatever was said inside the class room could be heard and seen from where she was standing. From where I sat I could see her crying, with her head bowed in embarrassment and shame. Our teacher then proceeded to tell the rest of us how poor and wretched this girl was and how she didn't have any clothes or food. He then told us that she probably had nits and the rest of the girls shouldn't get too close to her. Then he called her inside to take her place in class. She must have been broken- hearted as she sat alone and weeping quietly. She couldn't be consoled and after our first lesson the teacher took her around to the Office, presumably to seek the headmaster's wisdom on the situation. We didn't see her at school after that and I don't think anyone asked what had become of her. I've never forgotten her, or the difference in the way we were treated in our new country, as 'new chums'.

Chapter 3

QUINNY WAS AT the bike racks when I went to pick up my bicycle for the ride home. We pushed our bikes to the school gates and I could tell he wanted he wanted to talk about the incident in the playground when the supervisor had been shouting at him. I don't know why he spoke to me about it. That was the first time I'd met him but I tried to appear interested. He paused for a moment and then he said, "How did you know about the way I talk?"

"You mean Spoonerisms?" I asked.

"Yeah, roonerspisms." he answered excitedly.

I laughed but he didn't seem to mind.

"It's only when I get excited or a bit flustered," he said.

"Well," I replied, "It's when you talk back to front. That's what's called a Spoonerism."

"How did ya know?"

"I read it somewhere. It was named after Dr. Spooner." At this moment I was very happy to have always been surrounded by books as a child. I still love all kinds of books.

"Did he invent it", asked Quinny.

"Don't know. I answered. Probably."

"Well I'll be...." Quinny said. Spoonerisms eh? Good old Dr. Spooner. I'm gonna tell Mum and Dad about this."

"Do ya play footy?" He asked.

"Yeah." I lied.

"What sort?"

"Eh?" I had no idea there were 'sorts' of football. I had heard someone once, talking about Aussie Rules.

Rather than show my total ignorance of sport and being in Australia, I said, "Aussie Rules."

"Ahh, he growled. That's a weird game."

"A weird game?"

"Yeah," he said emphatically.

I allowed this comment to sink in for a moment and then replied, "What do most people play then?"

"Rugby League of course." Quinny replied, as though speaking with a backward child.

"Well of course I play that mostly," I answered as we pedalled towards home.

"What position do ya play?" He then asked.

I was so glad to stop outside my house at this point. I was getting out of my depth. I waved and said "See you later."

"Yeah see ya." he replied. "I live just up the end of the street." He waved as he rode on.

I asked my big brother Godfrey all sorts of questions about Rugby League that night. He suggested that calling people names wasn't a good idea.

I told him, "Quinny calls people names."

He said, "That doesn't surprise me."

When I asked him what he meant, he rolled his eyes, looked at Mum and said, "Forget I mentioned it. Some people are like that."

I was going to be prepared for my new friend Ronald Owen Quinn tomorrow. I'm sure I saw Mum and Dad share a quizzical look as I asked my brother these question, though they didn't say anything.

When I rode my bike out of our gate on on my way to school the next morning, Quinny sat on his bike waiting for me.

"What took ya so long?"

"I was just having breakfast. Why?"

"We never have breakfast. Dad says it's a waste of time.

"Don't you get hungry?"

He didn't answer, he just asked another question as we rode along Garborough road.

"What's your Dad do?"

"He's a Builder." I replied.

"Is he, you must be rich. Does he play footy?"

"Not now, but he used to play Rugby League," I lied.

"What team did he play for." was the next question.

I didn't bother answering him but asked, "What team do you play for?

He answered with obvious pride, "Brothers."

"Oh." I answered.

As we pedalled on I tried to figure out what a team of brothers would look like and made a mental note to ask my brother big brother. I had struggled with this concept of multiple brothers before when told about the Catholic brothers at the College up the road near the Garborough Bowls Club. I wondered if the same brothers were involved with Rugby League as well. Be patient with me. I had enjoyed a very sheltered childhood and Churches generally, can hold many mysteries for a young Anglican boy. Oh well.

When our Religious Instruction classes were called out on the parade ground and we all filed into our various denominations, I was aware that I belonged to one of the big two religions in Australia, maybe the whole world. Quinny belonged to the other and never the twain shall meet. All of the 'other' groups were seen as nothing more than sects, or fringe dwellers and not to be seriously considered. This situation was perfectly normal and acceptable in the late Sixties. We also stood respectfully before the flag and sang God save our Queen with all our hearts and at the top of our voices. This was a wonderful time for white, middle class Australians. We were Colonial and make no mistake, we had a class system which people never mentioned in polite circles. I believe the same class system is alive and well in Australia today.

Foreign names certainly weren't the norm and didn't sit well in the general community. Anglo-Saxon names were the common fare and accepted as cash everywhere. Classes were separated into work- related pigeon holes as ever and most folks seemed quite comfortable with the status-quo. Coloured people were treated with indifference as long as they stayed in their place, or ignored altogether. Even though dark coloured indigenous people must have been prominent in outback areas of Australia, I don't remember seeing them in South-Eastern Queensland. I certainly wasn't aware of any on the Redcliffe Peninsula. If indigenous people were seen, it was only in a cameo appearance, like a walk on walk off bit player. I'm only commenting here on what I remember seeing as a young boy and I don't mean to upset anyone. I'm striving to portray an honest and open view of a particular time and place and it's affect on young Australians. I never witnessed any hatred or dislike aimed at any particular group. Most seemed to be judged by the adults, on how hard they worked and how 'decent' they were. 'Ratbags' of any colour or creed were scorned in the community. Ratbag is a wonderful and descriptive Australian slang word.

It is a word which describes quite adequately a raggedy, annoying, non- productive individual who tends to be a loose cannon. What a great slang word for a new chum to learn and use.

We arrived at school and slotted our bikes into the bike racks. I removed my shoes and placed them in my schoolbag ready for the day's play. Quinny didn't wear shoes. He told me once that he didn't have any. I think each person in my family, both child and adult, would have possessed three or four pairs of shoes to cover most occasions. Walking around with bare feet all of the time made the bottom of the feet as hard as old leather. Quinny could stand barefoot on bitumen road on a hot summer day without any ill effect. He wasn't Robert Crusoe in this. Many people, including adults didn't wear shoes, even during the winter months.

"Dad says I've got feet as hard as boot-leather." Quinny stated proudly as we strode across the playground.

"What do you mean a boot-leather?"

"Like boots...you know?"

"Yes," I assured him I did indeed know.

"Did you finish your homework?" I asked.

"Nah, Dad said homework's a waste of time. Anyhow, I 'll see you at little lunch." He ran off in the direction of the office. I was left wandering up to my class wondering what sort of Dad this was. I was thinking he was totally different from mine. I didn't know why at the time but I started wearing my shoes more and more when at school. With the benefit of hindsight I can see that times were beginning to change. At Garborough State School times began to change, when three British kids attended for a while in the final year of Primary school. They went on some years later to become rich and famous. They also wore shoes.

I was learning to play the guitar by this time and we talked together about music. They left our school soon after and that was the end of our association. It's a pity, because we could have stayed in touch. These days it would have been called networking. It did encourage me to continue playing my guitar and as soon as Quinny learned I could play, he thought he should also. Quinny had a plan. Actually he had heaps of plans. He was always having ideas and plans.

"We could start a band." he said.

"But you can't play anything or sing." I replied.

"You could show me. Think of the girls we could meet."

I did think of the girls we could meet, so I decided to form a band. We would just need some members and maybe some talent. I knew I could do it but in my immediate circle of friends I couldn't see any likely musicians. This was the era of the four-piece band and the singer-songwriter. I was going to be both. It was C, F, Am and G and clever rhyming for me.

Chapter 4

I REMEMBER AT the onset of my teen years I became mildly interested in the make up of other families. I think this is a normal response among young people and sleepovers, after school visits and such, are the result of this new found curiosity.

The Quinn family, consisting of Ronald Owen's father Adrian, mum Joyce, his older sister Jenny and younger sister Elaine, lived just up the road from my place. A clean, neat, low-set weather board home with clean neat gardens. It had a carport on one side which contained the neat little car. They had a not so clean and tidy Blue Cattle dog which like most of it's breed, enjoyed chasing cars..... and bikes, birds cats and other dogs who came too close to his territory. Inevitably of course, this dog's name was Bluey. Quinny's father's pet name for the dog was 'you stupid beast'.

Our home, which housed me, my father John, mother Sarah, older brother and sister Godfrey and Abigail and younger brother Simon, was a weather board house with reasonably neat and tidy gardens and lawn. Out front was a white fence and blue iron gates. Also out front was our dog which was a boisterous Springer Spaniel called Leo. In the double-doored garage lurked our Ford Prefect 100E. Leo's party trick was to run in and out of any open door, including cars, with his large, furry and wet muddy feet.

At times like this I discovered he had several pet names as well, one being 'you great hairy beast'. This epithet would be applied to many, by many, as we entered another age of long haired musicians. Quinny was wiry and energetic but when I first met his parents I was struck by their apparent weariness. Thin and tired was the way I would describe them. Mrs Quinn was a nice lady and very friendly from the day I first met her. She was working in the kitchen or at the sink whenever I saw her.

She was always smiling but In a tired way, according to my memory and her two daughters looked the same. My memories conjure up images of prettiness and pleasantness which made a young boy feel very comfortable.

Mr Quinn, however was a different kettle of fish. He was tall, thin and weary in a policeman sort of way. He was the Senior Sergeant at the Police station. Mrs Quinn said he worked long hours and overtime, whatever that was. He was what my mother would have called, an ill-mannered and uncouth person. He always seemed to be swearing and one of his most endearing qualities, at least in the mind of a young boy. This was truly intriguing stuff. He would always say, whenever Quinny and I were hanging out at his place, "I hope you two boys aren't playing up. I'll be on your case if ever I catch you."

This sort of hinted threat was very effective back in the day, in controlling errant youth. Many youngsters were sent home to their parents after being found straying from the straight and narrow. This was a far more desirable situation than allowing young folks to run amok unchallenged and ending up before the courts.

I was to find out personally sometime later, that another effective way of policing youngsters was to bundle them into a Police car at the point of transgression and drive them home to their parents for discipline. A rough push would usually be employed, to help the offender into the vehicle prior to transportation.

Don't get me wrong, the real crims were treated very forcefully by the Police and rightly so. With the benefit of hindsight I can see the result of the pressure of Police work on the faces of Quinnie's parents. Sometimes it can bring great stress into the whole household.

To the young people in every era however, the Police are just ever-present and their brief is seen as spoiling everyone's fun. One thing I must add, is this. We always respected the Police, especially when it was 'a fair cop'. Concerning the Traffic Police, we had a different view. Their brief, in our eyes, was definitely to spoil our fun at all costs.

Having said that, many vehicles on the road back then were held together with wire and probably running on re-grooved tyres. Safety certificates were non-existent in Queensland and the road-worthiness of a vehicle, or otherwise, was a totally personal thing. The safety laws of New South Wales and some other states were seen as draconian, to say the least. How dare the Government require the driver to present their vehicle to an inspection station every year.

In later years we also adopted this policy and the uniform colour of the 'Southern' Police. Our khaki Police uniform went by the board in favour of their blue. To the average Queenslander, anyone from down south was considered 'different', and not to be trusted.

The ideas of southerners were generally thought to be left of centre. Ah, those were the days, weren't they? Weren't they?

Quinny and I had just walked into he lounge room of his house, where Mr Quinn was sitting reading the paper. He said loudly," You know Joyce, that Prime Minister wouldn't know if it was day or night in my opinion".

"Oh, Adrian." Mrs Quinn replied from the kitchen.

I marvelled secretly at this wonderfully descriptive language, even though I had no idea what he meant.

I hadn't heard the Prime Minister of Australia described in this way in my own house and Quinny himself didn't bat an eyelid. I assumed he must have felt the same way. Either that or he didn't even hear what had been said. I realised I had never heard anyone talk about politics at home, especially in such an emphatic and colourful way. We sat in his bedroom and talked about his plans to get a guitar. My big brother had bought me my first guitar and I remember how proud I was as I took it out of the box and held it in my arms. Dad would drive me to the music lessons in Cornelius street where the guitar teacher gave lessons every Thursday. The teacher came from The College of Music and drove from Brisbane every week to teach. I asked Dad one day as we drove along, what he thought about our Prime Minister. He looked at me with raised eyebrows and replied,

"He's a good man and a good Prime Minister. Why?"

I told him about him about Mr Quinn's opinion. His laugh echoed around the car for quite a while.

"Your mate's Dad must be a Labour man." he said with a smile.

"I didn't know you were interested in politics." Dad added.

"I'm not really", I answered. Then I asked, "Are you a Labour man Dad?"

"No son, not really," He smiled. "I believe a man should be able to be a free agent in his life, with a minimum of interference from Government agencies".

He then added, "Some people do need the Government to look after them."

That's where the subject ended. I didn't know what a Labour man was but I smiled as well. Dad knew stuff. I thought it important that a boy should know, whether his Dad was a Labour man or not.

The lessons went well. We were learning a well known instrumental. Our first 'Pop' song. I was amazed as I watched our teacher playing and it made me determined to play well every time I watched him. His guitar was a beautiful old American made Gibson. It made my guitar look and sound a bit feeble but

I didn't really care. Even though my fingers were sore, I was just happy to be there playing. As my memory drifts back to those early days, I'm so glad to have had the opportunity to learn to play the guitar. I think I was born to play the guitar and sing. My big brother must have recognised this when he decided to buy me my first instrument.

Quinny was having some trouble advancing his own musical career. The next day at school he told me he had asked his father to buy him a guitar.

"What did he say." I asked as we parked our bikes.

"He said he didn't want me to grow up to be strange like these Pommie bands." Quinny replied.

"They're not strange, they're just blokes in bands." I told him.

"We know that Matty," he said, "But Dad doesn't."

"Do you reckon he'll buy you one?"

"Mum said she would have a talk to him." said Quinny.

"I know, what about If I come around and play him a song? That way he'd see what we're trying to do. You know, start a band. He might want to join."

Well, Quinny thought that was pretty funny and we both laughed all the way to the class rooms.

"You know Matty, that might not be a bad idea." he said with furrowed brow.

"Dad'll be home this arvo, can you come around?"

"I should be able to. Anyway, I'll see you later." I replied. We parted ways and went to our separate rooms. Well, he went to his room and I went to my verandah desk.

That same afternoon after school I asked Mum if I could go and sing a song or two for Quinny's Dad. I told her about our clever plan to sway him into sponsoring his son's musical career. She thought it was an excellent idea and gave me the Ok. With my guitar tucked under my arm I walked up to Quinny's place. On the way I learned a lesson about guitar players and girls.

There was a beautiful girl with long shiny black hair, who lived in the house on the corner of our street. She had never shown much interest in me before but when I walked past she waved from her front garden. I of course changed course immediately and went over to join her at the front gate. She said, "You're Matty aren't you?"

"Yeah." I replied in my best 'muso' manner.

"I didn't know you played guitar," she said, looking at my instrument.

"Yeah, I've been playing a while," I pretended.

"Will you sing something for me?" she asked from the top of her marble pedestal.

By this stage of my musical career I had a repertoire of three songs so I was able to say.

"Ok." I was never shy with a guitar in my hands, even as a young lad.

With one foot up on her gate and the guitar on my knee, I launched into a Jazzy version of 'Blue Moon' and I nailed it.

When I had finished she put her hand over her mouth and then said, "You're pretty good."

I'm sure she had tears in her eyes. Her mother had been watching and listening to the impromptu concert and clapped from the front door. I blushed, said "Thanks," and walked off up the road with a wave. I think I was walking on air. I was supremely confident and in awe of the power of music. I approached Quinny's front door. I was beginning to feel quite the troubadour.

Quinny's Mum ushered me into the lounge room where her husband sat reading his paper.

"Adrian, young Matthew has brought his guitar around to sing us a song."

"Eh," he replied without looking up from the page.

"Do you remember me talking to you about buying young Ronald a guitar?"

By this time Quinny's sisters had entered the room to witness the musical presentation and it's effect on their father. Something happened just after this, which almost caused me to lose my composure. Mr Quinn blew the loudest and longest raspberry just for fun.

"Adrian, that's very embarrassing." said Mrs Quinn. "Now what about some manners please, if you can manage it."

The girls just giggled. I sat down on a chair and struck a loud C chord. I was always confident with a guitar in hand. Under normal circumstances I trod lightly around Mr Quinn. I knew the rest of the family were with me, so I threw caution to the wind. I started singing 'A little Bitty Tear'. I fixed my eyes on the friendly face of Mrs Quinn and ploughed on through the number until the end. There was a short period of complete silence and then everyone except Mr Quinn clapped.

"Don't ya know any Australian songs?" he asked with a laugh.

I almost collapsed at this point until I remembered that 'Waltzing Matilda' could be played using the same chord structure as Blue Moon. I figured that was about as Australian as you could get, so I started playing and singing the only verse I knew. Luckily Mr Quinn knew all the verses so he finished the song with me accompanying him. Then everyone joined in and we all sang it together one more time. I didn't have to sing any more because Mr Quinn stood to his feet and made an announcement.

"I've just had a brilliant idea," he said. "I think young Ronald could learn to do that easily Joyce. Why don't we get him one of those gittars so he can learn?"

Quinny's Mum rolled her eyes as she adjourned to her kitchen saying, "That's an excellent idea Adrian. I'll see about buying one tomorrow."

Young Ronald had a grin from ear to ear. The girls were both smiling at me. I was thinking, 'so this is how mothers work their magic'. Mr Quinn returned to his paper without saying another word.

Mrs Quinn and the rest of the family thanked me as I headed home with my guitar on my back. I didn't have a carry case for it yet. The beautiful girl with the long black hair stood at the gate and waved to me as I walked past. I had to ask myself as I waved back, "Do days get any better than this?"

Chapter 5

I DIDN'T KNOW whether we were 'well off' or not when I was young. I suppose it's all relative anyway. We'll always be better off than some families and worse off than others. Those families who had wall to wall fitted carpets throughout the house, a car and a telephone were considered to be fairly well off. If one or more of the parents played regular golf and took the occasional air flight for work or pleasure, plus enjoyed a flushing toilet inside the house, the family was thought to be quite wealthy. If some sort of ocean-going pleasure craft and a caravan were added into the mix, then that was just out of this world. Many homes didn't yet have a television and even if they did, it may not have been a '21incher.' Having a transistor radio powered by batteries enabling us to have music wherever we went, was considered quite the in thing, particularly for trendy teenagers. I loved listening to music on the wireless, especially the 'hit parades' with which the disc jockeys would entertain us, exposing us to all the overseas music at the twirl of a dial.

The world was shrinking rapidly as our T.V. News programs sans ads, took us into the other States of Australia and the nations of the world. This would be through 'Newsreels', which could be weeks or even months old. These Newsreels would also be show during the interval period at the movies. Churches and pubs were full, while Doctors waiting rooms and Hospitals were comparatively empty, at least in Queensland. Then we were invaded by the 'southern sick' attracted to our free hospital system. We were all terribly up to date with what was going on in the world even though we weren't very interested in a lot of it. After all, not much of it affected us here in Australia. As offensive as the thought may be to many Australians now, the class system was alive and well in the nation then and I believe it still is. Across the world in England, before we came to Australia, the definition of the words 'well off' were different again.

Generally, if someone was said to work in the city, they would more than likely be a professional person like a Banker, Lawyer or Solicitor. This group would be considered well off. They would probably commute into London by train with hundreds of other types doing the same thing for the rest of their working lives. They may have never learned to drive or owned a car but still be thought of as well off. The tradesmen did Ok but they didn't yet know their worth yet in the scheme of things, and no one was about to tell them, for fear of upsetting the status quo. Tradesmen today of course, can be some of the highest earners in the community.....but still only Tradesmen. The Landed Gentry, of course were doing pretty well but the Hoi-Polloi were becoming weary of their airs and graces, and taking every opportunity to pull them down. Having a history of attending the right school was still very important and could set the young person on the road to success. Of course, this situation remains the same today, even though we still hear folks bleating about the benefits of a State School education, compared with that of the English Public school or the Australian Private school.

Those who were low in the pecking order, with no talent or qualifications, particularly if they lived in one of the big cities, were really struggling. They weren't struggling as we might think of it in today's terms but they were literally fighting every day, for their very existence on Earth. If they did find somewhere for themselves and their families to live, it would more than likely cramped in a single room with no heat, no running water except what came through the roof and no toilet other than a filthy shared earth-closet in the back yard or a bucket on the landing. A person's accent would also denounce them and relegate them to a certain type of behaviour. The scale by which an individual was judged started with the polished Oxford accent at the top and proceed down hill to that of the North of England and the East end of London. This was life, even in the 50's and 60's, for many in England.

When we came to Australia, my brother and I stood out, not only for our crew-cuts but also for the way we spoke, our accent and diction. We learned that there was a rounded, cultured accent in Queensland and a sometimes a harsh broad accent. The harsh broad Australian accent tended to grate on the nerves somewhat but for the sake of convenience we decided to mimic it and I suppose over the years we came up with some approximation. It can be difficult for a new chum to fit in, especially when their speech patterns are so different from the locals. I've found it easier to fit in a country where the English language, 'she aint spoke at all mate'.

My understanding as a youngster was that England ruled over the nations of the world and certainly over the oceans of the world. Biggles and Algy and friends (all white of course), ruled the air, outwitting their 'swarthy' opponents with ease. The saying 'the sun never sets on the British Empire', rang true. If not for the expansionism and boldness of British explorers, the world in general, would be in darkness. Anything that wasn't made in England was extremely suspect in quality and British Engineering and Science were second to none. Of course it goes without saying, that our sportsmen were considered unbeatable unless another team cheated, or played in an unsportsmanlike manner. We thought we had the best sailors, car racers, motorcycle racers, footballers, cricketers, golfers, writers, artists, not to mention breeding.

At the risk of mentioning breeding, we had Kings and Queens and their families, which later became 'The Royal family'. What, to a young English boy living in the Colonies, could possibly go wrong? Why do these Colonial countries keep wanting independence?

They just don't know when they're well off. I embraced these thoughts with all my heart, even though I considered myself a Christian. Weren't all English people Christians and weren't all true Christians Anglicans, I asked myself? Good, I thought, that settles it then.

Since those days of course, I've learned that there are no different races but one race, which is the human race, which in turn consists of many people groups. These different groups, according to the Bible, and now geneticists also, are all descended from common ancestors.

Therefore we shouldn't use terms such as us and them, but the inclusive we when discussing national groups. I have heard some well-meaning spokespersons for groups, when talking about the negative effects of racism, refer to their group as 'my people'. This term is as divisive as many other racist comments and can only serve to feed racists' attitudes, as they attempt to identify or define their own 'people'.

However, thoughts such as these didn't trouble the minds of a young boy back in the day. I'm not sure anyone gave this subject much attention back then and I'm sure it wasn't a cause for general discussion. Later, in the 70's, racism became a cause celebre, with many of the inevitable rent-a-crowd jumping on the band-wagon, just to enjoy the resultant public notoriety, and, of course to oppose any Tory government. I do recall Quinny's Dad voicing his opinion one day when I was visiting their house. He said, for the benefit of anyone who would listen, "These hippies...

they're not even black and they're protesting. They're as white as I am, it's got nothing to do with them."

I didn't understand what he was saying back then but on the surface it seemed like a reasonable statement. Suffice to say, we youngsters considered ourselves to be living in a country which our worthy ancestors discovered, liked and took, (read conquered) because they could. We saw nothing untoward about that, after all, it was quite big and it wasn't being used for anything at the time. I didn't understand Mr Quinn but I have to admit I was intrigued by the manner in which he spoke. I didn't hear this kind of talk at home. There were other things which intrigued me about Quinny's Dad.

One day as I was leaving I waved goodbye to him as he watched T.V. In the lounge room of the Quinn house. As usual he was eating peanuts from a container on his lap. He must have decided, for some obscure reason, to share his philosophy for doing so on such a regular basis.

"Young fella", he said, "These are good for you. All the experts say crunchy food is best for you. It's good for your brain."

From the kitchen I heard Mrs. Quinn quietly say, "Oh Adrian".

I filed this jewel away with another one of Mr. Quinn's other favourites, "Boys, It's the squeaky wheel that gets the oil." It took me quite a while to consider the magnitude of the latter saying but I did master it and use it even now. The peanut one, not so much. I must say, I thought they were both shaded by one of my Dad's sayings, and it must be spoken with a broad 'Geordie' accent, "Aye lad, there's brass in dirt."

It means of course that there is a lot of money to be made, being involved in doing things that other people consider too dirty. Another one that's right up there and self explanatory is, "That lad's not right in't' heed." Head is pronounced 'heed' up North. I grew up loving this talk. Mind you, if I'd spoken like that I would have received a severe caution from Dad.

My mother didn't talk like this, although I heard her say 'my giddy aunt' once when frustrated by someone's behaviour. If opposites attract then it's no surprise that Mum and Dad ended up together in England in 1935. Dad was from the Country and Mum was from the Town, in every sense of the words.

Chapter 6

"WUN RON MATTY," shouted Quinny as he rushed toward me down the pitch.

I took off and just made it to the other end as the ball came in from mid-on. It was a direct hit and scattered the stumps.

"No more quick singles Quinny," I shouted. "You'll get me run out."

This was the school competition of 1961. Quinny was a natural with any sort of ball or any sort of bat and excelled in these games. His judgement was always perfect, in spite of his speech impediment which caused him to lapse into spoonerisms when excited. The wicket keeper started to giggle but he soon shut up when I turned and gave him the look.

"No more." I snarled, forgetting my big brother's advice about never losing my cool and immediately regretting it.

The keeper started crying. His captain at first slip said, "There's no crying in cricket Johnson, so that's enough."

By this time we all had to shut up because the bowler had started his run-up and I was facing. He was fast. I managed to get some bat on it and we ran another single. This put Quinny back on strike and there was no way that keeper was coming up to the stumps. From the other end I watched the fast-bowler thunder in and watched Quinny despatch him over the square-leg boundary for six runs. He did that three more times in a row, turning to wave to the keeper each time. This won the game for us and it made me happy to have seen Quinny let his bat do the talking. Both teams gathered in the shade of an old mango tree at the side of the school cricket oval. It was one of four trees which served as viewing areas and changing sheds for visitors and school teams. The visiting team politely clapped us as we gathered to shake hands.

I've always had a super-powered conscience, even as a youngster and when it came time to shake the hand of the wicket keeper I noticed Quinny walk straight past him, without even giving him a glance.

I apologised to him for snarling at him and shook his hand. He apologised for laughing at Quinny. It was all lost on my mate, who just made a snorting noise and walked off rolling his eyes. I learned something that day. The wicket keeper, whose name incidentally was Tishe O'Prince, became as close a friend as a boy from another school can be. I don't know what country his family came from with a name like that but I didn't care. We always enjoyed a joke whenever we played games in future fixtures.

Quinny said later, "Dad reckons he's a foreigner with a name like that."

I didn't answer. What was there to say? His family and mine were different, which made us different but we were mates. It came to light later that the opposing captain had reported the exchange to his Principal and if I hadn't apologised off my own bat, so to speak, I would have been dropped from the team. We live and learn even at a tender age. I decided I would never lose my cool again. Quinny still did.

In the game of cricket there is a certain requirement regarding manners and etiquette.

These days, it seems to have gone by the board. Some nations try to keep the level of on-field behaviour above the gutter level but not many. The modern game reflects the appalling drop in behavioural standards across the board, maybe even reflecting a lack of training in the home.

When we played Rugby League for the School team we were both glad there were no such niceties involved. It was a rough game played by tough people and it was so much fun. We were allowed to be as rough and uncouth as we possibly could be. What a dream game for a young boy to be involved with. These were the days of unlimited tackles, which meant the forward pack got to do a heap of work in the ruck. Then, when the ball was within striking distance of the opponents posts, the ball was spun out to the flashy back line, for them to perform their wizardry and hopefully score a try.

This was really hard work but so much fun. In those days a player had to be big, strong and fearless to play in the forward pack. The scrum was a means of gaining possession of the ball and even gaining ground, if the pack was strong enough and the hooker was clever enough.

The front rowers had to be powerful enough to overpower the opposition forwards and support the weight of the hooker, as he raked for the ball with both legs. If a lad showed some speed and dash, he was allowed to play in the back line as a centre or winger. He would, more than likely, be in a position to test himself against his opposing player with the chance of scoring a try, if swift and elusive enough. Those who played in the forward pack thought it a good game if they walked from the field covered in sweat, dirt and blood. Quinny and I both started in the forwards but I was later played in the centre position, which wasn't as much fun but the back-line boys seemed to attract more attention from the female fans. Ho hum, you win some, you lose some.

Quinny lost interest in the game after we were split up. That was a sad thing because the Garborough School team went on to play in the finals of the Inter-school championships that year. He missed out on our magnificent wins, the glorious defeats, the bus trips and claimed he didn't care. He said he had more important things to do but I think he just needed to do stuff with someone else and not on his own. At times when I was at his house his Dad might say, "How are you boys goin' at footy, orright?"

He obviously never mentioned his drop-out to his father for his own reasons. I didn't question him about it but just said "Yes," and nodded my head in unison with Quinny.

"Have you scored any tries yet?" he would ask.

"I said, "Yes, a couple Mr Quinn," and got a foul look from Quinny.

"Good, what about you boy?" He asked his son.

"Nah," he replied "I don't really care about tries, I like guitar now." My mate turned and walked away from his father and into his bedroom, slamming the door behind him.

"Well, I'll be blowed, that's a weird thing for a boy to say," said Mr Quinn as he walked to the lounge room.

I opened Quinny's bedroom door and walked in. "Shut the door Matty, will ya," he hissed at me. "What did you say that about football for."

I stopped dead in my tracks. I said "What the...?"

"Don't say anything else to Dad about the footy, alright?" He asked.

"Ok, if that's what you want."

"Thanks mate," he said. "Hey, let's play guitar for a while, ya wanna?"

"Ok, for a while." I replied. Having a mate was becoming as difficult as it was fulfilling. Quinny took his guitar out of the box and said, "Can you show me another chord?"

I showed him where to place his fingers to play a C chord and he began to strum it.

"Tap your foot in time with your strumming," I suggested. This was the way my guitar teacher taught me to co-ordinate and keep a beat. I thought it would be good for Quinny's playing as well. He sat on the bed with furrowed brow, tongue sticking out and provided me with one of the funniest sights I'd seen, though I didn't laugh.

I had been showing him some chord formations since the day he was given his guitar by his Dad. I had been there at the presentation, along with his Mum and two sisters. His mother had gone to the music shop and bought the guitar, which was the same brand as mine, except it was Sunburst finish instead of a Creamy colour. We had to wait until Mr Quinn came home from work because Mrs Quinn wanted him to give it their son. No one even asked me whether I would teach him to play the guitar. I thought he would be coming to lessons with me.

Mr Quinn thought proper lessons would be a waste of money. I got the job but I didn't really mind too much, because I had plans of forming a band and Quinny was to be another member of my band. While the mother and sisters smiled at their soon-to-be guitarist son and brother, he was handed the guitar shaped box by his father.

"There ya go son, you'll soon be another Elvis," he smiled.

Jenny and Elaine, Quinny's sisters clapped their hands and cheered, while his Mum's face was beaming with pride.

"Thanks Mum and Dad," he said with a grin.

"We want to make music like the new bands that are coming out now," I said.

"You mean like the English bands?" gushed Jenny.

Mr Quinn looked at me as though I had just flown in from another planet, so I hastily added, "We'll be singing Elvis songs as well." He turned, grunted and departed. "Oh Adrian," said Mrs Quinn.

I had to get my thoughts together quickly. I found myself staring at Jenny as though I had never seen her before. I was suddenly struck by her stunning looks and noticed she was looking at me in a different way.

Did she feel pity for me, or was it some other look I had as yet learned nothing about?

But wait, this is Quinny's older sister, what am I thinking?

As Quinny sat on the side of his bed strumming his guitar my mind was reeling with new thoughts. Fortunately, watching him did bring my thoughts into focus. I realised he couldn't strum and tap his foot together, or even to the same beat.

"Hold on mate, you're kidding aren't you? You're joking right?" I asked. Kids can be very tough with each other sometimes. Can't they?

"What?" asked Quinny.

"Well, you're not following a beat," I told him.

"Yeah, I am" he replied.

"But your strumming and your foot are supposed to be following the same beat, not different ones mate." I said.

I must admit that even though I wasn't laughing, I did have a fairly big grin on my face. I had thought everyone could keep a beat until this moment.

"Well you can go home show off. Just 'cause you can do it." he retorted.

"Alright, cool down, we can have another go at our next practice. Ok?"

"I'll see you later," I called out as I walked from his room and headed for the front door. "Bye Mrs Quinn," I said as I walked past the kitchen.

"Bye Matty," she replied without turning. I couldn't help feeling that Mrs Quinn always seemed so tired and sad. Special occasions involving her children were the only times I'd seen her look happy.

As I walked down the front steps and into the garden I noticed Jenny lingering by the Hibiscus bush. She didn't say anything. She just placed her hand on my shoulder and kissed me gently on the lips. Her lips were soft and warm. There was a sweet perfume in the air and the world stood still. She slipped away before I could speak, which is probably just as well. I doubt that anything I could have said at that moment would have improved the experience, or even made sense to any linguist in the world. I floated out of her front garden and into the street, unaware of my immediate surroundings. Apart from the kisses of my mother this was the first time I'd been kissed by a female and now I knew why all of those love songs I loved so much, had been written. I walked home past the house where the girl with the long black hair lived. She just happened to be standing there when I passed by. She walked to the gate and waved.

She then beckoned me and I sauntered over to where she stood. Her long, black hair shone in the sunlight. I stood before my beckoning angel and rested my hands on the top of the gate. I tried to say hello but all I heard was someone make a squeaking sound. I realised with horror that it was me who had made the noise and quickly cleared my throat. I thought it best to say nothing and appear stupid, rather than trying to speak in my lovestruck condition and sound stupid. This turned out to be a wise move and gave me time to gather my thoughts.

"Matty, what school do you go to," she asked

"Why?" I asked suavely.

"I just wondered that's all."

I felt I'd disappointed her somehow with my slow wit and resolved to concentrate harder on the conversation.

"I go to the school up in Eversleigh Road. Where do you go?"

"I go to the Catholic college," she replied, with a toss of her raven hair.

I recognised that my mind was in some sort of altered state at that moment but carried on. "That's why we don't see each other much." I replied with obvious and brilliant deduction. Her mother then called her name.

"Antonia!"

"Coming mother," she replied.

"See you later Matty," she said with a smile. Then she touched my hand.

With another shake of her hair she was gone. I assumed she'd gone back to heaven with the other angels. Such was the state of my mind at the time. Her name was Antonia and she was a Roman Catholic girl. I walked home with the sun shining and the birds singing just for me.... and Jenny and Antonia of course.

At home I sat in my bedroom and wondered what was going on. Why have these stunning creatures decided to take an interest in me? Here I am not yet 14 yrs of age, and my whole world was changing. Suddenly, instead of being the hunter, always admiring girls and seeking their company, I seem to be the hunted. Girls are interested in me. My younger brother entered our shared bedroom and said, "Why are you sitting there like that?"

"I think I'm in love with two girls," I said, without thinking. One learns never to confide in ones younger brother in these matters.

"You are." he grinned. "Who are they?"

Now, I might be slow but there's no way I'm sharing this information with anyone now, especially after his reaction.

"Mind your own business and keep your nose out," I said as menacingly as I could.

"Awww, don't tell me it's Quinny's sister. You're joking," he laughed.

"No! Of course not," I answered. Why would it be?"

"You can't go with your best mate's little sister, that's why."

"Why not! Any way it's not her." I said. I wasn't going to let on it was Quinny's older sister that I was interested in.

"Who's the other one?" he asked, not accepting my strenuous vocal protestation.

"It's no one you know, so just mind your own business." I wasn't really lying.

The chances of him knowing the girl up the road were very slim indeed. Anyway, I decided to play my cards close to my chest about girls when in the presence of my little brother. Apart from anything else, he was nearly old enough to be a competitor in the love stakes. We are only 11mths apart in age and I love him dearly but 'all is fair in love and war'. Mum's the word from now on.

PART 1
THE VERY EARLY
YEARS IN ENGLAND

Chapter 7

IT'S 1935 AND a young Roman Catholic girl named Sarah Dubois is settling into Peace Hall farm in the Blaney Beck district of Northern England. Her parents, Carlos and Sarah Dubois of Stopford Brook had brought her to their friends farm to recover from a recent bout of pneumonia. The fresh country air would be most beneficial, the doctor had told them, for her recovery. The younger of two daughters, she was a frail but beautiful creature given to the arts of poetry and music. Her long wavy auburn hair glistened in the cold morning sun as she sat on a garden seat at the front of the house writing one of her poems into a leather bound notebook. The garden seat was located in a sheltered nook, surrounded by various flowering shrubs. Edward Lofthouse and his wife Thora, the owners of Peace Hall, had farmed there for generations. They were friends of the Tyndale family who had farmed next door for a similar amount of time. The Tyndale's farm was called Old Tun farm. Both farms were involved in mixed farming which consisted of growing feed and crops, running sheep, cattle (for dairy and beef) and pigs. At that time Shire horses were still being used alongside the new-fangled tractors and it wasn't unusual to see horses and carts travelling the country lanes, where motor cars were beginning to prevail. Thora Lofthouse was an accomplished pianist who had been engaged by the Dubois family to teach the two girls. It was through this period that the two families had become friends.

Big Bill Tyndale had heard talk of this young Dubois girl from the local publican. 'The Cross Keys' was a clearing house for local gossip, like all country pubs. It was about this time that the pronunciation of Dubois became Dooboys, with the heavier North England emphasis on the 'u' and the 'ois'. The Dubois became the Dooboys throughout the farming villages for the duration. This proved a never ending source of annoyance to Carlos Dubois, who dreaded the thought of his daughter being surrounded by 'those farmers'.

Tyndale, as always wondered what, if anything, he could gain from this new situation, which lay well and truly within his sphere of influence. He knew his two sons would have learned of this town girls presence at Peace Hall by now but is there any way he can gain from the knowledge. The publican had said "Aye, this Dooboys fella's an Engineer from't' mine. Pretty well orf th' say. His dowter wouldn't be much good on't' farm eh?"

"Nah, thee's probably reet Brian." replied Bill Tyndale with a wink.

"She'd be weak as dishwater," he added as he walked to the door.

As Bill Tyndale drove slowly home in his Standard 9 Tourer, he made the decision that he had nothing to gain by allowing his family to become involved with the town girl. He would discourage his sons from meeting her. He was sure one of the local girls would prove to be more useful to them as wives and such. Since his wife had died his two daughters had been looking after him and the lads as well as working on the farm. This is the sort of girl he wanted for his sons. His daughters Margaret and Mary were bright girls, both younger than the boys but educated in the ways of the world by their long-suffering mother. His wife Maude, known as Missy throughout the district, was an educated woman. She fell in love with Bill Tyndale at a local dance at the Stopford Brook Town Hall. Her family were farm owners. They were probably one of the biggest land holders in the Blaney Beck area. Those who watched the relationship develop, knew that Big Bill Tyndale was only too aware of their prominence in the farming community. Her family had been dead against the marriage but she was headstrong and the ceremony went ahead. She loved her man and he loved the new status the union gave him, along with the bonus of having a bed warmer and unpaid farm hand.

Over the ensuing years, child birth and farm work wore Missy down to the bone and one severe winter seven years back, she didn't rally from the pneumonia that racked her feeble body.

The Doctor wasn't talking softly to Bill when he was finally called to her bedside.

In the dim light of the farmhouse parlour where the fire wasn't even lit in order to save Bill's precious money, Doctor Douglas confronted him. "Why didn't you call me earlier?"

"Tyndale, you've worked that woman to death and kept her in this cold house all these years. Why don't you light the fire man? You'll have all the children sick next."

"Aye Doctor, I'll trouble ye not to trouble me with thee fine opinions."

"Tyndale, I'll need some information. Was your wife born in 1895?" he asked.

'Aye, that she was, on May the eighth," replied Bill Tyndale quietly.

Doctor Douglas had been in practice around the Whitton-Le-Wear area for many years and he knew most of the families personally. He'd even delivered many of them in childbirth in their homes, including the Tyndale children.

"If you take another wife Tyndale, I'll be watching. I'll be watching how the children come on also." the Doctor took his calling very seriously.

would wake alone in the darkness to find his cold supper on the table before him. No matter the hurt Missy may have carried, her husband had never struck her and she had never refused him his place in the marriage bed. The children were usually asleep when he stumbled cursing, up the stairs to the bedroom.

He would mumble and grumble to himself.

This night John found sleep to be elusive, as thoughts of the day tumbled through his mind. Missy sobbed quietly to herself in the darkness, as she lay beside her snoring husband. She too, would never show her tears.

Chapter 8

IT'S SATURDAY THE 16th of May 1916 and Bill Tyndale and Missy Anne Lowther are married in the Church of England, Beckley Dell. It was a special Spring day. Blaney Beck church was much too small to contain the well-wishers, particularly the large Lowther contingent. The War years were not going to cramp their style. The bride was beautiful, in the manner of a small, delicate English bird with dark bright eyes. Her new husband was, in her presence, charming and sociable. Many thought he was in awe of her beauty and inner strength. No one doubted their love for each other.

Though the war had taken many of the local lads as conscripts, hundreds had volunteered, grabbing the chance to escape the drudgery and meagre wages of the farm labourer. To many town folk, life in the army was a hard one but to the poor farm labourer it was the first time in his life he had done no strenuous work. Unlike his life on the farm, he even got paid when it rained and a separation allowance for his dependants. Farm labourers were glad to get off the farm, where they were no more than serfs toiling for the benefit of the farm owner, who was in effect his lord. The risk of death or injury wasn't considered, after all it always happened to 'the other poor fella'. Mechanised warfare was being brought to bear now on the battlefields, especially on the front in France, in the form of the new English Tanks. The Battalions raised from the English countryside were still happy to go to war. They didn't, or in many cases couldn't read the reports of the carnage in the front lines. The German generals, even though their army was mowing down the allied forces by the thousand, with specialist Companies of machine- gunners, thought it unfair of the British to be using tanks against their troops. When reported in the newspapers back home in England, this gem of Germanic thinking caused much merriment at a desperate dark time.

It had been common practice in farming communities, in 1915 for farm owners to turn their farms over to their sons to avoid them being conscripted. If Bill's father hadn't done this, the farm would have virtually died for lack of supervision and labour. Bill Tyndale and many other farm owners were protected in this way. The farmers still talked about the pre-war agricultural depression which struck English farms. Much good arable land had been returned to grazing.

In Britain in 1914, before the outbreak of war, the farmers only produced a very small percentage of the wheat the country needed. In that year when war was declared, it was harvest time and the Government encouraged farmers to once again start ploughing up their land for crops. The Army then descended on the farms and took the horses and remaining labour in their thousands further hampering farm productivity. With fewer horses and men to tend the fields even weeding had to be done by hand. This was back-breaking work. Nitrate fertiliser wasn't available because Nitrate was needed for ammunition, so the ground became poor from constant cropping. Crops were generally poor. It was a constant battle for the farmers, to do their bit for the war effort.

Though Missy Lowther had been born into a well to do farming family and was accustomed to the problems the land-owners faced she was so happy to marry her man and share in the Tyndale farm and it's problems. Even though he knew it cast him in a bad light, he did allow his new wife to work in the fields weeding. She worked alongside the women and children who were hired to make up for the lack of farm labourers. Bill, and the other farm owners, payed these workers a mere pittance and made them work long hours. He begged Missy, not because she was pregnant with John but so he could save face. George Lowther, Missy's father had also expressed his distaste of the situation when speaking to him at the local Market.

"Dinna gan out there lass. Thee'll have me run out't village soon," he pleaded.

She relented and settled back to enjoy the life of a landed lady who carried the first child of Big Bill Tyndale. Bill's chest grew in proportion to his wife's belly during that period. The Tyndale's had a Vauxhall Prince Henry garaged near the house as well as a Tilbury carriage in the Cart shed by the Byre. It was in this latter conveyance that Bill would take his wife for gentle trips about the country lanes of the district. He had been able to hide his carriage horse when the army horse-hunters had come calling and he was proud of his fine carriage and horse whenever they stepped out. The farm had stables for six horses but Bill had been given permission to keep only two of his shire horses. The other two were taken into the army for the war effort. He never saw them again. In an effort to keep up productivity, he bought the first Saunderson tractor in the district. This enabled him to achieve his field work targets with the bare minimum of available labour. It was housed in a newly built shed next to the garage. The car was reserved for longer trips. He and Missy enjoyed their outings and the status this they were able to show to all and sundry. A picnic basket would always be taken whether in the car or carriage and enjoyed at various locations. Bill didn't consider saddle horses to be necessary, even though he was quite able to afford several if he cared to.

It was during these trips in the Tilbury carriage that they felt most relaxed and happy together. Sitting on the river bank below the church in Wharton Mead, or by the stone bridge over the beck on the Blaney Beck road in the shade of the ancient Oaks, they enjoyed some of their happiest times. As the time for Missy's confinement drew near and Winter closed in, their trips became less frequent. Missy had immediately taken steps to have the telephone connected when she moved into Old Tun farm. Old Tun farm was one of the last farms in the area to be connected to Electricity

As it happened it was one of the last farms to be connected to the telephone in the district also and Bill Tyndale still didn't see it's worth.

"Folks chatterin and chunterin int't' thing." he'd grumble.

Doctor Douglas had visited Missy four times during her pregnancy and was on alert for a call from Bill when necessary. The weather was quite mild now that Summer was here and the twilight hours lingered until late in the evening. It had been a severe and prolonged Winter and everyone was glad of some relief. Life in the country, in the well to do families, went on by and large, without much interference from the war overseas. The farming families didn't do without food, and even the inflated black market prices could be more readily afforded by them. 1916 had been a bleak year for harvest but the farm owners generally weren't feeling the pinch like the poorer folk, particularly in the towns and cities. The country folk looked 'hale and hearty' compared with their city cousins.

Missy had been restless most of the night, tossing and turning. Bill rose early and made a cup of tea for her and by the time he had taken it to her her waters had broken. She stood beside the bed in a pool, with a wet nightdress sobbing.

"What're ye deein' out t' bed lass, get back in," said her husband. She could see he was very concerned.

"No, I don't want to make the bed wet," she responded, shaking her head.

"I'm callin' Douglas," he shouted running downstairs.

His wife went to the bathroom to change her clothes. She then covered her mattress with waterproof sheet, re-made the bed and awaited further developments. The parlour clock struck four o' clock just as her husband re entered the room.

"He's on his way lass. I'll fetch another cuppa for ye, that's cold now"

She let out a long sigh as he plunged once more down the stairs. Farmers she thought, cope much better with animal births, than with the birth of their own children.

Missy called out to her husband and grimaced at the added pain. "Bill, will you telephone my mother and ask her to come here?"

"Aye I will, he shouted from below. D'ye no' think she should've been here these last few weeks?"

"Yes, yes, I didn't feel this close." Came the irritable reply.

It was four thirty when Missy heard a car pull up outside the house.

"Is that Doctor Douglas?" She called to her husband.

"Aye it's him," he called out to her.

"Thank the Lord," she breathed to herself. The pains were becoming more insistent now.

Dr Robert Douglas drew up to the stone wall of the house near the front gate. He didn't drive a shiny new car. It was an AC 10 open two seater and it was covered in dirt and dust from his rounds. Many of his patients lived in the country along unsealed roads. This was his fifth visit to the see Missy since setting up his surgery in Stopford Brook a year ago. He sat for a few moments gathering his thoughts. It had only been a few days ago he had been reading the works of a doctor from Aberdeen who had been a Navy surgeon in the 1790's. He had demonstrated that infection was the main factor in the prevalence of the deadly childbirth fever. This was an illness killing one in three mothers during and up to a year after childbirth. He had also studied the findings of an American Physician, which reinforced his own views on the dangers of infection during childbirth. He decided, since reading these studies, to take extra care with infection control when delivering babies.

Not all of the Doctors in England agreed with these findings on infection causing death through Puerperal Sepsis. Many medicos openly ridiculed the findings of these two men. Not much was known by his colleagues in the establishment, about bacterial transference in these early years of the Twentieth century but for young Dr Douglas this was a revelation.

A big ruddy faced man waved to him from the front door. He returned the wave and taking his bag in his hand he walked through the open gate to the door. Bill Tyndale thrust out his huge hand in welcome, "'Ow d'ye do Doctor."

"How do you do Mr Tyndale.."

"Does thee need owt before we gan upstairs Doctor?" enquired Bill.

When Douglas had first come to the district he had some trouble understanding the local dialects. He was finding it easier now.

"Yes please Mr Tyndale, hot water and the cleanest bed sheet you can find. Oh, and a towel or two."

"I'll take ye upstairs afore I gather it up then."

The two men passed through the kitchen and parlour to the stairs.

"Mr Tyndale I must stress that everything I asked you for must be absolutely clean.

Understood?"

"Aye I understand thee." replied Bill Tyndale.

They entered the bedroom and Missy smiled at them both.

"I'm very pleased to see you Doctor Douglas," she said with a smile.

"And I you Mrs Tyndale," replied the Doctor.

Again Missy's face contorted with pain. The contractions were coming more often now and each time they were much stronger.

"I'll leave thee to it Doctor. I'll bring up't' water and cloths directly."

He was accustomed to the birth and death of animals but he didn't like to see his wife distressed. The Doctor didn't answer, he was busy listening to the baby through his stethoscope.

When Tyndale re-entered the room with the hot water, sheet and towels, Doctor Douglas said, "Pull these curtains back and open the windows. Let's get some fresh air in here."

Missy was looking very stressed now and her pale face was bathed in perspiration. Her husband completed his task and left the room as quickly as possible.

A car was heard to stop outside. Missy called out," Mother is that you?"

"Yes dear, I'm here," she answered from the front door.

Bill met George and Ann Lowther at the door. They had just made the journey from their farm in very quick time. Some of the trip had been made across the fields to save time. Mrs Lowther nodded in Bill's direction and pushed past him as the men shook hands. She liked Bill Tyndale but not enough to delay her dash to her daughter's bedside.

She said, "How do you do Doctor," and gently kissed Missy on her forehead.

Now involved with washing his hands and fore arms in a saline solution, which he had prepared himself, he acknowledged her with a nod and a smile. Mrs Lowther then went over to the hand basin in the corner of the room and wet a flannel with cold water to place on her daughter's brow.

"The child is coming quite quickly. Mother and baby are doing well Mrs Lowther."

He then placed a sheet over Missy from the her waist down, as was his custom and washed her with saline solution also. All was well.

Downstairs Bill Tyndale and George Lowther sat at the kitchen table and drank tea.

The parlour clock struck five thirty a.m. The day had well and truly begun.

"I shouldn't worry too much Bill, she's in good hands with Robert Douglas. He's nobody's fool you know." said Lowther. "I've heard good reports about him."

"Aye I'm no' vexed about it George," replied Bill. "I ken she'll slip it easy."

"It'll be over before you know it," said George.

George spoke again, changing the subject, "I hear that Lloyd George is talking about putting the women to work in the fields. He's calling them the land army."

"The land army thee says. "Aye, I heard that 'n' all," replied Bill. 'It's sure to help us farmers a'right, but they'll want learnin'."

"Yes we'll have to train them." said George.

"Ow much will the' want payin'." asked Bill.

"You're a canny lad Bill." said George Lowther with a grin. "Always watching the pennies. We'll pay them a fair wage but it won't be as much as the men."

"Aye, that should do t' job nicely then. At least it'll get t' work done. Will the' be able to work tractors d'ye ken." Bill asked the other man.

"Yes, I'm sure they will, they drive cars now." mused George Lowther with a smile.

His musings were interrupted by the sound of a new-born baby crying. Both men rushed to the bottom of the stairs. On the landing Ann Lowther stood with a beaming face. "We've a new baby boy gentlemen and they're both well. You can come up soon, the Doctor's not finished yet."

"What do you think about that, Bill Tyndale?" called Missy from the bedroom.

Her voice sounded weak but steady.

"Aye, that's champion, just champion," said Bill Tyndale with a grin.

"Congratulations lad," said George shaking Bill's hand.

"An' thee an' all," said Bill.

"It's yet a quarter past the hour but I think we could take a wee dram." suggested Bill.

He walked to the cabinet and took out a bottle of his best single malt for the occasion. His father in law wasn't about to say no. It was a rare enough occasion that Bill Tyndale would be parting with his drink. They sat at the table and Bill poured them both a respectable measure of whisky in his best glasses. George raised his glass and offered the toast.

"Here's all the blessings on you and yours, may you always be the first and not the last. May you and your children prosper and remain in good health."

"Thanks George, the same to you and yours," said Bill Tyndale.

"What will the lad's name be, Bill?" Asked his father in law.

"John, his name'll be John." he replied. "John Tyndale."

Chapter 9

OVER THE NEXT few years Missy Tyndale gave birth to three more children. William was the next born, then Margaret and finally Mary whom Bill nicknamed 'young Missy'. As Mrs Tyndale took on more and more physical work around the farm and became run down in herself, she had also suffered three miscarriages. In 1928, after only 12 years of marriage, she contracted pneumonia. Many home remedies were tried by her husband and by the time Doctor Douglas had been was called by young John, it was too late. She was just too weak to rally.

John was seventeen now and a fine strong bright young lad he was. He, like the other children loved and respected their father but deep down he nursed a powerful resentment over the death of his mother. He knew his father could have done more to help her through her illness. John had watched his father grow into a mean, lonely old man, even though he was only 39 years of age. His grand-parents on his mother's side, George and Ann Lowther were very upset about the death of their daughter. George in particular held Bill Tyndale responsible for his daughter's death, saying on many occasions,

"It's his negligence that caused this."

Mrs Lowther encouraged him to stay involved with Bill Tyndale for the sake of the children.

"I know he loved Missy with all his heart. It seems the more children they had, he found it too difficult to find enough love within him, to go around everyone all the time. He is a man with strong but limited love and he can't change."

She had shared this opinion with her husband just after her daughter's funeral, hoping to temper his anger. He had agreed to stay involved for the sake of the children and as he expressed it,

"To watch that fellow."

Doctor Douglas had shared his opinion about the incident, with George Lowther one night over a quiet drink. As they sat by themselves in the Lowther's drawing room he had ventured his personal thought that Bill Tyndale had been too slow to call him to his sick wife. He added, "If it hadn't been for John's call, I wouldn't have arrived there when I did."

"Now George, This is merely my personal opinion and it won't change anything."

"No, it won't, but I think sometimes that man is not himself." said George Lowther quietly. "I know he loves his children but there's something dark inside him. His father was the same."

George Lowther and his wife were very dedicated Christian folk and not afraid to live their faith. On the day of Missy Tyndale's death Douglas had promised her husband in no uncertain terms, that he would be watching the development of his family very closely in future. George and Ann Lowther would also be watching the development of their grand children.

"You knew his father then, George?"

"Yes, old Bill was just the same. He was a hard man and very tough on his son."

"The grand-children seem to have benefited from your daughter's gentle influence." ventured Robert Douglas.

"Yes, they're lovely children alright." Their grandfather smiled.

The two friends chatted in the warmth of the fire until late.

"You'll stay for the night Robert? It's much too late to drive home now."

"Thanks, that's a good idea," replied his friend. "I'll call in at the Tyndale place on the way home tomorrow, just to say hello."

John Tyndale thought it about time he paid a visit to Peace Hall farm. He'd been thinking about the mystery girl who was staying there. His younger brother William claimed to have seen her from a distance but wasn't forthcoming when pressed for more detail. All he had said when John asked what she looked like was, "She's no' too bad."

He rode along the narrow roads toward Peace Hall farm. Patches of sunlight shone through the overhead greenery. The roads were lined with immaculately built and maintained dry stone walls and old rustic gates. Hedges were more the exception than the rule in this part of the country.

It was Saturday today, so he hadn't to go to work. He would go to Lofthouse's farm on the pretext that he needed some help with his motorcycle. It had belonged to Mr Lofthouse until he had given it to John to ride to his work. He would then. He had no doubt, be introduced to the mystery girl. The noise of his motorcycle engine echoed off the stone walls as he rode along. The sound was music to his ears and he wore a big smile. He had a feeling this was going to be a special day. The motorcycle itself was special even though it wasn't new. It was a BSA B35 250cc with a chrome tank with green coloured side panels and even electric lights.

John was blessed with a high mechanical aptitude, so was able to keep it running the way that it should. He rode along the lane way to the house and leaned his motorcycle against the garden wall. Mr Lofthouse came outside and met him in the garden. John had worn his best suit and shoes to impress Miss Dubois. He also wore his full length leather coat, of which he was very proud.

"How do you do this fine morning Mr Lofthouse," said John.

"I'm well John. I heard thee coming along the back road. I'd ken the sound of that Beeza anywhere."

"Oh aye," answered his young neighbour.

"How can I help thee lad?" asked Lofthouse.

John was busy looking for signs of Miss Dubois and not really listening. He had forgotten all about his clever ruse, about the reason for his visit.

"I um, er..." was the only answer he could come up with on the spur of the moment. He was sure he had seen a movement at the upstairs window. Had the curtain moved?

"Are you looking for something?" asked Mr Lofthouse.

He knew very well why young John was at his house. He had received a telephone call from Bill Tyndale, requesting in no uncertain terms that the two young folk, would not be allowed to meet. Now, while Edward Lofthouse was not a vindictive man, he felt it appropriate to honour the wishes of his friend and neighbour. He also had to consider his friend Carlos Dubois, who would surely want to vet any of his daughter's would be suitors.

John dragged his gaze away from the front windows and said to Mr Lofthouse,

"I was wondering er..what er.. what tyre pressures you found best in the Beeza?"

"Really?" said Mr Lofthouse. He was barely concealing a smile now.

John's gaze had once again returned to the widows and front door of the house, looking for any sign of the mystery girl.

"Aye," replied the young man absent mindedly.

His attention had been taken to another movement at one of the top floor windows. Did he see a pale face, a flash of auburn hair?

"About thirty psi should just about do it. Replied Lofthouse. Anyway young lad

I've work to do, so you'd better be on your way home lad.

"Aye," replied John.

He then asked, "Are you at home on your own today Mr Lofthouse?"

He hated lying to the boy. He just nodded.

"Oh aye," returned John. He realised by now that he was being mislead but had no idea why.

"I'll see you later then Mr Lofthouse." He turned and walked back to his machine. Thoughts tumbled through his mind. Why hadn't he been invited into the house? Where was Mrs Lofthouse, after all, she couldn't drive herself. Had he seen someone at the window?

He started his motorcycle and waved to Lofthouse who was still in the garden. As he snicked it into gear, he stole another quick look at the upstairs window. Yes, another glimpse of that beautiful pale face and the tumbling auburn hair. She is there. As quickly as the vision came, it went. He turned and rode up the lane, away from the house with mixed feelings. His heart was singing but his head was spinning. Why hadn't he been allowed to meet this beautiful girl? If he wasn't allowed to see this girl for some reason, then why hadn't someone told him. It would have saved him this embarrassing visit to Peace Hall farm. Mr Lofthouse must think his head's as soft as porridge. All of these negative thoughts soon disappeared however and his attention turned to the image of Miss Dubois. The picture of her brief appearance at the window was seared into his brain. It made him more determined to see her and he rode home as if in a dream.

Bill Tyndale's late wife Missy, had been a Christian woman and had insisted her children be brought up as good Christian boys and girls. Some of their father's traits however, were handed down to the children, which is after all, the norm. They were innocents and like their mother, had no guile in their characters. They had been brought up to be honest and open in their dealings with their family and others.

Their father had been brought up differently by his own father. Bill Tyndale was forced to be stealthy and secretive just to survive his father's abuse. Missy's influence had been like a breath of fresh air in his life and he missed her desperately. His problem was that no matter how hard he tried, since his wife had passed away he found himself slipping back into the dark place where he used to dwell. To see the happiness of his children though, was a deep desire.

John saw Dr Douglas drive his car through the farm gateway just as he approached.

He followed him down to the house and parked alongside him, leaning his motorcycle on the wall by the front garden gate.

"How do you do?" he said to the Doctor.

"Well, how do you do young John? I see you've been enjoying a ride this fine morning."

"Aye, I've been over Peace Hall way." John had no secrets to keep from this dear friend of his mother.

"And how are Mister and Mrs Lofthouse, John? They have the Dubois girl recuperating there. Did you meet her?"

"No, There was only Mister Lofthouse there. No one else."

John was very happy to hear this information and listened intently as the Doctor spoke.

He noticed his father walking towards them from the direction of the milking shed.

"She's a patient of mine. If you like I can arrange for you to meet her. She's a lovely girl."

"Yes please," was all John could say. He believed in miracles and he thought this latest development must be one.

His father joined them at the gate. "How d'ye do Doctor. To what d'we owe t' pleasure this lovely morn?"

"Good morning Tyndale. It's a short social visit only."

"Aye, come in t' house then and we'll share a cuppa."

Bill Tyndale led them into the house and sat his guest at the kitchen table. Douglas knew that those whom Bill considered friends would be seated in the parlour but he didn't care. He was mainly here to see the children and didn't particularly concern himself with the thoughts of his host.

"John, go and fetch thee sisters and tell'm to be sharp about it."

"Aye father," replied John and left the room.

"Have you been keeping well?" The Doctor asked Bill.

"Aye, I'm well enough," he replied.

John re-entered the room with his two younger sisters.

"Ye lassies fetch us some tea. Thee can drop t' fancy coat lad and find summat to do."

John left the room without answering his father. The two men sat at the table quite obviously merely tolerating each other.

"Are you girls well?" enquired the Doctor as they prepared tea.

"They're fine enough," answered Bill Tyndale.

Margaret turned to the Doctor and replied. "Yes sir we are quite well thank you."

Mary smiled and nodded, saying. "Thank you Doctor yes we're well thank you."

"Aye I told thee so Doctor, we're all well here." said Tyndale.

The cups of tea were dutifully placed before the men while the two girls were dismissed with a casual wave of Bill Tyndale's hand.

"Thank you girls," said Dr Douglas as they left the room.

They didn't answer.

"Has thee been kept busy this last while Doctor," asked Bill, as socially as he could.

Douglas ignored the question and said, "I'd like to make an arrangement to visit your family."

"Why does thee need to do that Doctor?" asked Tyndale, placing his cup noisily on his saucer.

"It's merely a general health check up, nothing to be concerned about. It's been a while since they were checked."

Bill Tyndale was annoyed at this unwelcome intrusion into his business but didn't want to appear churlish to the other man.

"Their grandmother is aways checkin'em thee kens." he said defensively

"Yes, shall we make it the middle of next week, say Wednesday?" answered the medico. He finished his tea and stood.

"Now, if you'll excuse me Mr Tyndale, I must be going on my way. By the way,

I didn't see young William. Is he well?"

"Aye, out checkin t' wall down near t' beck." said Tyndale.

Douglas made his own way to the door and thanked his host on the way.

"Thank you mister Tyndale, I'll see you later in the week. It will be in the afternoon."

"Aye we'll all be here." answered the farmer.

Douglas knew Mrs Lowther had been visiting the family, mainly for the sake of the girls. They where not yet teenagers and had their own special needs as young ladies. He knew Bill Tyndale would be glad of this help, even if under protest. The district nurse also attended the local farms on a regular basis. As he drove out of the farm gate he thought about John Tyndale and the Dubois girl.

The next time he visited her at Peace Hall farm he made a mental note to politely enquire about Carlos Dubois rules, concerning his young daughter Sarah and the local farm lads.

Margaret found John fiddling with his motorbike down at the cart shed. One of the dogs lay close to him. Molly was the oldest dog on Old Tun Farm and John was her favourite human. She lay contentedly close by and chewed an old turnip

"What do you want?" He asked his sister.

"I need to tell you something privately." she answered.

"What is it Maggie?"

She came closer, kneeled down beside him and whispered.

"Dad telephoned Mr Lofthouse after you were gone this morning."

"So what?" Asked John.

"Well, I overheard him say that you weren't to be allowed to meet Sarah Dubois."

"What d'you mean."

"It's true John, father thinks you're too young to be involved with a girl. He said it will affect your work."

She stood up to leave and added, "Don't say anything about this to father, He'll belt us all if you do. You know that."

"Aye I won't. Thanks Maggie for telling me." His voice wavered slightly as he spoke.

Chapter 10

CARLOS DUBOIS SAT in his office overlooking the Barrington Colliery, where he served the Company as an Engineer. Coal mining in the Stopford Brook area had been declining steadily since the Great Depression in 1932. Unemployment was at high levels and many mines had shut down altogether. Barrington Colliery had managed to survive and even prosper due to its up to date and efficient production policies. These policies were, in no small part, put into place because of Dubois clever Engineering plans involving the study of time and motion. This was one of the last deep collieries in the district still operating profitably.

His view was substantially black and grey in colour, dominated by two large Iron framed Pit heads. Gathered around the base of the Chimneys, like chicks around a mother hen, were a jumble of grimy buildings, including the tall Engine houses and Pump house. Across the road and down the hill toward the Gaunless River, stood three rows of Miners cottages. These too had taken on a grey colour over the years, from the dirt and coal dust. On the other side of the Coal mine ran the main Stockton Courtenay rail line. Travellers to Durham by rail crossed the River Wear over the Newton Cap viaduct.

Ezra Barrington, the owner of the Colliery, attended Saint Wilfrid's Catholic church with his family every week. Carlos

Dubois and his family attended the same church and they had become friendly. Through his contacts at Stopford Brook Town Hall, Barrington had arranged an interview on Dubois behalf. He would be able to take a position as Council Engineer, as soon as he finished his present tenure. With the Coal mines in decline, Barrington saw it as his civic duty to help his employees in any way he could. Carlos was a friend as well as an employee, and he had a young family to support. He had worked for the Colliery for the last fifteen years and was much loved by the Barrington family.

His wife, Hannah was a teacher at St Wilfrid's Catholic school and very focused on her two daughters receiving a sound education. She and Carlos agreed that their daughters should not be involved too deeply with boys until the age of 21yrs and then not to the detriment of their prospective careers. These lofty ideals were quite the norm for the era but like parents of any time, Carlos and Hannah would forget the effect young love had on themselves, at their own first meeting. They had fallen madly in love and had, against the wishes of Hannah's family, been married after an indecently short courtship. He had been seen as a foreigner upstart in Stopford Brook at the time but was accepted now. Stopford Brook still has a low proportion of foreign born citizens compared with the rest of the nation.

These issues didn't stop them becoming successful and gaining some prominence in the district as a family. The Roman Catholic church has always been well represented in the town.

Irish labourers drawn to the district by the promise of work in the Coal mining and Manufacturing industries boosted the Catholic population. In the neighbouring town of Shildon large numbers were employed in the Railway Engine works. Church membership brought a closeness and power to the congregation, even those in the lower classes. The local priest made it known that the ministry of the church would be based on the book of Galatians in The Bible, Chapter 6 and Verse 10.

'Therefore, as we have opportunity, let us do good to all, especially to those who are of the household of faith.' NKJV.

The Reverend Little had been able to send a donation of One hundred and twenty two pounds to the Irish church, for help in their 'time of trouble'. This money was all freely given by members of St Wilfrid's.

One cannot overestimate the influence of the Church in the general morality of it's members and constituents. However, mankind finds itself in a fallen state, with some more fallen than others. The Roman church tended to ease the burden on those of her flock who stray, by ushering them into the confessional as often as possible. Then they would ease the guilt of those who strayed. Money and indulgences would then change hands, salving the conscience of those involved but doubling and prolonging their feeling of guilt.

Such was the religious climate into which the daughters of Carlos and Hannah Dubois were thrust. There are those who would say the girls' upbringing was strict, while others would call their early life safe and secure. Both views are probably true. For even the most minor indiscretion the girls would feel the sting of Carlos's tongue. Bad manners or tardiness in their school work or music lessons, would place the girls in his firing line. These altercations caused much grief for Hannah Dubois, who was thrust into the role of peacemaker on many occasions because of her husband's temper.

This volatile disposition seemed to be handed down from his forebear Dubois, of Malta, who was himself a fiery politician and writer, who spent most of his life serving the Knights of Malta. The book he wrote is an analysis of the reign of Grand Master de Rohan; the second part reports the invasion and the occupation of Malta by the French.

Carlos had high expectations of himself and felt he had fallen short of the expectations of others. He was a lowly Engineer who was soon to lose his position at the Colliery, he hadn't scaled the dizzy heights of politics and he hadn't written a book. Hannah knew he sometimes felt a failure. Even though unsure of his own worth, Carlos Dubois considered himself and his family to be several steps above the farmers of the land. He knew he was more in the class of the landed gentry. Hannah had her doubts about his ideas however. She never voiced her doubts and it sometimes led to unresolved conflict between them. It wasn't that she doubted his claims of class but more that she saw a kind of snobbery that her upbringing denied. Her father, Paul Hall had owned his own Manufacturing business in Darnley. He bore no pretensions of grandeur, believing all men and women to be the same under God's heaven.

Under these circumstances Carlos quite often suffered inner turmoil, which caused him to lash out physically and mentally at those he loved the most, his family. His younger daughter Sarah, was a wild and rebellious girl who was more like himself than he cared to admit. His older daughter Clare took after her mother and didn't clash with him as much. This in turn caused him a feeling of terrible guilt which he kept inside himself, not allowing the world to see his weakness. Many families suffered in this way during this period of industrial unrest and unemployment in the North-East of the Country. Not all men and women faced uncertainty in the same way but they did face it together for the sake of their families. Appearances counted for everything in some social circles. Others, not so much.

It was on the Sunday following young John Tyndale's visit, that the Dubois family had arranged to call on their daughter at Peace Hall farm. They hadn't seen her for almost a month and even though Doctor Douglas had telephoned them several times to report on her progress, they were looking forward to the visit.

They were also excited to be spending some time with their friends Edward and Thora Lofthouse. They had been only too happy to take on the responsibility of looking after their youngest in her time of illness. The journey to their friend's farm by road had been uneventful.

Carlos was quite proud of his 1930 Austin 16/6 Saloon, and even though it wasn't new it was very comfortable and dependable. It had always been kept safe and secure in it's own garage next to their house in Stopford Brook. The three of them alighted from the car to be greeted by their friends and Sarah who rushed through the garden gate to hug her mother. She then proceeded to hug her sister, while the adults exchanged greetings.

"How d'you do Carlos, Hannah. You're both looking well," said Lofthouse smiling. He and his wife shook hands with their friends. Thora Lofthouse invited them inside.

"Mother, may we stay in the garden for a while?" asked Sarah, holding Clare's hand.

Hannah Dubois said, "Yes dears, that will be fine. Please don't wander away."

"Yes mother," the girls replied in unison.

"Did you have a pleasant journey?" enquired Edward Lofthouse as they entered the house. "The weather's been perfect for you today, hasn't it?"

Lofthouse always felt slightly uneasy in the presence of Carlos Dubois. He did class him as a good friend but the man was very difficult to talk to. He always gave the impression that his mind was somewhere else and he wasn't really listening to what was being said. The conversation would sometimes seem one-sided. When his friend did answer, it was quite often the answer to a question that was asked earlier and not to the one being presently asked.

Lofthouse passed it off as a trait exhibited by Academics generally, like absent-mindedness. The conversation between the two sisters outside in the garden was rather one-sided also.

Young girls generally find it difficult to keep secrets and the telling of secrets mostly requires a standard but necessary preamble.

"Can you keep a secret?" asked Sarah of her sister.

"Of course, you know I can," answered Clare.

In truth Sarah knew nothing of the sort. She knew very well that her sister was capable of changing secrets into juicy gossip, at a moments notice. However, things being what they are, all young girls know the power of a secret lies in the telling.

"Do you promise?" asked Sarah.

"Of course," whispered Clare, wide-eyed.

"Cross your heart and hope to die," added Sarah as the clincher.

"Of course," Clare repeated.

"No, it doesn't work if you don't say it," said Sarah. There was an urgency in her voice now, which only served to whet her sister's appetite.

The necessary oath was duly repeated, with several Robins bearing witness.

"What's the secret Sarah," asked Clare.

They were sitting on the garden seat surrounded by flowering Broom shrub and Hawthorn. This is where Thora Lofthouse would sit and read a favourite book, when the weather was fine. At this time however it was being used for very serious business indeed.

"There's a beautiful boy," said Sarah, satisfied now that her sister had fulfilled the necessary requirements.

"You've met a boy!" exclaimed Clare, loudly enough to scatter the little birds.

"Shhh, hissed Sarah. It's a secret Clare."

They looked furtively around the bushes toward the house.

"Sorry but I'm so excited. Who is it? What's he like? Have you kissed him?"

Clare would not be surprised at anything her sister did, especially now she was feeling better.

This secret was turning out to be better than she ever could have imagined.

"No, I couldn't get close enough to him." replied Sarah.

She wasn't about to admit to her sister that she had only seen John Tyndale from behind the curtain of her bedroom.

She pressed on with the revelation. "He rides a motorbike."

"What!" exclaimed Clare. Once more the Robins took to the wing.

"Are you girls alright out there?" came a voice from inside the house.

"Yes mother," called out Sarah, glaring at her sister.

Clare sat with her hand over her mouth and eyes wide open, barely able to trust herself to whisper, "Tell me, is he handsome? I simply know he is. Where does he live?"

The little Robins returned and continued to share Sara's secret in the sunshine.

"Yes he is very handsome and he lives over those fields at the next farm," answered

Sarah. "You can just see the roof of the house in the distance above those trees."

"Oh where? I can't see." Clare stood on the seat and looked in the general direction of Old Tun farm.

"It doesn't matter Clare. Trust me it's over there." said Sarah. The only reason she knew the general direction was because she had plucked up the courage to ask Edward Lofthouse one day.

"Yes," he replied with a smile, "There's Linburn beck between us and them."

"When will you see him again?" begged Clare.

"I don't know Clare. I just don't know but I will see him again."

"Mother wants to bring you home with us today," said Clare.

"What!" shouted Sarah. Once more the Robins took to the air.

This time their mother opened the front door and walked into the garden.

"Girls what is going on out here. What's all the shouting about?"

"Nothing Mother, we're just enjoying ourselves," said Sarah quickly.

"I'm glad you're feeling better darling. We'll take you home today if you feel up to it. Would you like that?" asked her mother.

Sarah fainted on the spot. When she came to her senses she had been lifted off the grass, carried upstairs and placed on her bed. She opened her eyes to the feeling of someone gently stroking her hair. Her mother had placed a wet flannel on her forehead and was looking down at her.

"Darling, are you alright? You gave us all a terrible fright."

"Mother I can't come home yet." whispered Sarah as weakly as she could.

Sarah knew she must appear ill at all costs, if she wanted to see the Tyndale boy again. next week. "Mr and Mrs Lofthouse are very happy for you to stay and your father agrees."

"Oh thank you mother. I'm sure I'll be much better by then." Sarah managed a weak smile but her heart was pounding. This meant she would have time to learn more about the Tyndale boy on the motorbike. She didn't want to deceive her mother and father, or be secretive but she said,

"I don't think I'm ready yet mother," she whispered, holding her hand to her brow.

"Yes dear, we telephoned the Doctor and he suggested we leave you here for another week."

Doctor Douglas was complicit in these arrangements for his own reasons. He loved the Tyndale children and didn't feel at all guilty about helping them rise above their present circumstances, even if it went against the wishes of their father. He knew, only too well that Bill Tyndale could be mean and controlling. Douglas was certain, the blame for the death of the children's mother, could be laid partly at least at Tyndale's door. While endeavouring not to be a busy body, nevertheless he had made it his business to bring some light into the lives of these children whenever he could. If enabling young John Tyndale to meet

Sarah Dubois, in the presence of a chaperone of course, would bring some happiness to them both, then he would do it. These two young people from different walks of life, could only benefit from meeting each other, surely. He didn't mention any of these thoughts to Dubois on the telephone of course, he merely stated his own medical opinion.

Sarah waved bravely and smiled triumphantly to her family, as they drove away from Peace Hall farm. She stood at the bedroom window and she was sure her sister had winked at her as she walked to the car.

Chapter 11

"WHAT ABOUT THOSE poor people over in Mardale, Edward?" Thora Lofthouse sat with her husband at the breakfast table, "It was in the newspaper yesterday."

"About the flooding of the village, you mean dear?" he answered.

"Yes, and all the land around it as well. Good land it was." said his wife.

"They did need to build the reservoir dear. We all need water to drink."

"Well I think it's disgraceful putting all those people's homes under water and all that land. It's a waste. The old Church went under the water as well you know."

"Some say that Mardale itself was a waste dear." said Edward Lofthouse with a smile. He gave his wife a wink over his cup of tea.

"Now Edward, it isn't very nice to say that. Think of those poor people watching their homes go under the water. What if Prime Minister Baldwin decided to do the same thing around here. What would we do Edward?"

"I would probably start to build a boat dear." said Lofthouse.

"Oh Edward Lofthouse, you're incorrigible." With this Mrs Lofthouse rose from the table and went to call Sarah to breakfast. Lofthouse returned to his newspaper.

It was King George V Jubilee year and the national celebrations hadn't been as lavish in the North as elsewhere in the land, even though the King and Queen were universally loved. Most folks were more concerned with the rise of a new military Germany in Europe.

"I fear we have more to worry about than the Manchester Water Board dear." said

Lofthouse as his wife returned to the table. "This Hitler fella is going to cause a great deal of trouble if we're not careful." He threw the newspaper onto the sideboard in disgust.

"Not now dear, not at the table. Sarah is on her way down."

"Good morning dear. Did you sleep well?" enquired Mrs Lofthouse, as Sarah sat down.

"Yes thank you, good morning Mr and Mrs Lofthouse."

"How are you this morning Sarah? You've seemed much stronger these last few days."

"I'm feeling much stronger now, thank you." she answered. "As a matter of fact I think I would like to go for a walk today If you don't mind."

"What a splendid idea. Perhaps I could accompany you." said Lofthouse.

"We could walk across the field and down to the beck." he added.

"Yes please. Is that in the direction of that other farm?" asked Sarah, feigning disinterest.

Thora Lofthouse fixed her gaze on her husband. She knew what he was up to.

"Yes, Old Tun is on the other side of the stream." he answered, meeting his wife's gaze with a smile.

Sarah was smiling on the inside. This walk would allow her to see where this interesting motorbike boy lived.

Mr and Mrs Lofthouse had decided to allow Sarah some freedom during the final week of her stay with them, under supervision of course. 'Walking will help to bring the roses back to her cheeks' Mrs Lofthouse had said. She also had said to her husband, "That John Tyndale is a lovely boy but don't you be matchmaking, Edward Lofthouse."

"The way the weather is holding, I think you'll have a wonderful walk." smiled

Mrs Lofthouse. "Now come on, eat your breakfast, you'll need your strength."

Mrs Lofthouse had insisted Sarah stay in bed for two days after her fainting spell. The Doctor had recommended it when speaking to her husband on the telephone on Monday morning.

Sarah was beginning to think her time at Peace Hall farm would run out before she had a chance to investigate her surroundings. She needn't have worried. The good Doctor had expressed his view that some social interaction may be good for her, when speaking to Lofthouse. "Now Lofthouse, he said. These children should not be isolated from the rest of the world forever. They're bright and clever children and they must see that there is a big beautiful world out there. If they are chaperoned, it should be beneficial for all concerned."

Lofthouse agreed but pointed out that the girl's parents may not see his point of view.

"It will only be for a few days and the young lady will be going back to Bishop Auckland." said Douglas. "I will call in to see how the young lady is feeling later in the week."

It was with this mindset that Lofthouse walked with Sarah through the gate into the fields. The sun was shining and the recent rain had freshened the grass, making it perfect for walking.

The fields were dotted with Sheep and frolicking lambs, while dairy cattle grazed in the sunshine. "This is so beautiful," said Sarah. "I've never been able to walk in the country like this. There is so much space, not like where our house is."

She had not enjoyed such freedom for as long as she could remember. Two farm dogs had joined them on the walk and ran about them excitedly with tongues hanging out. They loved to chase the hares through the fields, never being able to catch them. She laughed as she watched them play. Lofthouse too, laughed at the sight.

There was someone else in the fields that day. Young William Tyndale was checking the windbreak high in the top field, when he heard the excited yelping of the Lofthouse dogs over the other side of Linburn beck. He saw Lofthouse walking across the field and with him was the girl with the flashing auburn hair. William's dog with twitching nose, also surveyed the distant walkers.

"Well that's just grand Jess. I think we'll be taking a run down t' beck as soon as we're done here." The dog looked at him as though she understood what he was saying.

Lofthouse had seen William's blue Fordson tractor in the distance up in the high field and he wondered whether they would bump into each other. He knew William and he knew he would have seen him and Sarah walking towards the bottom field. As they drew nearer to the stream he wasn't really surprised to see the tractor moving slowly down the hill in the direction of the beck. His two dogs ran on ahead. They too saw and heard the distant tractor making it's way down the hill. Sarah, who was walking ahead hadn't noticed the tractor immediately but when she did, she waited for Lofthouse to catch up to her.

"Who do you think that is Mister Lofthouse?" she asked.

"I think that will be young William Tyndale," he answered, his hand shading his eyes. "I'll introduce you to him if you wish."

"Yes..., that should be alright." said Sarah quietly.

As they walked closer to the stream, her uncertainty melted away and she became quite excited to be meeting John Tyndale's brother.

"Is he younger or older than the one with the motorcycle?" she asked.

"How did you know he had a brother with a motorcycle darling?"

"Oh..., I must have seen him somewhere, or heard you speak of him," answered Sarah quickly.

"Yes, of course," said Lofthouse. "That must be it." He then added. "John is the eldest, William is the younger and then two younger sisters."

"I see, that's a nice family, isn't it?" said Sarah.

"Do you see them very often Mister Lofthouse?"

"No Sarah, not often enough."

Across the beck stood an old stone bridge with a gate at either end. The bridge had been built more than 300yrs ago, when the two farms were one large holding. It was a beautiful example of the Stonemason's art, in a country where Stonemasons were held in high regard.

Lofthouse and Sarah stood under the trees on the bank of the stream. The crystal clear water tumbled and gurgled over ancient stones. As it flowed it filled deep still pools, which are scattered along it's way. The sunlight painted a speckled scene under the shady trees. William seemed to respect the peaceful scene too much to bring the clattering, smoking tractor close. They watched as he stopped a distance away and walked to the edge of the stream with his dog. The sheep, cattle, corn buntings and tree sparrows payed little attention to the two farmers and the young auburn haired girl.

"How d'ye do Mr Lofthouse," he called out.

"Fine, I'm fine William, meet us on the bridge will you?"

William stumbled on an unseen tuft of grass. His eyes were fixed on the beautiful Sarah as she walked towards the bridge. He was thrilled to finally be meeting this mystery girl. More importantly he was meeting her before his brother John, who was presently at work miles away.

They met in the middle of the bridge where William and Lofthouse shook hands. Sarah stood behind the big farmer, gazing steadily over the wall at the water. She felt quite nervous.

"He turned toward the girl, saying gently, "Miss Sarah Dubois, I'd like you to meet William Tyndale from Old Tun farm."

She stepped around Lofthouse and held out her hand. William stepped forward and gently took her hand in his large rough mitt. He felt his face redden as he mumbled a greeting.

"How d'ye do miss Dubois."

"How do you do Mr Tyndale, "said Sarah quietly.

William dragged his eyes away from the girl of his dreams and leaned on the wall beside Lofthouse looking into the water below. Sarah stood to the other side of Mr Lofthouse and slightly to the rear, where she could study this Tyndale boy. The men talked about the farming business but Sarah had other things on her mind. Lofthouse could tell William had also.

Sarah could see William was handsome with dark curly hair. He wasn't as handsome as John and maybe not as tall but broad of shoulder and strong. Her inspection completed, she too leaned on the wall, looking down at the stream. The dogs were playing in the water, splashing around and chasing each other through the shallows. Grey Wagtails in the trees scolded them.

"Them beasts are daft as brushes," said William laughing.

He looked at Sarah and she laughed also. Lofthouse joined in and soon they were all laughing and feeling at ease with each other.

"We'd best be away now William, or Mrs Lofthouse will be looking for us."

"Aye, Nice to meet you Miss Dubois," said William.

"And you Mr Tyndale," said Sarah with a smile.

He turned and walked back to his tractor, which rattled patiently where he had left it up the bank. He would have looked back but didn't want to appear rude at their first meeting. He did turn when he reached the Fordson and waved to the others who were still on the bridge. He whistled Jess, who ran and jumped onto the carry-all as the tractor moved away. He turned to wave again but Lofthouse and Sarah were walking beside the beck among the trees and he couldn't see them clearly. He drove on up the hill with a huge grin on his face.

He was still grinning when he drove the tractor into the farm yard. His father heard him coming and opened the gate.

"By gum lad, thee looks a bit happy," he said to his son.

William had made the decision to keep the news of his meeting with Sarah to himself. He didn't want anything or anyone, especially his father, to spoil the experience.

"Aye it's a lovely day sure enough." he answered.

"We'll see how lovely 't is when thee's finished muckin' out 't pigs lad," replied Bill Tyndale shutting the gate.

William said nothing. It would take more than his father's misery or pigs, to bring him down today.

Meanwhile back at Peace Hall the walkers had just returned home from their walk.

"How was your walk this fine day," asked Thora Lofthouse.

"It was wonderful Mrs Lofthouse, just wonderful," said Sarah.

"It has certainly put roses in your cheeks. You as well Edward," she joked, slapping her husband playfully on the shoulder.

"You'll never guess who we ran into down at the beck, Thora."

"Tell me now, who did you see down there?" she asked.

"We saw William Tyndale Mrs Lofthouse and I met him," said Sarah excitedly.

"Well, well, well, did you now,?" replied Thora Lofthouse looking intently at her husband. "Did you indeed?"

Lofthouse returned her look with a smile. In a stage whisper he confided, "Don't worry, I'm sure she's more interested in young John and his motorcycle."

Chapter 12

"FATHER, WHO WAS our Uncle Joshua?" asked Margaret Tyndale. The family sat together in the parlour of Old Tun farm, one warm Summer evening. Bill Tyndale sat beside the empty fireplace in his comfortable chair, a glass of whisky by his side.

"Why's that lass?"

"I found an old letter from him in this drawer. It's addressed to you from Uncle Joshua."

"Aye, he'd be your great Uncle, he lives in America. He's my Uncle Josh. He wrote that t' me years ago. It was the first letter I ever got from anyone...and the last I'm thinking."

"Can I read it?" asked Margaret excitedly. Her brothers and sister joined in.

"Yes father, can she please?"

Their father thought about it for a moment, then said, "Fetch it hear lass I'll read t' bits you might be interested in."

He put on his spectacles, cleared his throat and stood to his feet beside the mantle piece.

"Now, this is about part of the family that sailed to America and never came back."

"What happened?" asked Mary.

"Why didn't they come back?" asked William.

"If you'll stop blatherin' I'll tell you." said Bill.

The room fell silent in anticipation. Their father didn't interrelate with them very often and they wouldn't miss this opportunity to enjoy some time together.

He began to read from the letter, in which his Uncle Josh explained the circumstances leading up to the time, when part of the Tyndale family settled in America.

"'The South Darnley pits fell idle. Most of their coal was burnt to produce coke, which in turn powered the iron furnaces but with no iron being produced there was no need for coke. Hardship set in among the work force, along with resentment at the power of the iron-masters Many people felt that their must be a better way of life away from the North-East.

In 1865 The Iron Worker's Union began making preparations to send out of the country, all who wanted to get away from the lockout. In late March 1865 the local newspaper noted, 'Emigration finds favour here, as at Spennymoor and about the same number, nearly 200 individuals, seem determined to leave the Country as soon as possible.'"

"That's the same paper we get now," said Mary.

"Aye lass," said Bill looking over his reading specs.

"'Agents representing American companies and landowners, toured the district offering inducements to anyone who wanted to leave for a life in a new country.

These industrial factors persuaded many of the 20 families of the Tyndale clan of Beckley Dell to consider leaving the area. Mother, from Blaney Beck, had married John Tyndale, a prosperous farmer and merchant in Beckley Dell, in 1826. Together they had 10 children. All of us were baptised in the Church of England.

In 1855, missionaries from the Church of Jesus Christ and Latter day Saints, which had headquarters in Wharton Mead, came calling on us in Beckley Dell. Mother desired to join them. She and the others were baptised into their Church by one of the members.

Ten years later she felt called to move to Salt Lake City in America, where the church also known as the Mormons, was building a model town. She took us with her and some of the grandchildren. Father and five of my brothers and sisters stayed on the farm. I don't think father had any intention of following us but mother never talked about it. In April we were among the many passengers who boarded 'The Norfolk' bound for New York City.

Mother said that many of the other passengers were paying for their passages with loans from the Perpetual Emigration Fund. She said we were fortunate that father was well off enough to pay the costs of the journey. No matter what the folks back there might say, father was never against mother following her faith.

We arrived in New York in May and began the 1,000 mile journey by rail and riverboat to Nebraska. Along the way my niece Charlotte died. My brother Robert decided to settle in Pennsylvania because his wife was pregnant again. From Nebraska we set out on a 1,100 mile trek. With the money father had provided we bought two wagons and eight oxen to pull them. We walked beside the wagons even when it snowed on the plains. Our belongings took up most of the space. We had to be constantly on guard against marauding Indians. The leader of the wagon train said they resented us crossing their lands. I don't know why.

We reached Salt Lake City in November. It took us 8 months from there to here. We have settled in a frontier town called Hailwood 50 miles from salt Lake City, where we are building our home. As you grow up, I hope you remember your American family.

Love, Uncle Josh.'"

"How old were you when you got this letter father?" asked William.

"I would have been about ten years of age lad," replied Bill Tyndale.

"Did you write a letter back?" asked John.

"Ye ken I'm not much at writin' letters lad." answered Bill. He was carefully folding his letter and placing it in the envelope.

"Put this back in t' cupboard lass," he handed it to Margaret and removed his spectacles. John broke the silence with a question,

"So we have all these relatives in America that we don't even know," asked John.

"I'd like to sail to America one day," said William.

"When thee's got nowt to do here lad, ye can go eh," his father answered.

"As for now ye can all go up to your beds and good night." he added.

As they walked up the stairs John said to his brother, "I don't think father's keen on you ever leaving this place Will."

"Aye, I think you're right," he answered as they wandered to their rooms.

"I'm going to be the one stuck here looking after the farm aren't I." William said as he slammed his bedroom door.

"Don't give up on your dreams brother," John called after him.

Down in the parlour Bill Tyndale spoke to the empty room, "Well Missy, the bairns are growin' and them without a mother to help. What should I do lass? What can I do?"

That night his dreams were peaceful, filled with his late wife's gentle voice. She had been the light of his life but now he needed to share his life with a companion, another woman. In his dream he told her this and was sure she gave him affirmation of his new-found desires. In reality, had she been alive, she would have called him a silly old fool.

That night all of his children dreamed of far away places.

It was a pleasant walk across the fields for Margaret and Mary to attend Marsley Hall School near the village. It had been a boys only boarding school in the 1750's but was now a co-educational establishment with provision for boarders. It had always been a Church of England school and was one of the largest in the district.

As they walked across the old stone bridge at the bottom of the bank the next morning, Mary spied a piece of paper wedged in the wooden gate on Peace Hall side of the beck.

"What could this be?" she said unfolding the paper.

"Read it out loud," said her sister.

"It says, 'Girls, would you ask your brother John to call at Peace Hall farm. Midnight at the old cottage. Please keep this a secret.' "It's signed S.D." added Mary.

"S.D. Who could that be?" asked Margaret.

"It's that girl. The one at Lofthouse's place!" exclaimed Mary.

"Yes, I think you're right and she wants to meet John. It's a secret letter."

The girls walked on, chattering with excitement.

"She must have sneaked down here sometime yesterday, maybe even last night." continued Margaret.

"She must be in love with John...how exciting!" said her younger sister.

"Now Mary you mustn't say any thing to anyone. Do you understand? You must promise me."

"I promise. I won't say anything, don't worry."

"Especially to father." added Margaret sternly.

It seemed an eternity to the girls, before the final school bell rang and they were able to head homeward. They were both keen to tell their big brother the exciting news.

As they crossed the corner of Lofthouse's field, walking towards the bridge, Margaret gazed towards Peace Hall farm. To her surprise she noticed a figure in a long white dress standing in a grove of trees behind the house. She thought it must be the young Dubois girl. As she watched, the girl took off her white bonnet and waved it in their direction. Margaret paused for a moment and returned the wave. Mary was walking ahead and hadn't noticed the exchange. Her elder sister didn't mention anything to her about the incident.

There was someone else watching that afternoon. Someone standing with his dog in the shade of the trees, by his beloved beck. This stream was his quiet place. Somewhere he could sit and dream away from the drudgery of farm work. As a young lad William Tyndale had found a sheltered spot between the rocks and a large willow, where he could run to and hide from his father. It was a safe haven which was protected in most weather conditions. He had made it more so by placing tree branches and pieces of dead wood as a rough cover over the hollow. Whenever he had gone missing as a child, his dog would have quickly followed his scent to their private place at the stream and given him a severe licking. From his position beside the stream he could see most of the surrounding countryside. This was an ideal place from which he could watch his sheep and cattle, even in bad weather.

Late the previous evening he had been under the trees looking out over the fields, for any sign of a troublesome fox, which he had reason to believe was moving too close to his lambs.

It was a cloudy night but the moon was still showing through in patches on the fields. He was just about to go home for supper when he saw a movement along the wall near Peace Hall farm. A slightly built figure dressed in dark clothes and an old hat pulled low over their face moved stealthily towards the stone bridge. This person was too small to be Lofthouse and he knew Mrs Lofthouse would never be out in the fields this late.

He caught a glimpse of a pale face as the figure moved through a patch of moonlight.

Even from a distance he could see it was the girl from Lofthouse's place, Sarah Dubois. He drew a sharp intake of breath. What should he do? It was obvious she was on a secret mission of some sort. If he made his presence known it would frighten her, so he decided to keep his peace and remain still among the trees. He watched as she made her way toward the gate on her side of the bridge, amazed at her speed across the ground. She had managed to stay close to the sheltering walls around the field taking advantage of any cover to be found.

"She must have sneaked out when they went to bed," he whispered, to nobody but his dog. The dog didn't appear to be particularly interested and lay quietly at his feet.

Sarah Dubois had no idea she was being observed as she placed her note in a crack in the old wooden gate. Her pale skin was flushed with exertion now and her breathing laboured. She looked quickly over her shoulder toward the farmhouse and smiled to herself to see it still in darkness. Her heart was pounding and her eyes sparkled. She had sneaked out of the house when all was quiet, to put her bold plan into operation. She knew she had to act quickly and secretly if she was to meet John Tyndale before going home to Stopford Brook. If her plan wasn't successful who knows when she would get another chance?

William watched her move swiftly through the moon shadow toward the farmhouse. He then moved slowly down the stream to the stone bridge and crossed over to the other gate, keeping low. He took the note and sat on the bridge with his back against the wall. His hands shook as he read it and he could even smell her perfume on the paper. When he read the contents of the note his countenance fell and his shoulders drooped. What should he do?

He loved his brother and his conscience wouldn't allow him to destroy the letter, which was his first impulse.

He replaced the note and headed back home with his thoughts tumbling. When he entered the kitchen he found the house in darkness and everyone in bed, except his father who sat in the darkness with his glass of whisky.

"Did ye spy t' fox lad?" he asked William.

William's heart skipped a beat. He'd completely forgotten about the fox during all of the excitement.

"No, I'll check again tomorrow night." he answered.

"Thee must be blind lad." replied his father quietly.

He didn't answer but went straight upstairs to his bed. He dreamed of an auburn haired girl in fields of green. During the night he decided to remove the note from the gate. If he allowed his brother to meet this girl he would never get a chance to get close to her. His infatuation with the girl overcame his conscience. He would go down to the bridge in the morning and destroy the letter. He felt no guilt. However, as fate would have it, one of the horses went down with a difficult foaling early that morning. When he had finished with his work it was too late to retrieve the note. The horse, the foal and the fox were happy but he was quite miserable.

Chapter 13

JOHN TYNDALE WORKED for the Stonemason Andrew Howe, who was known in the district as And. Howe. His yard was situated on the Whitton-le-Wear road near the crossroads. It was about an acre in size and on it was his cottage, a large work shed and several small sheds, all built from stone. Large blocks of Sandstone and Granite were stacked around with many smaller pieces scattered outside the workshop. Granite and even Marble was available from various quarries around Stopford Brook. Traces of these local stones had been discovered in ancient Roman ruins in the district. The locals had used these ruins as a source of readily available building products for hundreds of years.

By 1935 however, the powers that be were beginning to take a very dim view of the recycling of Roman artefacts. The new restrictions were slow to take effect in the North East and John Tyndale rode his motorcycle past several antiquities as he made his way to the workshop every day. Many of the farms in the area had Roman stone and marble included in their construction. Waste not, want not was the order of the day and the material 'cost nowt'. A diesel powered crane and tractor were parked on the concrete outside the shed, beside some grand looking columns leaning against the wall. Howe liked to tell folks his family had been in stone for many a century. Everyone knew his family had been in Roman stone for many a century.

John loved his work and was very good at his job. Competent stonemasons were few and far between in 1935 and he was kept quite busy. And Howe and the other workmen liked his work and thought a lot of him personally.

One morning Howe came from the office and said to John, "Now John, ower in t' brambles and long grass thee'll find an old stone lintel."

He pointed in the direction of a seldom used section of the yard.

He continued, "I ken as a lad my Dad dumped it there. I haven't seen it since."

"Tek Dusty with thee in t' lorry and fetch it to t' shop will ye?"

"Aye Mr Howe," John replied.

He called out to Jim Rhodes the labourer, "Dusty, drop what you're doing and come with me."

The lorry was a 1926 3ton Commer Karrier which was still giving sterling service in spite of it's age. It still looked presentable in it's dark blue and yellow livery, carrying the name of Howe and Co. Stonemasons. Howe was loath to buy the new 1935 model when this one was still doing the job.

Dusty ambled over to the lorry. He was a short stocky man 60 years of age and had worked for And Howe's father since just a lad. He wore his cloth cap at a jaunty angle and was fit for his age with a twinkle in his eye and a sprightly step.

"Aye young Tyndale, what's t' job lad." he asked.

He'd known the Tyndale family all his life and referred to all of the children as 'young Tyndale'.

"Somewhere over here there's a stone lintel lying in these bushes." said John.

He pointed at the general area in the far corner of the yard.

"I'll fetch a scythe," offered Dusty.

"Aye lad that's where it'll be. I ken we dumped a load of stone from the old monastery over there years ago." Dusty said as the lorry rolled to a halt.

"Stand back young Tyndale." The labourer stepped forward and swung the scythe with powerful strokes, until most of the prickly bramble bush was cleared away.

The two men stomped around with their heavy boots until the older man shouted,

"This'll be it lad. It's only about four foot long. We can heave it on t' lorry."

"Ha'way lad." said Dusty taking hold of one end.

They lifted it onto the vehicle and drove over to the workshop where the boss was waiting.

"Aye that's it lads. Now give it a good clean up. Toby Griffiths wants us to tek it ower to one of his jobs. That's why I never throw nowt away. Nowt's worth nowt ye ken, it's all worth summat."

"Aye Mr Howe," answered John.

"Thee's right an' all," muttered Dusty.

As they cleaned the stone lintel they uncovered some lettering which read, 'DEO INVICTO'.

"Well, would you look at this inscription" said John.

"I think it's the name of t' fella that carved it out of t' quarry centuries gone." answered the older man.

"It's in Latin, something about God I think." ventured John.

"What is?" asked Dusty.

"The writing. It's Latin, like in Italy."

"Oy up, ye think he was a foreigner then?"

"Never mind Dusty. It's not important, but I think it's very old." said John with a wry smile.

"Aye, but it's still good for t' job sure enough lad." answered Dusty, giving the stone a slap with his leathery hand.

The ancient stone lintel which had stood across the door of a monastery, would soon grace the front doorway of a house built by Toby Griffiths & Sons of High Etherley.

"That's fine lads, if he doesn't want t' writin' he can turn it ower," said Howe.

"His job's in Beckley Dell in t' estate near t' old rail bridge." he added.

"Tek it ower now and ye'll be back before knock off time. Now off ye go," he said with a wave.

"Bye the way John, ask him when he wants those sills and half-bullnose sections for that job."

"Aye Mr Howe." he answered, climbing into the cab of the lorry.

Even though he wasn't yet 18yrs of age John was And Howe's right hand man when dealing with builders in the district. On the way to Griffith's site in the lorry Dusty said,

"Andy Howe'll charge him a pretty penny for t' lintel and his father got it for nowt off t' old monastery ruin years back."

"That's the way to make money alright. My father always says there's brass in muck."

They both laughed as the lorry rumbled along the road between the dry stone walls. Their precious cargo would soon be built into another wall, for who knows how long. Their business concluded they drove back to the yard to finish their working day. Autumn was just around the corner and the days were beginning to close in. The lights were on in the office when they parked the lorry for the night.

"See thee tomorrow lad," said Dusty as they parted ways.

John headed for the office, while he headed for his bicycle and the ride home.

"How'd thee go lad?" asked Howe.

"Fine Mr Howe. He'll be ready for the rest of his stone on next Monday."

"Excellent, I'll see thee on the morrow lad. Mind how ye go on that contraption of yours," he said to John.

Mr and Mrs Howe worried about John riding his motorcycle. He was known to ride the narrow roads at speed. The local

Policeman had stopped him the other morning and warned him of the new 30mph speed limits through the village. They may have worried more, if they'd been aware he was saving his money for a bigger and faster BSA 500cc, which he'd seen at the dealership in Stopford Brook.

He fired up his trusty machine and put on his leather great-coat while the engine warmed up. With a wave he roared out of the gate and onto the Blaney Beck road towards home. His headlight cast a warm yellowish glow on the narrow country road. His sisters had walked up the driveway to meet him and he stopped beside them.

"What're you girls doing up here?" he asked.

"We wanted to give you this, said Margaret. It's a secret note for you."

She handed him the note and he read it in the motorcycle light.

"Where did you get this?"

"It was down at the old bridge this morning," said Mary.

John thought for a moment, then said, "Tell them you came to meet me for a ride on the motorbike. Jump on the back and I'll run you back to the house."

"Thanks girls, for doing this."

They loved both of their brothers very much but sensed this was a special secret, to be shared between the three of them for the time being. John let them off at the front gate while he went to put his machine in the shed. He took the note from his pocket and read it once more. He could hardly believe his eyes. Sarah Dubois wanted to see him. His heart skipped a beat at the scent of the perfumed paper. When he entered the kitchen he was unaware of the huge smile on his face.

"Thee looks happy to be home lad," said his father.

The girls who were sitting at the table, giggled. A quick look from John silenced them.

"Aye father, it's always good to be home," he replied still smiling.

"It's not that good brother," said William standing by the fire. "By the way, did you girls enjoy your ride?" He fixed them with an enquiring stare. He had a suspicion what had taken place in the driveway but said nothing. John went up to the bathroom to get ready for dinner. The conversation around the dinner table touched on the usual subjects of the day.

At the end of the meal William leaned back and said nonchalantly, "I think it's going to be very cold outside tonight."

No one knew of course, that he was aware of the contents of the note and John's plans for later in the evening.

John was puzzled by his brother's remark but simply answered, "Yes".

"Aye ye'd be a fool to be out tonight alright," said Bill Tyndale. He left the table and sat in his chair by the fire, with a glass of single malt whisky.

John held his nerve but wondered if everyone knew his secret. The girls shared a glance.

"We'll all be warm in our beds though, won't we?" she said with a smile.

"I'm off upstairs. said John. I've some reading to do."

He didn't notice the smirk on his brother's face but Margaret did and wondered about it.

"Is everything alright William?" she asked.

Her brother merely smiled without answering. His jealousy smouldered inside him.

John didn't come out of his room for the rest of the evening. He was thinking of his meeting with Sarah Dubois at the cottage near Peace Hall farm.

Chapter 14

THE COTTAGE NEAR Peace Hall farm stood about a hundred yards away from the main house beside a small stream. It had been abandoned since the main house was built many years ago.

The locals knew it as the Honeymoon Cottage, because it was built by Harold Lofthouse in 1624 for his new bride, in the first years of Peace Hall farm. A wooden bridge leading to a stone footpath still crossed the stream and lead to the front door. Though derelict, it was still a solid building. The once glorious garden was overgrown and the cottage was covered with Climbing Roses and Blue Wisteria. The moon struggled to shine through the clouds, presenting a hauntingly beautiful night time picture. The silence that surrounded the cottage was broken only by the tinkling stream and the distant call of a fox. Two cats ran across a patch of moonlight towards the tractor shed. The main house stood in darkness.

The cottage, because of it's beauty and history was known locally as a thin place. 'Thin Place' was the name given by the ancient Celts to those places which were so special, that the veil between Heaven and Earth is thin. It may be a certain mountain or section of coastline, or an area of woodland but mostly an ancient building. John Tyndale walked through the wooded tract at the rear of the cottage and slowly opened the small iron gate to the overgrown garden. He held his breath, senses alert and listened. He walked slowly to the back door, opened it and passed into the silence of the room. Beams of moonlight struggled through the small windows occasionally flooding the interior with a ghostly greyness. He held his breath again as the front door slowly opened allowing a small figure to enter. The person wore an old coat and Trilby hat. John recognised it as Lofthouse's old clothes. His legs turned to jelly as the shadowy figure stepped into a patch of moonlight and removed their hat.

The moonlight glowed on her auburn hair as it tumbled across her shoulders. She tossed her head and smiled at him as she crossed the room. He looked into her sparkling eyes and felt her breath on his face.

"Hello John, I'm Sarah Dubois." Her eyes dropped to the floor momentarily. "I've been wanting to meet you since I saw you at the house." She looked into his eyes. "I hope you don't mind me asking you here."

John's tongue seemed to be stuck to the roof of his mouth but he managed to say,

"Hello Sarah Dubois." He smiled at her and held out his hand awkwardly. She took his hand and held it.

"You're shaking you poor thing. Are you cold?" she asked.

He wasn't cold but trembling to be in the moonlit presence of this beautiful creature.

"No, I'm Not cold at all Sarah, as a matter of fact I feel quite warm." He wanted to touch her flowing hair and her pale smooth skin. What he did next surprised him and delighted Sarah. He slowly raised her hand and gently kissed it, as he looked longingly into her soft brown eyes. Sarah sighed and stepped closer to him. She pressed against him and looked up at his face. He felt her slim body tremble against him. They stood together in the moonlit cottage for several moments, until John put his arms around her slender waist and held her tightly. Without speaking, he kissed her gently on her forehead. Sarah raised her face to his and then he kissed her on the lips. They stood holding each other until Sarah pulled away.

"I must go, before I'm missed."

"But when will I see you again?" asked John, with his arm out stretched toward her.

"I'll find a way," Sarah whispered. She put on the old Trilby hat, slipped quietly through the front door and into the night.

John stood for several minutes in a state of wonder, then he retraced his steps out of the back door and into the trees, where he began his walk to Old Tun farm. His thoughts were swimming, his heart was bursting with joy. The grass sped beneath his feet as he began to run through the fields shouting her name "Sarah Dubois! I kissed Sarah Dubois!" As he approached the farm, he did quieten down somewhat and sneak into the house. All was quiet as he crept upstairs to his room. He had never experienced such a feeling before. He wanted to shout and sing and wake the whole house. He didn't have to wake his sister Margaret, who had been lying awake waiting for his return. She quietly crept to the door of his room and said in her softest voice, "Goodnight John, sleep tight."

"Goodnight sis," he replied, climbing into his bed.

He knew his young sisters would pester him tomorrow, for information about his romantic moonlight tryst. Sleep didn't come easy to John that night as the excitement coursed through his veins. When he finally fell asleep, his dreams were filled with visions of the auburn haired girl in the moonlit cottage. John woke early, free of any tiredness his late night may have caused. His father prepared a cup of steaming tea for him and they sat together in the still of the morning enjoying their breakfast. Bill looked out of the window and spoke,

"T' weather's closin' in lad. Thee'll need t' coat today on t' motorbike. It'll rain ye ken."

"I don't mind father. It's just water." replied John, still basking in the afterglow of his midnight meeting with Sarah Dubois. Bill Tyndale looked at his son, raised his eyebrows but said nothing.

William was the next one to come downstairs, followed by the girls.

They all sat at the table with their breakfast. William decided to test the waters,

"Did I hear someone downstairs about midnight last night?" he asked without raising his head from his plate. He knew very well he could stir up a hornet's nest.

"Did ye hear a din? I didn't hear 'owt lad." said Bill.

"We didn't hear anything," said the girls.

"I didn't hear anything," added John.

"It must have been some old fox prowling around," said William with a big grin to his brother.

The girls laughed as John replied, "Yes you'd better be careful, foxes can be dangerous at night, little brother."

"What're ye all blatherin' about?" asked Bill as he rose from the table.

"Thee's all daft as brushes." He smiled as he headed for the door and donned his overcoat and cap. "I'm down to see t' foal. Won't be long." He slammed the door closed behind him.

"Why did you say a stupid thing like that, William?" asked Margaret when they were on their own.

"Ask yourself why John's boots have fresh mud around them little sister." Replied William, pointing to his brothers boots.

"You'd all better shut up. All of you do you understand!" shouted John, looking straight at William. "I don't know what you think you know but if you know what's good for you, you'll forget it brother."

The menacing look that John gave his brother, was enough to frighten William and the sisters at the other side of the table into silence.

John went to the door, put on his riding gear and strode outside slamming the door after him. They heard the motorbike roar up the driveway.

After a lengthy strained silence, young Mary said, "William, do you know something you aren't supposed to know?"

Her brother's face reddened, "I know more than you think," he replied sullenly.

"About what, William?" She knew her brother very well and she knew he was a terrible liar. She pressed on with her question. "What do you know about last night," she asked.

"Mary!" said Margaret urgently, "You'll say too much."

Mary had already seen the tell-tale signs on William's face however and needed to ask no more questions. She knew he knew about John and Sarah.

"Sis, I need to see you upstairs." She took Margaret's arm and led her upstairs o her room.

"He must have seen the note. He knows," she whispered to her sister.

"He couldn't have... could he?" answered Margaret.

"Why not? It's his favourite place down at the beck. Don't forget he was down there after the fox the night before last."

"That's true. What a detective you are Mary. We'll have to tell John," said Margaret.

"We'll tell him tonight." said her sister.

When the girls went back downstairs William had left the house to start his jobs also. They tidied away the breakfast things and cleaned up, before getting ready for school. They heard their father come in downstairs, complaining about the cold drizzling rain.

"Thee'll need to rug up lassies. It's right nasty out there," he shouted up the stairs.

They come downstairs and put on their wet weather oil-skins, ready for the walk to school across the fields. With a kiss from their father they left the house and headed across the muddy yards toward the back gate. They waved to William who was busy in the tractor shed. He looked but didn't return their wave.

"He'll be alright when he takes time to think about it," said Margaret to her sister.

"Don't worry about William, he'll get over it." She put her arm around Mary as they walked down the field toward the bridge.

As they stepped across the stile onto the grass beside the road, a car drew up beside them.

"Good morning girls, are you keeping well?" It was Robert Douglas, on his rounds.

"Yes thank you Doctor, we are," answered Margaret. The engine ticked over quietlyn and the air under the car was warm on their legs as they stood by the door.

"How are the boys?' he asked.

Margaret, ever the enterprising one, saw an opportunity to help her big brother in his affairs of the heart. She was aware of the concept of 'go-betweens' in romantic novels and she was prepared to utilise the concept to her brother's advantage.

"They're fine thank you Doctor....well John isn't so well actually."

"Really, I hope it's nothing serious," replied Douglas with real concern in his voice.

Margaret relayed a condensed version of the affection which had grown between Sarah Dubois and John, stressing the need for secrecy. Before Robert Douglas could reply she added,

"If it's not too much trouble Doctor, I wonder if you could express John's best wishes to Miss Dubois if you happen to see her in your travels?"

Mary's heart was in her mouth at her sister's audacity. What was she thinking?

She needn't have worried. Douglas roared laughing and said, "I would be happy to do that for you and for the lovely couple. I will be seeing her today as a matter of fact."

"Mum's the word eh?" he touched his nose and winked.

The wide grins on the girls' faces warmed his heart on that cold miserable morning.

"Now, I must be on my way ladies. Good morning to you both."

They were sure they heard him laughing as he drove away. Since the untimely death of the children's mother, he had committed himself to helping the children broaden their horizons in any way he could. He was looking forward to sharing this mornings experience with George and Ann Lowther, the children's grandparents. As he drove down the narrow road, he had another brainwave and turned into the lane leading to Peace Hall farm. It must be time he called in to see his old friends George and Thora Lofthouse. The 'game was afoot', as his favourite fictional detective Sherlock Holmes would say. He smiled at the thought.

Chapter 15

BY THE SPRING of 1936 the world was changing. King George V had died leaving his son Edward to rule for only a short period. He abdicated, leaving George V1 on the throne. That year became known as 'the year of three kings'. The Nazi party in Germany had deprived all German Jews of citizenship, while the world looked on with only mild interest. War clouds were on the horizon, while Adolph Hitler was charming the nations with his preparations for the X1 Olympiad. Some city folk were talking about Schrodinger's cat and Quantum mechanics.

John Tyndale had paid 59 hard earned pounds for a second hand BSA 500cc Blue Star from McClellans, the dealership in Stopford Brook. He had sold his old motorcycle for a canny price and was very happy with his latest acquisition. It was the realisation of a dream he'd cherished for two long years. As well as being more powerful and faster, it had a pillion seat. On this motorcycle he would be able to take Sarah Dubois for rides in the countryside.

If all of his dreams came true, this would be their freedom machine. He was eighteen years of age now and considered a responsible, trustworthy young man by those who knew him. Because of the behind the scenes efforts of others, the courtship of Sarah and John had progressed in leaps and bounds. It was

Springtime, when a young man's thoughts generally turn to love. John Tyndale was very much in love and every waken moment was taken up with thoughts of the auburn haired girl from Stopford Brook, who had stolen his heart.

Doctor Douglas and Mr and Mrs Lofthouse had acted as referees for the boy but the most helpful in influencing Mrs Dubois in John's favour, was an invitation to a gathering at George and Anne Lowther's country home. Theirs being the only home in the local district with a ballroom large enough. It was a private Debutante party on behalf of Sarah and Clare Dubois. Many of the surrounding land-holders were invited to attend with their families.

It was a glittering affair held in early Spring which gave the young men and women a chance to socialise in a chaperoned situation. Anne Lowther and Hannah Dubois shared the planning and preparation, with Hannah keen to make sure her daughters met the brightest and best of the young gentlemen in the County. In the few times she had met John Tyndale of Old Tun farm, she had been impressed by his general demeanour. All of Bill Tyndale's children had benefited from the teaching of their late mother, Anne Lowther's daughter and were able to impress in the highest social circles. Bill's property and income placed him in the upper middle class but he wasn't interested in 'airs and graces'.

In due course the two debutantes in their white gowns were presented to the guests. Sarah danced her first dance with her father while Clare danced with George Lowther. After the first dance, the local boys and girls lined up to dance as directed by Lowther's housekeeper, who was acting as head chaperone for the evening. She had also fulfilled this role when Bill Tyndale had been courting Missy before they married. The lights burned brightly late into the night, as local dignitaries and gentry danced, laughed and flirted together.

The kitchen staff mixed gallons of wine punch and a barrel of Dandelion and Burdock was delivered from Feckletons of

Billingsley, for the young folk. Venison pies, game dishes of all sorts, roast meats, pheasant and pastries kept the guests fed. The dining room table groaned under the lavish presentation. Towards the end of the evening several men and women gathered in the drawing room for a quiet drink. Cigars were offered and many partook.

"Well Lowther, thee's really done it this time. What a party this has been," said Bill Tyndale with a puff of his cigar.

"It's wonderful to see the young people enjoying themselves, isn't it Bill?" answered George. "Where are the other children tonight?" He received no answer.

"It's been a very enjoyable evening," added Carlos Dubois. Hannah and I appreciate what you and Anne have done for the girls this evening. Here's cheers," he said raising his glass to Anne and George.

"Cheers," everyone repeated.

Bill Tyndale edged to Carlos Dubois side and said, "My lad John seems to be entranced with that young lass of thine, Dubois,"

Carlos Dubois turned and said, "Do you mean Sarah, Mr Tyndale?" he asked.

"Aye, young Sarah. She's a fine looking lass for sure."

"She is indeed a fine girl Mr Tyndale, as is her sister Clare. Your children are a credit to you also Sir," said Dubois. "I have no objection to your son visiting Sarah, We would be happy to receive him Tyndale," added Carlos Dubois.

"Aye, as you say, as you say, "answered Bill Tyndale lost in thought.

"Is that your answer man?" asked Dubois.

Bill was running through his usual mental check list of pros and cons concerning John's interest in Sarah. Would it be of any benefit to himself? The answer was no.

"Aye, that'd be fine but only very occasionally. You see he has a desire to stay on t' farm for life thee kens."

"Are you saying he wants to be on the farm for the rest of his life man? Is that what you're saying Tyndale?"

"Aye, does thy lass like to work on t' farm Dubois," asked Bill.

"Work?" said the other man, as though he had spoken a dirty word. I'll have you know Sir, we haven't raised a farm labourer." Dubois turned on his heel and left Bill Tyndale standing by himself.

George Lowther approached Carlos Dubois.

"Carlos, are you alright? You look pale." he asked his friend.

"George, your son in law is an oaf, if you don't mind me saying so."

"What has happened?"

"Well, he has suggested, in no uncertain terms that young John is just in the marriage market for a farm worker, not a loving wife. He believes his son isn't interested in being much more himself." Dubois added.

"Carlos my friend, let me assure you John Tyndale is an honourable and ambitious young man who worships the ground upon which Sarah walks. Take no notice of Bill.

He is as you say, a Philistine. A good man but a Philistine."

"Come, have another drink with me," he said, putting his arm around the other man's shoulder.

In the ballroom Sarah and John had managed to dance together most of the evening, without many interruptions. They sat together enjoying a cool drink under the ever watchful eye of Miss Jackson, the housekeeper.

"Miss Jackson would you accompany us onto the balcony? We would like to sit down in the fresh air for a while," asked John.

"Certainly Master Tyndale. We could go outside for a short while," she answered.

John placed Sarah's shawl around her shoulders and they walked outside.

The Lowther's 'Bell Hill' had been built around the same time as nearby Silverton Hall in Staindrop and they looked similar except for the ballroom and balcony at Lowther's house.

They were stylish homes and quite large but were still essentially farm houses used in conjunction with the everyday business of farming. Several Spaniels and Retrievers had the run of the place with their muddy feet, while quite often a visiting shooting party may gather in the drawing room in their hunting clothes. The byres and stables, while not being next to the house were still fairly close, filling the air with the unmistakable smell of expensive livestock.

John took a deep breath and looked around. The glow of light from the ballroom and the pale moonlight shone around the garden. Sarah's pale skin and the fire of her hair caused him to lean close and whisper, "You look very beautiful Sarah Dubois."

Sarah smiled and reached for his hand across the table. They held hands looking into each other's eyes, until Miss Jackson cleared her throat as a warning.

"Your time is up. We should go back inside now."

Miss Jackson led the way, which allowed the two love-birds to hold hands a little longer as they followed her. Mr and Mrs Lowther stood at the side entrance. They were thanking the guests that were leaving. Carlos and Hannah Dubois stood with them. The butler carried the hats and coats of several guests, from an ante- room. Bill Tyndale beckoned to John and went to stand with the Lowthers. Doctor Douglas and his wife intercepted John and Sarah as they walked to the door.

"I was just saying to Robert what a lovely couple you make. If ever you would like to come for a visit just let us know. I mean both of you together. Won't you?' Eve Douglas was a classic matchmaker and made no bones about it. She had been heard to say on several occasions,

"Good Lord, if nothing is done these country folk would take forever to get on with it. They're so slow."

It was a sentiment that John Tyndale agreed with wholeheartedly. His confidence had grown, particularly in the presence of Sarah.

"Thank you Mrs Douglas. Rest assured I'll keep that in mind," he replied softly.

He heard George Lowther ask his father why the other children hadn't been present for the festivities and he heard the reply that he had always heard as a child, "Well ye ken I don't like to leave t' place unattended in t' evening."

"Good heavens man, make sure you bring them out occasionally. It's good for them and as their grandparents we would love to see them here," said Lowther quietly, as he shook Bill Tyndale's hand. 'We would love to have them holiday here."

"Aye," said Bill. "Nowt would get done then."

Others gathered around the door chatting. There seemed to be more socialising at this point in the evening than earlier.

"You think about what I've said Tyndale. If you like, I'll send over one of my men to keep things ticking over while the children are here. Free of charge." added George Lowther.

"Aye, I'll think on it George," answered his son in law.

He turned to John and said, "Ha' way lad, let's be getting home. Thee can drive t' car for us."

Goodbyes were said and the two men left the house, John with a final wave to Sarah. On the way home Bill said to his son, "Thee kens this lass won't be much of a worker lad. Doesn't thee?"

"Yes father but I'm not looking for a worker." Then, with a new confidence welling up inside him he added, "I'm looking for a wife and one day Sarah and I will be together."

Neither man said any more as they drove toward Old Tun farm.

Chapter 16

THE DAYS WERE longer and warmer now and John would ride to the Dubois house in Stopford Brook in the evening to visit Sarah. With Miss Castle the maid as chaperone, they would walk in the open fields behind the house holding hands. The fields sloped gently down to the River Gaunless. One evening they noticed there had been some earthmoving taking place that day. This was part of the Government's new prosperity measures for the North. A new estate was being built. The newly erected sign told them it was to be called 'The Willows Estate'.

"I hope the boss gets some jobs here. I'll be working just around the corner from your house if he does." said John.

"That would be wonderful," said Sarah. "Do you think he will?" she asked excitedly.

"It'll take a while before they can start building. The roads will have to be done first."

"I'm going to ask your father if I can start taking you for short trips on the motorbike.

Maybe we could start riding slowly on these roads when they're finished, just until you get used to it,"

"Yes, let's do it. Let's do it soon John. I really want to," said Sarah

Her eyes were sparkling now as she looked earnestly into the face of her beau.

"I'm also telling him of my intentions to become engaged to you to be married," added John.

Sarah let out a squeal of delight and threw her arms around John's neck, with no thought at all of the chaperone. The maid walked implacably onward. She did stop however and turn around when the hug lingered too long for decency. She said nothing but the two love-birds got the message and un-entwined themselves.

"Oh John we must pray that Daddy agrees," whispered Sarah.

"They will say you're too young," said the maid, having overheard the last portion of their conversation.

"Oh, but Miss Castle we could have a long engagement. Many couples do these days," suggested Sarah.

John stopped and looked at Sarah's crestfallen face, "We'll cross that bridge when we come to it," he said firmly.

"I will pray for you both," said the maid with a broad smile.

As they walked and talked, John couldn't shake the fear that something may go wrong with their plans. That night his sleep was troubled but his fears melted away with the warm morning sun.

At work, he told And Howe about the new estate in Stopford Brook. And said he had been aware of the planning stages for a few months, and had discussed it with some of the local builders. Some of his friends had already won contracts there. He also said there would be brickwork as well as some stonework to do on the new houses.

Dusty Rhodes said, "We'll have to be on our metal on those jobs. It'll be good experience for thee young Tyndale. Bricks and stone both."

"I can't wait," was all John could say.

That night at home Margaret and Mary wanted to hear everything about the Ball at Lowthers.

"Did you dance all night?" asked one.

"Did you hold her in your arms?"

"Did she hold you in hers?" asked the other.

"Did you kiss her?"

Of course all of these questions were asked when their father was out of the room. William was busy in the carriage shed. John then brought out the heavy artillery,

"I'm going to ask for Sarah's hand in marriage."

"You girls must keep this secret now. Do you hear me?"

There was silence in the room. John had never seen his sisters so dumbstruck.

The girls began to whisper over and over again, "John's getting married,... John's getting married," They laughed and clapped their hands.

"No, no we have to get engaged first. Now be quiet...please." interrupted their brother.

"Yes, yes of course," said Margaret with her eyes wide.

"Won't you have to ask father and Mr Dubois?" asked Mary, the ever practical one.

"Yes...I just have to wait for the right moment," replied John.

Don't you have to be twenty one years of age?" asked Mary.

"I don't know how it all works," answered John.

"I'll find a book in the library at school. A book on etiquette will tell us the right way to go about it." said Margaret.

"That's a great idea sis. Now, you must go about your business before they come inside. It's a secret, you must promise not to say anything to anyone." said John sternly.

"We promise," they replied.

"Good luck finding the right moment John," wished Margaret.

When his father and brother walked into the kitchen after finishing their job, they were talking in undertones without any regard for John's presence.

"I'm here in the room you know," he said loudly. "What are you discussing?

"Ye ken were talking about ye and t' lassie," answered his father. "We dinna think she's right for thee lad."

William said nothing. He busied himself making cups of tea.

"We?" asked John. "You've both been discussing my future without my presence?"

"Aye lad thee seems to have tekin' leave of thy senses." his father said, sitting down at the table.

John was flabbergasted and merely sat shaking his head. Finally he said,

"What do you think you know about me and Sarah?" he finally asked.

"Your brother tells me thee's been seeing her secretly ower t' Peace Hall cottage,"

"Father! I told you that in private," interjected William. "I'm sorry John," he said to his brother.

"No matter brother. I'm not upset by it. My mind's made up about Sarah....and she loves me. That's all that matters."

"Is that so?" said Bill Tyndale. "If ye cannae wed a local farm lass who can workon t' place, then what's t' point in leaving farm to ye!" he shouted.

"It'd be more use to young William here," he added with a wave of his hand.

"No father, this isn't right," William interrupted. "John's your eldest son."

"All I'm saying is this," began Bill Tyndale, "Thee needs to have a think about what ye'll be doing." He was looking straight at John when he spoke.

"That's all I'll be saying on t' subject. Just have a think lad. Thee could end up wi' nowt."

With this last remark he rose from the table, went into the parlour and sat in the semi-darkness drinking his whisky.

"I'm sorry John. If I hadn't told him he wouldn't have said those things."

"Don't worry William I'm glad you know now. By the way, how did you know?"

"The night I was hunting the fox, I saw the Dubois girl leave the note on the bridge. I read it and replaced it."

"I'm glad it's all out now," said John. He stood up and gave William a brotherly hug.

"I'm off to bed now anyway. Goodnight William it's been a long day."

He walked through the parlour to the stairs and paused. "Father, if you knew Sarah, you would love her too. Good night," he said to the lonely figure sitting in the darkness. He received no answer. Sleep eluded him for a time that night.

Chapter 17

THE FIRST DAYS of summer brought heatwave conditions to the North of the country and the Stopford Brook area was no exception. One particular day which seemed to go on forever, John rode his motorcycle to the Dubois house. The heat was such that the tar was melting on some of the roads, leaving a soft black mess to negotiate. All creatures in the countryside sought some relief from the heat, in the shade of trees hedges and walls. The heat was almost intolerable late in the evening, as he knocked on the front door. He was welcomed by the maid and shown through to the drawing room where the family sat relaxing after their dinner.

John Tyndale had a plan and his face was set with determination.

"John, How nice to see you," said Hannah Dubois.

Her husband rose and shook John's hand. The girls did the same and returned to their seats. Carlos Dubois was in his shirtsleeves and the ladies in light summer clothing but even so they were all quite flushed with the heat. John had never seen Carlos Dubois so informally attired.

"Isn't this weather going to cook us all?" he said to John.

"I think you're right sir," answered John. "Even the roads are melting."

He glanced at Sarah, then said, "I wonder if I could speak to you privately for a few minutes sir?"

"Why, certainly John. Come through to the Library. Would you excuse us ladies?"

"Certainly Carlos. I'll ask Miss castle to bring you some tea." As the two men departed the room, Carlos and Hannah shared a look, as did Sarah and her sister.

John sat opposite Dubois with a coffee table in between. Small talk was the order of the day.

"I've noticed you've been working on one of the houses in the Estate," said Dubois.

"Yes sir, it's a Show home. Top quality all the way through."

"The work you're doing John, looks absolutely marvellous," said the other man.

"Yes, thank you sir. There is something I would dearly like to ask you sir," answered John.

A knock at the door interrupted their conversation and the tea tray was placed on the table.

"Shall I pour sir?" asked the maid.

"Yes please Mildred.

The two men watched as the maid poured their tea.

"Thank you Mildred, that will be all thank you." said Dubois.

John Tyndale could wait no longer for the right moment to speak. This is the right moment.

"Sir, you know Sarah and I have been spending quite a lot of time together."

"Yes John," answered Dubois.

"I've grown very fond of Sarah sir. In fact I love her very much indeed and want to marry her one day,"

A stony silence fell upon the library. Both men men took up their cups at this time and sipped their tea.

"I see. Are you asking for Sarah's hand in marriage?"

Before John could answer Dubois continued.

"If you are, there are some thing which need to be considered young man."

"I am asking sir, most definitely," said John earnestly.

"Yes, quite," replied Dubois, "Nevertheless, this matter is not as simple as it may appear to you John. Allow me to explain."

"Firstly," began the other man, "We must consider your respective ages."

"But sir..., began John.

Sarah's father held up his hand and smiled.

"Please John, let me finish."

"You are both still quite young to be making such a huge step. Have you spoken to Sarah about this? Does she feel the same way as you?"

"Yes sir, we both feel the same," answered John steadily.

"I see," said Carlos thoughtfully rubbing his chin.

"We must take into account your present earnings and assets young man. How do you propose to keep Sarah in the manner to which she has been accustomed?"

"I will earn much more as I gain more experience in my trade. Eventually I will have my own business." Explained John. "I will also inherit the family farm," he added.

Even as he spoke his father's earlier words rang in his ears.

Sarah's father spoke.

"John this is all very admirable but it only serves to illustrate what I've been saying.

These things of which you speak are all very much future events. For the time being, I'm afraid there is only one possible answer I can give to your request,"

John's shoulders drooped noticeably.

"Is the answer no, sir?"

"Not at all John. If you are willing to wait and court Sarah properly...we can talk about engagement. You may attend some special public functions together and attend church."

"You may take short rides together on your machine but only if Sarah wears the correct clothing for such a pastime."

"A motorcycle fall can be quite dangerous, as I'm sure you're aware."

"Yes sir, of course. I'll be very careful," said John quickly.

"May we go horse riding as well," he asked.

"Yes, but once again the correct riding outfit must be worn."

"Thank you sir, thank you very much."

"Now young man, you must understand. Any future engagement plans will depend on the behaviour you both exhibit. Do you understand?"

"Oh yes sir, I understand." answered John.

Dubois stood and held out his hand. As they shook hands he said, "In the light of this conversation, I will refer to you now as son... if you don't mind"

"I'd be honoured sir," replied John.

"Very well then. Say nothing about this to anyone until I've spoken to Mrs Dubois.

Let's rejoin the ladies, shall we?" he said.

He placed one hand on John's shoulder as they returned to the drawing room.

"Well, well. You two look very happy with yourselves after your little talk. Is there anything we should know?" said Hannah Dubois.

"No darling," said her husband. "Nothing to be concerned about at this time."

John was aware he was wearing a grin he couldn't hide, so he made his excuses and wished the family good evening. He was barely able to stifle a shout of joy as he walked down the garden path to his waiting motorcycle. He started the machine and with a wave he roared up the tree lined street. Once he had rounded the corner he did shout at the top of his voice, "Yes, yes,.... yes!!!The grin remained until he rounded the corner to th far

How could he share this momentous news with those he loved, especially his father? Maybe it's best to let sleeping dogs lie for the time being, he thought. At present his thoughts revolved around Sarah and their future. When he left her presence a major part of himself stayed with her. He now felt free to tell her how he really felt about her without holding anything back.

"Evening all," he said cheerily as he entered the kitchen. "You know it's still sunlight outside."

Before anyone else could speak Mary piped up with, "My teacher said we would have sixteen hours of sunshine today before it gets dark, because it's a heatwave."

"Thank you Mary," said John, "But I believe the sunny weather is all because I've just asked for Sarah's hand in marriage. Mr Dubois said we could marry but not straight away."

You could have heard a pin drop in the room. John couldn't quite believe he had told everyone without hesitation. He felt as though he could tell the whole world.

Mary spoke first, saying, "God has made this sunny heatwave just for you and Sarah."

She looked around the room wide-eyed.

Margaret rushed over and threw her arms around him with a squeal of delight. "This is wonderful, just perfect John."

William shook his brother's hand with a big grin and put his hand on his shoulder. All he said was, "You've done it, you've really done it."

"This lass must be special for ye to be so determined lad," said his father.

""D' ye ken what thee's doin'? He asked, looking intently at John.

"I don't know much but one thing I do know. I love Sarah Dubois and one day I will marry her."

"Thee's officially courting then?" asked his father.

John stood tall and said firmly, "I'm courting Sarah officially."

His father strode across the room towards John and held out his hand. He shook his son's hand and with a soft smile said, "I'm glad for ye son. I ken thee'll be very happy."

"Now, while we're on t' subject I've got news for ye all. Thora Lofthouse's sister and me, we've been getting friendly. Thee all kens how lonely I've been since thee mother's passing. Well, we've set a date to marry."

If John thought he had dropped a bombshell with his news, this statement from his father eclipsed it by far. The warmth left the room, leaving a chill in the air.

"We don't want another mother," said Margaret defiantly

"No, father," added Mary with tears in her eyes.

"Listen ye bairns, no one could ever replace thy mother. She'll be my wife, not thy mother. D'ye ken?"

John said, "Have you thought this through father. Have you thought, if you go ahead with this, what could happen to this place if you die before her?" The shoe was on the other foot now as John raised this important question with his father, regarding the inheritance of the children.

"I hope she doesn't think she'll be in charge around here," said William.

The two girls, by this time in tears, had run upstairs to Margaret's room where they endeavoured to digest their father's news.

"I won't even talk to her," said Mary. "I don't care who she thinks she is?"

"If she's mean we can go to live at grandfather's house," replied Margaret. She placed her arm around her sister as they sat on the bed together. "I'll never call her mother."

They could here raised voices downstairs but the men weren't speaking loudly enough for them to hear what was being said.

"What is this woman like?" asked John. "Is she a good worker?"

His father glared at him. The sarcasm in John's voice hadn't gone un-noticed. William gave a smile as he realised what his brother was saying,

"Yes Dad, she'll have to be able to work." he said.

"When ye ken Elsie you'll like her an' all, thee'll see." answered Bill.

"Cannae ye be glad for me like I was for ye?" he asked, looking at John.

John was touched with compassion for his father as he pleaded for his son's understanding.

"Yes, I am happy for you father. When will we meet Elsie?"

"Is she a spinster father, or a widow?" asked William.

"She's a spinster. A Lofthouse like Thora Lofthouse was."

John shook his father's hand, "Congratulations father I hope you're both very happy together.

"When will your wedding take place?" he asked.

"In the Autumn. The end of October lads we'll be wed." he replied with a smile.

"Would ye two lads share a wee dram wi' me afore bed?"

"It would be a pleasure," answered John. "Certainly father," said William.

Both boys were happy to be close to their father, even if only for a drink. They retired into the parlour where the single malt whisky was taken from it's cupboard and poured into three glasses.

"Here's all the best lads," toasted Bill Tyndale.

"All of the blessings," added John raising his glass.

"Cheers," said William.

As John walked past Margaret's bedroom door toward his room, she called him inside.

"John what's going to happen?" She had tears in her eyes.

He called both of the girls to his side and hugged them for several moments.

"Don't worry, I'll make sure everything is alright. We'll all stick together no matter what." he assured them. "Now go to bed and sleep tight, both of you."

John slipped into his bed saying to himself, "It certainly has been a long, long day."

Chapter 18

THERE HAD BEEN much talk by the older farmers in the district of a cold winter being expected. Fortunately the Spring and Summer had been very warm, allowing for a good crop of hay to be stored. Nevertheless, at this time of year preparations were made in case the predictions of the locals came to pass.

"Me bunions is givin' me trouble," one local man was heard to say, "We'll be snowed in for Christmas to be sure."

"The squirrels is layin' up late. I reckon t'll be early next year we'll see some terrible foul weather," said another.

John was working at the new estate in Stopford Brook. The builders were all working as long as possible while the weather held. Once it closed in there would be very little they could do. He would call in to see Sarah on his way home and sit with her in the drawing room as closely to each other as they dared. The door was never to be closed when they occupied the room alone. There was a moment when John leaned close to Sarah and kissed her gently, as long as he dared.

He whispered to her, "I will love you forever."

A moment later Carlos Dubois entered the room.

"Well son, It's quite dark and chilly outside. Hadn't you better be heading home?"

"Yes sir you're probably right."

He dragged himself away from his beloved and headed for the door. Mr and Mrs Dubois had made him very welcome at their home since the night he had pledged his love for their daughter and Carlos quite often referred to him as 'son'.

Mildred the maid however, had been heard to mutter jokingly, "Anyone would think that boy doesn't have a home to go to."

"Tomorrow is the big wedding day. We will all be at the Blaney Beck Church of England for your father's wedding." said Carlos with a smile.

"Yes sir," answered John. He was busy putting on his leather coat, helmet, gauntlets and goggles for the six mile ride home. He knew it was going to be a cold and miserable trip. He shook Dubois hand and went down the path to his motorcycle. It took several kicks to start because of the icy cold night but soon roared into life. John lowered his goggles, flicked on the headlight and rode off into the night.

"Saint Christopher watch over him on his travels," said Dubois under his breath.

Saint Christopher had his work cut out for him that particular evening. The weather was cold and icy, as were the roads and narrow lane-ways through places like Etherley and Toft hill. Along Emms Hill lane towards Old Tun farm John thought his limbs would freeze and his extremities drop off, he was so cold. Passing through the low lying parts of the road was akin to driving through an ice bath, which even halted breathing temporarily. By the time he swung his machine through the gateway and along the drive his hands and feet were numb. He could barely feel the controls of the motorcycle as he rode inside the machine shed. As he came to a halt, his leg because of the severe cold, refused to work quickly enough and bike and rider fell on their side onto the wooden floor. He switched off the still running engine and struggled to his feet. It was anger and frustration that gave him the strength needed to lift the motorcycle onto it's wheels and then onto it's stand. He stood with his face to the rafters composing himself, before walking across the frosty yard to the back door.

The warmth of the kitchen from the fireplace was almost painful on his bare hands and face, after he had removed his riding garments. He stood with his back to the fire while his body thawed out a bit. Margaret came from the parlour, concerned for his welfare.

"Are you alright? It must be freezing out there." she said, as she sat at the table.

"It is a bit cold sis. I must have become a bit soft over the Summer." answered John with a grin.

"Father's in the parlour, the others have gone to bed. I'm off to bed now you're home safely," said his sister.

"Come here and give me a hug Maggie," He smiled, holding his arms out.

As they embraced he said, "Are you ready for father's wedding tomorrow?"

Without looking up, she stared into the fire and after a pause said, "I'm as ready as I'll ever be."

"That's the spirit. Don't worry sis, It will be alright, I promise. Off to bed now and don't forget to say your prayers."

They walked hand in hand into the parlour where Margaret climbed the stairs, "Good night John, good night father."

"Good night," echoed the two men.

John sat in the chair next to the fire rubbing his hands together briskly.

"Best ye have a wee dram to warm ye before bed lad."

Bill Tyndale rose without waiting for an answer and poured his son a measure of whisky.

"It's a bit nippy for that contraption this night lad, dinna ye ken."

"It's not too bad," lied John, gratefully accepting the drink.

He closed his eyes and enjoyed the warmth of the liquor as he swallowed his first sip.

"Ye can take t' car to t' lass's place when the weather's like this If you like."

"Well thanks father. I appreciate that," said John.

This offer from his father was a surprise. Bill Tyndale was not the man for loaning or borrowing. John put down the change to his father's pre-wedding mellowness.

"Here's to your wedding tomorrow," toasted John raising his glass, "Good health."

"Thank you son, you're a good lad. I hope t' Vicar's got t' fire lit when we get there. That Church gets mighty cold." said Bill.

The thought of it was enough to cause a shiver through John. He downed the rest of his drink.

"Good night father," he said, standing to his feet wearily.

"Aye lad, see thee in t' morning."

Stillness fell upon the house.

The morning of Saturday the 24th of October 1936 dawned crisp cold and clear. All except William were a trifle tardy leaving their beds. He was up early looking after some late lambing ewes in the high field. If the weather worsened, he would be bringing the lambs into the kitchen for some warmth and hand-feeding. It wasn't the first time and wouldn't be the last he'd do that.

He too was thinking about his father's wedding and how it would affect things around the farm. He wasn't overly concerned, because he knew only too well his father was a canny man and not taken to losing his goods and chattels. As a matter of fact, he thought to himself, Elsie Fredericks would need to be strong to survive a marriage to Bill Tyndale. He smiled at the thought, as he drove his tractor up the bank towards the yard gate. The dog ran on ahead, jumped through the gate and lay on the sacks in the shed, next to John's motorbike.

It was a small gathering at the Blaney Beck Church of England that afternoon, to solemnise the marriage of Bill Tyndale and Elsie Fredericks. Only the immediate families of the Bride and Groom were invited. Doctor Douglas was best man, Thora Lofthouse the matron of honour. George Lofthouse gave away his sister in law but at the altar when asked by the Vicar, "Who gives this woman to be married to this man?" Some thought Lofthouse was rather slow to answer, "I give this woman."

He loved his younger sister in law very much. She had lived the sheltered life of a spinster and words like 'lamb to the slaughter' came to mind at the thought of her marriage to Bill Tyndale, whom he had known all his life. However, as time would prove, he needn't have worried.

Elsie, though not pretty in the classic sense, the way Missy had been, was nevertheless a handsome woman and intelligent with it. Prior to the wedding plans, she had been a teacher in Courtenay but had spent her early years growing up with her brother at Peace Hall. She was not unaware of the finer points of farming, or the history of the Tyndale family. She was, as Thora Lofthouse had said on many occasions, 'no shrinking violet'. Bill liked to think that she had fallen for his roguish charm, while others in the district were of the opinion she was a classic gold digger. Only time would tell.

The ceremony was very pleasant and even the children enjoyed it. The reception was held at Peace Hall farmhouse, around the vast dining room table. The Tyndale children had long been accustomed to being seated at the table with the adults and did so on this occasion. Food and drink were plentiful and the afternoon celebrations melted into the evening.

"Another toast to the bride and groom before we all head home," hinted Lofthouse.

May they and theirs live long and happy lives," he said.

"Here's to a long and happy life Elsie," said Thora Lofthouse to her sister. She looked straight past Bill Tyndale and raised her glass to her..

The Doctor raised his glass to the Tyndale children who were sitting at the far end of the table. The two girls gave a little wave, while William and John raised their glasses in return. Earlier in the evening he had told them to call if they needed to talk about anything. The Vicar had said the same thing.

As the guests were having final conversations at the door, Thora Lofthouse drew Mary and Margaret aside and said quietly, "I have an idea. Would you like to stay for the night? I have spare night dresses for you and plenty of room. You know you're always welcome here."

Margaret looked at her sister and said "Oh, yes we would love to but..."

"I'll go and ask your father," suggested Mrs Lofthouse.

"Bill," she said, "The girls will be staying here with us for the night. We will bring them home tomorrow sometime."

The girls noticed that there wasn't much asking involved in the conversation but they saw their father nod his head and wave to them.

"When Mrs Lofthouse talks, people seem to listen," said Mary to her sister.

"I like Mrs Lofthouse," whispered Margaret.

"It's all arranged girls. You'll stay here until sometime tomorrow. Now make yourselves at home."

She turned back to her other guests, saying, "Now make sure you're all rugged up before you leave."

"Thee'll be needing t' chains on t' wheels soon gentlemen, when t' weather gets foul,"

"I fear you may be right Tyndale," answered Douglas. "I think we may be in for a hard winter."

The menfolk were outside, removing the blankets and canvas covers which they needed to place over the automobile engines, to stop them freezing. Even this precaution wasn't successful in the depths of winter, when all water had to be drained from the engines cooling system prior to lengthy stops and replaced when restarting. A cover over the outside of the radiator when driving, also helped keep engine temperatures up.

"I'm still using a cupful of glycerine in my radiator water. I think it helps." Said Douglas.

"Aye, I do likewise," answered Bill Tyndale.

"I'll call in on you sometime soon Tyndale," said the Doctor helping his wife into the car.

Both cars were ticking over nicely now and Bill Tyndale walked his new bride to his car. Robert Douglas and Eve his wife waved goodnight, as did the folks at the door. The cars slowly made their way along the driveway to the road, until the tail lights were lost in the darkness. The night was deep and it settled over the countryside like a dark frost covered blanket.

Chapter 19

EXPANSIONIST POLICIES ESPOUSED by Japan in their aim to dominate Asia and the Pacific in 1937 seemed to usher into the world a new kind of madness. Japan was already at war with The Republic of China. Since their defeat in the First World war, Germany had bitterly resented the loss of all colonial territory And some home territory. Germany also had strict controls placed on it's development of armed capabilities after the First World war by the treaty of Versailles, which would be ignored. The other nations in Europe did not want to see a recurrence of Germany's belligerent ideals. The German Empire disappeared during the revolution of 1918-1919 leading to the development of the Weimar republic. Later, in 1933 the Nazi Party became all-powerful politically with Adolf Hitler as leader. Germany was then under the rule of a totalitarian single party led by the Nazis.

Ten years earlier Hitler had attempted to overthrow the German government. When he eventually became Chancellor of Germany, he abolished democracy and espoused the New World order of the Third Reich. Other European nations looked on with horror and trepidation. A lack of strong leadership in these nations led to a series of 'wishy-washy' treaties being signed, while Germany's armies began to invade their neighbours and annexe their lands.

Adolph Hitler merely shrugged his shoulders and adopted a, "Who me?" attitude pretending the rest of the world couldn't see. In actual fact, some political leaders like Britain's Prime Minister, rather nobly gave Hitler and his 'indiscretions' the benefit of the doubt. When the balloon did go up, as they say, the Prime Minister was ousted in favour of Winston Churchill. In hindsight, it proved to be very much a case of 'cometh the hour, cometh the man.'

In February 1936, newspapers across England carried a message from Adolph Hitler, with a front page photograph of him in his Nazi uniform. His message to the world at large said,

"'Let's be friends," and included the line, "I appeal to reason.'"

In the parlour of Old Tun farm Bill Tyndale snorted, "I wouldnae trust that Jerry as far as I could pitch 'im." He threw The Daily Mirror down on the floor in front of the fire.

He looked at John and said, "I ken there'll be trouble lad and it'll affect thee most."

"Why's that father?"

"Why? Because when that Jerry starts summat wi' us ye'll be t' age t' Army'll come looking for. That's why."

"Don't you think they'll have enough volunteers?" asked William.

"Mark my words lad. If this gets bigger t'Army'll come knocking. They did last time."

"You mean the last war?" asked John.

"Did you have to go to the last war father?" enquired Margaret.

"No lass, I had to run t' farm. Our William would have to an' all." he answered.

"Father, does that mean William would stay but John would have to join up and go to fight?"

John placed his hand on her shoulder and gave her a smile.

"It all depends if they bring in t' conscription. They're just talking about it at t' moment." said her father.

"Conscription?"

"Yes, that's when they force you to go to war," answered John.

"Do you think it'll come to that," asked William.

"It's all up in t' air for now, all up in t' air," sighed Bill, staring into the fire.

Such was the subject of discussions in many English homes at this time. It was a time of uncertainty across Europe. Snow still lay very deep against walls, buildings and hedges in the North-East. The roads and lane-ways between Old Tun farm and Stopford Brook were quite often impassable except by heavy vehicles. Snow ploughs and gritters were working overtime. Two blizzards had swept across the North country in the last two months causing havoc. Telephone lines had been down and travel all but impossible for days on end. The beck at the bottom of the field was mostly frozen and ice flows partly blocked the Tyne, Wear and Gaunless Rivers.

The short days and bad weather had made it almost impossible for John to visit Sarah as often as he was accustomed to. His work on the new Willows Estate had ground to a halt. They were still busy in the shed at And Howe's yard with masonry work carving lintels and blocks. John was still able to get to Blaney Beck on his motorcycle, by running in the tracks left by tractors and trucks. He did strike deadly patches of black ice, which caused him to slide off the road into some ditch or hedge. He suffered no injury and the motorcycle proved its toughness. On three occasions the weather closed in while he was at work. He had to trudge home across the fields on these evenings, leaving his machine in the work shed. There was more work to do on the farm as well, with all of the stock inside most of the time. The spreader was kept busy shifting piles of steaming manure and used hay. Sleet and drifting rain had turned some fields into mud.

In the towns and villages it wasn't so bad. In Stopford Brook the roads were kept clearer by the movement of traffic and the Council was able to keep up with the snow and ice more easily.

Most shoppers weren't deterred by the bad weather and trod warily along the slippery footpaths to and from the shops.

The Dubois household wasn't disadvantaged by the foul weather. Carlos could walk to the Council Chambers and work on his engineering projects no matter what the weather. One of his pet projects, was designing a more efficient method of salting and gritting the roads in the County. It was still a very labour intensive job with lorries driving slowly along the roads with a blade on the front, while labourers with shovels stood on the back. The men spread the mixture of salt and gravel with an accurate well-practised sweep of their shovels. The Council Lorries, like other vehicles were shod with snow chains on the wheels, to improve traction. Rail locomotives carried huge ploughs on the front during heavy snowfall, keeping the track clear.

Sarah Dubois sat in the warmth of the drawing room with her mother, while her sister Clare practised her piano exercises. Outside the front garden was covered in a blanket of white.

Robin Red-breasts fluttered around the hedges, about their business.

"Mother," said Sarah.

"Yes dear. What is it?" Hannah Dubois was aware her daughter had something on her mind. Sarah had been moping about with her mind on something for days.

"Well, we are Roman Catholics. Isn't that correct?"

"Yes darling. Why do you ask?"

"Well.... you were Church of England before you married Daddy, weren't you? Did you change churches to marry him?"

The piano playing stopped abruptly and silence fell on the room. Sarah's mother knew where this conversation was leading. It was a subject she and Carlos had discussed since Sarah and John had been seeing each other. Clare sat quite still at the piano.

"Yes Sarah," she answered steadily. "I had to change faiths in order to marry your father."

"Why do you ask sweetheart?" asked Hannah Dubois

"Is that a rule of the Roman Catholic church mother? Do those who aren't Catholics have to change their religion to marry a Roman Catholic?"

Silence reigned supreme again, then Mrs Dubois, aware that both of the girls were looking at her said, "I'm not sure whether it's still a rule. We'll have to ask the new minister but why do you ask?"

"Oh, no reason, I was just thinking about something," answered Sarah.

"Are you concerned about yourself and John perhaps? You must remember this is 1936 and the church is very modern now." her mother said.

"But what about father?....he's not modern." said Sarah frowning.

"That's enough Sarah. Don't be disrespectful when speaking about your father."

"Clare! Aren't you supposed to be playing the piano?" said Hannah Dubois sternly.

They both knew this wasn't the end of the conversation. The attitude of the Roman church concerning mixed faith marriage hadn't changed, no matter how modern the world may be. Any children brought forth from such a union would be nothing but illegitimate in the eyes of the Church. Sarah had heard about these things from the other girls at church. She had been so happy to tell her friends of John's and her betrothal but was soon brought down to earth.

"No one will stop us getting married," she had told her friends defiantly.

Mrs Dubois left the room leaving Clare and Sarah alone. Clare was still practising but had so much she wanted to ask.

"Do you think John will become a Roman Catholic to marry you?" she asked.

"I would never ask him to. I would rather join the Church of England." her sister replied.

"I don't hear any music being played," said Mrs Dubois from the other room.

Her heart was breaking for Sarah. She knew from personal experience the turmoil that lay ahead. It was always assumed by the Roman church, that the non-Catholic 'other person' will be so besotted, that considerations of church membership would be a non issue. The change over then being assured without a murmur. Hannah Dubois held these troubles in her heart.

"Don't worry sis' I'm sure it will all work out for you both," said Clare, as she re-commenced her practice. Sarah didn't reply but took her novel again from under the cushion and immersed herself in the story. The novel was called 'The Clermont Hotel'. It was written by Imogene Cross and had been the catalyst behind Sarah's concerns and questions. The protagonists were a young engaged couple in New York, who were experiencing insurmountable problems with the doctrine American Apostolic church and the Roman Catholic church. During these troubles they would meet at The Clermont Hotel in secret. When their secret was made known to the girls parents by a well-meaning housemaid, they called off the engagement and forbade the couple to see each other again. In the story the couple had eloped and married elsewhere. Sarah hadn't finished the novel yet but she found herself thinking about the couple in the story more as each day went by.

The Dubois maid, Mildred Castle had loaned Sarah the novel, stressing that Sarah not mention it to her parents. Mildred felt sorry for Sarah, knowing the difficulties that lay ahead with her marriage to John. She knew of a girl in her village who had been excommunicated by the Catholic Church for marrying a boy from a different denomination.

"I'm not trying to lead you or nothing Miss Sarah but it's a good book," she had whispered, as she passed it to her in the garden two weeks prior.

In the novel, the young couple in New York were a bit lax in their morals thought Sarah, with much kissing and fondling taking place during the time of their assignation. This had affected her also but only in making her want her beloved with even greater passion. They had been separated by the weather a great deal during the last month and her heart yearned for him. She retired with the book to her room, where she lay on her bed reading to the sound of the piano downstairs. Her eyes gradually grew heavy, until she rested her head on her pillow and dreamed her dreams.

She woke with a start. "Sarah, you have a visitor," called her mother from outside the door.

"Who is it mother?" she asked sleepily.

"It's John. He's braved the elements to come and visit you darling." Sarah's drowsiness fell quickly away as she straightened her hair and clothes in the mirror.

"I'll be down straight away," she answered breathlessly.

She ran down the stairs and along the hallway to the sitting room, noting his motorcycle clothing on the hall-stand. John was standing when she entered and her heart skipped a beat when she saw him. She walked past her mother and took him by the hands. Emboldened by her dreams she said, "My darling. I've missed you more than I can say," and kissed him.

Mrs Dubois cleared her throat and headed for the door. "I'll be across in the drawing room if you need me. I'll send Mildred in with some hot tea for you. John must be frozen."

He was frozen but the moment he felt Sarah's kiss he started to thaw from deep inside. This was the moment he had been dreaming of for weeks.

"Sarah it's so good to see you." He glanced at the door and took her in his arms kissing her passionately.

He gazed into her upturned face for what seemed like an eternity, then said,

"Come, sit and we'll talk for a while. I need to hear your voice"

They sat together on the a divan near the fire. They kissed again and their lips stayed locked together for a longer period, than some would consider proper. Their enforced parting had made them more hungry for each other than ever. A polite cough startled them and they turned to see who had entered the room. It was the maid carrying a tray of tea and scones. Mrs Dubois followed her into the room.

"This will warm you John, after your long cold ride," she said.

The maid placed the tray on the coffee table and left the room. She gave Sarah a smile as she left but said nothing.

"Thank you Mrs Dubois. That's very kind of you," he answered.

John and Sarah had been seeing each other for quite some time now and they were trusted to be together without a chaperone for longer periods. Talk of an official engagement was gaining momentum.

Chapter 20

THROUGH THE SPRING and Summer of 1936 John Tyndale was able to work long hours, particularly on the new Willows estate in Stopford Brook. For around 700 pounds one could purchase a large two storey home with quite large front and back gardens. For a small deposit, a family could enjoy the pleasures of their own home. Those families who had already taken up residence, had proudly fixed name plaques to the front of their homes, such as 'The Oaks', 'The Willows', or 'Auckland House'. The area was a hive of activity and represented a time of prosperity and excitement.

John had taken Sarah for short rides around the estate roads so that she could become accustomed to being on the motorcycle. Edward and Thora Lofthouse had bought a new leather coat and gloves for Sarah as a gift. John bought her a leather helmet and goggles. They were almost ready for the open road. Sarah loved the motorcycle and wrapped her arms tightly around John whenever they went riding. Their first ride alone, away from Stopford Brook, was to Peace Hall farm to visit the Lofthouses. The Dubois family stood in the front garden and waved as they left and the Lofthouses waved from their front garden as they arrived. They were welcomed with tea and sandwiches in the garden.

"What a beautiful ride we've had," Sarah said excitedly to Thora Lofthouse. She took off her helmet and her wavy auburn hair sparkled in the sun as it fell to her shoulders.

"It's good to see those roses in your cheeks again young Sarah," said Edward.

"I hope you haven't been going too fast John. These machines can be quite dangerous you know," Mrs Lofthouse said.

"Oh Thora," said her husband. John is every sensible and skilful rider. We don't need to worry."

Carlos and Hannah Dubois had also stressed the need for care when they had left.

John didn't have the heart to tell either family that Sarah wanted to go fast.

"Will you be taking Sarah over home to see Elsie and your father?" asked Thora Lofthouse.

"No Mrs Lofthouse, not this time. We're expected straight back to Stopford Brook from here. Mr and Mrs Dubois will be waiting." John replied.

"I see, never mind. Maybe next time then."

John was making sure there would be a next time, by being punctual on this, their first solo trip. Mrs Lofthouse glanced at her husband and they both rose from the garden table.

"Edward darling, may I see you in the house for a few minutes please?" said Thora Lofthouse to her husband with a smile. "Excuse us dears. Will you be alright on your own for a few minutes?"

They both walked into the house leaving the two love birds in the garden by themselves. No sooner had the Lofthouses entered the house than Sarah threw her arms around John's neck and kissed him. She then drew back with her eyes sparkling and stared into John's eyes. He then embraced her and passionately pressed his lips against hers. Time stood still.

"Do you remember that night in the cottage John?" asked Sarah.

"I sure do," was all he could say.

"I wish we could go back there one night," she said.

Before he could answer the Lofthouses came out of the house and sat down at the table. They all said their goodbyes and as determined as ever Sarah asked, "Do you think we could come and visit you again soon."

Sarah had plans. They included John and her and the honeymoon cottage.

"You're both welcome here any time. Just let us know when you want to come and visit." Then Thora Lofthouse said the words that Sarah had been hoping for. "Perhaps you could come and stay the night with us.

"Oh I don't think father would allow that," replied Sarah.

"We'll see. I'll speak to your parents darling. Good heavens it's not as if you'll be running away on some secret rendezvous now. Is it?"

"No Mrs Lofthouse. It isn't is it?"

Meanwhile Edward and John had wandered over to look at the motorcycle.

"How's she going? Asked Edward.

"Just brilliant mister Lofthouse. Just brilliant," replied John.

"You know young John." he began. Mrs Lofthouse and me, we're so happy to see you and Sarah together. If there's anything else we can do to help you, just let me know."

John shook the other man's hand and thanked him for everything. He called to Sarah,

"We'd better be going now. We don't want to be late getting back."

They thanked The Lofthouses again for the coat and gloves, as they sat on the idling motorcycle. They waved as they rode along the driveway. As they passed the cottage they both looked across the little stream and thought of their first meeting. Sarah gave John an extra squeeze and he had a wide grin on his face as they rode onward to the road. They were both lost in their thoughts as they rode through Toft Hill and Etherley. John was thinking of asking Carlos Dubois about the time of an official engagement to his daughter. Sarah was thinking of The Clermont Hotel in the novel and the Honeymoon cottage at Peace Hall.

Back at the Dubois house everyone was excited to hear about the motorcycle journey. Sarah, still wearing her riding clothes, including her leather helmet, was talking to her mother and Clare in the hallway. Her enthusiasm was plainly evident. "It's the most wonderful day I've ever had," she said. Her sparkling eyes and the colour in her cheeks, were enough to convince anyone of her happiness.

"I'm so glad you enjoyed yourself my dear," said her father. "How are the Lofthouses? Well I trust."

"Yes Daddy, they're very well....and they asked us both to come and visit again. And they asked us to stay the night next time."

Nothing more was said for some time. Mildred and Mrs Dubois helped Sarah remove her riding clothes while Carlos Dubois stood just outside the front door with John.

He said, "John, I'm very pleased to see you and Sarah enjoying each other's company."

John smiled. He felt under enormous pressure to please Sarah's father, in order to ensure an official engagement to her in the near future.

"Thank you mister Dubois. I love her very much."

Then came a reply John wasn't expecting. "You do realise John, that nothing must interfere with Sarah's church attendance. Don't you?"

John paused for a moment before replying. He shouldn't have been surprised at this statement from Carlos Dubois but it did temporarily knock the wind out of his sails. The invitation from Mr and Mrs Lofthouse had left him and Sarah in a buoyant mood and this was a cold dose of reality.

"Yes sir," was all he could say. Had he offended Carlos Dubois somehow?

"Are you two men coming inside or are you staying on the porch for the evening?" asked Hannah Dubois.

Her husband stepped inside and went to his study but John remained at the door.

"I think I'll get going Mrs Dubois. I have an early start for work in the morning." He said. He smiled and asked, "May I call on Sarah tomorrow evening?"

"Of course John. Of course you may," replied Hannah Dubois.

Sarah turned to face her love, on hearing his strange request. Normally he wouldn't ask such a thing. It would be taken for granted that he would call to see her as often as possible, without asking each time. "What is the matter John. Are you alright?" she asked.

"Yes my sweetheart," he replied with his usual big smile. "I'm just a bit tired," he lied.

He touched her gently on the cheek with his gloved hand and walked down the garden path to the motorcycle. He didn't look back in case they saw the disappointment in his eyes. He was too late however. Sarah had already seen the sadness behind his smile and was wondering what could have happened.

Sarah and her mother stood at the door and watched John as he rode away up the avenue.

"Mother, what has happened? John looked as though he had been stabbed in the heart."

"I don't know my dear, perhaps your father can shed some light on the subject. I'll speak to him later."

To say Sarah was perplexed by this latest development would be an understatement but she was soon to be enlightened by her sister, who had overheard the conversation between John and her father on the front porch.

"Sarah," called Clare, as her sister walked down the hallway toward the stairs. Clare was on the landing. "Come up to my room, I have something to tell you." She beckoned and ran to her room. Clare was sitting on the bed when Sarah entered.

"What is it sis?" she asked sitting down beside her.

144

"Well," started Clare, "I know why John seemed so sad when he left."

"How do you know?" asked Sarah.

"Because I overheard what he and father were saying on the porch. Or rather, I heard what father said to John."

"What Clare. What did he say to John?"

"Well, it was about you two staying overnight at the Lofthouse farm."

"Go on." said Sarah.

Clare took a deep breath and said. "He said you wouldn't be able to stay overnight because you may get back home too late for church the next day."

"What!" cried Sarah standing suddenly to her feet. "John would never do anything to displease mother and Daddy. Why would Daddy say such a horrid thing?"

Clare, flushed with wisdom said, "You know Daddy. He doesn't like to see people enjoying themselves too much."

"Don't you tell anyone that I told you this Sarah. Promise?"

"I promise," murmured Sarah as she walked from the room. She was already deep in thought.

Sarah's relationship with her father had always been a stormy one. They loved each other dearly of course but seemed to clash over some things. John was strong and tough but she knew he could be hurt.

He would see this comment from her father as some kind of rebuke, even a criticism. In her room she sat and thought. What should she do? Should she confront her father, or keep the peace? Her mother did say she would speak to her father, so perhaps it would be better to say nothing, until she saw John tomorrow evening. He would know what to do. Yes, that's what she would do. She returned to her novel The Clermont Hotel, where she would revel in the freedom that the young New York couple enjoyed. She knew in her heart, that she and John would soon enjoy this kind of freedom.

Chapter 21

THE DISAPPOINTMENT JOHN had felt when leaving the Dubois house soon melted away as he rode the country lanes back to Old Tun farm. He wasn't one to dwell on set-backs. It was a beautiful summer evening and lately the North-East hadn't had much opportunity to enjoy the outdoors. His heart sang in tune with the engine of his motorcycle, as the evening sunlight and shadows flickered across his face. He was already looking forward to seeing his love tomorrow evening.

He walked into the kitchen after parking his machine in the shed and divesting himself of his riding clothes. "Good evening all," he said cheerily. "Hasn't it been a wonderful day?"

Bill Tyndale, his new wife Elsie, William and his two sisters all sat round the large kitchen table. It looked as though he was just in time for supper. Everyone greeted him as he took his place at the table.

"Thee always looks glad when thee comes from t' lassie's house lad," said his father grinning

"It's true love," said young Mary nudging her sister.

"Did you have a good time at the Lofthouses?" asked William.

"Yes, we had a wonderful time," replied John.

Elsie didn't say anything. She just smiled at the interaction of her new family. Since her marriage to Bill she had enjoyed getting to know the children. Being Thora Lofthouse's sister, she still visited her sister enough, to know about the love match between John and Sarah. She also knew Carlos Dubois enough, to know he could be a miserable 'so and so'.

"I'm off to bed straight after supper tonight," said John.

"Aye lad. And Howe'll be trying to make hay while t' sun shines I ken," said Bill.

"Are ye still on t' new estate?"

"Yes father, we've still months of work there," answered John.

"I fear t' weather might get in t' way lad."

"Autumn's soon upon us John," said William. Though he was always involved with farm work, he was very proud of his big brother's success in the building trade.

They all enjoyed their supper together while the darkness closed in outside. Soon it was time for John to day goodnight as he made his way to the stairs. William didn't see why his brother needed to go to bed early to prepare for an early start, after all he started his farm work early every morning.

"You builders must be soft," he joked with his brother as John left the room.

Elsie followed John into the parlour and placed her hand on his arm. She spoke to him quietly, with a smile. "Just remember young John. The path of true love never runs smoothly."

He grinned and said, "Thanks Elsie. I'll remember that. Good night." he leaned over and kissed her on the cheek. He was asleep as soon as his head hit the pillow. As usual, his night was filled with dreams of his beloved Sarah.

As he and Dusty Rhodes the labourer drove to Stopford Brook in the morning, John had to endure the light-hearted banter of his workmate in the cab of the Lorry.

"Did yer lass enjoy t' ride yesterdy lad," asked Dusty with a wink.

"Yes Dusty, she enjoyed the ride," said John with a roll of his eyes.

"What's her Dad think of t' all then," asked the other man.

John thought for a moment, then said, "He thinks it's brilliant Dusty." He looked at his workmate with a big grin.

Of course John was just leading the other man on. He wasn't about to admit there was a slight hiccup in his plans. Both men laughed anyway, probably for different reasons. Now that Dusty was on the subject of women, he regaled his young friend with some news he had heard at The Cross Keys pub the other night.

"A feller down t' pub was tellin't' publican Brian about a picher he'd seen in France last year," he said."

"Was it any good?" asked John.

"He said it was, even if he didn't talk the French language. "He was sayin' how rude it was"

"What!? John turned to the older man expecting him to be joking.

"He said it's true. She was runnin' about everywhere with no clothes on at all. She'd left her clothes on her horse."

"Did she? On the screen?" asked John

"Yep, that's what he said. Then t' hoss ran off." Laughter filled the cab of the Lorry.

Dusty waited for a while, then added the 'piece de resistance'.

"You'll never see anythin' like that round 'ere. The picher I mean. Not allowed. She was nekked."

"What!? Exclaimed John. "No." He turned to look at the labourer this time.

Dusty laughed at the look of surprise on his young friends face.

"That's what he said. He weren't jestin'lad. Can you imagine it?" said the older man. John could imagine it and was doing so. Being a farm lad he was familiar with animal behaviour but this information was something entirely new and exotic.

The men passed through Stopford Brook lost in their own thoughts.

"I saw a snap of that girl on the screen," said Dusty as they stopped outside the job.

"What does she look like," asked John.

"Dark hair, black flashin' eyes. A grand lookin' lass," the other man replied with a grin.

"Anyway enough of that, let's get these walls up. It'll take us all day," said John.

Around the streets of the estate, other gangs of men were working on houses in various stages of construction. Many homes were finished and some were already occupied. As John worked, his imagination was filled with images of him and Sarah together, down at the deep hole at the beck. An imaginary blanket appeared on the soft grass and they lay together in the warm sunshine, passionately in love.

His reverie was interrupted by the call of, "Tea up lad." Dusty stood with the Thermos flask of tea for 'smoko'. John was snapped back to reality and climbed down from the scaffold.

"Thanks Dusty, let's sit for a while." he said.

The two work mates sat and talked as they enjoyed their hot tea together.

"Will thee be seein' t' lass tonight lad?" asked Dusty.

"Yes, I'll go home and get cleaned up first like I usually do," answered John.

"It's good to see thee happy, young John," said his friend.

"Does thee ken when ye'll be engaged?" asked Dusty.

"Her father wants us to wait until we're older and I'm making more money."

"Aye, It's always like that lad but if you want summat bad enough ye'll get it. Keep on askin'. Keep on knockin' as they say in t' Bible," said Dusty.

"You know the Bible?" asked John.

"Aye lad, thee'd be surprised what I ken."

"I probably wouldn't you know. You must be as old as Methuselah."

"Aye, and as wise lad. I'm wise enough to tell you summat young John" said Dusty laughing.

"And what may that be oh wise one." asked John.

"Love your lass more than anythin' else in t' world and tell her so every day. Remember lad, love is both visible and invisible."

"What?

"That's all I'll say on t' matter lad. Just heed what I've said and you'll do fine."

"I think I understand what you're saying Dusty. You've been happily married to your wife for years, so you must know what you're talking about," said John.

"Ha'way now young Tyndale, let's get this job done t' weathers lookin bad again," answered Dusty.

John had another reason for wanting his working day to finish. He wanted to see Sarah.

September was nearly over and so far they had been lucky with the weather in the North-East, but some of the old farmers were predicting rain and floods for October. Down South the weather was still holding.

The Speedway World championships had recently been held at Wembley Stadium, with an Australian having won, an Englishman coming second and an Australian third. John had a great admiration for the Australian racers.

Chapter 22

BY THE CHRISTMAS of 1936 the North-East was beginning to claw it's way out of the depression which had held England in it's grip since The First World war. Most of the larger landholders had been relatively isolated from the worst of it and been able to support themselves. Unemployment had been very high around the country for years, mainly in the North, with the poor forced to go without coal for warmth and food for sustenance.

Government investment in road building and housing had eased the situation but many unskilled workers still faced the spectre of unemployment. One of the greatest boosts to employment prospects came in the form of a massive re-armament policy, in the face of the rise of Nazi Germany. In spite of a blizzard across the North from the end of February and well into March 1937, many industries were either re-born, like Coal and Steel in Sunderland and Hartlepool, or new industries were established. A clothing factory was established in Middlesbrough. A Plywood factory and Food factory were built in North Shields, while a Plastics factory had been built in Billingham.

This increased activity filtered down to And Howe the Stonemason who was securing more bricklaying contracts, thanks to John's skills with a trowel. Later in the year the company would branch out as full-blown building contractors with John as foreman. John's status and earnings grew exponentially. The biggest problem in the North, as ever, was the bad weather. One literally had to make hay while the sun shone. William dreamed of a warm sunny place to live as a farmer and John longed for a warm sunny climate for building.

One of John's particular talents was the construction of stone walls and Byres, which were so prevalent in the North-East and the Dales area.

And Howe was forced to purchase another Lorry to cover the extra distances involved, as word of John's skill spread further afield. It was a new Bedford WHG Tip Truck, finished in the same dark blue and yellow colours as the Commer. The new signs on the Lorry read Howe and Co. Stonemasons & Contractors. John was the only one of the Howe employees allowed to drive it. He also maintained the vehicles for And Howe. As the business continued to grow, John's responsibilities grew also, having to supervise the extra tradesmen hired by his employer.

Spare time was at a premium, with Sarah and John cherishing the hours they could spend together. He generally visited the Dubois home on Sunday afternoon, when he and Sarah would spend time together in the garden if the weather was fine. If not they would sit in the drawing room enjoying each others company. Carlos and Hannah were allowing them more private time these days, which gave John the confidence to approach Mr Dubois regarding an official engagement to Sarah. The two men spoke in Dubois study one Friday evening.

"Mr Dubois, I believe it's time for me to ask for Sarah's hand and to be officially engaged to be married." said John.

"Son, I've been waiting for you to ask me this question for quite a while now. I think it would serve the needs of respectability for you to be engaged. I'm sure there are many people looking on, who must wonder about your intentions." replied Carlos Dubois.

"Has there been something said?" asked John.

"No, not at all my boy, not at all."

"I and Mrs Dubois will be happy to announce your engagement at the earliest convenience. We believe you to be an excellent prospect as a husband for Sarah. I know you will keep her in the manner to which she has become accustomed."

Carlos rose from his desk and held out his hand to young John. "Allow me to be the first to congratulate you," he said as the two men shook hands.

"Now let's call a meeting in the drawing room to announce the news to the family."

Mrs Dubois, Clare, Sarah and the two men gathered in the drawing room. Even Mildred the maid had been summoned to attend. John was in somewhat of a daze. He couldn't believe how agreeable his future father in law had been.

Dubois said," Young John has an announcement to make," and then he sat down with the rest of them.

John duly cleared his throat and then spoke, "Mister Dubois has given his blessing for me to ask Sarah for her hand in marriage, commencing with our official engagement." Sarah immediately leaped to her feet with a scream and wrapped her arms around Johns neck. Then she hugged her father and thanked him. Clare and Mrs Dubois followed suit with tears and laughter while Mildred clapped her hands.

"Congratulations!" they all shouted. Hannah Dubois hugged John as soon as Sarah had released him, saying, "I'm very happy for you both and I know you'll be successful in every way. Carlos and I have watched you develop into a fine young man in the time we've known you."

Sarah remained standing at John's side holding his hand. She looked up into his eyes and whispered "I love you." He replied, "I love you too Sarah Dubois."

John then turned to Mr and Mrs Dubois and said, "With your permission I would like to take Sarah into Stopford Brook and buy her an engagement ring as soon as possible.

I think tomorrow morning would be an excellent time for us to go," added John quickly.

"As soon as you purchase the ring I will make the public announcement," said Mrs Dubois.

Sarah and John hugged and kissed on the porch for quite some time before John said,

"I must be going now my darling, I will see you in the morning."

"Oh must you go?" cried Sarah holding him tightly.

He kissed her passionately and then donned his motorcycle gear. "Until tomorrow," he said as they parted.

Sarah stood and watched until the motorcycle roared out of sight, then walked inside the house.

When John arrived home, he gathered his family together and told them the news.

"Father, Elsie, William, Margaret, Mary I have an announcement to make."

"I think I know what it is young John," said Elsie unable to keep still in her chair.

"What is t' lad, "asked Bill.

"Tomorrow I'm getting engaged to Sarah, officially. There'll be a notice in the newspaper"

There was much merriment at his announcement, with hugs and kisses. William shook his brother's hand as if he was using the water pump. Margaret and Mary danced about singing, "We knew it, we knew it, they're so much in love."

Bill, much to John's surprise gave him a great bear hug. "All t' best lad. I'm very glad for ye." The sound of laughter echoed around Old Tun farm until late into the evening. Bill's stock of Single malt was severely depleted by bed time.

Bill and Elsie stood at the stairs as John went up to bed. He was still wearing a grin from ear to ear.

"We all love you very much," said Elsie. "We want to see you both here as many times as possible in the coming months. Don't forget now young John."

John drove the car to Stopford Brook the next day, where the ring was duly bought from Alexanders Jewellers. He drove Sarah to the river bank with Mildred in the back seat as chaperone. Mildred took a short walk while John proposed to Sarah.

"I will love you and no other forever. Will you accept this engagement ring as token of my love for you." Tears ran down Sarah's face while he spoke.

"Yes darling, I love you more than anything. I always will."

He slipped the ring on her finger and they kissed hungrily until Mildred returned to the car.

When they returned to the Dubois home, Mildred prepared a light luncheon for the family. They all sat down and enjoyed the moment. Mrs Dubois had prepared the announcement for the newspaper. She read it out to them.

"Mr J Tyndale and Miss S Dubois.

The engagement is announced between John, eldest son of Mr and the late Mrs Maude (Missy) Tyndale of Old Tun farm Blaney Beck, and Sarah, eldest daughter of Mr and Mrs Dubois of Stopford Brook."

"I will arrange a small engagement party," added Hannah Dubois with a smile.

Chapter 23

IN 1938, AFTER a beautiful white Christmas, the weather in the North-East was warm and dry from February through April. Those involved in the farming and building industries, were making hay while the sun shone. Germany invades Austria and gas masks are supplied to the civilian population of Britain. Later in the year some newspapers reported.

'Only a miracle can avert a war'. An ageing Prime Minister tells the nation that they now have 'Peace in our time'. The Nazis in Germany destroy Jewish lives and property as the world looks on.

"There's nowt good comin'outa' this lad," said Bill Tyndale throwing the newspaper on the floor with disgust. They'll be callin' up young lads for t' army soon. Ye mark my words. Yon Hitler's insane."

He was talking to his family after reading about the invasion of Austria by the Germans.

"Sarah's over at the Lofthouse's for a couple of days," said John trying to ignore his father's prophecy.

"Why don't we organise a get-together Bill?" asked Elsie. Knowing her husband would not want to organise any such thing, she continued, "See what you can arrange while you're over there John. Will you?"

"Of course I will," he answered. "We'll have a bit of a knees-up."

No one knew that Elsie and her sister had been involved in some shameless matchmaking for a few weeks now. It was Thora Lofthouse who had invited Sarah for a visit, knowing full well that John wouldn't be able to keep away. They too were aware of the war clouds over Europe and were trying to hurry up the marriage process between John and Sarah.

Hannah Dubois wasn't keen on long drawn out engagements either and had said as much to the Lofthouses on several occasions. Carlos Dubois, however, was in no hurry to see his daughter walk down the aisle, no matter how much he liked the prospective groom. He was very much in favour of long engagements. Such was the situation as John parked his motorcycle outside the garden gate at Peace Hall farm. Sarah ran out to meet him.

"I heard you coming a mile away," she said throwing her arms around him.

Sarah guided John to the seat in the arbour and they sat down. With John being so busy this year, they hadn't had as much time together as they would have liked.

"I've missed you so much," said Sarah. "I'm sure I'll go mad if we stay separated like this."

John saw the frown on her face and kissed her firmly on the lips. He drew away and said,

"It won't be like this forever darling. Don't worry, everything will be alright. Now, I'd better go inside and say hello to Mister and Mrs Lofthouse. I've something to tell them."

Hand in hand they walked to the door. John paused to knock but Sarah dragged him straight nside.

"John, I thought I heard a motorbike. It's good to see you. Sit down." Thora Lofthouse proffered two chairs and they both sat down at the large dining room table. Edward Lofthouse nodded to John "How do you do young John," he said with a wink.

"I'm very well Mister Lofthouse. Especially since I've seen Sarah," he replied.

The Lofthouses both laughed. "I'll make us all a nice cup of tea," said Thora Lofthouse.

"Edward and I had such a lovely time at your engagement party. Why don't we have a small party here, now that Sarah's visiting? We don't see much of you these days Sarah."

"That's just what Elsie said Mrs Lofthouse," mentioned John.

"Really! Well I never. Did you hear that Edward?" said Thora. "I think it must be meant to be."

Her husband didn't answer. He watched the young couple as they stared into each other's eyes.

"I've been tidying up the old cottage and doing some renovations," he said.

"Really!" exclaimed Sarah, her eyes wide. "May we see it?" she pleaded.

"Let's have our tea first and then I'm sure we can go down and have a look."

Mrs Lofthouse placed the refreshments on the table saying, "I'm sure we don't have to go down there Edward. We're very tired today aren't we? The young ones can manage on their own. Yes?"

An almost imperceptible glance was shared between the older couple, before Edward Lofthouse said, "Yes, I do feel a bit tired actually. Do you think you could have a look by yourselves?"

"I'm sure we could manage," answered Sarah a little too quickly.

"Very well, that's what we'll do then," said Mrs Lofthouse sitting down at the table.

She smiled as she poured her husband's tea. "Hasn't the weather been beautiful?"

Everyone agreed that it had been very beautiful indeed. John and Sarah seemed to be overcome by thirst as they gulped down their tea. Good manners prevailed though and soon Sarah said,

"If we may be excused we'd love to go and see what you've done to the cottage." Then she added as an afterthought, "I've never seen inside the cottage."

On hearing her remark, the last mouthful of tea got caught in John's throat, causing him to cough violently.

"Are you alright darling?" said Sarah, slipping her arm around his shoulder.

She smiled ever so sweetly at him, frowning with concern.

"Yes, I think I'll be alright now," John managed to say.

"You must be very careful you two," said Thora Lofthouse smiling. "You've just seen how accidents can happen so easily."

She showed no sign on her face, of the kick she had just received under the table from her husband.

"Enjoy your walk bairns," she said cheerily to Sarah and John, as they made their way through the front door.

"We will thank you Mrs Lofthouse," replied John with a wave.

The sun was shining, the birds were singing, as John and Sarah walked down the road to the honeymoon cottage. They held hands as they walked and laughed together. Thora Lofthouse stood at the door and watched them with a smile and a sigh. Her husband walked up quietly behind her and put his arms around her waist. They would have dearly loved to have children of their own.

"Do you remember the lovely times we spent in honeymoon cottage my dear?" he whispered in Thora's ear.

"Oh yes my love, I remember as though it were yesterday," she answered. "Didn't we have some wonderful times there Edward?"

"So many my love," he answered, kissing his wife gently on her cheek.

They turned and walked back inside the house together.

"Oh John! Just look at it. It's so beautiful. Look at the flowers growing everywhere.

Look at the beautiful honeysuckle vine." They walked across the small bridge through the front garden of the cottage. Bumble bees hummed around the daisies, carnations and pansies as the couple stood on the threshold gazing into each other's eyes.

"Come on then slow coach. Let's go inside," said Sarah excitedly.

John opened the door and sweeping Sarah up in his arms, carried her inside.

"What are you doing, we're not married yet Mister Tyndale," said Sarah in mock horror.

"Just practising Miss Dubois," he answered with a grin.

They walked spellbound through the little cottage. Edward Lofthouse had returned it to the beauty he remembered, when he and Thora used to spend their own precious time there together. Since the day it was built the cottage had known nothing but love and it was a palpable presence in the place.

"Do you remember the night we first met here John?" asked Sarah holding his arm.

"No, I don't think I do....," John replied with a frown.

"Why you beast." laughed Sarah, "I should box your ears John Tyndale," laughed Sarah. John was laughing now, with tears rolling down his face. He took her in his arms and swept her off her feet.

"How could I ever forget that night. I go weak in the knees when ever I think about it.

I will never forget that night. I love you Sarah Dubois and I always will."

He kissed her gently and carried her to the small divan in the front room. They sat holding each other until Sarah spoke. "John, close your eyes and tell me what you feel in this place."

"Well," he replied, "I can feel your beautiful soft skin and..."

"Oh don't be silly," said Sarah. "You men are simply beasts. Can't you feel the love and warmth in this place?"

"Yes dear, I'm just teasing you. I think that's why I want to kiss you again."

He took her face in his hands and they kissed. They kissed until they were breathless. Sarah broke away and quickly stood to her feet straightening her clothes

"We must go back to the house John. I feel as though I'm being swept away in a raging torrent," she said running her hands through her hair. Since I've been wearing this ring I feel.... I want everything to be right. Do you know what I mean John?

Please say you do."

John stood to his feet and took her in his arms. "I do know what you mean darling and I feel exactly the same way. Don't worry, everything will work out for the best."

They took one more look around, straightened each other's clothing and hair and headed back to the farm house holding hands.

"The cottage looks absolutely beautiful Mister Lofthouse," said Sarah.

Thora Lofthouse answered for her husband, "I'm so glad you liked it. Do you like it young John?"

"Yes I do. It has a very warm feel about it. I love it. I mostly remember it from when I was young, being overgrown and lonely. We used to think it was haunted as kids."

"I think it is haunted, "said Sarah.

"Oh, what do you mean lass?" asked Mr Lofthouse.

Sarah smiled and said, "I think every stone is haunted by a spirit of love."

"I think you're absolutely right sweetheart," said Thora Lofthouse.

As it turned out, it was agreed that the engagement party would be held at Peace Hall farm. Close friends and family were in attendance. The Lowthers, Doctor Douglas and his wife Eve, And Howe and his wife also attended. The large dining room at the farmhouse was filled to overflowing with chattering laughing guests. They all toasted John And Sarah and wished them all the best for their future.

Some of the menfolk talked about the Test cricket. Bradman had been scoring runs at will, but as Bill Tyndale said to Robert Douglas,

"Aye these Australians aren't too bad but what about Len Hutton's 364 runs?"

"It's amazing what the BBC can show us on the television these days Tyndale."

"And have ye seen t' news about Hitler on t' television?" asked Bill Tyndale.

"I don't like the look of it Tyndale. It looks bad to me. said Robert Douglas. I think we don't have the politicians to deal with it. They don't seem to have the where-with-all to deal with this man Hitler."

The two friends at the party weren't the only ones concerned with what was taking place in Europe. People from all walks of life were talking about it and those who remembered the First World War, were worried. The Government was continuing with the build up of armaments and a new Aircraft Carrier called The HMS ARK ROYAL had been launched at Birkenhead

Chapter 24

IN 1939 ALL madness broke loose in Europe. The British Government, rather than dealing head on with the Nazis, decided on a series of feeble efforts to placate the ever aggressive Adolph Hitler. Finally Hitler persuaded the British Prime Minister to allow The Sudetenland, part of Czechoslovakia, to pass into the hands of Germany. When the Nazis invaded Poland, (a nation which had a war pact with the British) on the 1st of September, Britain and her allies were at war with Germany. On a beautiful summers morning on the 3rd of September, at 11am the Prime Minister announced that Britain had declared war on Germany. People started digging bomb shelters and sewing black-out curtains. The prime military age had been set at 18-41 yrs of age with conscription set in motion earlier in the year. Only those employed in essential industries would be exempt from military service. John Tyndale received his call-up papers.

The Tyndale family sat around the kitchen table. The papers sat in the middle where Bill Tyndale had thrown them during their conversation.

"Those warmongers!" he shouted. "Now we're all deep in it, 'specially thee. Still, if thee goes now thee'll have it ower soon."

The others weren't saying much. That which they had dreaded for most of the year had finally come to pass and already impacted their lives.

"Where do you have to go John,' asked Mary in a tiny voice.

"I have to report to Barrowthwaite for training sis. That's all I know," He replied placing his hand on her arm.

His little sister had tried to be brave but burst into tears at the thought of her brother having to go to war.

"I don't want anyone to be upset about this. I'll go and do my duty and like father says, I'll be back before you know it," said John.

"Does William have to go as well?" asked Margaret.

"No. Someone has to look after the farm, "answered William.

Elsie spoke, saying, "The sooner you go lad, the sooner you'll be back."

This was the prevailing attitude around the nation. People generally thought the war would be over quite quickly. Some thought before Christmas.

"Well, if I have to report to headquarters on the fourteenth of August. That's three days time, I'd better get busy."

"Aye lad, thee'd better get crackin' and visit some folks before thee goes," said Bill.

John made his way to Stopford Brook to visit Sarah. There were more military vehicles on the road now and they were generally in a hurry to get somewhere. It had been a very hard Winter but the rest of the year through Spring and Summer had been quite mild. In early August John found the weather beautiful for riding his motorcycle.

"John No!" was Sarah's reaction when he told her of his conscription. "What are we going to do?" They sat alone in the front garden of the Dubois house. For the two lovers the day lost it's brightness.

"What will I do if something happens to you? If you're lost I'll surely die," she added.

"Nothing will happen to me darling. It's not going to be much of a war they tell me."

"Daddy said it's going to be a beastly affair which could drag on for months," said Sarah, her voice wavering.

"We'd better go in and tell your parents I suppose," John rose from the garden seat with a deep sigh. He took Sarah in his arms and said, "Don't worry, it will be alright lass."

"Are you sure," Sarah asked as they walked inside.

"I'm sure darling. I'm sure."

"I believe this war will last for a much longer period than most people think John," said Carlos Dubois gravely. "I'm thinking we may be at war for years, not months as some are saying."

Sarah's face fell as she listened to her father speak. When would she see her true love again?

"When do you leave? Where do you go? Asked Hannah Dubois.

"I report on Monday morning at Barrowthwaite headquarters." answered John.

"That's only three days!" cried Sarah. "They can't do that. Daddy you must do something."

Of course there was nothing Carlos Dubois could do for his eldest daughter on this occasion. In any case, he was well aware that John was quite prepared to do his duty. He was a fine young man and he, with many others like him, would answer the call. At 21 yrs of age John was now a fully qualified Builder and able to make his own decisions. Soon, however, he would have to get used to others making decisions about his life.

"Mr Dubois, I have to visit my grandparents tomorrow. Would you mind if I take Sarah with me?" asked John.

"Not at all son, that will be fine. You may take the car," Carlos answered.

"Thank you sir. Until the morning then."

Later, John and Sarah sat in the garden contemplating their future. He placed his arm around her and she lay her head on his chest.

"Sarah, I've been thinking," said John.

"Yes my love. What have you been thinking."

"I think we should be married before I go to the war."

Sarah sat up quickly and looked into his eyes.

"That is exactly what I have been thinking," Sarah whispered. "But we don't have time to be married, do we? Don't forget, I'm not yet of age," she added.

"But you will be next year," John protested.

"Daddy won't allow it until I'm twenty one darling. He already told us that."

"I'll go and speak to him now," said John resolutely standing to his feet.

"No my love! Not now. It will cause such a fuss and I'd like some peace before you go away," begged Sarah, taking him by the hand. They sat talking until the midges from the river bank started to bite.

"Until I see you in the morning my dear," said John kissing her on the forehead.

"Take care on the way home my love," whispered Sarah.

The following morning they rolled up at the gates of Bell Hill and drove slowly along the tree-lined driveway. Mr and Mrs Lowther, John's grandparents, met them at the front door. Mrs Lowther's face showed the concern she felt, for the well-being of her eldest grandson.

"Come inside you pair of love-birds," she said after the welcome. "It's so good to see you both."

George Lowther took his grandson aside into the privacy of the drawing room and gave him a hug. He took a small Bible out of his pocket and gave it to John.

"I'd be proud if you take this with you lad. I've always carried it with me."

"You will find all the comfort you need within the pages of that book," he continued.

"Thank you very much grandfather, I'll treasure it," said John.

"Follow orders and keep your eyes open wherever they send you lad," said Lowther.

Anne Lowther and Sarah came into the room. Mrs Lowther said, "We've prepared a picnic basket for you and there's a Tilbury and horse waiting outside. You can take a run around the place, maybe down by the river, as long as you're back in time for luncheon."

"Off you go now and enjoy yourselves," added George Lowther.

"What a lovely surprise," said Sarah. "How beautiful."

The grandparents ushered the couple outside and waved from the front steps as the carriage drew away up the lane-way. John knew his grandparents property like the back of his hand and drove the one-horse carriage straight to his favourite spot. He stopped under the shade of an ancient Oak overlooking a quiet bend in the river, where the water gurgled over the rocky bed. He helped Sarah out of the carriage and they spread their blanket on the soft grass.

A herd of Lowther's Jersey cows looked on but soon lost interest. The carriage horse picked at the fresh grass, enjoying it's time out of the stable.

"Oh John, this is absolutely beautiful," smiled Sarah.

"It sure is. I've taken some lovely trout from this stream over the years. Grandfather used to bring me and William here fishing." said John, gazing at the water.

Sarah sat on the blanket and patted her hand beside her. "Come and sit beside me my love."

John took off his jacket, rolled up his shirtsleeves and sat down beside her. Sarah immediately removed her bonnet and shawl and lay back on the blanket while John reclined next to her on one elbow.

"I love you Sarah Dubois," he said quietly. He gently stroked her face. She took his hand and kissed it.

The animals in the meadow were left in no doubt that these two people were seriously in love, as they saw them kissing and petting under the old Oak tree. The time and the river passed. Sarah suddenly spoke,

"I think we had better have our picnic now John, we don't want to waste all of this lovely food and drink."

No matter how passionate she and John became, she never let herself go too far. She knew exactly what she desired, marriage and she would have it. The time was not so easy to plan any more, in the present circumstances, but the place had been fixed firmly in her mind since the first time they met. She rose and straightened her hair and clothing. John walked to the river bank and composed himself. They sat together on the blanket and enjoyed the Thermos of tea and sweetmeats which Anne Lowther had prepared for them.

"Who lives in that cottage over there?"

"That's Morrison's place. He's been the game-keeper here for as long as I can remember."

Sarah gazed at her surroundings, deep in thought.

"What a heavenly time it's been John. Hasn't it?"

"I'll always remember this day," said John with a smile.

Chapter 25

"STAND UP STRAIGHT you lads! Shouted the Sergeant roughly. "You're not in the local Pub, you're in the Army now."

The new conscripts were lined up outside the administration building of 'C' Company 2nd Battalion Darnley Light Infantry, at Barrowthwaite. This intake had netted 152 new soldiers for the Battalion, with some to be absorbed by the Engineers.

"Wish I was in t' Pub," murmured the young man standing next to John.

"Shut up that man, or I'll come over there and shut you up!" shouted the Sergeant.

He looked like the sort of man who could do any 'shutting up' that may be deemed necessary. He was a stocky man, of medium height in his mid-forties, with no neck to speak of. He had a Roman nose (it roamed all over his face) and his face showed the scars of many a battle. His hands were the size of dinner plates and he had one cauliflower ear. John was sure this man had a mother who loved him but the man to whom the Sergeant had spoken wasn't so sure and did shut up forthwith. The Sergeant's name was Larson.

John had decided to heed his grandfather's advice as soon as he walked through the C Company gate, 'follow orders and keep your eyes open lad', he had told him. It seemed like pretty good advice. He and the man who had the run in with the Sergeant, were billeted in the same hut with eighteen other conscripts.

"What's your name?" asked John as they stored their new gear.

"Vivian Edwards....they call me Bev," said the other lad.

"Pleased to meet you Bev, I'm John". They shook hands.

John saw no reason to query his new friend about his nick-name. It was the start of a friendship which would last through thick and thin.

Bev's nick-name had caused him trouble ever since he had received it from one of his Uncles, as a lad. He'd had to fight because of the teasing it brought with it but he'd become quite a good fighter because of it. Many had learned this the hard way over the years.

"I could change my nickname I suppose," he told John one day, "But I've sort of grown attached to it. I'll bet everyone calls you Tinny, he added."

"No, not really," said John laughing.

"Well, from now on I'll call you Tinny."

"That's fine by me Bev."

And as the saying goes, 'that was that'.

John found the training interesting and compared with his normal work, the hours weren't too bad at all. Even though the Government had been involved in a massive re-armament program for nearly three years, many units were suffering shortages of equipment. Many of the new soldiers had to use pieces of wood and water pipe to train with, instead of rifles. One didn't receive his uniform until basic training was almost finished. There weren't enough vehicles to go around. One of the Officers had to pack his holster with paper because he hadn't yet been issued with a pistol. Many units lacked niceties like compasses and binoculars.

In spite of these shortages the training went ahead and the conscripts were moulded into a fine Company of fighting men. Their basic training was planned to finish in late September.

Sarah knew this plan and was well aware that her betrothed could be pressed into active service any time anywhere. She wasn't the sort of girl to let her dreams slip into obscurity without a fight.

"Mother, when do you think John and I would be able to marry?" she asked, as they sat together in the dining room. She was very direct in her manner. Her mother saw this attribute as one of her own. Hannah Dubois knew her husband always struggled with outspoken females and it was his attitude which always led to violent outbursts of temper in their home. She and Clare seemed to be able to work around these situations but not Sarah.

"Sweetheart, you know your father won't even consider your marriage until you are of age."

"But mother, we've been together for almost four years.... and engaged for more than a year of that time. I'll be twenty one next year." replied Sarah.

"You won't be twenty one until May Sarah. That's seven long months away."

"Mother you know they could send John to war in October! What if something happens to him before we have the chance to marry?"

"Don't shout at me Sarah, I am not your enemy. I've spoken to your father about this and he won't change his mind."

"Mother, I will marry John before he goes to the war. I'm quite prepared that he may die but I will not be separated from him any longer. I would rather be a widow than an old spinster," said Sarah defiantly. "I am not a child. We've done everything father has asked of us since we met and I think enough is enough."

"I don't know what to say to you Sarah. Would you rebel against your father's wishes?" Sarah didn't answer her mother. She was much too angry to speak civilly, so would keep her peace.

"I'm going to my room mother," she said as she rose from the table.

Through tear-filled eyes Hannah Dubois watched her fiery daughter leave. Deep down in her heart she knew what Sarah had been saying was true but she could see trouble ahead.

Sarah stood in her bedroom looking out of the window over the garden. Tears began to roll down her cheeks until she threw herself onto the bed, her body racked by a huge sobbing fit. Finally, as she calmed she fell asleep. As she woke and opened her eyes, she noticed the novel called The Clermont Hotel which was still on her bedside table. She took it up and flicked quickly through the pages. "Yes, that's it!" she exclaimed. "That's the answer."

The heroine in the story was forced by circumstance to elope with her lover and Sarah was going to elope with John. Her face was set with a determined look. She carried the book downstairs and returned it to Mildred the maid, who had loaned it to her a while ago.

"Did you enjoy the story miss Sarah," asked Mildred.

"I did indeed, Mildred. It was very enjoyable...and informative," answered Sarah.

Unbeknown to Sarah, Mildred had heard the earlier conversation between Sarah and her mother and didn't think it interfering to say, "The couple in the story weren't going to have their love denied miss." She closed the kitchen door and whispered to Sarah, "They eloped you know miss Sarah. They were right passionate those two. Right made me blush the things they got up to they did."

"Yes, quite," said Sarah absently.

"Anyhow miss if you need anything just let me know," Mildred said, busying herself at the sink.

"Thank you Mildred, I shall" replied Sarah.

Mildred smiled as Sarah left the room. She loved the two girls and had watched them grow up since babies. She respected Carlos Dubois but resented the way he dominated the household. She had been privy to many torrid arguments over the years, most of them as a result of Dubois violent temper. She knew he had been physically abusive, particularly to Sarah who didn't pander to his tantrums. She always wanted to protect the girls. She herself wasn't frightened of Carlos Dubois but it was more than her job was worth for her to interfere. This new turn of events gave her the a chance to help Sarah and secretly stand against her employer, if only in a covert manner.

Mildred had heard of a place called Gretna Green up on the Scottish border, where a couple may legally marry without parents permission and without being of age. She made it her personal quest to find out more about this town, for future reference. One of her friends, a Butler, happened to work at the house of a prominent Solicitor in Stopford Brook and was able to debate with his employer concerning the Law. A few well aimed enquiries could aid dear Sarah in her plight.

True to plan, later that same week, the information Mildred was seeking came to her hand in the form of a note, delivered to the scullery door by the Solicitor's stable boy.

The note written by the hand of her friend, read as follows,

Dear Mildred,

The Scotland Marriage Act of 1939 now forbids marriages of the type you describe. However, this new legislation does not come into force until the 1st of July 1940. I hope this information serves the purpose you envisaged,

Yours Faithfully Andrew Russell,
Stopford Brook

Mildred threw the lad a rosy red apple for his trouble and closed the door after him.

"Surely the Lord himself is in this," she said softly.

She made her way upstairs to Sarah's room and quietly knocked.

173

"Come in," said Sarah.

Mildred entered and closed the door after her.

"What is it Mildred?'

"Well miss, I've some information here that you may find interesting. There's a town called Gretna Green up on the Scottish border where they have different rules about them that elope to get married." she whispered. "There, now I've said it."

"But why did you bring me such information Mildred?" asked Sarah quietly. Her heart was in her mouth as she stood and approached the maid.

"Oh no reason pet. Just for the sake of education...you understand." Mildred winked at Sarah as she spoke. "This is our secret now." She then threw the note on Sarah's bed and left the room.

Sarah took the note and read the information. "This must surely be the Lord's work," she breathed. It's an answer to my prayers.

"But there's no time to lose, I must make a plan." she said firmly.

It was a difficult time for her. She had to keep her thoughts from her mother and father her dear sister. Deception didn't come easy to Sarah but when tough decisions had to be made she was determined to make them. She wasn't without money. Carlos Dubois had always given his daughters a generous weekly allowance.

She had no doubt that John would be able to support a family when they did eventually marry.

"I must run away from home, find John and marry him before he goes to the war."

This is the thought that drove Sarah, to begin putting her plan into motion. She would write a letter to John telling him of her thoughts. Mildred would post it for her on one of her many outings. However, her conscience was troubling her and she decided to tell her mother and sister about the idea but only after the letter was sent. No wait, she would leave a letter for those who need to know after she has left. For Sarah's plan to come to fruition successfully Edward and Thora Lofthouse would have to be entrusted with the information about the elopement. The Honeymoon cottage was pivotal for Sarah and the use of it on her wedding night, would be the realisation of a long held dream.

"I must speak to the Lofthouses," she said quietly to herself.

She didn't realise that Clare was standing right behind her at the time.

"Why do you need to speak to the Lofthouses Sarah?" asked her sister.

"Oh!" exclaimed Sarah whirling around with shock. "Don't frighten me like that. I didn't know you were there sis."

"Please don't ask me that Clare. I don't want to lie to you." said Sarah holding her sister's hands. "Just trust me and don't say anything to mother yet."

"What's going on Sarah? What are you being so secretive about?"

"Will you swear to keep my secret if I tell you and will you cross your heart?"

Of course I will," answered Clare.

Sarah took her sister by the hand and led her into her bedroom closing and locking the door behind her.

"You aren't pregnant are you?" asked Clare wide eyed.

"No! We've never done that," cried Sarah. "That's a horrid thing to say Clare."

"Alright I'm sorry but I've a feeling it must be a momentous secret sis."

"Shush," said Sarah. "The walls have ears you know." Clare giggled and put her hand over her mouth.

"Sit down here with me and I'll tell you my secret but you must promise not to say anything to anyone," said Sarah sternly.

A few moments later Clare's delighted scream echoed through the house, out of the open door and up the avenue outside.

Hannah Dubois called out at the bottom of the stairs, "What's going on up there you girls."

"Nothing mother," came the reply from Sarah.

"Stop that screaming. You'll have the Police on the doorstep." Hannah Dubois said.

"I told you to be quiet," hissed Sarah at her sister. "That isn't being quiet."

"You're eloping," whispered Clare. "That's a wonderful secret." She hugged her sister, bubbling with joy.

"I'm so happy for you Sarah. Do you need any help?"

The two sisters whispered for quite a while as sisters do, until every minute peace of information had been revealed and discussed at length.

"You really do have to contact the Lofthouses somehow sis," said Clare quietly.

"I'm sure they will help you," she added.

"Why don't you let me telephone them for you and sound them out?" asked Clare.

"That's a good idea sis. Would you?"

"Consider it done," said Clare. She hugged her sister tightly. "This is so exciting."

Chapter 26

SERGEANT LARSON HAD finished 1st in the Isle of Man motorcycle TT in 1936 but only 2nd in his marriage to Gladys Smith of Croydon. He was a fine leader to his young charges however, and they were progressing through their training with flying colours. The troops were being trained to drive cars and lorries, ride motorcycles and how to carry out basic maintenance on the vehicles. These tasks came easily to John due to the wide range of mechanical experience he'd gained looking after his own motorcycle, And Howes lorries and his father's farm machinery. His machine was currently housed alongside the Company's BSA M20 on the base.

On one of their motorcycle training days the Sergeant asked John to give the others a riding demonstration. Well actually, Sergeants don't ask private soldiers to do anything.

Sergeant Larson shouted, "Tyndale! Show these boys how it's done. Ride this motorcycle around that field for us. Now watch carefully you daft lads."

Larson had placed some marker flags in a slalom pattern for John to negotiate as a riding demonstration. He raced around the course without putting a wheel wrong, kicking up great clods of earth and grass. He roared the machine back to the watching lads of C Company and skidded to a halt in front of Sergeant Larson.

"That wasn't so bad. Now go back and show us how slow you can do it without putting your feet down." said Larson with a grin.

When John had complied and returned, the others were then shown how to ride. Some of the lads proved more adept at handling the machine than others. When it came time for Bev to try, everyone was unaware that the throttle was getting sticky when wide open. Intent on copying his mate's speedy ride he tore around the course and flat out past the gathered troops.

His face was red, his eyes wide and he was shouting what the other lad's thought was a blood curdling war cry.

As he flew past they realised his war cry was, "How do I stop this crazy thing?"

The motorcycle ended up wedged in a hedge, while Bev flew over the handlebars and landed in a farmer's field surrounded by admiring sheep.

"Edwards! Bring that machine back here immediately! Shouted Sergeant Larson.

"It won't start Sir," replied Bev.

"Then carry it or push it son. Help him Tyndale." said the Sergeant.

A cheer went up from the lads as the motorcycle was pushed back to the group, followed by much laughter.

"Tyndale, get the machine running again. Meanwhile who can tell me what that man did wrong?" Much wisecracking and chatter followed, while John fettled the BSA.

"Now that you all know what not to do, I hope you don't forget it," said Sergeant Larson as they made their way back to the course. "If you can't stop the machine, simply turn off the ignition."

"Yes Sir," they all shouted in unison.

One unfortunate young lad was overheard to ask his mate, "What's the ignition?"

Larson grabbed him by the ear and dragged him over to the motorcycle and pushed his face down near the headlight. "There's the ignition you cloth-eared farm boy. Now don't forget it." He didn't forget it. Neither did his ear. Army sergeants weren't known for their genteel manners.

When John received the letter from Sarah his reaction to it was predictable. He was over the moon at the thought of marrying her. He did have some misgivings about eloping but time was of the essence and war made many things acceptable that normally would not be.

"Are you saying you're going to ride all the way up to Gretna Green and back in one day Tinny. That's well over a hundred miles each way man," said Bev Edwards. "Sarah must be a bonnie lass for all that trouble lad."

"She is Bev. I'd walk that far to marry her," replied John.

"When does all this happen?" Bev asked.

"She'll be waiting at the front gates when I ride out to go on leave." said John.

"What! That's next Tuesday!" his mate yelled.

Sergeant Larson told the boys they would be headed overseas when their leave was over and they must tell no one of the troops movements in the near future.

"Except for you Tyndale you lucky lad. You can tell your new wife if you get any time to talk on your honeymoon. Her name's Sarah isn't it?"

"How did you know that Sir. It's supposed to be a secret."

"There's no secrets around the lads, you know that my boy," smiled Larson.

"Three cheers for Tyndale lads. Hip hip hooray!"

When the noise had died down Bev looked at his mate and winked. He wasn't going to let John's wedding go by without making a fuss.

"You couldn't resist telling the Sergeant could you?" said John.

"Never mind that Tinny. You'd better get that bike of yours tuned up before Tuesday. And you'd better make sure the lights are working mate. You're going to need them."

John did spend time fettling his machine and checking tyre pressures on Monday night. He also checked the lights. Sergeant Larson had allowed him to fill the petrol tank of the motorcycle with top grade fuel to send him on his way to Gretna Green the following morning.

"I'm happy for you lad. You just mind how you go tomorrow, there'll be quite a few Armed forces vehicles on the road and you know how badly they can drive."

That night in the Mess the Sergeant addressed the lads as they enjoyed a quiet drink together.

"Tomorrow you'll go on three days leave. When you come back here bring nothing with you that you can't carry in your pack. We'll be doing some travelling and we'll be travelling light. Make sure you say your goodbyes because you may not see your people for a long time. Remember, don't be late at the gate."

"Yes Sergeant!" shouted the lads.

"Tyndale, front and centre!" shouted Larson.

"The lads have had a whip round for your wedding," The Sergeant handed John a package wrapped in brown paper and tied with a bootlace. He opened it amid a cheerand grinned when he saw the contents. The package contained a flask of Scotch a woollen scarf and a bar of chocolate. "For energy Tinny," Bev said. "You're going to need it."

"In more ways than one," laughed the Sergeant with a wink

"Thanks everyone...I was going to say I'll miss you, but I wont,"

"You'll all see each other soon enough and you'll be C Company of the Second Battalion Darnley Light Infantry. Don't forget it and make sure you behave like a soldier of the King whenever you're in uniform." said Sergeant Larson.

"Three cheers for Sergeant Larson!" shouted Bev.

Larson said, "Thanks...my lovely lads. Now go back to the hut and get some sleep." Then he left the room.

Most of the lads found sleeping difficult. Tomorrow morning they'd be seeing their families again, if only for three days. When John eventually got to sleep, his dreams were filled with visions of Sarah Dubois, who was soon to become his bride.

Chapter 27

SARAH WORE HER best slacks and left the house ostensibly to visit the High street with Mildred for some shopping. In a small carry bag she carried toiletries and her best frock. The maid carried Sarah's leather coat and other riding clothes in another small bag.

"It seems a bit early to be going to the shops ladies," said Hannah Dubois with a loving smile, as the two of them walked to the front gate. Mildred carried Sarah's small bag. Hannah knew her daughters and her maid and it hadn't taken her long to figure out what was going on in her household.

She was secretly delighted and did everything she could to facilitate the adventure, even to the point of telephoning her friend Thora Lofthouse to make some discreet enquiries. She knew Sarah's love for the Honeymoon cottage at Peace Hall farm. Sarah had shared with her mother on many occasions, her desire to honeymoon there with John. Sarah didn't know that Mildred had been coerced into confessing her own part in the elopement, by Hannah Dubois one morning in the kitchen.

"You know Mildred," said Hannah. "I sometimes think it would be better under the circumstances, if Sarah and John were to elope."

Mildred dropped the cup she was holding and suffered a coughing fit. Hannah Dubois continued when Mildred had recovered.

"If this were to be the case I would hope someone would take the responsibility to see they did so with safety. I will hear nothing more said on the subject."

Hannah Dubois looked steadily into Mildred's eyes for a moment, turned on her heel and walked out of the kitchen.

Mildred said nothing but heard the message loudly and clearly. With those few words, Hannah Dubois had placed on her the responsibility of aiding Sarah and making sure she was kept safe whatever her plans. There would be no more discussion about the situation. Despite her easy relationship with the Dubois family, she knew her place and had no doubt about the repercussions should she fail this secret task.

Sarah and Mildred didn't have to wait very long for the Coach which would carry them to the gates of 2nd Battalion Darnley Light Infantry in Barrowthwaite. Mildred stood with Sarah outside the iron gates and awaited the appearance of Private Tyndale on his motorcycle. There were many others waiting for the appearance of their own particular soldier.

"I'm so excited Mildred. I can't stop shaking," said Sarah.

They watched as dozens of young soldiers poured out of the Base but still there was no sign of John. He was busy unravelling yards of rope from around his machine, put there by his mates during the night as a pre-wedding gag. "Those lads," he mumbled to himself as he worked.

"Here I'll give you a hand lad." Sergeant Larson had walked in and burst out laughing. "My lovely lads," he said with a smile.

The job was soon finished and John on his way to the gates.

"I can hear him coming Mildred. He's coming out now." Sarah was unable to conceal her excitement and was almost jumping on the spot. She was all set to go, already wearing her coat. John rode out of the gates and stopped at the kerb wear the two of them stood waiting. Sarah was wearing her bottle green slacks and her auburn hair flashed in the morning sun. John leaped from his motorcycle and took her in his arms as he kissed her.

A loud cheer went up from a group of the other lads who were hiding behind a hedge on the other side of the road. They had been waiting to see Sarah and by the comments they were very impressed with their mate's betrothed.

"How did you get a beautiful girl like that Tyndale?" shouted one of the lads.

"She's too good for you Tinny," cried another.

Sarah blushed at the good natured jibes. They were all laughing and joking until the voice of Sergeant Larson rang out, "You lads had better get on your way. Now hop it you lot!"

She quickly put on her leather helmet and goggles, and kissed Mildred goodbye. John sat on the machine with the engine running with his bag strapped to the fuel tank. As they roared off he waved to his mates, wearing a grin which was smeared with Sarah's lipstick. As he waved to Sergeant Larson who was standing at the gate watching, he saw him give the thumbs-up signal. They were on their way to Gretna Green. Sarah hugged John tightly around the waist as he urged the motorcycle through the streets past the Castle and out into the countryside. Hedges and walls flashed past in a blur as they rushed along the highways and byways. The boys had studied the Army maps with the help of the Sergeant and come up with the best and shortest route to Gretna.

John pulled in at a small Pub in the village of Romaldkirk to talk to Sarah and check the motorbike. They sat together at a table outside and enjoyed a hot cup of tea.

"Are you alright honey?" asked John. He took her by the hands across the small table.

"I'm so happy sweetheart. I've never felt better."

"Clare has organised with the Lofthouses to stay there when we come back from Gretna Green," said Sarah. "They're both very excited to be able to help us."

"Good. I'm glad about that," said John. "I'll bet Clare has told everyone by now."

"Yes my sweet," said Sarah. "I think our secret is well and truly out."

"Well then, let's get on our way. We have a couple of hours to go yet."

The towns and villages fell behind them as they pressed on. Alston, Tindale through Weardale, Brampton and Longtown. Finally they rode into Gretna Green and stopped outside the ancient building, where the wedding ceremony would take place. They walked arm in arm to the open door and John called out to the Smithy.

"Any chance of a wedding taking place mister Blacksmith?"

The Smithy, spying John's uniform replied, "Och I'd be glad to marry ye. Fetch yer bonnie lassie inside lad. Are ye off to the war?"

The short stocky Scot came and shook John's hand.

"There's been a few of you Army lads through here fer marryin' with their lassies."

"I can see ye love each other. Did ye bring some brass thee noo?" he asked John.

"Yes I did sir," answered John.

"Och aye the noo. I'll be off to fetch the witnesses then." With that he left the building and returned with his wife and three other people.

"Come ower here to the anvil noo, and we'll get tae it," said the Blacksmith with a warm smile. The couple did as they were asked and stood before the anvil. Sarah turned to John with tears in her eyes and said quietly, "I wish mother and father could have been here."

The ceremony was duly performed and witnessed. A form was produced and signed.

"In the presence of God, I noo pronounce ye husband and wife before yon witnesses." said the Blacksmith solemnly.

"Ye may noo kiss yer bride laddie," said the Smithy's wife with a wide toothy grin.

After the couple had kissed the Smithy took John aside and they completed the financial side of the transaction. "That'll be two pund an' ten shillins thank ye lad and all our blessins for yer time at the war."

Sarah and John both thanked the Smithy and his wife along with the friendly witnesses. Outside at the motorcycle they hugged and kissed. John wiped the tears from Sarah's eyes and they set off for Peace Hall farm. They shared a feeling of elation with a tinge of sadness. Sarah hugged her husband tightly as their motorcycle roared along the road through the lengthening shadows. John would gladly have stopped at any of the village Pubs for the night but he knew Sarah had a dream of spending her wedding night at the honeymoon cottage. They stopped at an Inn and rested for a while wrapped in each other's arms, enjoyed some hot tea and scones, then continued on their way. Weariness was their ever-present companion.

The lights of Peace Hall farm loomed through the dusk and excitement grew as they rode to the honeymoon cottage. At last thought Sarah, this is our moment.

"Mr and Mrs Lofthouse are waiting for us. They've left a light on in the cottage," said John over his shoulder. "They must have been listening for us coming."

He stopped the motorcycle next to the couple and they both dismounted stiff and sore.

There were hugs and congratulations, even some tears from Thora Lofthouse.

"We're so happy for you both," she said as John and her husband shook hands.

"Edward and I would like you to have some supper with...."

"Darling," interrupted Edward Lofthouse, "I'm sure they would like to get themselves sorted first and maybe have a rest." He winked at his wife and smiled.

John leaned the motorcycle against the fence and opened the gate for Sarah.

"Mrs Tyndale welcome to the honeymoon cottage," he said.

Sarah walked through saying, "Well, thank you Mister Tyndale I'm sure.

"We'll see you later then Mister and Mrs Tyndale," called Sarah Lofthouse. "We've so much to talk about."

The young couple thanked them again and walked to the front door through the garden.

John opened the door, scooped Sarah into his arms and walked her over the threshold kicking the door shut behind them. He stopped in his tracks, still holding Sarah in his arms. A fire glowed in the hearth, the table had been set for two and from where he stood they could see that the upstairs bed was made up. A lamp glowed softly beside the bed.

"Oh John this is beautiful," whispered Sarah. "They've worked so hard to make it special for us. Aren't they darlings?"

"That they are," said John as he walked up to the bedroom and deposited Sarah onto the bed. They took off their heavy clothing and dived under the covers, where all tiredness slipped away in the passion of their honeymoon night. The release of pent up emotions and years of desire was theirs, until finally they finally fell into a deep rapturous sleep.

"Wake up sleepy head." John stood beside the bed with two cups of steaming cocoa.

"What time is it?" asked Sarah sleepily.

"About midnight I think, he answered. "This will have to serve as our supper my love."

"I don't want this night to end, so this is an opportunity to start our evening all over again," laughed John.

"Oh you are awful Mister Tyndale," giggled Sarah.

The next couple of days they enjoyed their time together walking across the fields, lying together in sunny secluded grassy hideaways. They walked to Old Tun farm and spent time with the family around a specially prepared luncheon. Under Elsie's supervision Bill was on his best behaviour, prompting Sarah to say, "He's like a big soft teddy bear." The second day, Edward and Thora Lofthouse drove to Stopford Brook and brought Hannah Dubois to see her daughter. They fell on each other's neck when they met, with tears of happiness and laughter.

"How is father?' asked Sarah.

"He hasn't taken it well dear but give him time to understand."

"That's just the thing mother. We don't have any time left. John is off to the war in a couple of days."

"I know darling. Don't worry about things you can't change, just enjoy the time you have together. We're living in very dangerous times. There's even talk of the Germans invading England. Can you imagine?"

"Mother, please tell Daddy I love him," said Sarah.

"I shall darling," replied Hannah Dubois. Then she changed the subject as tears welled up in her eyes. "Isn't it wonderful of the Lofthouses to allow you to stay here when John goes overseas?"

Sarah nodded, wiping the tears from her own eyes with the aid of her mother's handkerchief.

"Cheer up darling. I'm sure everything will be fine," said her mother.

"Come on let's go downstairs and find the others." she added with a smile.

Carlos Dubois had taken the news of the elopement very badly indeed. He hadn't spoken to anyone at home since he heard the news. His bitterness knew no bounds and he decided to speak to Reverend Little about an annulment of the recent marriage, or even having his daughter ex-communicated from the Church. In the Priest he found an ally.

"This is preposterous!" thundered the Reverend, pounding the desk with his fist.

"And you say this boy isn't even of The Faith Dubois?" he asked.

"No Father, he's a Church of England lad," replied Carlos Dubois.

"Well Dubois, if they have children, you know the Church will dismiss them as illegitimate. Don't you? Protestants!" shouted the Priest.

"I understand what you're saying Reverend and I agree with you. I think my daughter should be cut off from the Church for her wanton behaviour, as an example to others."

"What an excellent idea Dubois. You're a credit to the Roman Catholic Church. I'll see what I can do, said Father Little. "I'll have to contact my superiors," he added.

"There'll be some indulgences in this for you....and for the rest of your family. We'll have to talk further about the salvation of Sarah. These things can be quite costly to you financially you know," said Father Little gravely.

"Yes Father, I realise that. I must do what the Church requires of me," answered Dubois, his eyes on the golden cross above the Priest's head. He felt much better already. This would satisfy his need for redemption.

In his mind, the money he would have to pay for these indulgences would be well spent, taking away the threat of purgatory which hung over his family because of Sarah's rebelliousness.

However, he'd reckoned without the condemnation which would fall upon him when his wife heard about his plans concerning Sarah. Hades hath no fury like that of a mother fighting for her children. As the Bard would say,' The best laid schemes of mice and men....'

Chapter 28

MRS SARAH TYNDALE stood at the roadside with her mother. Many other women, some with children, were present also. They waved as the convoy of Army lorries passed by, carrying John and his fellow soldiers to the Courtenay Railway station. It was the beginning of their journey to France via Tilbury docks in London. It was September the 30th 1939 and a bright clear Autumn day in Barrowthwaite.

The journey by rail seemed never ending and by the time the train reached Tilbury the next day a stiff breeze had blown up under a leaden grey sky. A fine drizzle swept across the Thames River, soaking everything which wasn't covered. The men of the 2nd Battalion Darnley Light Infantry were to form part of the 2nd Infantry Division. Hundreds of soldiers filed up the gangway onto the coastal freighter which bore the rather ironic name 'Spirit of Peace'. The rain continued and white capped waves tore across the English Channel and up the river.

"Sod this for a lark," said Bev, as he and John stood shivering against the lee-ward rail. The men stood around on deck, with their their kitbags. It was still drizzling rain but there was much laughing and joking going on. To many of the soldiers this was no more than an adventure. They were going to a phoney war in which there hadn't yet been a shot fired.

"Where are we going anyway?' he asked John.

"France of course, you flannel head," replied his friend.

"I know that. I mean where in France?"

The man on the other side of Bev answered his question. "We're off to the border of France and Belgium mate."

The man who spoke was a Londoner whose accent gave him up as one born within the sound of The Bow bells. He had a rain-soaked cigarette hanging out of the corner of his mouth.

"You geezers are a long way from home," he said to Bev, noting his 'Geordie' accent.

"Me name's Ronnie. Ronnie Milford. I used to work just over there in the Custom shed before they 'scripted me."

John and Bev introduced themselves, then listened as their new friend told them stories he'd heard on the docks, about French girls.

"Right friendly they are lads," he said with a wink.

Sergeant Larson interrupted Ronnie's ribald revelations. "I want all of you boys in C Company to stay together in this area. Do you hear me? Don't move from here." The area he referred to was fairly well sheltered by a bulkhead and several lifeboats, so they were happy to stay where they were. "Smoke 'em if you got 'em,' he said.

The ship was now making it's way out of the river and into the rolling swell of the Channel. The vessel soon took on an uneasy motion, which had many of the soldiers faces in various shades of green with seasickness. Many vomited over the side. Some lads forgot to remove their hats before doing so and lost them to the wind, incurring the wrath of their Commanding officer and the Pay clerk. As the ship approached Calais it had to stand off until another vessel disgorged its soldiers and their equipment onto the jetty. Thousands of British and French troops along with vehicles filled the town and outlying regions.

"Have a gander Bev, this is bedlam. Just look at them all," said John.

"This looks like serious stuff alright Tinny, and we'll soon be in the middle of it."

"Cor blimey lads I fink the party started without us," laughed Ronnie Milford.

No sooner had The Spirit of Peace nudged alongside the mooring than Sergeant started rallying his men and they joined the line taking their first step onto foreign soil. They took their place in a large shed near Command Headquarters and waited while the Sergeant was briefed.

"The Germans are building up to the East of Calais," he told them on his return.

'They're sending us as reinforcements to a small village called.....'' he paused and closely scrutinised a map he had been given. "...Oost-Cappel."

"Who, what Sarge?" asked Bev Edwards with a grin.

"I'll repeat the name for you people that are flannel-eared," said the Sergeant.

"Oost-Cappel!"

"Now get your gear ready!"

Outside the building they climbed into three Lorries and began the drive to their destination.

The roads were packed with traffic of all kinds, mostly headed North. Several Divisions had already taken positions along the River Dyle and the River Dendre but the men of 2nd Infantry Division, including 2nd Battalion Darnley Light Infantry were to take their positions to the West of Dunkirk. It was their job to stop the Germans if they made a push towards the Channel.

As yet there had still been no fighting and many referred to the situation as 'the phoney war'.

Even so, Britain was taking no chances and was building defensive lines just in case of an invasion. Eight thousand concrete gun emplacements had been built along the Kennet and Avon Canal, which stretched 87miles from Bath to Newbury. The waterway was to be used as a barrier to any invading force from the South.

All road signs throughout the country had been removed and citizens advised to hide or destroy any maps they may have in their homes, to avoid giving aid to an invading force. An Army of volunteers which became known as Dad's Army was pressed into service in case Hitler's Armies decided to cross the Channel.

John, Bev and their comrades bounced along the country roads of France on their way to Oost-Cappel. They were to spend the next few months reinforcing the villages defences and engaging in reconnaissance missions to gauge the strength of the enemy. They were destined for a small camp in the field behind the Church. As the vehicles passed through the guard post, which stood at the gate in the thick hedge surrounding the field, one of the men observed,

"We're gonna freeze in them tents when winter comes. We're gonna be colder than them folks in that graveyard."

No one answered. They all knew what he said was true. The nights had been getting colder as Autumn took hold of the countryside.

"Everybody out!" shouted Sergeant Larson. "We're home."

Rifle Platoon of C Company stood at ease outside the C.O.'s tent and awaited further developments, while the Lorry drivers unloaded the Mortars and Radio equipment. The Commanding Officer walked from his tent. The men stood to attention at the Sergeants command and saluted.

"As you were men," said the C.O. "I'm Lieutenant Cleary. We are part of several Brigades involved in the defence of this sector and we are ordered to hold this position until further orders."

"That will be all Sergeant, said Cleary.

"Attention!" shouted the Sergeant. The men quickly responded.

The tall thin Lieutenant turned on his heel and re-entered his tent.

"Fall out men and find yourselves a tent!" shouted Larson.

They were directed to a cluster of two-man tents. John and Bev took one closest to the hedge seeking some shelter from the wind. Another Platoon was set up further down the field near the trees. Between the two was located the stores van and a rudimentary Mess tent. The Sergeant told the men they would have no use for such niceties as food, because they would be out on patrol most of the time.

"And no fraternising with the local girls either you daft lads," said Sergeant Larson.

"What's fraternising Sergeant?" asked one likely lad.

"Quiet, that man," Larson replied.

"Yes Sergeant," came the answer. The men carried on tenting.

Ronnie Milford, whose grasp of the English language was rudimentary to say the least, had taken on the task of instructing the lads in the use of the French language.

"Yer gotta remember that these French girls are lookin' for damore an' that," he said to his young listeners.

"Looking for what Ronnie?" asked Bev with a laugh.

"Damore mate. It's French for larve. You know what I mean," he answered with a grin.

Ronnie pressed on with the French lesson, ignoring the jibes of his detractors.

"This is what you say when you meet a French girl." he continued. "Voules vou le promenard avec mire nest pars."

The young lads were very impressed by Ronnie's eloquence. One of them pressed him for more information. "What does that mean Ronnie?" asked one gullible lad.

"It means somefink like "Your country is very beautiful," he answered his unfortunate listeners. "This will create in them a very pleasin' attitude towards you," he assured the young soldiers.

"You're useless at French Ronnie," said Bev, who did possess some knowledge of the French language. "What?" asked the Londoner.

"Ronnie. The lads are going to hear the word useless quite a lot if they follow your advice mate."

Padre Francis Dudley-Earl interrupted the conversation as it proceeded downhill. His concern for the Spiritual well-being of the lads was deep, as was his knowledge of the French language.

"You chaps needn't worry about speaking to the locals. Have you forgotten what the Lieutenant told you about fraternising with the locals already?"

"What's fraternising Vicar?" came a voice from the ranks. The Padre ignored the voice.

"The only place you may speak with the local people is when you attend the Church which you see on the other side of the wall."

"Furthermore if any of you wish to attend the Church you may only do so in my company. Do you understand?"

"Yes Sir," came the reply.

"Carry on chaps," said the Padre as he left the group to continue their unpacking.

A couple of the lads on watch at the Camp gate, had attempted to establish cordial relations with an elderly lady as she walked past their post. With his best smile, one of them said to her,

"Voulez vous le promenade avec mois n'est pas?"

The young man's French was much better than Ronnie Milford's but still received Bev's predicted response from the old lady, "Idiot!

This event severely curtailed any further attempts by the soldiers, to converse with the natives.

Chapter 29

THESE EARLY WEEKS and months spent by the Platoon around Oost-Cappel, were soon swallowed up in the routine of camp life and endless reconnaissance missions. Seven long months passed by. An observation post had been established in the Church tower. This was manned by several teams of less than enthusiastic soldiers who were initially excited to learn that they could see the Germans quite easily through their field glasses. They weren't so excited after one of the men pointed out that the Germans were probably watching them as well.

Quite often on these patrols, the Platoons of C Company found themselves so close to the scouting Germans they could here them speaking. Sergeant Larson had noted a huge build-up of German Cavalry troops and Artillery batteries to the West of the village. Large numbers of Transport support vehicles were parked behind a temporary H.Q. He had no doubt there was trouble coming and shared his feelings with Lieutenant Cleary.

"If the Germans make a move towards the Channel they'll go straight over the top of us. We won't be able to hold this position Sir."

"We will do our best Sergeant. We are part of a defensive line and we must hold."

"Yes Sir, of course," answered Larson.

The Sergeant knew, in spite of his orders, that C Company might slow down a German advance at best and suffer annihilation at worst. The lookouts in the Church tower became even more skittish, when a single projectile from a German rifle passed cleanly through the roof of their precarious perch.

"Very funny Fritz!" shouted one of them in a Westerly direction.

After that incident the Camp was on high alert around the clock.

"I don't like the look of this Bev," said John to his mate. "I think we're in for it."

"I reckon you're right," he answered quietly.

They had taken their turn in the tower and could plainly see the build up of German troops which now stretched as far as they could see. The enemy front was now established to the North and South West, as well as due West of Oost-Cappel.

"We won't be able to protect these poor blokes. We won't even be able to protect ourselves when they come marching through here." observed Bev.

"Anyway, if we were meant to protect the village we should be on the Western side, not here," he sneered.

"I reckon our boys at headquarters have been out manoeuvred by the Jerries," said John.

The British Generals had indeed been outmanoeuvred by the German hierarchy. They believed they had time on their side, thinking that Germany would be weakened by a planned blockade. The men of C Company had no way of knowing until it was too late, that the German Army had pushed into Belgium at the River Dyle. It was the morning of May the 10th 1940 and Hitler's forces had begun the Blitzkrieg.

The two friends were just climbing down the stairs of the tower after their watch, when all hades broke loose. Artillery and mortar fire between the Germans and the allied Brigades rocked the old Church building. The Rifle Platoons of C Company were right on the front line

John and Bev had just reached the bottom of the narrow winding stairs when they were thrown to the floor by an explosion. An enemy artillery shell had obliterated the Church tower. Smoke and debris filled the interior of the building and part of the ceiling was burning.

"Good grief Bev, move yourself out of here," shouted John.

They headed outside into the graveyard through a small side door. They took cover behind a large headstone as German mortar shells landed in the field where they had camped.

"Listen. There's a Tank coming down the road!" Bev yelled. They ran to the front wall of the Churchyard and peered over the top. John crouched behind him.

"They won't come too smartly. They'll soften us up first!" shouted John over the noise. Allied artillery screamed over their heads creating carnage behind the enemy line.

The screams and shouting from their own Camp could be heard as the enemy Artillery zeroed in on their mates. Smoke and dust almost blotted out the morning sun giving the two men excellent cover.

"We've got to get back to the Eastern side of the building. We're sitting ducks here," yelled Bev.

"Not yet," shouted John. "Let's see if we can pick a few off first,"

With that, he scrambled off to another position that gave him a good view of the Panzer Tank and Infantry which had stopped half a mile down the road. He raised his rifle and began picking of any German soldier who hadn't bothered to find cover behind the tank. Bev took up a position behind a nearby headstone and began his own attack on the enemy Infantry.

"We'd better move before they get a fix on us," yelled Bev.

He pointed to the rear of the Church building and they both scurried to a new position.

They could see the open field from this spot and what they saw made them duck down very quickly. A Company of German soldiers, crouched low, was making it's way towards the Churchyard where they were hiding. They were only 400 yards away from their position.

"We've got to slow those Jerrys down," croaked John. He suddenly realised he was very thirsty. Thick black smoke drifted across the field but the two friends could still see clearly enough to loose a few judicious rounds at the advancing enemy. A combination of the Company mortars and their own marksmanship, stopped the German troops in their tracks. Bullets whined over their heads as the Germans began to target their position.

"We'll have to move again," shouted John. He crawled to the rear corner of the yard and took cover behind a large pile of soil. Bev ran low and rolled behind the dirt as a Mortar shell exploded only 10 yards away. They still had their heads down as another one went off, destroying the wall where they had been taking cover only a minute ago.

"These fellas are onto us," hissed Bev.

"They didn't like you shooting their friends," laughed John.

He noticed a side door which had swung open from the explosion in the tower.

"Let's swing through the Church and see if we can get back to the Camp," he shouted.

They crouched and ran to the open door, diving through into a small store room. It was relatively undamaged and they could see a doorway which led into the main building. If they could run through to the other side, they could re-unite with the rest of the Platoon. The fight was raging outside and most of the stained glass windows were blown out by this time.

There was a large ragged hole in the roof of the building. Occasionally the sunlight struggled through the smoke and dust, lighting up the scene of devastation within. The noise of the battle seemed to take on a greater intensity as it echoed around inside the Church.

"What's that noise?" yelled Bev.

"Are you serious?" answered John. "Really?" he yelled back.

Bev ran to the corner of the room and there in the corner in a cardboard box was a white Terrier cross with a litter of new pups. "You poor lass," he said as he looked at the trembling animal.

"Come on, there's no time for that!" John shouted to his friend.

"I'm going to cover her up," Bev shouted in return.

With that, he took hold of the heavy cupboard door which had been blown from the bottom of the collapsed stairwell and positioned it over the dog's box for her protection. The whole building was shaking now as the enemy pounded it with mortar fire. Plaster, and pieces of stone and timber ricocheted around the room. Smoke and dust were thick now and fire had taken hold of the timber panelling around the interior of the Church building.

"We've got to go....right now!" yelled John.

The German front line now stretched for miles to the East and West of Oost-Cappel and were moving North towards the English Channel. Spitfires, Stukas and Hurricanes filled the skies, while the ill-prepared British and French troops on the ground made a valiant effort to stop the German advance.

Cannon fire from the enemy Tank slammed into the corner of the building, instantly destroying the Vestry in which they sheltered. In the midst of the flame, the deafening noise and the flying rubble, they were hurled to the floor under the collapsed ceiling and part of the roof. The two friends were knocked unconscious. John came to much later and found himself covered in dust but able to crawl around in the space between the fallen ceiling and the floor. He grabbed his rifle and moved over to his fallen comrade.

"Bev are you alright?" he whispered hoarsely.

He shook his friend's shoulder and was glad to hear Bev groan in response. John saw the dog carrying one of it's pups through a hole in the wall to the graveyard outside. He shuffled towards the hole dragging his friend with him. The fresh air on his face felt good and as he peered outside at ground level. The dog returning for another of her pups, wagged her tail and licked him on the nose. Bev had partly regained his senses as they lay sprawled in the long grass among the headstones. John noticed the Terrier mother carrying one of her pups through a broken gate into an overgrown garden. The dog paused for a moment and looked back at him as though waiting for him to follow. He half dragged and half carried his groaning friend and followed the dog into an old stone garden shed, where he sat and took stock of their situation. He found himself smiling through the dirt and grime which smeared his face. The mother and pups had nestled into a pile of old pew pads, under a bench in the corner. She was safe for the time being.

"What happened?" asked his friend. "I've got a blinding headache," he groaned.

"I'm not surprised. A church fell on your head," laughed John. They both laughed momentarily at the sight of each other covered in French Church dust.

"Are you good to go mate?" asked John. "We've got to move quickly now before those Jerrys get here. We must have been out for hours."

Bev spied the dog under the bench and breathed a sigh of relief. "Good girl," was all he said. She wagged her tail in response.

"Grab your rifle and follow me," John whispered.

Without a backward glance he ran to the Northern wall of the Churchyard, leaped over it and looked around the deserted Camp area. The Bedford supply lorry had gone, as had all of the gear the men could carry. What couldn't be carried had been destroyed, to prevent it falling into the hands of the enemy. By this time Bev lay by his side and let out a low whistle.

"They put up a brave fight here didn't they Tinny?" he whispered.

There were mortar craters everywhere and all of the tents were destroyed.

"Over here," said John and ran to the side of a bomb crater. Partly covered in soil, the body of the Chaplain lay slumped over a dead soldier whom he had been praying for when another mortar shell had landed, killing him instantly.

"They must have been in one big hurry to leave these blokes behind!" shouted Bev. The bombardment was intensifying now and they could hear the Tank moving forward again.

"Come on, run!" shouted John. They both sprinted for the far boundary wall with bullets whining over their heads, as they dived for cover behind it.

"We've got to find our boys," panted John.

Stuka dive bombers were wreaking havoc on the withdrawing troops as they endeavoured to secure a position from which to launch a counter attack. The two friends ran fearlessly in the direction of the circling enemy aircraft about a mile to the North.

"That must be where they are Tinny," shouted Bev. The two men ran across another field to the far hedge. Even if they could have seen their pursuers, they didn't have time to return fire. They broke cover and ran across the next field, all the time coming under heavy fire aimed at their retreating comrades. Many dead farm animals lay in the fields among the bomb craters but the boys saw no more dead mates.

"Come on. Keep moving Bev," shouted John. Bev was slowing now as his head injury started to bleed again. The blood and perspiration mixed and ran in rivulets through the dirt on his face. They ran towards a red bricked barn, keeping low and dived into a ditch near the open doors. "Cover me. I'm going for a look," whispered John, who leapt to his feet and ran through the large wooden doors. He stood with his back flattened against the wall, as he waited for his eyes to become accustomed to the dim light inside the building. There were several pieces of farm machinery scattered on the dirt floor, and a stack of hay bails but the object that caused his eyes to light up was an old motorcycle among the junk.

John nearly jumped out of his skin as Bev dashed into the barn from his hiding place.

"Keep an eye on the farmhouse while I check this bike, John whispered.

"The whole place looks deserted. They must have heard the Germans coming and hit the road," answered Bev.

"Just keep an eye out. I don't want any more surprises," said John

"If you know any prayers you'd better pray them," John said to his friend.

His heart was in his mouth as he as he dragged the machine out of the junk. The air battle still raged overhead and the thunder of the artillery outside continued.

It was an old BMW motorcycle covered in dust and John held his breath as he checked the fuel level in the tank. He stood back and grinned at his friend. "It's got fuel in it," he hissed triumphantly.

"Will it go?" asked Bev urgently.

He watched John fiddle with the engine and crossed his fingers as he saw him stomping on the kick-starter. The old engine gradually wheezed into life belching a cloud of blue smoke but it kept running. John swung his leg over the machine and directed Bev to the rack on the back.

"Get on mate. I'll take you for a ride to the coast for a picnic," shouted John with a laugh. He shifted the hand gearshift into first gear.

The two men on their old iron steed roared down the dirt lane-way beside the farmhouse and onto the road heading North West. There were the bodies of many soldiers on the side of the road and dozens of bomb damaged vehicles. They didn't slow until they ran into a traffic jam a couple of miles up the road. Near the small town of Berques they were slowed by large volumes of troops, both on foot and in various types of vehicles, travelling the narrow country roads towards Dunkirk. Negotiating the many canals in the area was extremely difficult.

"How in hades are we supposed to find C Company amongst this lot?" shouted Bev.

John didn't answer. He didn't have an answer. He realised that many of these men would have been separated from their Platoons the same way they had been.

"Get over here you dozy blighters, and fall in!" Shouted the unmistakable voice of Sergeant Larson. He was taking cover with a group of soldiers near a road bridge across one of the many canals in the area. John leaned the machine against the wall of a Cafe and the two men pushed their way through the line of soldiers waiting to cross the bridge.

"Good to see you boys. Get over here and keep your heads down!" yelled the Sergeant over the noise. "The Lieutenant went off with Sigs. They're on that roof over there!"

He pointed to the roof of the Post Office building across the Town square. The Lieutenant and the radio operator could be seen above the Parapet. Lieutenant Cleary was looking back along the road as he listened to the voice of the Commanding Officer of the Field HQ. The men saw him wave to the Sergeant and point to the road leading South. Just as he and the radio operator headed for the door to the stairwell on the roof of of the Post Office, a Bomb hit the building, showering the line of troops below with rubble and shrapnel. From the cover of the wall on the other side of the square, the platoon saw the horror unfold and the damage it caused. Only a moment before, a line of men had been withdrawing to another defensive position and now the roadway to the bridge was filled with stone rubble and injured men.

"You two come with me. The rest of you go and help those poor blokes! Roared the Sergeant. John and Bev followed Sergeant Larson as he ran towards the bombed building.

"The Germans are trying to blow this bridge. They want to stop us reforming a counter attack! Yelled Larson amid the confusion.

The whole top floor had collapsed into the lower floor. Dust and smoke filled the air as the ancient timber burned furiously.

They saw the bodies of Lieutenant Cleary and the Sigs operator amongst the burning roof timbers. They could do nothing but turn and run from the destroyed building back to the road.

They ran back to the rest of the Platoon.

"We've got to help get this road cleared and get these injured men under cover! Shouted the Sergeant to the Platoon.

Before long, the body of men had the road cleared and a First-aid station established in the Place de la Republique which was a substantial building in the middle of the square. Larson's face was grim as he surveyed the scene outside. Hundreds of men, some in vehicles, were endeavouring to make their way over the narrow bridge to the North of Berques. Once over the canal they would destroy the bridge behind them and set up another front to stop the German advance. Since the death of Lieutenant Cleary he was in charge and he made his first decision.

"We've got to go and defend that road to the South and give them time to cross over that canal boys! Shouted Larson. "Follow me!"

Keeping to fields and ditches, they headed South. The Panzer Tank approaching them on the Southern road was causing much of the destruction with it's cannon. The withdrawing convoy including Field Ambulances was being harried by the pursuing Germans. Many of the troops heading for Dunkirk on this road were wounded and most out of ammunition after their run-in with the enemy. The men of C Company retraced their steps toward the village of Quaedypre, under sporadic but accurate

Air attack. Three of the Platoon had to drop back with shrapnel wounds, lucky to be able to walk.

The enemy was doing it's utmost to stop the successful withdrawal of allied soldiers from the area. It didn't take long for the Platoon to see the approaching Tank. There were only twenty Infantrymen walking with it. Sergeant Larson divided his men into two groups. One group in the trees on one side of the road and the rest, including John and Bev, in the trees on the other side.

"Wait until they're next to that dead horse in the ditch and then let them have it with all you've got," he instructed the boys. "You, you and you come with me," he said to John, Bev and a man called Nobby Clark. They worked their way on the inside of the hedge along the field towards the spot where the dead horse lay. The men lay in the long grass near the carcase and waited for the approaching Germans.

"Cor what a pong," whispered Clark.

Larson ignored him. "When the shooting starts stay under cover and watch out for stray Germans. The ones our boys might miss will try to run into the fields, so don't let them but stay low. Then follow me. We're going to stop that tank." he whispered urgently.

The crackle of the Platoon's Lee-Enfield rifles sounded from the trees and more than half of the German foot soldiers fell dead. The Tank commander, taking advantage of their relatively unthreatened position, was travelling with the hatch open guiding the direction of the gunner. He fell dead, slumped forward on the turret, his lower body blocking the hatch. The boys could hear loud shouting from inside the Panzer and the Machine gun barked in the general direction of the tree line. Four of the German soldiers ran through the hedge and into the field where the friends lay waiting.

They were cut down with a burst of rifle fire before they knew what hit them. On the other side of the road another four were shot by the men in the wood as they ran into that field.

John broke through the hedge and walked calmly across the front of the Tank and fired two rounds from his Webley service revolver through the driver's view port directly into the gap. He flinched as he heard a shot from behind the Panzer as Nobby Clark despatched another German soldier hiding behind the vehicle. He watched as Sergeant Larson dropped a grenade down the open hatch of the tank and jumped down beside the tracks. John and the other men dived into the ditch for cover just as the grenade exploded, killing the rest of the crew inside their metal tomb. The whole incident had taken little more than ten minutes.

"Back to Berque on the double now. They'll be swarming all over us soon!" shouted Larson.

They ran back along the road to join up with the rest of the Platoon, then continued on back to the village where the fighting had escalated. The Germans were right on their heels with more Panzers and Infantry following. They reached a deserted house on the edge of the Square and took cover behind a thick stone wall facing back down the road. The sky above the village was filled with tumbling allied and enemy aircraft engaged in dog fights. The rattle of their cannon and machine gun fire adding to the rumble of bomb and high explosive artillery rounds hitting the village of Berque.

"If we can hold these Jerrys up for a while, that bridge will be cleared boys! Larson shouted. "Make every shot count!"

The Platoon spread themselves out along their position and waited for the enemy ground troops to show themselves.

"Tinny, take Bev and see if you can get up in that tower," shouted Larson.

He pointed to the large building in the middle of the square. From there they would have a perfect view of the road the enemy would use. The two friends ran as fast as they could to the Place de la Republique and burst through a side door. Once they had gained access to the tower, they darted up the spiral stone stairway to the top. From their elevated position they could see what they judged to be a Battalion of men and Tanks halted on the outskirts of the village.

"Sarge, there's too many. We need to fall back!" John yelled to the Sergeant.

"We'll cover you while you move!"

The Sergeant waved back to them and then it all broke loose. Two bombs fell directly in the Square with a huge thud throwing debris across the area and blowing the windows out of the surrounding properties. One fell next to the wall where the Platoon had taken cover adding to the dust and smoke.

"I reckon they've blown the boys to bits Tinny," shouted Bev.

"The Jerrys are on the move mate. They'll be on top of us soon," yelled John.

The enemy was about to enter the Town square and an eerie silence fell as the bombardment temporarily ceased.

"I can't see the boys Tinny." said Bev quietly.

"Aagh!" shouted John with frustration.

John was busy taking aim at the first few German soldiers as they walked past the position where their friends had taken cover. They were stepping around the rubble and attempting to hide in the huge crater the bomb had left. The first two men fell victim to John's unerring aim.

"Cop that you Jerrys," he said coldly.

"Come on, we've got to go now Tinny!" yelled Bev heading to the stairs.

A Panzer Tank began to make it's way across the pile of rubble into the Square.

"Run for the bridge!" yelled John at the top of his voice.

The friends scampered down the stone steps, out of the door and using the building as cover, ran towards the canal.

"Look, it's the bike," said John. "It's still there."

He ran to it and swung on the kick-start. The engine sprang into life with a cloud of blue smoke. At the same time, a high explosive cannon shell smashed into the building they had just vacated. Bev didn't need an invitation to jump on the back of the machine. John gunned the motorcycle onto the bridge, with both wheels clearing the road as they went over the hump. Dodging bombs and damaged machinery, they joined the stragglers heading North-east towards the coast.

Chapter 30

THE CLOSER THE friends got to Dunkirk the more congested the roads became. They stopped amid the noise and smoke, on the low cliff overlooking the Dunkirk beach. Temporarily overcome by the sight before them they stood transfixed. Stuka Dive-bombers screamed above them, strafing and shelling the thousands of men assembled on the sands. As far as the eye could see to the left and right, vehicles and equipment stood deserted on the sand hills and promenade. Many hundreds of soldiers were milling about awaiting orders or trying to link up with their comrades. There was a huge withdrawal taking place. Battleships, Cruisers and small craft stood off the beach while under attack from enemy aircraft and Artillery. A jetty had been built out from the beach enabling troops to make their way to the rescue ships and even as they walked along these planked walkways, the enemy raked them with cannon and machine gun fire.

They followed the directions of an officer and made their way down to the beach where they took some cover under the meagre cover of the bank. Machine gunners set up their weapons in the sand to fire on the marauding murderous enemy aircraft, which were constantly bombing and firing on the beach. Even though clouds of thick black smoke drifted over the scene of horror providing a smoke screen, there was really nowhere to hide. The larger rescue craft were unable to get close to the beach because of the shallow water. Bold volunteers from England with their own small pleasure craft came in close to lift off as many as they could and ferried them to the bigger Naval craft. Some 'little ships' carried rescued soldiers all the way across the English channel, braving the attacks of German Stukas, to Dover and other small coastal towns in England. Lines of men snaked out into the water up to their armpits waiting to be picked up.

Many bombed ships drifted off shore burning until they sank. These wrecks made the job of the rescuers even more difficult, as they attempted to navigate close to the men in the water. Brave soldiers, including John and Bev, fired back with their rifles at the strafing German aircraft as they swooped along the beach. Anti- aircraft gun emplacements pounded the attacking Stukas. British Spitfires shot down scores of German fighters but were outnumbered. French, Belgian and British soldiers were involved in bloody counter attacks and defensive pushes in a sickle formation around the Dunkirk area, eventually halting the German advance. This didn't stop the constant air and artillery barrage which rained down on the men trapped on the beach and hundreds died without cover of any kind.

Officers with drawn pistols patrolled the beach with orders to shoot any man pushing in ahead of his turn to board a rescue boat. They weren't needed, as the men dealt out summary justice to anyone found attempting such a cowardly act. The officers in charge of clearing the beach and filling the rescue vessels worked tirelessly for three solid days and nights, with no thought for their own well-being. It was in the afternoon of the second day, that John and Bev were ordered to take their place in one of the lines of men wading into the water to take their place on a rescue boat. Neither man had relinquished their rifles and as they shuffled into deeper water they held them above their heads. However, as minutes stretched into hours, the wading men couldn't hold them any longer and were forced to sling their weapons in the water.

"I forgot to tell you Tinny," shouted Bev. "I can't swim!"

"Hang onto my pack and think like a fish!" yelled John.

A very real fear had swept over many of the men, who like Bev had never learned to swim. The oily waves were building up and threatening to knock them off their feet. The dead bodies of many of their comrades either drowned or mutilated, bobbed about in the water, bumping up against the line of waiting soldiers. Nothing could be done for these men and the bodies of hundreds of them were never even found after the conflict. A flotilla of small boats edged closer, with volunteer helpers taking the men's outstretched arms and pulling them on board. A fishing boat out of Dover picked them out of the sea, along with 8 others. Palls of black smoke from burning wreckage drifted across the scene, as they made their way out into the channel. They had to make their way through other vessels of all shapes and sizes and even though they had the smoke to hide their escape, it made the skipper's jobs extremely difficult. Enemy dive-bombers were still targeting the rescue ships until they came under the protection of Spitfire squadrons closer to the English coast.

"Thank heavens for you blokes," said John to the skipper of the boat. The skipper of the small boat, a big ruddy faced man, stood against the wheelhouse window

"We're thankin' the Lord for you chaps as well," he replied. He peered grimly into the distance. One of the men died before reaching England. The back of his uniform was soaked in blood when they rolled him over. He'd been hit by a piece of shrapnel but no one knew when. His war was over.

Many of the men on deck were shaking uncontrollably now, with a combination of the cold and delayed shock. No one spoke. They just stared silently at the misty English coastline ahead.

"It looks like we've made it Tinny." Bev broke the silence, shouting over the noise of the diesel engine rumbling below deck and the wind blowing across the bow of the boat.

"Aye, I think we have this time lad, I think we have." Bev looked at his friend.

John's face was set like a stone and he thought he saw tears in his blood-shot eyes. The closer they came to the Port of Dover, the more animated the men became. Their rescue was becoming a reality at last. Off the beams they watched other boats carrying their cargo of returning soldiers, making their way through the entrance to the harbour. Any celebrations at their safe delivery were held firmly in check, by the memory of the carnage on the beach at Dunkirk and the suffering of those still fighting there. Many French, Belgian and British Divisions and Battalions were still held a tenuous line around Dunkirk and gradually withdrew to the coast where most of them were rescued.

The German thrust had commenced on the 10th of May 1940 ushering in a period of savage attacks and counter attacks. Three weeks later Germans had gained the ascendancy as they pushed through Holland, Belgium and France as far west as Calais. They weren't able to take Dunkirk but did secure the ground to the South of the town. They pushed the British Army from central France all the way back to the coast and by the 1st of June 330,00 allied troops had been rescued from the beaches of Dunkirk. 11,000 dead, 40,000 captured, 50,000 vehicles lost including Tanks, 9 Destroyers, 200 marine vessels and 177Aircraft destroyed.

The enemy toll amounted to 30,000 dead and wounded, 100 Tanks and 240 Aircraft destroyed.

In the thoughts of some, it had been a gallant withdrawal and so it had. In the minds of some of the soldiers on the ground and the citizens of the subsequently occupied nations, it had been a 'deadly shambles.' There was still a strong feeling across the English nation to make Hitler's army pay for it's treachery and plans were already afoot to do just that.

The returning soldiers were handed blankets and given a hot cup of tea on disembarking their rescue craft. They were then ushered into a large building to be de-briefed and if possible to be re-united with their Command. The injured, no matter what their nationality, were treated in makeshift hospitals. Some soldiers didn't recover mentally from the time they spent, at what became known as The Battle of Dunkirk. Others were more than ready for a return bout against the German

Many Battalions had been decimated during the conflict, some totally depleted. After the re-organisation at Dover the two friends were split up into different Regiments.

Bev, with the remains of C Company, was attached to the 14th Brigade to be based in Dorset. John was taken North by train to Whitby, where he would placed in the newly formed Royal Engineers Bomb Disposal Unit to work throughout the North East.

BACK IN ENGLAND
JUNE 1940

Chapter 31

WHILE IN FRANCE John had developed a liking for French cigarettes and he quietly enjoyed his last one, while staring out of the window at the countryside he had missed so much. The train, loaded with soldiers and civilians lurched it's way towards Courtenay, where he would enjoy one week glorious leave at home before his re-deployment. His mind was filled with thoughts of Sarah. There had been no mail getting through to his Company all the time they had been in France. He hadn't heard from her since leaving Barrowthwaite almost nine months ago and his heart was aching for her. He had sent her a letter from Dover three days ago and hoped it would reach home before he did. He had asked for someone to pick him up at Courtenay Railway Station.

Since arriving back in England he had been struck by the number of Posters advising the public to be mindful of secrecy during this time of war. They carried messages like, 'The walls have ears' and 'Loose lips sink ships'. The news of The battle of Dunkirk and the subsequent withdrawal, had shaken the British people, driving home the reality of Germany's expansionist programs. Farms were working at peak production now, to keep up the necessary wartime food supplies. The English countryside was a hive of activity. The Land Army once more had been pressed into service, bringing back memories of the First World

War for many. Many women were working in the manufacturing industries, filling the void left by those sent to fight for their country. As the train approached Courtenay, John noticed that much land hitherto unused, was now being cultivated to grow food crops. The North East was currently enjoying fine warm summer weather, which lifted John's spirits.

Memories of his involvement in the recent horror, was for the time being pushed to the back of his mind.

As the train pulled into the Station, he scanned the platform for his father and Elsie but the place was packed with people. Most of them were soldiers on the move. He stepped down from the train carrying his kitbag and headed for the waiting room.

"Hey up lad we're ower 'ere," he heard his father shout over the din of the crowd.

He caught a glimpse of him through the waiting room and headed for the exit.

"Hey father," he said and shook his hand. They both showed the usual lack of emotion found among farmers in the North East. Elsie however, had no such inhibitions and threw her arms around John kissing him on the cheek. Big Bill picked up his son's kitbag in one hand and slung it into the back of the car.

"The car's looking a bit old and tired," remarked John with a grin.

"Aye lad and so are you," replied Bill. John noticed for the first time, the concern and stress showing on their faces. "I reckon thee's aged ten year and lost two stone." Said his father. Elsie nodded gravely in agreement.

"Don't worry, I'm alright," smiled John. He thought his father had aged also.

Most of the traffic they encountered on the way to Peace Hall farm was Military. John noticed very few private vehicles were out and about.

"How's Sarah?" he asked, enjoying the view of familiar roads and lane- ways leading to the farm.

"Right as rain lad, right as rain," answered his father quietly.

Bill stopped the car outside The Honeymoon cottage while John climbed out and then he and Elsie continued along the driveway to the farmhouse. He stood looking at the cottage which was surrounded by a riotous display of bright flowers and shrubs. With his heart pounding in his chest he walked across the small stone bridge with his kitbag. "There she is!"

Sarah rushed from the front door, meeting him in the garden. For several moments they stood in each other's arms oblivious of the world around them. Face to face, heart to heart at last.

Sarah spoke first. With tears streaming down her face she sobbed "I was so happy to get your letter yesterday. I thought something terrible had happened to you. Did you get any of my letters?"

John placed his finger on her lips. "I didn't get any letters my love. None of us did."

He kissed her, the taste of salty tears on her lips, mixed with his own as they ran down his face.

His arms were still wrapped tightly around Sarah's waist. She then took him by the hand and led him inside to the bedroom.

"Don't make any noise darling. I've a surprise for you."

"What the...,"

"Shush," Sarah whispered. "Open your eyes now. This is your new son, Godfrey.

He's just two weeks old."

John opened his mouth to speak but uttered no sound. He reached out his rough calloused hand and touched his babe's tender face, causing him to stir in his crib.

"He's beautiful," he whispered. "I didn't know...." His voice trailed off.

A lone tear ran down his face and dropped onto the front of his uniform.

"Hello little man," he said quietly. "I'm your Dad."

Sarah sad "You sit on the bed and hold him, while I and get your bag and make us some tea. By the way, I chose John for his middle name."

John closed his eyes and savoured the scent of his wife and new-born baby. Sometimes closing his eyes brought in a flood of dark chilling battle images but at this time, his mind was filled with pure joy.

"Let's go outside and sit in the sun for a while honey," he smiled at Sarah.

"You go to the garden and I'll bring out our tea darling," she answered kissing him on the forehead.

Sarah returned with the refreshments and sat beside her husband. "The baby's still asleep," she said.

"I've something to tell you honey," said John.

"What is it. What's the matter?" asked Sarah.

"I've been re-deployed into The Corps of Royal Engineers. A week from now I'll be a part of 3 Bomb Disposal Company based in Whitby."

Sarah didn't answer immediately but John saw the tears well up in her eyes. He took her hands in his.

"I'm coming with you," Sarah answered. "We'll be together."

"But you can't come.."

"I'm not going to be apart from you as long as you're serving somewhere in England," replied Sarah defiantly.

"Now I don't want to talk about it any more. Let's enjoy our time while I'm on leave. We'll cross that bridge when we come to it." John took her in his arms and held her tightly. "Don't worry honey. Everything will be alright."

"We heard a rumour about the massacre of British prisoners in France by the Germans while you were away," whispered Sarah. "I prayed for you all the time."

Keep praying for me honey, wherever I go."

"What's the situation with your father lately honey?" asked John, changing the subject.

"He and the Reverend Little have taken a stand against us. Reverend Little has told father that we are in danger of hades flames. He said even the children aren't saved without being Christened in The Church," Sarah looked at John and smiled.

"I know in my heart that isn't true," said John. "I think I'll go and talk to your father. That Priest is just stirring trouble."

"Mother still supports us though. A funny thing happened while you were away, I still don't know whether it was coincidence or an answer to prayer," said Sarah excitedly.

"Mildred went along to an evangelistic gospel meeting in Stopford Brook Town Hall with one of her friends and after the meeting she asked the Speaker some questions about marriage and the Church."

John threw his head back and laughed. "Mildred's just cheeky enough to do that."

"Anyway," continued Sarah with a smile. "He told her that a Christian couple need not be married in a Church as long as they are married in true conscience before God."

"Did she ask him about the children?" asked John.

"Well," said Sarah thoughtfully. "Because we believe in God, we should still have our children dedicated or Christened and bring them up in the Church."

"Why don't we do that in the Church of England then honey?"

"I think that would be a good idea," answered Sarah. "We could do it before you go away again."

In the warmth of the garden, as the birds and bees went about their business, talk of the mundane soon faded and their thoughts turned to love. Sarah took John by the hand and led him into the cottage. Her world was now complete again and the rest of the world didn't matter.

The days passed in blissful happiness as they walked the fields with the baby in his pram. They visited Old Tun farm enjoying the company of family. Edward and Thora Lofthouse drove them to Stopford Brook to see Sarah's mother in one day during the week and she fussed over her daughter and the baby. John's BSA had been stored a the farm while he was in France and he took several opportunities to ride around the district, enjoying the familiar sights and smells of the countryside. Most of the time though, they spent alone in the Honeymoon cottage at Peace Hall farm treasuring their time together.

Chapter 32

THE LUFTWAFFE DURING these early war years was dropping tons of bombs on London but also further North as well. Not only were they targeting Ports and factories but also civilian targets. Hitler saw these bombings as being of great value in demoralising the populace and bringing the country to it's knees. Simple tactics used by the British people, such as the vigilant use of blackout curtains made it difficult for the German Bombers to see the targets at night.

However, once the bombs hit and fires started lighting up the scene, there was no hiding from the dreadful carnage and many thousands lost their lives. Those millions who had their homes destroyed by the bombs, were forced to shelter in The Underground railway stations. Bombs were dropped in the countryside as well, in places like Dorset and Hampshire. Plymouth was very badly hit, as were Birmingham, Coventry, Bradford and Liverpool. The Hull Estuary was bombed with many of the bombs falling harmlessly into the North Sea. Further north, Tyneside and Teeside were bombed. One stray bomb dropped in the grounds of Willersley Castle down by the River Derwent in Derbyshire. Other than blowing a large crater in the ground, it did no damage. Many of these bombs that landed in unpopulated areas were usually dropped at night by bomb aimers who couldn't see their target because of blackout below. The number of bombs that fell in populated areas but didn't explode, posed a very real threat to the public as they attempted to go about their business among the ruins, after each attack.

Many Bomb Disposal Companys were established around the nation to defuse these unexploded bombs. These were usually attached to The Royal Engineers. John Tyndale found himself in 3 Bomb Disposal Company based in Whitley Bay overlooking the North Sea.

The Camp was situated on the cliff-top across the lane from the ruins of Whitby Abbey. It was surrounded by a high wooden fence topped with barbed wire. Many areas, particularly around the huts, were heavily sandbagged. A 40mm Bofors gun stood at the seaward end of the camp. The Engineers had made it even more lethal to attacking aircraft, by fixing a Bren gun to the top of the weapon. It could be fired independently of, or in conjunction with the Bofors. Any enemy aircraft attempting to fly near that part of the coast, had to risk flying through a barrage of hot metal from this gun emplacement, which had an effective range of 12-15,000 feet with a ceiling of 20,000 feet.

To the North, the rugged headland known as the Khyber Pass towered over the village of Whitby. The township stood on the banks of The River Esk inlet overlooking the harbour. To the South spread farmland above the beach. Captain James Cook was born near Whitby and would have been familiar with the coastline when working on the Coal ships as a 17yr old lad.

John Tyndale found himself admiring the same coastline as he leaned against the wall of St Mary's Church of England on the cliff-top. The nearby graveyard brought memories of his time in France flooding back. He wondered what had happened to the rest of his Platoon during the bombardment of Berque. Since returning to England he had continued making enquiries about their fate through The Red Cross. To date he had heard nothing positive about the Platoon but he did know the approximate location of his friend Vivian (Bev) Edwards, who was stationed somewhere in Kent. He thought of the dog and her pups, which Bev had cared for.

His reverie was broken by the sound of an explosion from the direction of the camp. He threw his cigarette to the ground and ran back to the gate. "What was that Shorty?" he asked the tall man on sentry duty.

"Dunno Tinny. It came from over at the trainin' hut." the man replied.

A pall of smoke rose from a sandbagged section outside the hut. A small group of men were standing about. Some were laughing. "It's alright. The Lieutenant was just showin' us how these new time delay fuses work," laughed one man. "Here, he offered John a cigarette.

"Let that be a lesson to all of you. Those crafty Germans don't like you and they're trying to kill you by using these delayed fuses. They can explode up to eighty hours after the Bomb has dropped. So don't forget it!" said the training Officer. "Our boffins have come up with a few gizmos that will help us to de-fuse them but remember..." He paused for a moment puffing on his pipe, "You're being paid huge amounts of money to do this job, so do it well every time!"

This last statement caused much hilarity because the British Tommy wasn't paid very much at all but behind the laughter one could see the tension on their faces. The Private soldier in 1940 was paid between 2 shillings and sixpence and 6 shillings a day depending on qualifications, while a Sergeant could expect to be paid up to 8 shillings and ninepence per day. Even so, allied Bomb disposal experts were involved in a non-stop cat and mouse game with the German fuse designers, as they tried to out-wit each other.

It was late September and the mild weather was holding. John had just been informed by his Commanding Officer of his promotion to Sergeant and the whole Platoon was being kept on high alert, as the enemy intensified it's Bombing campaign over England.

Sarah, with the help of her mother's maid Mildred, Thora Lofthouse, Elsie Tyndale, Minnie Lowther and Dr Douglas wife Eve, had taken a room in Whitby. She and baby Godfrey had moved into a small but comfortable attic room, overlooking the 199 stone steps which led from the village below to the Abbey on the cliff-top. She had promised to be near John wherever he served in Britain and she was doing it.

Stress was an ever-present companion of the bomb disposal squads around England and the Commanding Officers of these Companys did their utmost to maintain morale among the men. While discipline was paramount on the job, a less formal air was present at other times. It was during these rare quiet times that John's CO allowed him to stay with Sarah and the baby. The room which Sarah had rented was only a couple of hundred yards from the camp gate after all.

"Don't make a big noise about it Tyndale," was all he added.

There were strict blackout conditions around the nation and the North-East was no exception. Most bombs that fell near Whitby dropped into the sea causing damage to shipping and shaking those living in the area. The noise and heavy percussion of this ordnance, struck fear into the stoutest of hearts during the night raids. Sometimes Sarah wasn't able to get to the air-raid shelter on time and curled up with her son under the bed wrapped in a thick duvet. John could never be with her at these times because of his work but he had placed a ring of sawdust bags around the base of the bed for just such occasions.

He had thought about sandbags but was afraid the extra weight would put too much strain on the rafters. Mrs Toghill the landlady lived below them and he didn't want their bed to fall through the ceiling during the night. John and Sarah sometimes burst out laughing uncontrollably as they tried to keep as quiet as mice in bed. The elderly landlady smiled at their laughter. It reminded her of the happy times she had spent with her husband.

He had been a member of the local lifeboat crew lost at sea in the bad storm of 1927, while attempting to aid a stricken coastal freighter which had lost the power of its engines.

Whitby lifeboat station was kept busy rescuing survivors of bombed ships in the North Sea, setting out in all weather with no thought for their own safety. The same scenario was being played out all along the eastern coastline of Britain.

Whenever the weather permitted Sarah walked along the headlands and beaches in the area. It took her mind off the danger that surrounded John every day. She pushed the baby in a pram the lads in the engineering shop had made for her. They presented her with it one day as she stood at the camp gate waiting to see John. It was a fine piece of design made from scrap aluminium finished in aircraft black and khaki enamel with canvas bodywork. She was proud to push young Godfrey around the district in his new chariot.

Later that year John received some leave and they caught a bus back to Peace Hall cottage. Godfrey was a toddler now and interested in everything. He enjoyed the walks across the fields between Old Tun farm and Peace Hall in his pram. He gurgled with joy as he pointed at the cows and sheep. John and Sarah spent as much time as possible in between visits to Old Tun farm, sitting under the trees by the stream, down near the old stone bridge.

"E's a fine lad lass," said big Bill Tyndale to Sarah. He stood with Godfrey in his arms looking every bit the proud grandfather. "E's got t' look of y'self about him thee ken."

Elsie agreed. "He's absolutely beautiful Sarah."

William was in from the fields especially to see his brother and Sarah. He made out like he didn't care much about his nephew but he held him longer than anyone else. Even Mary and Margaret didn't hold the toddler as long as William.

Elsie said quietly to Sarah, "Are you sure you're not expecting another baby lass?"

Elsie and her sister Thora were both of the opinion that Sarah was pregnant again.

"You can tell by the way she's carrying herself," said Elsie.

Sarah had known for a few days but was keeping it a secret until seeing Dr Douglas. She had hinted at her condition to John earlier in the day, so she felt at ease replying, "Maybe."

"I knew it," squealed Elsie with delight. "Bill did you hear that? They're having another baby!"

Bill, who was enjoying a quiet chat with his two sons in the parlour, heard the commotion in the kitchen and temporarily forgot his northern England reserve. He hugged John, almost lifting him off his feet. "Why that's grand," he said with a grin. That news deserves a wee dram." He went to the drink cabinet and poured three glasses of Single Malt. One for himself and one for each of his sons. "Here's to the new bairn," he said swallowing the golden liquid in one gulp. William smiled at his brother, raised his glass and drank the whisky. John raised his glass to Sarah and finished his drink. He was delighted. They both knew there could never be any secrets in this family.

Chapter 33

THAT SERGEANT JOHN Tyndale was a brave young man could not be disputed. Those who knew him did not doubt his courage but none would consider him foolhardy. He and his comrades in 3 Bomb Disposal Company didn't consider themselves brave. They saw themselves as soldiers doing their duty for King and Country, protecting the general public from the threat of unexploded bombs. The Luftwaffe had been instructed by Hitler to bomb civilian targets indiscriminately, in order to spread panic and destroy the moral of the British citizens.

The men were kept busy at all times and in all weather even as far south as Grimsby disarming UXB's as they called them. It was during one of these missions that John Tyndale's bravery was noted by his CO. It was not the first time his dedication to his duty at the risk of his personal safety, had been mentioned in reports. One such report was featured in the London Gazette on 19th of November 1943. This was one of the episodes which led to him being awarded the George Medal for his service. The article described the work which involved Sergeant Tyndale between the 14th and the 22nd of June 1943.

'Sergeant Tyndale personally dealt with 43 SD2's (Butterfly bombs) in one week in June 1943. During this period most of the

Company Officers and Sergeants were in the Grimsby area. A typical way he had of dealing with these devices was as follows;

In Hainton Methodist Church one of these bombs had become lodged within the panelling of the Organ. He removed some panelling and placed a hook around the device enabling him to remove the bomb remotely. It did explode during the operation but only minor damage to the Church was caused. The Organ escaped undamaged. On the same day at 86 Fairmont Street he found a device in the front room.

He removed the furniture and fittings, then removed the device. One other bomb was found in a rockery. It was rather precariously balanced, so he built a wall of straw bales around it and detonated it. Although the house was only 5 feet away no damage was caused.'

Some of John's comrades lost their lives to explosions during the time he spent in Bomb Disposal Company but he and the other soldiers pushed the risk firmly to the back of their minds. Royal Engineer Bomb disposal teams were being confronted by more and more munitions fitted with anti-handling devices, e.g. the Luftwaffe's ZUS40 anti-removal Bomb fuse. This type of fuse had been specifically designed by the German forces to kill Bomb disposal personnel.

Later that same year a German Dornier Bomber crew making their way home to Frankfurt after a night raid on York and Hull dropped a 4000 lb bomb over Whitby. It missed its mark and buried itself in the sand about two hundred yards from Khyber pass cliffs without exploding.

"I need a volunteer. Tyndale, bring those two men and make sure they're armed with shovels," said the Lieutenant.

"I suppose hittin' it with shovels might work Sir," joked Corporal Smith.

"You can help us find out Smith. Grab a shovel," ordered John.

"Don't forget to put your fingers in your ears if it goes off Smithy. We don't want you to get brain damage," shouted one of the men. Another one yelled, "If his brains was TNT there wouldn't be enough to blow his hat off."

Everyone laughed at the good-natured banter. It helped relieve the tension.

"That's enough chaps, said the Lieutenant. Come on you boys, into the Lorry before the Navy boys beat us to it. The tide'll be turning soon"

As the vehicle drove out of the Camp gate, Corporal Smith stood on the back grinning, holding his shovel like a guitar. He was singing 'Don't Get Around Much Any More'. This brought more laughter from the watching men. American soldiers based in Britain had brought their own hit parade with them and their music was very popular.

Down at the beach the Bomb disposal crew began the 'long walk' to the device. Part of the tail fin was all that could be seen but they quickly identified it as a 4000 pounder.

"Start digging chaps. Sergeant, give me a hand with these sand bags," said the Lieutenant quietly.

By the time they had stacked a double row of bags around the site, the 3ft long Bomb had been uncovered.

"Ready Sir," said the Corporal.

"You chaps stand off behind the Lorry. Sergeant you come with me."

Before long they had removed the fuse and attached a remote detonator to the device. They re-covered it with sand and placed another row of sand bags around the immediate area. As they drove back to the cliff unrolling the detonator wire as they went, they noticed a row of onlookers lining the cliff top.

"If we don't move these people back they'll be in danger when we explode this thing," said John to the Lieutenant.

With that, he shouted to the crowd and waved them away from the cliff. Most left their vantage point immediately. The stubborn ones soon followed when the Lieutenant took out his Webley side arm and fired a shot into the air.

"That'll shift the busy - bodies," he muttered to himself. "Now, we'll drive round the headland and set her off."

The resulting explosion shook them to the back teeth and sent a plume of sand and sea water high into the air. A crater 10ft deep and 20 feet across was all that remained of the bomb. The North sea tides would eventually erase the evidence of the explosion but the crater remained visible for many months. The crew was smiling and joking as they cleared up and drove back to Camp but their jokes couldn't hide the stress in their eyes. That shadow would remain for many years.

There were two children to consider now that baby Abigail was born and Sarah found it more difficult to stay in Whitby to be close to John. Abigail was a blonde haired delight and John wanted to see her as often as possible. The honeymoon cottage was quite often empty, as Sarah spent time between Old Tun farm and her parents house in Stopford Brook. Her father had relented somewhat and she and the children were allowed back into the family home for visits. He tried not to show it but he was delighted to see them as often as possible.

Young Godfrey would toddle into his study and climb onto his knee as he sat at his desk.

No one actually knew what had brought about the change in attitude after the elopement but Sarah's mother told her of the time she had overheard a blistering argument between Father Little and Carlos, in the Church Vestry one evening.

Hannah Dubois told Sarah she had never seen Carlos so angry. Not even when he had learned of the elopement. "Darling, all he said to me was, No Roman Priest is going to put a curse on my family."

"A curse?" said Sarah in amazement.

"He must have said something about you and the children your father didn't like darling. That's all I know."

Sarah didn't press the matter further. She was happy that her relationship with her father was on the mend. She was able to leave the children in the care of her family or John's parents occasionally and spend time in Whitby with him. It was 1944, the War was now at its peak and 3 Bomb Disposal Company kept very busy. The Country was abuzz with preparations for 'Operation Overlord'. Troops from all Allied nations were massing around the ports in the South East of England, making ready for the invasion of the Normandy beaches across the Channel. The nation was ready to take their revenge on the German Army for the Dunkirk defeat and no effort was to be spared. Europe must be freed from the grip of the Nazis.

When Sarah stayed at the Honeymoon cottage she was keen to help with farm work alongside the women of the British Land army. There were plenty of volunteers to look after the children. Sometimes the Lofthouses watched over them but mostly Elsie Tyndale looked after them while Sarah worked on the farm. William kept Old Tun farm production at its peak while his father took more of a back seat role. He took every opportunity to spend time with his grandchildren, though Elsie said he would never admit it. This work helped Sarah keep her mind off the danger of John's situation.

It was at this time that John received notification that he and a small group of Award recipients from the North and Midlands, would travel to London to be presented with the George Medal by the King. Sarah would travel with him to attend the ceremony. The whole district of Blaney Beck and Beckley Dell were proud of their local medal winner and a large gathering of well wishers was present at the Railway station to see them off.

For the ceremony in London, John wore his best uniform and Sarah was resplendent in a Leopard skin jacket with a matching hat.

"You look beautiful honey," said John as they stood outside Buckingham Palace after the investiture.

They stood arm in arm in front of The Victoria Memorial statue as photographs were taken. Much was made of these ceremonies, as they were seen by the government as a boost to public morale. As they stood enjoying the moment a voice rang out from the crowd.

"Hey Tinny!"

John spun around at the sound of the voice. There, standing with the crowd of onlookers was a familiar face. "Bev!" shouted John. He dragged Sarah by the hand to the footpath. The two men shook hands and grinned at each other for what seemed an eternity.

"What are you doing here?" asked John. "Where's your uniform man?"

"I saw this notice in the paper and couldn't believe my eyes. John Tyndale getting a medal,"

John laughed and turned to Sarah. "Honey, you remember Vivian Edwards?"

Yes I do. I remember you from Barrowthwaite Vivian," replied Sarah with a smile.

"Please call me Bev. It's nice to see you again Sarah." The two shook hands.

Bev put his arm around an attractive dark-haired girl who stood beside him.

"I'd like you to meet my fiance Carlene Baron." Everyone shook hands again.

"I've heard a lot about you John," said Carlene. "Don't worry it's all been good," she laughed.

How come you're not in uniform Bev? Are you on leave or something?" asked John.

Bev reached down and tapped his lower leg. It made a hollow metallic sound.

"No!" exclaimed John and Sarah in unison. "What happened?"

"You're not going to believe this." he began. "I was with an Anti-aircraft Company down on the South coast just after we got back and I came home on leave." The two couples now stood in the park as Bev continued his tale. "I was walking along the High

Street one evening minding my own business, when round the corner comes this Lorry."

Sarah and John stood silently listening. "What happened then Bev?" whispered Sarah.

"Well, it was going so fast it ran up onto the footpath and knocked me down. I woke up in Hospital with the bottom part of my leg missing." He smiled nervously.

"You can call me peg-leg if you like."

"I certainly won't," answered Sarah. "That's a horrid thing to call you."

"You haven't heard the best bit yet though," said Bev.

"What's that?" asked John.

"Well, the speeding Lorry was on it's way to an emergency. It was an Army Lorry.

Get this Tinny. It was a Bomb disposal crew on their way to a job in the Square."

"What! Exclaimed Sarah.

"You're not serious." John said letting out a quiet whistle. "So you've been pensioned out."

"Now you know why I had to be here. I knew you'd be tickled by that." laughed Bev.

Carlene snuggled up to his side and put her arm around his waist. "I fink 'e should get a medal an' all," she added seriously.

"I think you're right," agreed John with a smile.

"There's a nice little caff down the street. Let's all go and have a cuppa," suggested Bev.

They spent the next hour chatting and drinking tea. Bev told them he was working at the Battersea stray dogs home and enjoying every moment of it.

"That doesn't surprise me mate," said John. "Do you remember the dog in the church with her pups?"

"Just before we got blown up you mean? I think about her all the time and hope she made it alright." said Bev. Carlene squeezed his hand and gave him a smile.

"Tinny, you'd be amazed how many homeless dogs we've taken in since the Blitz started. They just run the streets scared stiff. Some of the poor sods don't get over it." He said softly.

"'E's very good at 'is job is our Bev," added Carlene proudly.

"Well you two, we have to catch the evening train back home. We'll have to say goodbye," John interjected.

Bev walked outside the Cafe to whistle a Taxi. It was only then that John and Sarah noticed him limping slightly. "'E gets a bit wobbly when 'e's tired the poor fing," whispered Carlene. They all stood on the footpath hugging each other while the cabbie patiently waited.

"Until next time," they promised each other.

John and Sarah climbed in the Taxi clutching their overnight bag while Bev ordered the driver to Victoria Railway Station. A tear rolled down Sarah's cheek, as the cab driver picked his way through the bomb-damaged streets of London. "Oh John," she whispered quietly.

Chapter 34

IN EARLY SPRING 1944 Sarah was staying at Peace Hall farm with the children. Edward and Thora Lofthouse were enjoying looking after them. One wet and overcast evening the noise of aeroplane flying low over the farm woke the household. It's engines were running roughly and it seemed to barely clear the rooftop. The windows and doors of the farmhouse shook as it passed overhead. The children looked more excited than frightened.

Lofthouse said, "What the..." and ran to the windows on the western side of the house. "That thing's coming down for sure, in the meadow down near the stream maybe."

Next they heard a thump, followed by a crashing rending sound. Then silence. Sarah the children and Mrs Lofthouse stood on the landing in their dressing gowns listening but no other sound came except for the ringing of the telephone in the hallway downstairs. Mr Lofthouse dashed past them and ran down the stairs to answer it.

Suddenly a violent explosion from the field shook the house and the brilliance of the flash of light lit the faces of the children, as they looked up to their mother.

Godfrey's voice wavered as he spoke, "What was that noise mother?"

Abigail's eyes were wide as she listened. "Don't worry darlings, everything will be alright." said Sarah hugging them closely to her.

Edward Lofthouse could be heard talking on the telephone, though not clearly. He walked to the bottom of the stairs and called up to them. "The Police are coming over to Old Tun. I'm to meet up with them there, then Bill and the rest of us will go and find out what's happened."

"Make sure the doors are locked when I leave," he said to Thora, as he went to change out of his night clothes. She looked at him but said nothing.

As he drove along the driveway he saw the Police car pass along the lane-way towards Old Tun farm. 'They didn't waste any time,' he thought to himself.

At the Tyndale farm Bill and William stood in the cobbled yard looking across the bottom meadow towards the fire. The firelight played on their faces in the darkness. Sergeant Alf Bliss and three men joined them as Lofthouse drew up in his car.

"Evenin' lads," said Bill heartily. "It's a braw night for fireworks Edward. He gave Lofthouse a smile. "Is all well with t' wee'uns?"

"Yes Bill. Good to see everyone's alright here." Edward Lofthouse noticed Elsie and the two girls standing at the bedroom window. Their faces reflected the firelight from the burning aircraft.

"Righto lads, there's been a bombing raid on Tyneside tonight," interrupted the Police Sergeant. "We're to investigate this crash without endangering ourselves and wait for the Home Guard boys to get here."

"Now," he added. "Do exactly as I say at all times."

They passed through the gateway to the meadow and walked slowly towards the distant fire.

"It's down t' other side of t' bridge," said Bill Tyndale. He spoke in hushed tones even though the noise of the fire grew in intensity as they approached.

The Sergeant called a halt to their progress. "We go no further until I identify that aircraft."

He took a folded piece of paper from his tunic pocket and studied it intently for a minute. He gave a grunt of satisfaction and replacing it he said. "We must stay back here men. That's a German Junkers 88 Bomber and we don't know what ordnance is still on board."

"There's nowt t' could get me any closer than this Sarge," said Bill Tyndale with a smile. The rest of the men laughed. They too, had no intention of being blown up.

"Poor sods would have been burnt up," muttered one of the Constables.

"Righto lads, there's nothing we can do here. Back to the house," said the Sergeant.

He turned and proceeded up the hill. As Edward Lofthouse turned to follow, he thought he saw a slight movement in the shadow of an old Oak tree off to his right. He stopped momentarily and peered into the shadows. He saw several sheep bedded down there and gave it no more thought. "Ha'way Lofthouse, thee'll get blown up if thee doesn't 'urry," called out Bill Tyndale.

"I thought I saw something Bill," replied Edward Lofthouse as he caught up with the rest of the men.

"It"ll just be shadders from t' burnin' German junk," grinned Bill. "Or sheep," he added.

"I ken there's a bottle of Malt whisky in my pantry," said Bill Tyndale with a wink. "Aye, me and thee and young William'll have a wee dram together lad, afore t' Guard gets here."

By the time the And Howes Lorry arrived the fire in the enemy aircraft had all but subsided. Howe was the Officer in charge of the local Home Guard Platoon. He and Dusty Rhodes sat in the front of the Lorry, while two other uniformed Guards sat precariously on the back. The Police Sergeant and his Constables directed them through the gate, which led down to the meadow in which the wreckage lay.

The Police followed them in their vehicle. Bill Tyndale, William and Edward Lofthouse followed on foot. They weren't in any hurry after consuming several glasses of Scotch whisky each, while waiting for the arrival of the Home Guard. The headlights of the vehicles lit the immediate area. The front part of the aircraft and the inner section of the wings were destroyed by the fire. The tail section, with its white band and Swastika, stuck up in the air at a sharp angle to the ground. The nose and the two engines were partly buried in a grassy bank near the stream. The burnt bodies of the unfortunate crew were visible in the wreckage. Back up the hill towards the house a section of hedge had been destroyed where the stricken aircraft had first struck the ground in its death glide.

"I can't see the body of the Flight Engineer," muttered And Howe, as he swept the interior of the tail section with his torch. He had to stand on the roof of his Lorry and peer through the bottom hatch of the wreck. "We'll have a closer look in the daylight. Greeny and Johnson!" he shouted. "You two guard this thing until morning."

He walked over to the watching Police Sergeant and said, "I'll need your help in the morning Alf. We'll have to go over this thing with a fine toothed comb. I've called the Air Force boys and they'll be here as soon as possible."

"Righto And," the Sergeant replied.

"Bill, can I see you a minute?" he called out, beckoning Tyndale away from the others.

"What is it And?" asked Bill Tyndale.

"I don't like the look of this Bill. All of the crew members are accounted for except the Flight Engineer. The belly hatch of the plane was open when we got here."

"D' ye figure e's got away from t' wreck?" asked Bill.

"I don't want you worrying man but we won't know for sure until we can inspect the remains in the daylight," answered Howe. "Keep your eyes open until then."

"Aye And," said Bill. "That I will....that I will."

He turned on his heel and strode over to Lofthouse and Will. "Back up to t' house lads There might be a survivor on t' loose tonight."

The three men made haste back up the hill to the farmyard. "Will, take a shotgun and check around t' house. Shoot first and ask questions afterwards!" he added grimly.

"I'll be off home now Bill. I'll have to make sure everything is secure," said Lofthouse.

"Give us a call on t' phone when thee gets there man, so's a Ken thee's a'reet." answered Bill Tyndale. "And dinna stop for nowt on t' way home," he added.

Edward Lofthouse had an uneventful drive home and on arrival found everyone safe and well, locked securely in the house. He told his eager listeners what had been happening during the hours he'd been away.

"Did And Howe say we're in any danger?" asked Thora Lofthouse. She watched as her husband took the shotguns out of the gun-room and checked their loads.

"He thinks there's a possibility a survivor may be on the loose but we won't know until daylight. We'll take precautions until we know Thora," he answered quietly.

"I'll stay upstairs with the children," said Sarah. "You stay with Mr Lofthouse," she said to Mrs Lofthouse. Thora Lofthouse smiled and nodded. Sarah could see she was very concerned.

Will and his father stood at the door looking across the cobbled yard towards the barns and sheds. "If we keep our ears open, t' dogs'll bark loud if they see t'German about." said Bill. "Gan off to bed lad. I'll stay up for a bit."

"I f there's any shooting to be done, you call me straight away father," said Will with a grin. He headed off to bed with his shotgun in hand.

Mary and Margaret with their stepmother, stood wide-eyed with excitement on the landing.

"What's going on William? Asked Elsie. "Is everything alright?"

"Yes everything's alright," William answered gently. "One of the German airmen may have escaped the crash. We have to stay alert just in case."

"I don't think I'll sleep tonight," said Margaret.

"Can I sleep with you Maggie?" her sister asked. "Please."

"Alright then scaredy cat come on," Margaret didn't say so but she was glad of her sisters company that night.

Some hours later, in the early morning when it was still dark, everyone was awake again.

The dogs in the machinery shed were creating a fuss. They were barking and yelping at something.

"Ha'way lad let's see what all t' fuss is about," said Bill to young William.

"It might just be a fox father," whispered William as they made their way to the machinery shed. They kept to the shadows as they crept quietly up to the double wooden doors.

Jess and two of the other border collies ran out to greet them, in a high state of excitement.

"Who's in there?" called out Bill Tyndale. The dogs had quietened somewhat by this time, so Bill and William entered the shed.

The lamps they carried cast a yellowish glow around the barn. There were many areas of deep shadow behind the machinery but by this time the dogs had sniffed out every part of the building. The two men saw no intruders but they did notice John's motorcycle lying on its side near the hay bales. Will went over and righted the machine.

"It looks as though we've had a visitor tonight father. That German must have tried to steal John's bike."

"Aye lad. I reckon thee's reet," his father answered quietly.

Will laughed. "I reckon he would have got a hot reception from Bessie."

Bessie was one of the farm dogs who had been faithfully attached to John since she was a pup. Since John had been away at war she had taken to sleeping next to his motorcycle on one of his old haversacks.

"I'll wager 'e got a shock lad," answered Bill with a smile.

Bill's dog Jess meanwhile, was following a trail. She was sniffing excitedly around the gate to the top field. It had recently been ploughed by the Land Army girls but no footprints were visible in the lamplight.

"Ha'way lass," said Bill to the dog. "We won't find him tonight. Time enough in t' morning"

"Ha'way lad. Let's get back to t' house, I've some telephoning to do."

"He's probably out there in the dark watching us us right now," said William as they headed back to the house.

Bessie returned to her vigil beside John's motorcycle.

Back at the house, Bill telephoned Edward Lofthouse and told him of the latest developments. He also phoned the Police Station.

"He's probably trying to escape to the coast where he may stand a chance of being picked up by a U-Boat," said Sergeant Alf Morrow on the other end of the line.

"I reckon he'll try Peace Hall next Alf. Lofthouse and t' ladies are on there own there."

"I'll drive out there myself immediately Bill," said the Police Sergeant, without hesitation.

"Will they catch him," asked Elsie Tyndale as she pottered about her kitchen making cups of tea.

"If he comes skulking around here, I'll blow his square head off," said William with a grin.

Word of the crashed German bomber and the escaped crewman, travelled around the district as quickly as news does in country areas and many folks were awake all night.

"Will this War never end?" said Elsie wearily.

Chapter 35

FLIGHT ENGINEER ERIK Demel, the German airman, had indeed made his way to Peace Hall farm across the fields that night. He had a broken collar bone and a pounding headache as a result of a head wound he had received in the crash. The jagged end of the broken collar bone had pierced the flesh and skin of his shoulder and was causing him a great deal of pain and discomfort. The front of his uniform tunic was soaked in blood.

He lay watching from his hiding place in a greenhouse in the orchard behind the house. He cursed his luck even though he was alive and his comrades were not. An anti-aircraft battery had scored a hit on their plane as they had flown over Whitby towards their target in Tyneside. The crew thought they had escaped major damage but after the raid, on their way back to the Channel the pilot reported engine problems. "Wir haben oldruck verloren! Wir sinken! Englischers!" The Bofors rounds had inflicted more damage to the aircraft than they thought. The engines had lost all oil pressure.

More problems had arisen in the form of a burly Policeman, who was now patrolling the area around the main house. Daylight had started to paint the spring sky with tints of pink, pale blue and orange. Soon his hiding place would be his prison during daylight hours. Already he could see dozens of women in work clothes spreading out over the fields. Some were ploughing, others planting and picking while some attended to dairy cows. The countryside was abuzz with activity as the Women's Land Army continued their efforts to support the War effort. Demel's heart sank. He was effectively surrounded in the middle of nowhere. He attempted to move further into the building but the searing pain overcame him. His sight became blurred and he lapsed into unconsciousness. He was still losing blood.

In his escape plan the German hadn't regarded the persistence of the plucky sheep dog called Jess. She had joined the search party in the morning as the men had begun to scour the outbuildings, hedges and woods. They were all armed, with weapons of all shapes and sizes. The Police carried service revolvers on their belts for the occasion, along with their truncheons. Royal Air-force investigators were subjecting the downed German Bomber to a thorough investigation, while a small crowd of on-lookers had gathered along the top of the bank, where the hedge had been knocked down.

"Where's t' dog got to?" muttered Bill Tyndale.

He and William walked along the thick hedgerow behind the barns looking for traces of the airman. A shout went up from the top of the field. They'd found some blood from his wounds. The two men headed up to the area.

"He's definitely wounded. He must have been lying here watching us last night."

One of the Police Constables was speaking. He was a short man with a very long uniform.

He drew himself to his full height and pointed dramatically towards Peace Hall.

"That's where we'll find him!" the Constable shouted.

They heard a dog barking excitedly from the direction he was pointing.

"That's Jess," said Bill. "I'd know that bark anywhere."

The Constable blew his whistle and they all proceeded down the hill in the direction of the barking dog. With his short legs and long trousers, the Constable found it difficult to stay at the head of this fine body of men but eventually they reached the back garden of the house. Edward Lofthouse had taken a position between the old greenhouse and where his wife stood with Sarah at the back door. The children peered out from behind their legs.

As everyone stood back, the Constable raised his hand, blew his whistle and called out, "Now everyone stand back."

"Thank you Williams, I'll take over now," said the Sergeant from his position at the side of the house. He and Lofthouse had been observing the greenhouse since Jess had shown an interest in it.

"Come back lass!" shouted Bill Tyndale. The dog turned immediately and ran back to sit at his side. "Good girl," said Bill quietly.

"We know you're in there," shouted the Sergeant. "If you're in there come out with your hands up."

The Constable immediately blew his whistle with excitement, having kept it in his mouth since using it a few moments ago. The startled Sergeant looked back at him with a scowl and said through clenched teeth, "Put that away and keep the crowd back."

Constable Williams stood with his arms outstretched in front of the five people who stood watching. Tension mounted as silence fell on the scene.

"Throw your arms out of the door," shouted Sergeant Alf Bliss with all the authority he could muster. Edward Lofthouse who was standing right behind him, wondered at the Sergeant's use of the English language, and the German's understanding of it. He quietly shared his thoughts with Sergeant Bliss, "What if he doesn't understand English, Sergeant?"

"Comzen outen of the greenhouzen," said the Sergeant forcefully. One had to admire Sergeant Bliss's persistence, if nothing else.

"Thee'll have to go in and fetch him Alf," called out Bill Tyndale.

"One of the farmhands shouted, "Don't worry Sergeant. We's right behind ya""

"Stay behind the Sergeant, Edward," said his wife quietly from the back door.

The Policeman by this time, had crept close to the door of the greenhouse. He held his service revolver in front of him. To his credit, his hand was as steady as a rock. A loud oath, followed by a groan suddenly came from inside the building. Sergeant Bliss took a step backwards planting his size 12 boot firmly on the top of Lofthouse's foot. The resulting pain caused Lofthouse's trigger finger to flex, firing a shot into the air with a loud bang very close to the Sergeant's ear. His helmet was dislodged by the shot and fell at his feet next to the revolver he'd just dropped.

The Constable's whistle rang out again.

"You big oaf," groaned Lofthouse standing on one leg nursing his injured foot.

"Eh?" shouted Bliss. "That boomin' gunshot made me deaf in my other ear. Will you please be careful with that thing. We don't want any more accidents." he pleaded.

"Williams, If I hear that whistle one more time I'll come over there and....."

He regained his composure, retrieved his equipment from the ground and approached the door once more. Those who watched were impressed by the Sergeant's bravery as he slowly entered the old building. They held a collective breath as he disappeared inside.

He reappeared several moments later and said to Edward Lofthouse. "Could you telephone an Ambulance. He's here but he's unconscious."

"Certainly Alf," answered Lofthouse turning toward the house.

"Eh?" said the Sergeant.

Sarah and Mrs Lofthouse had darted inside with the children when the shotgun had accidentally discharged, so Edward Lofthouse limped inside to use the telephone himself.

"Don't say anything my dear," he said to his wife as she began to admonish him.

"Everything is under control. Now, I have to telephone for the Ambulance."

"Is the German dead?" asked Thora Lofthouse.

Godfrey and Abigail watched in wonder as the men carried the unconscious German airman in a sheet to the front garden, placing him on the soft grass. The sheet was covered in blood.

"Come away from that window you children, this instant," called out Sarah. "Oh, I wish your father were here. It's altogether too much."

Thora Lofthouse took Sarah in her arms and said softly "There there little one. You two love-birds will soon be together again. Try not to lose heart."

"Thank you Mrs Lofthouse," sobbed Sarah. "I'll be alright."

The injured airman still hadn't regained consciousness when the Ambulance arrived. Two Constables sat in the back with the man who was now their prisoner and he was taken to Stopford Brook Hospital for treatment of his wounds.

Flight Engineer Erik Demel's war was over and so was the excitement at Peace Hall farm. The onlookers who had gathered dispersed and things returned to normal. The downed Junkers 88 was taken away by Lorry to Thornaby Air base in North Yorkshire where it was studied by the Royal Airforce boffins. When Flight Engineer Erik Demel had recovered sufficiently from his injuries, he was imprisoned in Windlestone Hall Prison Camp at Rushyford Co. Darnley for the duration of the War.

Chapter 36

IT WAS THE week after 'D' Day and Sarah had travelled with the children to Whitby, where they would stay in her rented attic room for a while. The Company of Royal Engineers whose responsibility it was to administrate Bomb Disposal activities around the district, was now also involved in some grass-roots projects in Whitby. The construction expertise of The Engineers was needed, in the repair of bomb damage to vital infrastructure. Two nights previously a bomb had damaged part of the Southern sea wall which protected Whitby harbour from the savagery of The North Sea. Sergeant John Tyndale had been given the job of mending the stone and concrete wall. A select band of artisans governed by the tides, and aided by an ancient steam shovel operated by an elderly local named Gladstone, began the work of restoration. The weather was pleasant and the work peaceful, compared with the Bomb Disposal work which had kept the men busy for the last two of years.

From her attic window Sarah could see the workmen and the children pestered her continually to be taken to see Daddy at work. Godfrey was particularly interested in the Steam shovel and it's myriad of pulleys and cables. The noise the steam and the sparks held him entranced, as he stood and watched it heaving building materials into place, at the direction of his father. Sometimes the three of them would sit with the workmen at 'smoko' time and be given a cup of tea in a tin mug. To sit and watch their mother and father talking and laughing with each other and the workmen, was a happy memory that would always stay with them. Such memories were rare in this time of War.

The sketchy news which had filtered through to the men of 3 Bomb Disposal about 'Operation Overlord', wasn't good.

The invasion of Europe by the Allied troops, which had been launched from the Eastern coast of England a week ago had been successful but many soldiers had lost their lives on the beaches of Normandy. Their sacrifice would pave the way for the conquest of the Axis armies and there was a hope across Britain, that an end to the War was just around the corner.

Prime Minister Winston Churchill encouraged the British nation.

During the days and nights that John and Sarah were able to spend time together, they were able to shut out the rest of the world. They walked and talked down on the quay with the children, who were both walking of course and quite independent in their ways. Sarah knew that time spent together as a family was a luxury to be cherished, not to be wasted.

In the latter part of 1944 and the early part of 1945 Sarah found it impossible to leave Peace Hall and Old Tun, because she was so busy working with the Women's Land Army.

The Royal Engineers were needed in London and other parts of Southern England after this period of relative calm. Hitler's deadly V2 Rockets were now ready for battle and it wasn't long before 1,500 of them had pounded the nation. Thousands perished and thousands more were made homeless by this infernal weapon. 3 Bomb Disposal Company had been sent to Carlton Base in Cambridge. It was their job to clear away the damage caused by the Rockets in that County and rebuild essential infrastructure. Several V Bombs had exploded around Norwich. One had blown the main road to Great Yarmouth on the coast. Several others had exploded in farming areas while one had destroyed a school. Four V Rockets were UXB's, one of them on the beach at Harwich.

Lieutenant Morton Bacchus stood outside the Coms. Building addressing the men.

"We'll be down here until we've helped these people get back on their feet. The sooner we finish this work, the sooner we'll get back. Now, none of us likes being away from our loved ones but just think about our chaps in France at the moment. Do you think they're enjoying themselves? Ask your Sergeant about the time he spent in France. He'll soon tell you how bad it was. Now you've been called down here because of your training in defusing the new V Rockets. As usual the Navy boys have dibs in those below the high water line, while we will be responsible for those everywhere else. Now, remember what your mother used to tell you whenever you went out anywhere special. Remember who you are while you're based down here." He turned to John, "Carry on Sergeant."

"The places I went Sir, it was hard to remember who you are," said Corporal Smith, obviously shaken.

The Lieutenant gave no sign that he had heard Smith. He saluted and retired to the Coms. Building. He was under a great deal of pressure from High Command. If things continued the way they were in Europe, he and his men would soon be sent across the Channel to help clear up as the Allied Front advanced towards Berlin.

John raised the back of his hand to the Corporal and said, "Fall out boys."

He then said, "Don't antagonise him Smithy. He's the best friend you've got in this war."

"Yes Sarge," said Smith before hurrying on his way.

John Tyndale knew they could soon be at the front but the Lieutenant had sworn him to secrecy.

"'Why are you in despair, Oh my soul? And why are you disturbed within me?'"

Hannah Dubois gently quoted the Scripture to Sarah. "What is on your mind my darling child?"

"Mother I have a very bad feeling about this war. I think it will never end until it has taken John's life. I don't know when I will ever see him again."

The two of them sat together on the edge of Sarah's bed. Hannah had invited her daughter and the children to Stopford Brook to stay with her for a week. It would be rest for her from her duties with The Women's Land Army and an opportunity to be close to the family. Sarah sobbed quietly on her mother's shoulder. Hannah could hear the children playing in the drawing room with Mildred.

"You know John Mother, He won't shirk his duty for the sake of his own safety."

"The Lord will watch over him my dear," whispered Hannah. "I've been praying for him every night. Even your father has been joining me lately. What do you think about that?"

Hannah lifted Sarah's chin and smiled at her. He's really changed sweetheart. He adores having the children here and wants you to stay as long as you wish."

Clare placed her hand on her sister's shoulder. "It's true Sarah darling. Daddy has changed so much over these last few years."

"I wish I knew what he was thinking," whispered Sarah.

"Oh don't be silly sweetheart. He loves you just as much as he ever did. Now go and wash your face and come downstairs. We'll have some tea together."

Hannah Dubois and Clare left the room. Sarah stood and paced backwards and forwards from the window to the door.

She paused and looked out of the window. She remembered being on the motorcycle with John as they roared along the tree-lined avenue. She remembered how safe she had felt as she clung tightly to him. 'If only I could hold him now', she thought to herself but her arms were empty. She was so alone since they had been separated from each other. Even in her mothers house she felt isolated. She was used to sharing everything with John and now a major part of her was missing. She felt as though she was in limbo, with no joy or hope left. Tears once more, began to roll down her pallid cheeks, filling her eyes with their sadness. With her vision blurred by tears she stumbled down the stairs, losing her footing, she tripped across the landing and tumbled helplessly to the bottom. Hannah, Mildred and the children heard the thud and came running to the hallway, to find Sarah in a crumpled heap lying still on the floor.

"Sarah!" shouted Hannah Dubois. She knelt down and cradled her Daughter's head to her bosom.

"There's a big egg on her forehead," said Mildred. "Now try not to move her too much Mrs Dubois until the Doctor sees her. Children come with me now, Mummy will be alright."

Mildred ushered the children into the drawing room and left them in the care of Clare.

She then rushed to the telephone and called the doctor. When she returned to the scene of the fall she saw Sarah stirring.

"Mother, what happened?" she asked shakily.

"You just had a little fall darling. You're going to be alright."

"My head hurts." She began to sit up but had to lean on her mother.

"Try not to move too much Miss Sarah. Doctor Douglas is on his way," said Mildred kneeling beside her.

"Mother I can't see the Doctor sitting on the floor like this. What will he think?"

"Please help me to get up. I'll lie on the sofa." begged Sarah.

"But what if you're hurt Miss Sarah?" insisted Mildred.

"Oh, don't be silly Mildred. I'm feeling much better."

"Alright darling," said Hannah. "If you insist. But you must do it very slowly."

The two women helped her slowly to her feet and half dragged her to the sofa, while Clare and the children peered wide-eyed out of the drawing room doorway. Sarah moaned with pain as she was lowered onto the sofa. "I think I've hurt my wrist," she whispered. Her face was pale but lathered in sweat.

"I'll get her a blanket," said Mildred and dashed upstairs.

"Don't you fall as well girl," shouted Hannah Dubois after her. Seeing the children at the doorway she reassured them quietly. "Don't worry darlings, Mummy will be alright."

Mildred appeared with a blanket and placed it over Sarah who was now beginning to tremble.

"Go and make her a cup of sweet tea Mildred," said Hannah.

The maid dashed off towards the kitchen and reappeared in no time with the warm drink.

"Here Miss, you must drink this sweet tea," encouraged Mildred.

Sarah thanked her and drank the sweet beverage.

"Thank you. I think I feel a little better now but my wrist is really painful."

"That right wrist is really swelled up Mrs Dubois," said Mildred quietly.

"Where's that Doctor," said Hannah Dubois pacing up and down the hallway.

"I have a terrible headache mother," Sarah whispered.

"I'll fetch a cool face-cloth for her," Mildred offered, dashing to the laundry room.

The cool wet cloth was duly placed on Sarah's forehead. "Thank you Mildred," said Sarah.

"You're a treasure," she smiled weakly.

Doctor Douglas arrived and without hesitation walked through the open door to the sofa on which Sarah lay. Mildred retired to the drawing room on his arrival, with Clare and the children.

"Well Hannah, what have we here?" Without waiting for an answer he spoke to the patient. "Hello Sarah. Tell me where it hurts."

"She fell down the stairs Robert." she interjected.

"My head and my right wrist," answered Sarah. She winced with pain as the Doctor gently touched her injuries. Why did you fall down the stairs my dear?" asked Robert Douglas.

"She was crying so much she couldn't see what she was doing," Hannah answered for her daughter. As the Doctor continued his examination he asked Sarah, "What on earth would cause a young woman like yourself to cry so much?"

"She was....." began her mother. "Please allow her to answer for herself Hannah,"

"I was crying for John and this stupid War. I haven't seen or heard from him for ages."

"I see," murmured Robert Douglas. "I'm sure he's alright my dear. He's a very brave and resourceful young man. Have you been sleeping alright Sarah?"

"No Doctor, not really," she whispered.

"Is my daughter alright Doctor?" asked Hannah Dubois wringing her hands.

"Well," said Douglas standing to his feet. "She does have concussion and her right wrist is very badly sprained but I'm sure with the right treatment, she will recover."

"Oh thank God!" exclaimed Hannah Dubois.

"Yes, quite," replied Doctor Douglas. "Now, her arm must remain elevated in this bandage, with a cold compress on her wrist and forehead every two hours for three days." He drew Hannah to one side and spoke to her in a low voice. "I've given her a sleeping draught Hannah. I'll leave it with you. Please make sure she takes a dose every night. The girl looks worn out. I've seen her over at the farm working with the other women in the fields. That has to stop immediately. She has enough on her plate with two children to look after."

"Yes Doctor," answered Hannah.

Doctor Douglas took her by the arm and drew her into the library. He looked into her eyes.

"Is Carlos still angry and aggressive towards her over the elopement?" he whispered. Hannah wasn't offended by the question. The Doctor was a long-time family friend.

"Actually he's become much like his old self, Robert. Sarah is staying with us for a while."

"Good, very good. And what of John, do you know anything?"

"No, we haven't heard from him for quite a while now. It's the not knowing that's hard on Sarah," answered Hannah with tears in her eyes. Robert Douglas took her by the hands.

"We must continue to be strong Hannah. The Army is making good progress in Europe. I'm certain it will all be over soon and all of this turmoil will be behind us."

"John is involved in a very dangerous occupation Robert," said Hannah.

"That is all the more reason to keep things together while he is away. Do you understand?"

Robert Douglas gave her a smile. "This household needs to see you and Carlos united, strong and smiling," he said. "Keep your chin up and if you need someone to talk to just give me a call and I'll be here."

"Thank you Robert," smiled Hannah.

Sarah was sleeping when they returned to the hallway. "She must be moved to her bed now," said Robert Douglas. "If you go before me I'll carry her up to her room." He swept Sarah into his arms as though she were a child. "Good heavens there's nothing of this girl," he said as he took her upstairs to her room.

She made a pitiful whimpering sound as he laid her under the covers.

"I'll be back to check on her in three days Hannah," he said as he walked to the front door. "Good bye."

"Is Sarah going to be alright mother?" asked Clare. Mildred and the children stood behind her waiting expectantly for her answer.

"Yes darling but she needs plenty of rest." Godfrey and Abigail were happy after they saw the smile on their grandmother's face and ran into the drawing room to continue their games. "Come along Mildred, read us another story."

Chapter 37

ON THE 29TH of April 1945 Sarah received a letter from John.

'Dearest Sarah,

I've missed you and the children so much. I am in London at the moment. We are camped in a place called Downhills Park between Tottenham and Wood Green. We have been very busy here but the people are so cheerful in the face of all the danger. They have welcomed us every where we go. One bomb landed just across the road from the camp. Anyway I will be home for three weeks leave on the 3rd of May. Will you meet me at Courtenay Railway Station on that day. It will be an afternoon train. All my love John.'

The information John didn't include in his letter was that he was being sent home to recuperate after being cared for in The North London Military Hospital with a leg injury. His ankle had been fractured when a bomb crater had collapsed on him. He had been working on a UXB in the school grounds of Pankhurst College in Tottenham. Bev Edwards and Carlene had visited him a couple of times and had jokingly referred to the two of them as the dead-leg twins.

"You'll be hobbling about like me in no time Tinny," he laughed. Carlene dug him in the ribs and scowled at him. Bev added, "At least yours is only plaster from the knee down mate."

John was due to be up on crutches the next day. That's when he was told he'd be going home to recuperate. He was elated at the news even though his leg was hurting badly.

At Old Tun farm the house was a hive of activity with preparations for his return. The Tyndale family would be travelling to Peace Hall, where the Lofthouses had prepared an afternoon tea to celebrate.

Much to everyone's surprise Carlos Dubois had offered to take time from his work, to bring John from the Railway Station in Courtenay. Hannah and Clare were beside themselves with excitement. Sarah was waiting at the honeymoon cottage for John to return. Her wrist was still giving her pain and a supporting bandage had been fitted by Doctor Douglas, who thought there may be a hairline fracture in one of the bones. Today however, her heart soared and no heed was paid to the discomfort.

The Dubois sat in Carlos' shiny black Austin 16 and watched the train pull into Courtenay Station. "Come on you slow-coaches," said Clare breathlessly. "Let's go and meet him on the platform."

"Alright, we're coming," Hannah answered.

She was very apprehensive about the outcome of this meeting between John and her husband. The last time they saw each other Carlos had been extremely angry about the elopement. He had promised her he was over the incident. She knew John wouldn't be bothered what her husband thought one way or the other but she was a peacemaker at heart and wanted the best for all concerned.

Smoke and steam swirled around them as they stood on the platform. It was the Friday afternoon train and a mixture of armed forces personnel and other commuters poured out of the carriages with a banging of doors and windows. Porters loaded suitcases and overnight bags from the Baggage car onto their wooden trolleys.

"Where could he be mother?" asked Clare, as the platform began to clear.

A soldier on crutches emerged from the crowd and gave them a grin. Hannah Dubois saw the crutches and almost fainted. She staggered sideways against Carlos who supported her. Her face was as white as a sheet as he guided her to a bench near the Rail office.

"John," cried Clare and ran to him and gently placed her arms around him.

"Are you alright? What's the matter with your leg? It's alright isn't it John?"

The questions tumbled from Clare's lips in quick succession. John placed his hands on her shoulders. "Calm down it's just a break. It's in plaster, see." He rapped his crutch against his leg and Clare let out a huge sigh of relief. "When I saw you on the crutches I expected the worst I'm afraid," said Clare with a smile.

Hannah was just beginning to rally when she saw John tap his plastered leg with his crutch. She too thought the worst and wailed to Carlos, "Oh no, it's a wooden leg." She saw John and Clare approaching and whispered to her husband, "Don't say anything to embarrass him."

Carlos rose and offered John his seat. Clare knew what her parents must be thinking and stood with her hand over her mouth, barely able to hide her amusement. As John sat down Clare broke her silence. "Mother, John's leg is in plaster. He has a broken ankle."

"Oh, thank the Lord!" exclaimed Hannah Dubois. She and Carlos broke into laughter. Pretty soon they were all laughing uncontrollably at their mistaken assumption.

"I'm sorry," said John. "I should have realised the affect these crutches would have." "It's good to see you home, even if it is only for a while," said Carlos. He and John then shook hands. Hannah and Clare smiled at each other.

"Oh dear," said Clare.

"What is it girl," asked her father.

Well," began Clare. "What a shock Sarah will get when she sees those crutches."

"Carlos we must break the news to her gently, lest she faint also." Hannah said.

"I'll have to retrieve my kit-bag from the luggage office," said John, standing up.

"I'll help you son. We'll meet you ladies here." The two men wandered off to fetch the bag.

"I really think Daddy is trying to build bridges with John," Clare said to her mother with a smile.

"It's been my prayer for many a long year sweetheart, replied Hannah. "Many a long year."

When John and Carlos returned Hannah and Clare were very surprised to see Carlos labouring under John's bag. "Can you manage that alright darling?' Hannah asked her husband sweetly. Clare hastily masked an involuntary snort with a cough. Carlos did have quite a red face from the exertion. Manual labour was not one of his strong suits. He may have been short of breath but he didn't answer her. Clare and her mother exchanged a glance. John clopped along on his crutches, without showing any obvious thoughts about the situation. Back at the car, Carlos strapped the kit-bag to the luggage rack on the rear and stood back mopping his brow with his white silk handkerchief.

"Thank you sir, I appreciate that help," smiled John.

"It's a pleasure son. Now climb in, we must be going."

During the journey back to Peace Hall farm, Carlos and Hannah couldn't get a word in between Clare's constant questions and chatter. John didn't mind, he would soon be with Sarah and his daydreams rested with her.

"Your car still looks and runs like brand new sir," said John as the vehicle cruised silently along the road.

"It's hardly ever been out of the garage since this War started John," said Hannah.

"I'm sure Daddy loves this car more than any of us," laughed Clare.

Carlos just smiled to himself and winked at his wife. "Clare isn't serious darling. We know there must be quite a few things you love more than your car. Surely," Hannah giggled. They all joined in the joke and laughed together.

As they drove towards Peace Hill farm a lone figure ran to meet the car. With her auburn hair flowing and the pale blue dress she wore, Sarah was a vision of beauty, which had filled her husband's dreams for many long lonely months. She stood beside the driveway under the branches of an Oak and waited for the car.

"Is that a bandage on Sarah's arm?" asked John, with a look of concern on his face.

The car drew up beside her and she opened the door while it was still moving. She climbed inside, sat on John's knee and kissed him hungrily all over his face. Clare laughed at her sister and shouted, "Can't you wait a few moments longer Sarah, you've nearly smothered him!"

John cupped Sarah's face in his calloused hands with a huge lip-stick covered grin and said to her, "You are the most beautiful woman in the universe."

It was then that Sarah noticed the crutches. "What on earth are those for?" John replied, "What on earth is this for?" He pointed to the bandage on Sarah's arm.

Clare held up her hand in mock frustration. "Stop!" she called out with a laugh.

"You both have broken bones..... but it's nothing serious. "Alright?"

"Are you hurt? Where are you hurt John?" asked Sarah feeling his legs.

"It's just a fractured ankle honey....see?" He tapped his plaster cast with his knuckles.

"What about you? asked John. "What happened to your arm?"

"It's nothing darling really," whispered Sarah. "I'll tell you later."

"Why didn't you tell me about your leg," asked Sarah.

"I didn't want to worry you over nothing honey, that's why. Is that why you didn't tell me about your arm?" Sarah nodded. She was still looking at the plaster cast on her husband's lower leg. "I did think the worst when I first saw those crutches," she said quietly. She clung tightly to John's arm with her un-bandaged arm and looked into his eyes.

"We're a bright pair aren't we?" she laughed.

"Well," sighed Hannah. "I'm glad that's all sorted out. Drive on Carlos before these two love birds turn the car over with their jumping about." Carlos smiled and said, "Shut the door please. We're almost there."

A large group of friends was waiting for them on the lawns as they alighted the vehicle. Ladies in Spring dresses and bonnets, gentlemen wearing their best suits, all stood to welcome John. Godfrey and Abigail clapped their hands excitedly. When he walked into the garden on his crutches there were some concerned looks but he soon put there fears to rest.

"Don't worry everyone. It's only a fractured ankle," he assured the guests. Bill Tyndale, quite overcome with emotion, stepped forward and firmly shook John's hand.

"It's grand to have ye back lad," he said with a grin. For a home-coming in the North Country, it was a very emotional affair indeed.

Margaret and Mary hugged him while he shook William's hand. Godfrey and Abigail clung onto his trouser legs. He wandered about chatting to his friends, with Sarah on his arm and the children on his legs. Tables had been set in the garden and a light afternoon tea was served.

John found himself sitting next to Doctor Douglas and his wife Eve. The Doctor didn't mention anything about Sarah's fall but merely advised John to be careful and allow his injury to heal properly.

"When did you receive the bone fracture?" he asked John.

"About three weeks ago Doctor," he answered.

"If you have any worries about it just give me a call on the telephone, any time. How have your nerves been holding up?" the Doctor asked. He placed his hand on john's arm and peered into his eyes.

"What nerves Doc?" he joked. "Bombies don't have nerves."

"Well that may be so but you've been under some major stress over these last few years. If you need me for anything just let me know."

"Thanks Doctor."

Seated on John's other side were George and Anne Lowther, his grandparents.

"Your mother would have been so proud of you son," said his grandmother with tears in her eyes. George Lowther put his hand on John's shoulder and whispered,

"You and Sarah come and see us when you can. Bring the children with you lad. Grandma doesn't see enough of them. We're on our own now in the big house. It will be nice to hear them running about, like you and William used to. There are plenty of fish in the River. Perhaps young Godfrey would like to go fishing with you."

"Yes grandfather, I'll do that" promised William.

He took his grandfather's hand in his own and held it. He hadn't noticed how old and frail he and his grandmother were until now.

Edward Lofthouse took John aside and told him the whole story of the crash of the German Bomber and the escaped airman. "Well I tell you John, it was a fine kettle of fish."

"You can still see the burnt area down near the beck. I think it'll take ages for the grass to grow back again, blasted Germans," muttered Lofthouse. "It's good to see you again lad. How long will you be home for this time?"

"Two weeks Mr Lofthouse. Then I have to report to the Company at Barnard Castle," answered John. Even as John spoke he was looking around for Sarah.

Now that he was home he was loath to be away from her for more than a few minutes. "I think John is looking for someone special Edward," smiled Thora Lofthouse.

"I'm sorry Mrs Lofthouse, I don't mean to be rude," said John.

"I think Sarah is in the kitchen with Clare and the children," she whispered.

When John entered the kitchen Elsie Tyndale threw her arms around him and welcomed him home. "I'm so happy to see you again... and safe," she said.

Over Elsie's shoulder John saw Sarah beckoning him to the library.

"Thank you Elsie. Would you excuse me for a moment?"

He clopped his way over to the library and found himself alone at last with Sarah and the children. Sarah shut the door behind him.

"Come and sit down darling. Take the weight off your legs for a while."

Godfrey and Abigail each took one of their father's crutches to play with, while he sat down on the sofa with their mother. They sat in each other's arms for several minutes without speaking.

"I've missed you so much honey," said John quietly.

"I've missed you more than I can say John," said Sarah. "When will you be coming home to stay?" He wiped the tears from her face with a finger and kissed her firmly on the lips. "I don't know but I think Hitler and his cronies are just about washed up."

"Do you really think so?" John nodded and kissed her again.

They held hands and sat in silence gazing into each others eyes, until a rousing call from outside interrupted their quiet time.

Bill Tyndale shouted, "Come outside both of ye. It's time for t' toast."

Sarah smiled and sighed. "Come on children give Daddy his crutches back, we have to go outside for a while. She squeezed John's hand. "Don't worry, we'll soon be alone in our Honeymoon cottage."

They sat with his grandparents, George and Anne Lowther, enjoying their company. George would go to be with The Lord the following year.

Chapter 38

JOHN'S FIRST NIGHT home with Sarah in their honeymoon cottage was a night of bliss but also a night of laughter, as they gingerly moved about nursing their injuries. They slept late the next morning. Sarah woke later than John and she rose to find him standing on his crutches at the door of the children's room, quietly watching them as they slept.

"Aren't they beautiful?" whispered Sarah behind him. In an instant John whirled around in a crazed panic. Sarah stumbled back with a scream. "John it's me!"

The wild look in his eyes quickly faded and he fell to the floor beside Sarah, his crutches clattering against the wall.

"Honey, honey I'm sorry. I get a bit jumpy when someone surprises me like that.

I'm so sorry." He hugged her so tightly she couldn't breathe. "Darling," croaked Sarah.

"You're hurting me."

"I'm a stupid clumsy oaf. I belong back in the war," moaned John.

"John Tyndale don't you ever say that again. You belong here with us. You'll soon settle down again," said Sarah firmly.

"I would sooner die than hurt you honey," John whispered.

"I know," said Sarah.

The two children sat in their beds watching, as Sarah helped their father to his feet.

"Is Daddy alright mother?" asked Abigail.

"Yes sweetheart, Daddy's fine."

"You go and sit in the garden darling, while I get some breakfast for the children,"

Sarah turned and headed for the kitchen, trembling violently. Tears welled up in her eyes.

John walked through the back garden and sat on the stone wall at the rear of the cottage. He remembered the night he had passed that way to meet Sarah for the first time. He smiled and lit a cigarette. Through the trees to his left he could see the morning mist rising from the stream below the meadow. The view of the old stone bridge across the stream made him feel at home. It was Springtime and what could be more beautiful than this part of the English countryside in Spring? His eyes and heart had almost forgotten this beauty. He'd seen enough mud and blood and death and feared the visions of it filled his mind to the brim.

He sat with his eyes closed and his face to the tree tops. "Oh Lord heal my mind.

Give me peace again." he said aloud. Silence surrounded him, except for the bleating of some playful lambs in the meadow.

The throbbing of his injured ankle forced it's way into his thoughts and he winced with pain. A tractor rattled in the distance and a dog barked.

"John darling, where are you?" Sarah called. "Breakfast is ready."

He hobbled to the front garden and the rustic table and chairs he had built some years ago, under the Purple Beech tree.

"There you are. Come and sit down for a while. We'll have a nice quiet breakfast together." Sarah smiled. Her smile quickly turned to a frown, when she noticed the pain on her husband's face.

"Oh darling, that horrid leg is bothering you again isn't it?"

"I bumped it this morning when we were...on the floor."

"I'm going to call Doctor Douglas. You need some pain medication," said Sarah, pouring the tea. There was a certain tension in the air.

"Your grandmother took me along to a Mothers' Union meeting down at the Blaney Beck Church while you were away darling. They're a wonderful group of ladies."

"That's grand honey. I didn't realise until yesterday, how old she and grandfather are getting. They must be over eighty years of age now."

"I know, time goes so quickly doesn't it? Here, put your leg up on this chair."

"Ah, that's better," sighed John. "They asked us to take the children over to visit soon. Maybe do some fishing."

"I'd love that darling. I'm sure your father and Elsie would drive us there."

Sarah could sense John beginning to relax, as he sat enjoying the quietness of the garden.

"I'll get us another pot of tea. I won't be a minute." She kissed him gently on the forehead before leaving. John closed his eyes and allowed the peace of the morning to soak into his soul. Yellow bumble bees droned in the flower beds around him. The children laughed as they played together on the lawn. He found himself counting his blessings.

Sarah returned and sat down gently beside him. "Darling," she began. "I love you dearly but there is something I need to say."

"You can say anything to me honey," answered John placing his arm around her shoulder.

"Well...I know what you've been through these last six years and you aren't the same young man who went away to the War."

"What do you mean...."

"Just let me finish darling. You are a different person to the one who went away.....and I understand that. I still love you and I always will but something's changed."

"What are you say...." John started speaking but Sarah placed her finger on his lips.

"If you are suffering an illness in your mind that causes you anger problems, you must do something about it."

Sarah looked deeply into her husband's eyes before leaning her head on his chest. She listened to his heart beating. He said nothing for what seemed like an eternity then he said, "Don't worry honey. I hear what you're saying. I promise I won't bring this stinking war home to you and the children. I Promise. I'll talk to someone about the anger inside me. That's what you're talking about, yes?"

"Darling you don't mind me saying this do you?"

"No honey, I'd rather die than hurt you and the children."

One of the things John loved about Sarah was her forthright manner. Some thought her insensitive, particularly her father with whom she often clashed but John saw this trait for what it was. It was total honesty and he loved her all the more for it.

Spring time 1945 was warm and pleasant with the farms a hive of activity. William drove the new Fordson Major tractor and four-wheel trailer over the beck and crossed the field one morning, to the honeymoon cottage.

"Who wants to go for a ride this fine day?" he called out from the lane.

Sarah and the children were already in the garden and ran to the tractor.

"Come on slow coach, let's go for a drive," shouted Sarah to her husband.

John hobbled through the garden to meet them. "I'm coming. Hold your horses." He'd taken to using one crutch instead of two and he found he was able to cover more ground.

"All aboard!" yelled William at the top of his voice.

"Where are you taking us lad," asked John throwing himself onto the wagon.

They made themselves comfortable on some hay bales. The children squealed with excitement as the tractor and trailer bounced along the lane. As they drove past the Peace Hall farm house Edward and Thora Lofthouse ran out into the front garden waving their arms about and shouting.

"What's going on around here?" shouted John over the clatter of the tractor engine.

William turned around with a big grin on his face and shouted at the top of his voice,

"It's over! The War is finally over!"

"What? Are you serious?" John shouted back at him.

Sarah let out a scream that echoed across the fields as far as Old Tun farm. William could contain himself no longer. He stopped the tractor and climbed onto the trailer where they all jumped and danced together.

"Wait a minute. Tell us how you know lad," asked John earnestly. He held his brother by the arms and peered into his face. William laughed.

"It's Doctor Douglas. He heard it on the wireless and he's telephoning everyone he can think of.

"Remember this day children," said Sarah. "Tuesday the eighth of May 1945.

The end of the War!" Tears were streaming down her face.

By this time Mr and Mrs Lofthouse had caught and joined them.

"The Germans have surrendered lads," said Edward Lofthouse with a smile.

"Thank the Lord it's all over. I can't believe it," said Mrs Lofthouse. She too was crying.

Everyone except the children climbed off the vehicle and embraced each other. John found himself trembling uncontrollably and leaned against the tractor. He lit a cigarette. Squeals of delight could be heard across the fields as the girls of the Womens' land Army heard the news.

"Are you alright darling?" hugging her husband.

"Yes. Don't worry about me. He threw his arms around Sarah and kissed her passionately on the lips. Mr Lofthouse was standing nearby and stepped up to kiss Sarah also. William quickly lined up behind him.

"Just a minute I'm not kissing everyone in the district," laughed Sarah. She kissed William, the children and turned back to John. "Right, that's it. All my kisses are for you from now on." They kissed hungrily before William shouted, "All aboard for Old Tun farm.!"

Mrs Lofthouse said, "We'll come over in the car."

The rest of them bounced along the lane singing 'Roll out the Barrel'. As soon as they reached Old Tun farm and climbed down from the wagon they were surrounded by Bill and Elsie, Margaret, Mary and four happy Border collies wagging their tails.

"This is brilliant lad," enthused Bill. He even gave John a quick hug.

William and Margaret waltzed together around the dogs in the cobbled yard, while the others burst into song again, "Roll out the barrel, we'll have a barrel of fun."

"William, now look what you've done!" scolded his big sister. "You've left a big dirty hand print on the back of Mary's dress."

"Brilliant lads," grinned Bill. "I reckon this calls for a wee dram."

"I'll drive over to Bell Hill and fetch the grandparents," offered William.

"Aye, in t' car not t' tractor lad," answered Bill. "And be sharp about it.

I'll call 'em on t' telephone an' tell 'em thee's coming."

As they walked together to the house Sarah, her eyes wide, turned to John and said,

"Does this mean you don't have to go back?"

"Well no not quite. I still have to report to Barrowthwaite Barracks. I'll probably be de-mobbed from there but I don't know exactly when." He smiled at her, "Don't worry about it today honey."

Elsie welcomed them all into the sitting room and the chattering group were soon supplied with refreshments. Generally it was whisky or beer for the men and sherry or tea for the women. Soon William arrived with his grandparents and they were made comfortable.

"The whole district's gone mad," he said. "There's people dancing in the streets in Blaney Beck and the Pub's already full. Henry Chalmers was letting off fireworks down at the pond."

"We were going so slow through the village because of all the people," laughed Mrs Lowther, "Gertrude from the Post office walked alongside the car and told us they have already organised a street party for tomorrow to celebrate."

"I told you," William raised his whisky glass "The place has gone mad. Here's to us."

"Here's to us," they all agreed.

After several hours of merriment it was decided to call it a day and retire, ready for the street party in the village tomorrow.

The rafters rang to the sound of "There'll be blue-birds over the White Cliffs of Dover."

Even an occasion such as a street party to celebrate VE day, couldn't proceed without considerations of family feuds and class distinction. There would be a separation between one group of tables for the 'haves' and one for the 'have-nots'. One of the organisers, being fully aware of the prickly situation between some of the landed gentry, was heard to ask innocently,

"Do you know any farmers with a grudge?"

One of the local women said with a wink, "Are there any other kind?"

The Daily Mail had proclaimed the headline, 'VE Day. It's all over'. There were crowds celebrating in the streets all over Britain, USA, Canada and other Allied nations. Those servicemen and women fortunate enough to be home joined in the joyful celebrations.

A Warship in Sunderland harbour accidentally fired live shells into the town but fortunately no one was injured. Hymns were sung in Darnley market place. Keith Campbell a well known local Scottish soprano, sang Brittania Rules the Waves, Land of Hope and Glory and There'll Always be an England, to an appreciative crowd at The Town Hall. Some thought his strong Glaswegian accent added an interesting flavour to the songs. Later in the evening, he was reportedly involved in a scuffle with a small group of Scottish Nationalists in the lobby. The scuffle was soon forgotten however, after several more whiskies had been consumed by the lads. Campbell later enthralled his audience with a stirring version of 'My Auld Highland Croft'.

From the balcony of The Ministry of Health, the British Prime Minister made a speech on VE Day.

The Liberal Party, led by Prime Minister Winston Churchill lost the general Election a couple of months later. The Labour Party under Clement Atlee were elected to govern on a platform of full employment, a national health service and a 'cradle to the grave' welfare state.

THE POST-WAR YEARS

Chapter 39

BETWEEN 1945 AND 1950 John and Sarah Tyndale prospered in every way. John carried on working for Andrew Howe the Stonemason but this time as foreman. This work was mostly repair work on Private homes and Public buildings. There was so much repair work after the War, that the dream of nationwide full employment was almost achieved.

ICI built their new Wilton Works near Middlesbrough on the south side of the Tees. The Company already had a factory at Billingham on the northern side of the river. Construction began on the new Darnley Pines Mothers' Hospital while the Plastics Factory in Billingham was being extended. In many instances the shortage of qualified building trades people became problematic.

John was involved with his private work more and more, to the point where he had to leave Howe's and start his own Company. He commenced operations under his own name, simply, J. Tyndale Builder and Stonemason.

One of the first contracts he won was the building of 2 Council Bungalows on a plot on the outskirts of Beckley Dell. The Council was so impressed with the quality of his work on completion, they kept him busy for the next 2 years with various projects. The winter of 1946/47 was very severe, with blizzard conditions in much of the North. Fortunately for John he had a contract to build 50 pre-fabricated homes. These were constructed in a spacious factory in Stopford Brook, which prior to the War had been used for the manufacture of furniture. This meant he and his workmen could continue building, regardless of the inclement weather.

In 1948 their was much cause for celebration in the Tyndale household. A third child, a second son was born to John and Sarah in the Spring and rationing had come to an end around the nation.

"I'd like to call him Matthew whispered Sarah."

"Matthew is a good strong Bible name," answered her husband as they gazed down at the new-born babe.

"Then Matthew it is," said Sarah. "Matthew William I think." John nodded.

"So be it. Our William will be right pleased."

Eleven months later another son was born. He was named Simon and was his mother's pride and joy. Sarah gathered her family around her like a mother hen with her chicks.

By 1950 1.2 million new homes had been built by Councils nation-wide, plus 157,000

pre- fabricated houses of many and various designs by different building Companies. Some of these pre-fabricated homes could be bought for as little as 2,000 pounds.

5,000 timber framed houses were imported from Sweden by the Government and sited mainly in Kent. They were very smart in appearance and well constructed. Many building Companies started building homes from pre-formed concrete panels erected on concrete slabs. Many of these were not very attractive but certainly practical and strong.

It was in this bustling era, that John was able to establish himself as a competent and reliable Building Contractor. As well as the family Ford Prefect the Tyndale' owned a Fordson 10cwt Van, and a Fordson Thames 5 ton Lorry.

The business vehicles were now emblazoned with signs informing everyone that they belonged to J Tyndale & Sons Building Contractors.

The house Wyndham Hall, on the outskirts of Stopford Brook, was a spacious Victorian 6 bedroom home, set back from the road in 10 acres of land, with Stables, Garages, other storage sheds and out-buildings. They had purchased the house as a renovation project and had finished it to a very high standard over a period of 2 years. Black wrought iron gates and a lengthy gravel drive-way greeted visitors, presenting this particular Building Company as one of considerable substance.

Doctor Douglas had encouraged John and Sarah to engage in these projects together.

"This will help you forget the War and get back into the 'rat race'," Douglas had told him.

He had been correct in his treatment. John's anger issues diminished and he and Sarah became even closer, enjoying this quality time together. The *piece-de-resistance* was the addition of a patio to the rear of the house. They worked together on the project with the children helping and getting in the way, until it was finished. The table and chairs which John had made, were brought from the honeymoon cottage and placed on the new patio. This would enable them to sit outside in good weather and gaze across the field to the River Wear.

"We're so blessed darling," whispered Sarah. They sat on the patio in each other's arms, as evening fell. The children were in bed and all was peaceful but for the yelp of a fox down near the river.

She sat up and looked at her husband. "You still haven't got over the death of your grandfather have you?" Sarah was always spontaneous, to say the least.

"Not really honey, I have to admit. You know since grandfather passed away, father and William have been struggling to run both places." He smiled at her outburst.

"Do you miss the farm enough to go back and help them? You do remember your grandfather saying Bell Hill would be yours when they both passed away. Your grandmother is very frail you know. What will you do then? What will we do then?"

"Whoa, not so many questions, you're making my head spin," laughed John.

Sarah's mind was always busy and she tended to keep her thoughts bottled up until they tumbled forth like a gushing waterfall.

"I'm sorry darling,"

"No, not at all," he answered softly. "When that happens we'll have to form another Company, or bring the two businesses under one name I suppose."

"How will we run both businesses? It would be a nightmare," ventured Sarah thoughtfully.

"Don't worry honey, we could do it together. Maybe we could get a manager for Bell Hill."

"I would need help with the house," said Sarah with a smile.

"Your wish is my command honey." John grinned and kissed his wife gently on the lips.

"I know someone who could come and help me," said Sarah excitedly.

"Of course you do my love. Who is this willing maid?"

"She's a lady I met at the Mothers' Union meeting last week. She's a darling and so desperate for work. The children would love her. Her name is Vera McKenzie."

"Shall I telephone her to come for an interview tomorrow?"

"Of course honey, that would be grand. Now let's go off to bed, I've got that huge concrete slab to do tomorrow over in Spennymoor."

"I hope the weather holds for you darling," said Sarah as they walked arm in arm into the house.

"So do I honey. I can feel Autumn creeping in on us."

Without warning, with a laugh, John swept his wife off her feet and whisked her upstairs to the bedroom.

"Stop laughing so loudly, you'll have the children awake," giggled Sarah.

"Shush," she whispered as he kicked the door shut with his foot.

"John Tyndale you're a beast....and I love you," said Sarah as he placed her gently on their bed. Her shock of auburn hair flashed against the white pillow.

"You know," giggled Sarah, as he smothered her in kisses. You won't be able to act like a noisy animal when there's a maid in the house Mister Tyndale."

"We'll see about that lass," he replied with a lecherous grin.

The next morning Sarah woke alone. John had risen with the lark and left early in order to get his concreting done while the weather was favourable. She realised the possessions they enjoyed came as a result of hard work but resented not seeing enough of her husband. Even the children had given up asking her, "Where's Daddy?" Godfrey in particular missed his father and when not at school, wanted to go to work with John and the workmen.

"Maybe he'll want to take over the business one day," Sarah had said to him.

While John felt quietly proud at the idea, it made him feel uneasy for some reason.

"I hope life holds more for him than this," he spat out.

"Don't talk like that please John. You know I don't like it," replied Sarah.

She had reached out to touch his arm as he'd strode to the Lorry but her hand merely brushed against his jacket and he was gone. The morning she was thinking about was only a week ago and she was once again reminded, her husband's moods could still be volatile.

The Winter of 1951 was notable in the lives of the Tyndale family. The first and most telling was the passing of Anne Lowther,

John's beloved grandmother. The second was the worst snow fall for years. Huge drifts left the North of England virtually paralysed until as late as the following March. Both of these events had a dramatic effect on the family. Building work was reduced those jobs which were under shelter. This in turn lowered income for J Tyndale & Sons for several months. George and Anne Lowther bequeathed Bell Hill to John in their Will with the proviso that John, William, Margaret and Mary would share the proceeds equally, if it were ever sold. Mrs Vera McKenzie commenced work as House-keeper for the Tyndale household, soon after these events took place.

John was kept busy in the office most of the time now. The Company had purchased an old house next door to Miller's hardware store, in Newgate Street Stopford Brook. They renovated the building and converted it into an office on the ground floor. The side gate led to a large yard at the rear, with a storage shed and workshop area. The scope of Company contracts took them from Newcastle in the North to Richmond in the South and from the Pennines in the West, to most of the coastal towns down to Scarborough.

The English weather was the ever-present arbiter in their success, often crippling the Company's real earning power. Bell Hill however, was moving ahead strongly under the leadership of it's new manager Bev Edwards.

"But John, he knows nothing about farming," Sarah groaned when John told her of his intention to hire his friend.

John's reply to both was, "He's a quick learner, he's out of work and he's my friend."

Bev and Carlene took up residence in the rear wing of the house at Bell Hill, bringing with them nothing more than three suitcases a barrow load of hope and two Springer Spaniel pups.

"This one's for you mate. It's a thank you gift," said Bev handing it to John.

"But I don't...." he began to protest.

"No, don't mention it mate. I got them for us from the shelter before I left."

"Bev's a real softy inny?" gushed Carlene in her broad Cockney accent, as she looked around the elegant ballroom of Bell Hill.

Sarah was amazed at the way Carlene could speak and chew gum at the same time, without missing a beat. She thought to herself, 'this house has never heard an accent like that in it's three hundred years. Not in this countryside'. Carlene didn't say much as she and Bev were shown through the house but she did let out many wide-eyed whistles.

"Cor blimey Bev 'ave a gander at that Grand pianner."

Bev chatted to John as they walked from room to room and did his best to ignore her. They all reminisced over tea on the terrace and time flew quickly by.

"Can you drive alright with your dodgy leg Bev?"

"Yeah sure," his friend assured him.

"You'll find a Humber in the garage closest to the house. I'll draw you a map and you can drive over to our house for a visit tomorrow. After you get settled in I mean."

"That won't take us long mate laughed Bev."

Later as they drove out of the gates towards Stopford Brook, Sarah said,"Oh John,

I hope you know what you're doing. I love them both but... Oh dear," said

"Don't worry honey. They'll do fine. Morrison will keep an eye on the place."

Morrison was the game-keeper or 'Gillie'. He'd worked for the Lowther family all of his life and lived by himself in the cottage down by the river. His father had also worked on the Estate and his father before him. He would indeed keep his eye on developments. Morrison wasn't too keen on city folk, especially 'Southerners' as he called them, well within earshot.

Their puppy nestled peacefully on Sarah's lap all the way home.

"What shall we call him?" asked Sarah. "I know, we'll let the children name him."

And so it was. He was a Liver and White coloured Springer, so for obvious reasons the children named him 'Patchy'. Godfrey, who was now 12yrs of age thought the name a bit 'sissy'. He would rather have called him Rex but he was happy to let his younger siblings name the dog. He was happy to have a dog. He loved animals and enjoyed the chance to interact with them, whenever he visited the farms with his mother and father. John wasn't happy to have a dog at the house even though he was a dog lover himself.

"It might run on the road and get injured, or even killed. There's a lot more traffic about these days," was all he said.

Sarah replied, "What are you going to do when Abigail wants her own pony?"

"Oh my Lord," John groaned.

"Who are you and what have you done with the man I married?" asked Sarah laughing.

"I don't know, I think he's busy."

"See if you can find him for me, will you?" Sarah was joking but John knew she was serious about his behaviour of late.

"I'll see what I can do honey," he replied, as he wandered off to his workshop. Godfrey and Patches followed him.

"Godfrey, don't get in your father's way now!" Sarah called after the lad.

John watched his eldest son as he followed him into the workshop. Godfrey was quite a big boy, slender and wiry like his mother but not as stocky as Simon his younger brother. He was doing well at the Grammar School. John was very proud of his family and when he did have time to spend with them he was always surprised by the speed at which they had grown. Abigail would indeed love a pony, he was sure.

"Father, may I go and look at grandfather's old car?" Godfrey asked.

Grandfather Lowther's car was a Rolls Royce. A 1935 Mulliner bodied 20/25 with blue and silver paint work. It was stored in one of the garages on blocks, with a cover over it.

"Aye lad but don't forget to put the cover back."

Godfrey would lift the cover and sit in the rear on the plush leather seat pretending to be driven about by a chauffeur. He placed the pup on the seat beside him. For some reason the imaginary driver would always talk with the same accent as Carlene, the wife of his father's friend Mr Vivian Edwards.

"Where we off to today ven guvnor?' she would ask.

Young Godfrey thought her a stunningly exotic creature.

When he had finished travelling, he and the pup went back to the workshop. He sat on a paint tin while the Spaniel lay in a pile of wood shavings. He watched his father skilfully fitting pieces of timber together on a large work bench.

"What are you making father?"

"These are the new front doors for the house Chip."

John had taken to calling all of his sons by the nickname of Chip. It had all started when Sarah had mentioned they all looked like chips off the 'old block'. He quite often called Abigail 'My Little Miss'. Apart from this he didn't have a lot to do with the children. Even though he loved them dearly, he found himself following the example of his own father, encouraging and guiding only when needed. Godfrey was happy sitting in the workshop silently watching his father. Sometimes he would sit on John's old motorcycle, which stood in a corner covered with an old horse blanket. He loved the interesting smells of wood shavings, varnish, paint and turpentine.

This day he was about to learn a non medical method of treating open wounds.

"Blast," his father said under his breath. He had cut his arm on an exposed metal bracket and it was deep enough to cause copious blood flow.

Godfrey watched in horror as his father spat on the torn

bleeding flesh and immediately wrapped his not so clean handkerchief around it. He then lit a cigarette and kept on working as though nothing had happened.

"Mustn't get blood on the timber lad. It makes a stain."

Godfrey, feeling a little squeamish said, "I'm going back to the house now father."

"Aye lad," John Mumbled absent-mindedly.

The puppy, now covered with a coat of wood shavings, followed Godfrey.

THE WINDS OF CHANGE

Chapter 40

THE EARLY 50'S in the North-East weren't easy for everyone. Winston Churchill and Neville Chamberlain, who was a Darnley lad were Prime Ministers and dedicated themselves to re-building the nation. The 1951 Darnley County Development Plan called for the redevelopment or destruction of some 350 small villages, which had grown up around various coal mines.

These were referred to as Category 'D' Villages. Many of these were left to die with no assistance given, other than to direct the hapless inhabitants to Council Housing in other areas. Unemployment was high in the North, even though some relief came in the form of the fledgling Oil Industry with it's large Refineries and Infrastructure.

Those as fortunate as the Tyndale family of Wyndham Hall, weren't as badly affected as others because the Company was involved in many of the various construction projects.

The Coronation of Queen Elizabeth lifted the morale of the nation, with many being able to watch it on the newly developed Television. By 1956 even Rock and Roll could be heard on the wireless.

Father had built a wooden boat for us with oars and a sail. The four of us, plus Patches the dog, enjoyed many happy hours on that stretch of the river, totally isolated from the nation's problems. We had a library full of the classics and visits to the family farms to keep us amused Mother made sure we were happy at home. Her family was safe and secure at Wyndham Hall and other than her visits to the Church for her Mothers' Union meetings, she didn't mix with the people of the village. Even the daily trip to the local shop was made by Mrs McKenzie.

I remember in the Spring of 1957 father piled the family into the 1956 Fordson Van with pillows and blankets. The Prefect wasn't big enough to contain all of us. What excitement! We were going on our yearly holiday. This time to the seaside village of Staithes, where we would be staying at 'The Cod and Creel Inn', located on the promenade overlooking the harbour.

Captain James Cook was inspired by the sea, when working here in a Grocer's shop as a lad. I had no idea then who he was, or that I would live in the land that he had visited almost 200yrs earlier but I too was inspired by the sea in this village. I loved watching the fishing boats in the beck and the harbour. I loved sitting in the ones pulled up on the exposed mud at low water. The scent of the wooden craft and the salt water remains with me.

Father took us to visit the Lifeboat Station where I hung on every word, as the men related stories of raging North Sea storms that threatened to sweep the village away. There were faded photographs around the walls of these wild storms and some of the ships and crew that owed their lives to these rescue boats. The volunteers would man the oars in all kinds of weather in these open wooden craft to aid stricken vessels in the open sea. Many of the brave crew were lost to the sea during these rescue attempts. Amateur climbers would attempt to climb and sometimes get stuck on the cliffs, to the North and South of the harbour. We watched as the rescue team came with their ropes and pulleys.

Father and mother occupied their own room at the Inn while we children slept in another.

From our window on the top floor at night we watched them and the other holiday makers walking the promenade below. The lights on the seafront and the laughter from the bar downstairs, coloured the scene in a way I will always remember. During the day we were engrossed in watching the fishermen landing their catch.

When we returned home, two things happened that impacted the whole family in ways we could never have imagined in our wildest dreams. Firstly mother went on a trip to Llandudno with The Mothers' Union. It was Summer time and the weather in North Wales was beautiful, with blue skies blue ocean and I'm sure she returned with itchy feet. As usual the weather where we lived was somewhat less attractive, with one fine day per week on average.

I remember my father was having trouble completing contracts because of the bad weather. Secondly, mother produced some brochures while we all sat around the dining room table one evening.

"I've been reading about a place called Australia,' she announced. "The weather is always sunny and warm."

"Really. Where did you here about this honey?" asked father. He was genuinely interested. We all were.

"One of the ladies on the trip has friends who went to Australia and she said they're very happy there."

We all waited for more information and mother didn't disappoint.

"She said anyone interested in making the journey, should write to the Australian Migration Office in London."

The wind and rain beat steadily against the dining room window.

"There's no harm in finding out honey," father replied. "Let's have a look on the globe in the drawing room and see where this country is exactly."

We all filed in to scan the globe for the nation of Australia.

"It's down under," laughed my sister. "It's a wonder they don't fall off."

March 1958 was cold and wintry, with heavy snow mid way through the month. I was now 10 yrs of age. The last six months have been a whirlwind of change and frenzied activity.

Our move to Australia is now just around the corner. Father and mother have sold the house and most of their belongings. I heard them talking to each other about having to sell at bargain prices because of the urgent sale. Father built heavy duty storage trunks for the special things they want to take with them. These will travel across the seas in the Hold of The SS Orcades of the P&O Orient Line.

What would become of Patches? Uncle William offered to take him to Old Tun farm.

We children shed many tears over having to leave him but we know he will be happy there. Bev Edwards and Carlene returned to London after their successful stint managing Bell Hill. My elder brother won't be coming with us on the ship. He joined the Navy last year and is serving on a D Class Destroyer. He will find his own way to Australia in due course.

We all enjoyed a few days in London before travelling to our embarkation point. The City was an eye-opener for a family from the North Country. We attended Theatre matinees where we were treated to My Fair Lady and West Side Story. Most of West Side Story went over my head but it certainly impacted me. We also paid the obligatory visit to the London Zoo where we saw the Pandas and our first, if not our last Kangaroo.

Even though we were all terribly excited boarding this beautiful Ocean Liner, I was aware I was leaving my own Country and felt a heaviness in my heart. We boarded from the Central Parallel Dock at Tilbury which is situated about twenty miles downstream on the Thames River. The dock was a short but interesting train ride from London.

The SS Orcades was air-conditioned, with sheltered decks, a children's playground and the most wondrous attraction of all for me and my brother, a swimming pool. The internal fittings and design gave it a feeling of 'old world' luxury. I remember looking over father's shoulder as he read a pamphlet about the ship. Her construction had been completed in 1948. I felt a kinship with her already. She was 28,000 tons and cruised at 22 knots, even when her stabilisers were deployed. Mother and father occupied a 2 berth cabin, while Abigail and we two boys stayed in a 3 berth next door.

Many adults and some of the children on board suffered from sea-sickness on our journey to Australia but we didn't. As a matter of fact, I don't remember ever thinking that the sea was rough. I do remember being part of the group of passengers who had to be treated in the sick bay for extreme sunburn. Particularly on the shoulders. We learnt a new found respect for tropical sunshine as we wore our burns treatment bandages. There were many lobster-coloured people sitting in shaded areas nursing serious sunburn. They jealously watched others who frolicked in the sun, wearing hats and long sleeved shirts for protection. We very quickly became sun wise and tanned, to the degree where we no longer got sunburned.

Simon and I couldn't swim very well when we started our sea journey even though we used to splash about in the river at home. The swimming pool on the ship had a hand rail around the inside edge, for those who weren't confident in the water. We pulled ourselves around by this rail cutting the corners as we went. Pretty soon we were cutting the corner by even greater distances until we found ourselves actually swimming. The pool wasn't very big but in no time at all we could proficiently swim the length and breadth of it. Occasionally the water level would be lowered for the use of children and adults who couldn't swim.

We both sat back in the shade and watched these poor unfortunates, as though they were some kind of sub-human, non aquatic species. We were sun bronzed water babies and obviously of a higher order. My brother and I soon learned we could curry favours with the young Stewards, because we had an attractive young sister. Abigail was always the centre of attention with the young men, whenever she strolled the deck. One of the young lads whose name was Jim approached us and told us he would let us into the pictures free, if we would put in a good word with our sister. True to his word he showed us into a small room which contained several chairs, behind the screen. He and his mates must have used it from time to time for various purposes. We saw the movies in mirror image but we didn't mind. I've a feeling Abigail saw movies with Jim from this same room, when no one else was around.

Somehow we lads were invited to the bridge to steer the ship. I don't know how or why but what a thrill. I also remember dining at the Captain's table on more than one occasion. Unofficially we were shown around most of the ship from the bow to the stern and even the engine room by one of the Stewards. I remember stopping for a while at Port Said before travelling through the Suez Canal and seeing sunken Warships. The adults spoke unfavourably about the antics of some Arabs, who made rude gestures to the ladies standing at the rail of the ship as we passed. We stopped at Aden and I remember walking through the city with my parents. We were constantly accosted by locals wanting us to buy things from them. Subsequently all of the passengers were told by the Purser, not to venture too far from the ship on our walks. My memories of these walks, are all of wide-eyed wonder at the different sights, sounds and smells, in these exotic far away places. From memory our next port of call was Colombo. It was here we experienced our first tropical downpour.

We could not believe the deluge and the way it ceased as quickly as it had started. This tropical storm swept through, as we sat enjoying refreshments at a Tea room in Victoria Park. Balmy days crossing the Indian Ocean followed, when we enjoyed our Crossing the Equator Ceremony.

King Neptune appeared from somewhere, wearing his crown with his huge white beard and duly officiated. Those who were crossing the Equator for the first time, which was most of us, celebrated with ice-cream and a plunge in the pool. Certificates were then handed out. A great time was had by all, particularly the children as I remember. I think most of the adults adjourned to the Main lounge or the Aft Tavern after the ceremony. Presumably Neptune returned to his watery kingdom until another ship passed by.

We made landfall in Fremantle Western Australia and set foot on our future homeland for the first time. The blue and yellow Terminal building smelled of fresh paint. It looked warm and welcoming in the confines of the Port. From the ship we could see many fine brick buildings. We went ashore and rode a tram around the town, which to new chums felt like the wild frontier. We all felt excited at the prospect of living in this new land.

Many migrants left the ship here to start their new lives in Western Australia, but for us it was only a stopover. From here we would travel on The Orcades to Sydney, which would be our Port of disembarkation. We would then take a train from Sydney to Brisbane. Travelling across The Great Australian Bight we struck the roughest seas of our journey with mountainous seas and howling wind. Many were ill with severe sea-sickness, although our family wasn't affected by this *mal de mer*. From that time on, I stand amazed at the way vessels ride over and even through these towering waves.

The memory of the Orcades shuddering from stem to stern as it shouldered its way across the Bight, stays with me and my admiration for lone round the world sailors knows no bounds. I think I am one of those who love to 'go down to the sea in ships'.

We docked at Pyrmont in Sydney Harbour and I remember the excitement on board as the next phase of our journey began. Some would stay in New South Wales while others joined us on the rail trek to Queensland in the North.

My memory of this journey is filled with images of our first real glimpses of Australia. We passed through an amazing mixture of scenery, with ocean views ranging from Cobalt blue to turquoise in colour. We marvelled at the verdant rain forests, endless Gum trees, brown grass and even browner rivers lined with greenery and bird life. We saw Kangaroos, Wallabies, Emus, Cockatoos, Dingoes and flies. We were looked after by friendly Rail staff on the trip at various Railway refreshment rooms and I remember having a meal on a country platform at least once. We feasted on tea, watery cordial, sandwiches, scones and believe it or not, trifle. During these pauses on the trip North, we also saw millions of ants of all shapes and sizes, huge spiders....And did I mention the flies? It was not only a culture shock but also a nature shock. In short, our introduction to Australia was memorable and we loved every minute of it.

We were welcomed by the courteous staff at the Roma street Railway Terminus in Brisbane. Dad remarked on the beauty of the red-bricked station building. He always seemed to be admiring structures, wherever we went....and bridges, he loved bridges.

The final stage of our Journey was by car to Stafford where we stayed with relations before we set out upon the final leg of our journey to our home on the Redcliffe Peninsula. We had completed an amazing stage in our lives and another era was about to begin.

AUSTRALIA
SCHOOL DAYS END, WORK BEGINS

Chapter 41

IN 1962 QUINNY and I left the cloistered security of Grade 8 scholarship year at Garborough State School and entered the wide-open wild-west school life at Redcliffe High. Apart from having to wear a school uniform, we all felt very American and grown up indeed. We had seen our overseas cousins antics during their High School terms in the movies and we expected the same excitement. The gap between the cool kids and the plebeians became greater at High School but I noted that one could be cool and still excel academically. I decided to be one of the cool academic kids. I later found that a liberal dash of focus needed to be added to the equation. A ration of passion. Oh dear, 'the best laid plans of mice and men' and all of that.

With the benefit of the binoculars of hindsight I can see that each prospective student needs to be asked one simple question before setting out on their Secondary school life.

"What do you want to be when you grow up?" (read; If you grow up?)

We all learn that if we don't aim at a target we will never hit it. Sometimes we learn that lesson, when we actually should be learning to hit a moving target. Anyway, I didn't even see the target, which means I never even fired a shot. There are many distractions at Secondary school as most of you know and I was distracted by most of them. In my defence, it was the 60's. Much freedom was beginning to stir amongst the young and the young at heart.

Quinny's disinterest in the academic life increased in direct proportion to his exposure to the same. In no time at all he was headed for the door and employment at one of the local garages. However this was a minor distraction for me when compared with the major distractions of girls, cars, motorbikes and music.

The two of us had formed a band together with the addition of another friend, who like Quinny wasn't a good guitar player or singer. I believe their primary reason for being involved wasn't the music but their quest to meet girls. For a cool kid I was naïve. We played gigs at Church dances, School concerts, private parties and such. The name of our band was The Bystanders. We were a three piece guitar playing all singing all dancing modern folk-group, wearing black trousers white shirts and black bow-ties. I thought it would last forever but my two mates lost interest after they started work. C'est la vie.

My second year at High School was cut short after my brother Simon, who had started that same year, told me of a Painting and Decorating apprenticeship which was on offer with a local Tradesman. Lack of the necessary fun funds was causing me to lose interest in school work and I remember sitting in class one day taking part in exams. I had completed my question paper and was staring idly out of the widow at a merry band of Painters, who were painting the School building on the other side of the quad. What a wonderful life they seemed to be enjoying.

The steps we take and the decisions we make in our lives do not happen by mere chance. I believe, 'the steps of a good man are ordered by the Lord.' NKJV. Many and varied however are the consequences of our decisions, which remain hidden for our own good.

This time was very special time for me also. More than I realised at the time. I went home from school and informed Dad and Mum of my decision to become a Painter and Decorator.

To say they weren't impressed with my decision would be an understatement of great magnitude.

"You are staying at school, completing your studies and going to Teacher's College," said Mum.

"But...."

"No buts. Wait till your father gets home and we'll see about this, young man."

I thought this was a reasonable outcome. Dad was a builder. He understood the benefits of working in the Building Trades, especially in the presently booming climate of post-war prosperity. Surely he would more than likely be an ally instead of opposing me.

Later that evening Dad said he would make more enquiries about the apprenticeship.

The man who is seeking an apprentice is called W H Stubbington and apparently Dad had worked with him on one of his construction projects. Over the course of the next few days the decision was made. I would join Wally H Stubbington as an apprentice for a period of 5 years. Mum told him during the interview process of my flair for art. He pointed out that my flair for art may not be of much use when painting a roof. It could be said that my mother didn't think much of Wally Stubbington after that remark.

"What sort of Painter is this man John, if he doesn't consider artistic ability?" Mum was speaking rhetorically of course. I don't think Dad was going to answer anyway. They were both thinking about the huge step I was taking. I was only 16 yrs of age.

"At least he's English," said Mum looking out of the car window. "That's something I suppose."

Wally had come to Australia with his family around about the same time as we had. He didn't have enough money to buy a car but he had a bicycle, which he used for everything until he could afford one. One could have seen him with a ladder, paint tins and other materials he needed, hanging from his bike as he made his way to the job. It was a matter of making do with what he had and no one thought any less of him for it. He was judged on the quality of his work. These days of course we all need the best of everything, right now. By the time I joined him he had a very nice cream coloured 1957 Holden pickup which was his pride and joy.

It was the first motor vehicle he had owned and I was expected to be as careful as he in keeping it free from paint spots. The beautiful red seats were kept covered unless Wally and his wife were going somewhere special on an outing. Many workers used their utilities as dual purpose vehicles, as they were originally intended.

Wally Stubbington was a very astute business man and he was able to buy an attractive property on the cliff at Redcliffe overlooking Pelican Bay. In those days a boy was apprenticed to one man for a period of years and because they spent so much time together, the Tradesman had a huge influence on his young charge, in many areas of his life. Apart from learning the Trade, the young apprentice would learn about life issues from his boss. I learned how to relate to people, how to think independently, how to drink beer and the value of a good reputation.

The Painting and Decorating Trade used to be a valuable one, with many special finishes to master including Wallpaper, Graining and Faux finishes. We were taught how to manufacture Paint and other finishes for our own purposes, during our 4 years attending Technical College. We attended Tech. College one half-day per week in the boss's time for Practical training and one night per week in our own time for Theory.

Our Theory nights were spent at Kedron while our Prac. Training took place in the old Palais Building next to the Brisbane River near the George Street Bridge. We weren't required to attend College in the last year of our 5 year term. All Trades people of that era were comprehensively trained. There were no women that I knew of, who took up apprenticeships in the Building game. They wouldn't have been able to lift and carry the heavy scaffold we used back then. Quinny was working as a Mechanic's off-sider. He wouldn't receive any formal qualifications but he was happy earning a proper wage.

Unemployment was unheard of during those years, with the majority of people occupying their own home. Most of the new homes being built in the early years of my apprenticeship, were High-set Chamfer board on concrete stumps. Later on High-set brick veneer houses became popular, followed by a small number of Low-set Brick veneer places toward the end of the 60's. The popularity of these Low-set Brick houses, which were in effect built on the ground, gradually spread to Queensland from Victoria. Those of us involved in the Building Trade thought this type of house totally unsuitable for the Queensland climate. We also thought it foolish to waste space by parking a car or two inside the house, instead of outside or underneath. This type of house was however, cheaper and quicker to build making it easier to feed the needs of first-time home buyers. It was the time of a car in every garage or house and a banana tree, grape vine and chicken in every back yard. The backyard being big enough for the kids to play cricket or footy. Victa and Atco were the lawn mowers of choice and British cars were as popular as Holden and Ford.

'Populate or perish' was the catch-cry of the Australian Government and qualified European Tradespeople were invited to migrate down under.

Without people like my father, who helped bring experience, stability and expertise to Australia, the impetus of the Post war boom would have been seriously curtailed. One only has to look at the contribution of European and Continental workers have made, to the growth of Australian States to realise the truth of this. In the early years we were all aware of the Kanakas, who were 'black-birded' and exploited for the furtherance and profit of the Sugar Industry in North Queensland. Where would the giant Cattle and Sheep properties have been without Aboriginals being used the same way? When I first read the account of the life of Tom Kruse the famous Outback postman of the mid 50's, I realised that my idea of an Australian was built around people like him. Kruse and thousands like him were as much the builders of Australia, as those involved in the Construction Industry or any other.

As I grew up I learned there are people in many and varied walks of life of whom can be said to have 'built' Australia. This country however, soon began it's journey from being a country which was different from others, to a nation which is just like all the rest.

Nationalism became multi-nationalism and the love of many waxed cold, for the Australia of old.

Quinny and I loved the Australia of old. We felt safe and secure in our world. He gave up music in favour of unmarried married bliss with his girlfriend. Increasing numbers of girls were willing to enter into permanent relationships, without entering into the promises of marriage. Living together in de-facto relationships was becoming a common way of living, with women and men having 'partners' instead of husbands and wives. It turned out that I must have been searching for something permanent also but packaged in the old way.

Chapter 42

THE BYSTANDERS HAD passed away after the loss of two thirds of it's members and I was playing with another band called the Waterloo Wombats. A mate of mine from school had formed the band and we were doing covers of the music coming out of England.

He told me the name was a nod to the English Australian connection. I was 17 by now and living with some musician friends in an old house in Redcliffe. The house was in the middle of town and had been converted into a rabbit warren of small Flats and bed-sits. We cared for little but music and girls. Not necessarily in that order.

I was working at a real job while playing with the band, so I couldn't throw myself totally into this lifestyle. It was like living in two different worlds. The other band members had begun to refer to me as Captain Sensible. We were playing at the regular Saturday night Dance in the Redcliffe Town Hall, when another life changing moment took place. Usually these moments happen without warning and are sometimes quite subtle.

I remember it as though it were yesterday. We were playing 'I Wanna Hold Your Hand' when I caught the eye of a girl across the dance floor. I don't know, maybe she caught my eye. Anyway we caught each other's eyes all night, until she finally came and danced with her girlfriend near the front of the stage. She was a dainty, dark haired, dark eyed beauty and I soon found myself totally mesmerised by her. I had to consciously focus on the songs I was singing and playing, instead of just breezing through the way I normally did.

At the end of the dance as we were packing up our gear I noticed she was standing in the entrance foyer on her own. After I'd packed my Strat and Amp into the car which was parked at the rear of the Hall, I made a beeline across the empty dance floor towards her.

Our eyes met, not across a crowded room but across a large empty one. I realise it sounds like the king of cliché but the world stood still at that point and we stood facing each other in a kind of bubble.

"Hi, I'm Matty," was the best I could do.

"I'm Laura. It's nice to meet you," replied this beautiful creature.

"I love your dimples," I heard myself say lamely.

Laura merely smiled a perfect smile, while I for the first time in my life I found myself tongue-tied in the presence of a girl.

"Would you like a lift home?"

"Can you take my friend as well?"

I reluctantly took my eyes off Laura and looked around the foyer. Her friend was being chatted up by a couple of blokes near the front door. They wore the usual clobber, leather jackets and motorcycle boots. Laura beckoned to her friend to come with us but as the girl turned to join us one of the other boys grabbed her arm to stop her. He held her tightly enough that she couldn't break free. I could see the panic in her eyes. Before I could take a step Laura yelled, "Let her go you creep!" He looked at her and laughed.

I walked over to them with intention of talking some sense into their heads. They instantly let Laura's friend go and turned their attention toward me. Now I'm no fighter but I'm stronger than most and I had learned by now that the best form of defence is attack. Laura pushed past me and slapped one of them in the face. He immediately slapped her in return. Something snapped inside me and I punched the one closest to me in the face as hard as I could. He staggered backwards through the door and fell onto the pavement outside.

The other one hit me so hard on the chin. I saw stars and heard bells ringing. As I fell I instinctively grabbed his arm and dragged him to the marble floor with me. My head was pounding and I couldn't see properly but I managed to get one of my hands around his throat. I squeezed as hard as I could as we rolled around on the floor. I thought I would have to let go when he kneed me in the ribs but I held on. I heard screams and the sound of running feet as darkness started to cloud my mind.

"Matty, Matty....let go of him!" I heard someone shouting at me. It was Dougie, our Drummer. Someone slapped my face and I began to come to my senses.

"Let go of him," he shouted.

I realised I still had a grip on the throat of my assailant and released him. I felt Dougie drag me across the floor and sit me against the wall. He tipped a cup of water on my face and wiped my eyes with his handkerchief. A towel appeared from somewhere and I could see the concern on Laura's face as she gently wiped blood from my eyes.

"Are you alright now?" she asked.

"Never mind that. Are you alright." I staggered to my feet and saw Dougie bending over the bloke who had given me this blinding headache. My head felt like it was splitting in two. He was lying on the floor gasping for breath. He got to his feet with the intention of finishing me off but he couldn't stand without help and staggered back against the wall. His mate still lay prone on the footpath outside. The whole incident had only taken a couple of minutes. Dougie turned to me and said, "Run, before the Cops come. The manager's on his way as well." A small crowd of sight-seers had gathered around us by this time. A faulty fluorescent light flickered above.

"Thanks mate, I'll see you back at the flat," I took Laura and her friend by the arm and we headed outside past the one I had punched. He was being helped to his feet by a passer-by. We slid into the front seat of my trusty Austin A 40 Tourer and drove into the night.

I realised I was shaking and my head was pounding. I had trouble focusing my eyes. Laura sat in the middle next to me, while her friend sat next to the door.

"This is my friend Mary," Laura said, placing her hand lightly on my arm.

"I gave her a smile. I could taste blood in my mouth.

"I've got an Aunty called Mary. She lives in England." I said to her friend.

I drove into the front yard of the Flats and we all got out of the car. I reached into the back seat to grab my Guitar case and Amp. Laura said," We'll carry those for you. Come on Mary, you carry the Amplifier."

They placed the gear in the middle of the floor and we sat around the table together. Laura disposed of the empty beer bottles we had left on the table, while Mary gathered up the dirty coffee cups and placed them in the sink. I suddenly felt aware of the mess and casually wiped the table top with one of Dougie's shirts which I had picked off the floor.

"What a night girls." I said as I slumped in a chair beside Laura.

"I think you're getting a black eye," answered Mary.

"Matty, you could have choked that boy to death if your mate hadn't stopped you.

We couldn't get your hand loose." said Laura. "It was like you were in some sort of trance or something. We were all scared." Tears welled up in her dark eyes.

I placed my arm around her shoulders and held her.

"Do you think the Cops will come here looking for you?'
Mary asked.

"No.... I don't think so, Dougie will sort it out. He's good
like that." I assured them both. Dougie was a year older than the
rest of us kids and like a big brother.

"Anyway," I said. "It was self defence wasn't it?"

"Sort of," smiled Mary, "but you hit the other one first."

"He slapped Laura!" I glanced at the red mark on the side of
Laura's face. It wasn't too bad.

"I can't even feel it," she said.

"Those two won't say anything anyway," I mumbled. "They
won't tell anyone they got hit by a guitar player. They would have
been hurting a lot more if Dougie had been there when you got
slapped."

We laughed and the tension slowly ebbed.

I ventured to the bathroom to survey the damage. I had a gash
on my chin and my eyes were bloodshot. I took off my dirty shirt
and stuck my head under the shower while watching the blood
swirl down the drain. Laura had followed me into the room and
handed me a damp cloth.

"Press that against the cut for a while, until the bleeding
stops." I thought I was going to melt when she placed her hand
on my chest and kissed me.

"Thanks for looking after us tonight,' she whispered.

I heard the rest of the boys pile into the Flat and they were in
high spirits. We went out into the kitchen to join them.

"G'day girls," said Joe the Bass player as he spied Laura and
Mary. "What a top night eh." He flopped down on one of our
dilapidated lounge chairs and carefully rolled a cigarette. His girl
friend walked out of his bedroom wearing only a pair of knickers
and sat on his knee. Jimi Hendrix looked down upon the scene
from a poster on the wall.

"Come on you two It's time I took you home. Your parents
will be waiting for you."

I was being Captain Sensible again but this time I had an ulterior motive. I didn't want anything to come between me and Laura. I didn't want her parents blaming me for her being late home and putting a barrier between us. I had another reason also. An after the Gig, Saturday night party in this place can get a bit untidy and I didn't want to create a bad impression. Even as I was thinking this stuff I couldn't believe I was doing it. Suddenly I was being confronted with feelings I'd never had before. Girls had always been just that, girls. Not to get involved with on a permanent basis.

We squeezed past Johnny our front-man on the way down the front steps. He was sitting having a smoke with some girl.

"Hey Matty, great gig man. Aren't you going to introduce me to your new friends?'

"No I'm not," I laughed. No one was going to interfere with my plans. Especially lover-boy Johnny. Good old love 'em and leave 'em Johnny.

"Are you keeping both of them you greedy boy?" He yelled.

"Yeah, I'm keeping both of them away from you," I called back.

As I drove the girls home they told me how much they had enjoyed the Dance.

"Are you playing there next Saturday night?" asked Mary as I dropped them off at Laura's house. The front porch light was on.

Laura gave me a quick kiss on the cheek and called over her shoulder as they ran up the front path, "See you later Matthew Tyndale.

I realised then that I didn't even know her last name. What a smooth operator. Johnny and his girl had disappeared when I drove into the parking spot. They had probably adjourned to somewhere private for the evening. Our Flat was quiet for a change. Usually the music was playing too loud for the neighbours. We got regular visits from the Police. One night a young girl had followed Johnny home after a gig but it turned out she was too young. Her big brother, who was built like a lumberjack came to the Flat looking for her. He found her with him in the back of Dougies Panel van. Luckily one of the neighbours had called the Police and they got there in time to stop him turning Johnny inside out sans anaesthetic.

The following week dragged by with work as usual. I often called in to visit Mum and Dad after work for a chat, with the bonus of sitting down to a home cooked meal with the family. I'd always go back to the Flat to sleep.

"What's your new girlfriend's name?" asked my brother Simon from across the table.

"What girlfriend?" asked Mum looking at me.

"She's not my girlfriend. I don't even know her name."

"I know her name," said Simon with a grin.

"How?"

"Her little brother is in my class at school."

"What's her name then," I asked.

"Yes Simon, tell us her name please," urged Abigail.

"Alright keep your hair on. Her name is....drum roll please maestro...."

"Simon just tell us, said Mum. This is an exciting moment."

"Her name is Laura McPherson."

"Laura McPherson," I repeated softly.

"Look at him he's like a lovesick calf," laughed Dad. "You'll have to bring her home to meet us lad." Godfrey nodded in agreement.

"What? Not with him here." I pointed at my little brother.

"I'll behave. I promise." He batted his eyelids coyly and pursed his lips.

"That just makes you look silly," I said.

"That's enough, stop being an idiot Simon." Mum put her hand on my arm. "Bring Laura home soon, we'd all love to meet her darling. And please go to the Hospital and have them look at that cut. I think it needs sutures."

"Don't fuss over the boy Sarah, He'll be fine," Dad said.

Chapter 43

"WHAT DOES THE other fella look like?" laughed Wally Stubbington when he saw me.

"What the..! that's a decent cut on your chin." He examined the injury through his paint spotted spectacles. "It should have been stitched I reckon."

"I haven't got a clue Wally," I laughed. "I didn't hang around to find out."

"Come on, I'll take you up to my Doctor. See what he reckons about it."

He drove me down town in the Ute and the Doctor duly stitched up my wound.

"It's going to leave a scar," he said. "Were you defending a ladies honour?"

"Something like that," I answered.

"Good, then try to duck next time." Wally and the Doctor laughed.

We then drove back to the job. We were painting a house in Old Garborough Road near the Catholic College.

Wally had become like a second father to me in the time I had been apprenticed to him. The kindness of Mr and Mrs Stubbington would shine to the fore during the next stage of my life. The next stage included Laura McPherson.

To my way of thinking Laura was special and I didn't think of her the same way I did the other girls in my life at that time. The other girls were tied up with the Band and parties at the Flat. It was a strange situation. Without realising I had placed her on a pedestal, a position she had no desire to occupy. She told me one night, as we sat in my car outside her house, that she didn't want to be kept in a cupboard but to be with me wherever I happened to be. Until this moment I had been living my young life without restraint, seeking only pleasure.

Even as my tiny teenage mind struggled to understand this new development, I did have the where-with-all to grasp that Laura in essence, wanted to 'go steady'. The words 'going steady' back then had many connotations but the most telling one was that once the 'steady' deal was done, a pseudo-marriage understanding popped it's head up...so to speak. I know we didn't discuss these issues per-se but I'm sure the idea lay somewhere in the back of our minds and eventually advanced our relationship. Laura fell pregnant soon after.

Ever the free-thinking youthful optimists we were overjoyed. Our joy however soon gave way to worry, as we wondered what to do next. At this early stage neither of us felt as though we could broach the subject with our parents. Laura decided to share the secret with her Grandmother while I would tell Wally and ask his advice. However, Grandma immediately alerted her parents to the situation and the balloon as they say, went up. To say there were mixed responses to our news, would be an understatement to say the least. At this stage of proceedings Mum and Dad hadn't even met Laura.

Through all of the 'hubble bubble toil and trouble' we were united in our desire to be married and keep our baby. Many well meaning people had other suggestions, ranging from abortion to giving up our baby for adoption. One of the main snags to our marriage was that I at 17, was legally too young to be married while Laura at 16 was legally allowed. We weren't the first couple to find themselves in this situation but I was one of the youngest. After many trips to lawyers and later an interview with a Judge, we were given permission to wed.

Without the constant help and support of our parents none of this would have happened. Once the wedding plans could be made I know they were happy to see us together with the promise of a new grandchild to look forward to. Our joy knew no bounds.

I learned a new song about teenagers and weddings. We sang it at all of our Gigs from then on. We were married at the Redcliffe Church of England. Dad loaned us his car and we headed off to a Motel in Caloundra for a weekend honeymoon. Laura's father slipped a flask of Scotch into my jacket pocket, gave me a grin and shook my hand as I climbed into the car. I appreciated that gesture and never forgot it.

The Motel isn't there any more. A burger restaurant now occupies the site.

I was still on apprentice wages when our first child of a total of five was born in 1966. We named her Laura after her mother. The next ten years brought the births of our other dear children.

We had moved into a bed-sit over a shop on the beach road at Clontarf. There was just enough room for the three of us with the crib beside the bed, if we both climbed out of the other side. We had a million dollar view of Pelican Bay from our room and it is still there today.

I was able to work overtime for Wally to make more money and a Plumber I knew paid me for backfilling trenches on his jobs after work. This was done by shovel back in the day and I remember getting home and collapsing on the floor with exhaustion on many occasions. I get a twinge in my back even now just thinking about it.

The money from playing in the Band was handy but not the constant attention of stray girls. Musicians throughout the ages will testify to my 'plaint. It was around this time that work with the Band came to an end for a couple of reasons but I continued playing the guitar and writing. By the time the new baby was born we had moved to a Flat with 2 bedrooms and an office, which was the top floor of an old house in Redcliffe.

The landlady occupied the ground floor. I had met her when Wally and I painted the house. She was a wonderful person and we became very close to her during the time we lived there.

Good advice from Wally and hard work from both of us, enabled us to build a house of our own in 1969. We built on a block of land we had bought in Klingner Road Redcliffethe previous year. What an exciting time! Not many couples our age were able to accomplish this, even back then.

As I carried Laura over the threshold, we had unwittingly stumbled through the doorway to the mundane. In hindsight we were following the script from someone else's life. No matter how hard we worked or how successful we became, we always felt as though there was a bigger adventure somewhere else.... and there was. The Vietnam War was raging and the Australian Government was committed to increasing the Australian fighting force by conscription. They had decided to use a system, which was known as the 'Birthday Ballot'. All 20 yr old men were required to register for the ballot, which was a literal one with numbered marbles in a barrel.

Conscription was begun in 1964, not as a result of the War in Vietnam but as a response to the conflict between Indonesia and Malaya, which had the potential to spill over into Papua New Guinea. I was quite prepared to go and do my duty for my Country but my number didn't come up. If it did, the fact that I was married with children probably brought about my deferrment. A couple of my friends were conscripted to fight in Vietnam. They left Australia as light-hearted boys and returned as scarred cynical men. My father and his comrades would have been the same after returning from the Second World War. The iconic song 'Back home blues', sums up the effect the War in Vietnam had on Australian troops. In 1972 the Labour Government Prime Minister suspended conscription and to the dismay of many the scheme was never restarted.

I settled down to my life as a Contractor and worked hard to support my wife and family, which is no more than was expected of me. Laura took work from time to time whenever possible but mostly stayed at home with the children, which was no more than what was expected of her. In the early 70's we decided to take a working holiday to 'get away from it all'. We sold our house, bought a large Caravan and hit the road. On reaching Townsville in North Queensland I took a part-time job with a large Contracting firm as Foreman. Three years later I quit my part-time job and we returned to Redcliffeto settle down again. The Caravan was sold. We and the 5 children seemed to breeze through our free-wheeling lifestyle. Years later I learned they struggled with having to change schools so many times.

Quinny and I had drifted apart. Laura and I didn't collect many friends generally. The few friends we had back then are still our best friends today. As we followed a path of itchy feet we seemed to move as a phalanx, a kind of mobile tightly knit group under a turtle shell.

Unknown to us, in some ways 'Lost and in love' could have been our theme song. We were happy living in yet another house, in a Northern suburb of Brisbane. This was going to be our last move. We would settle down, I would continue Contracting and there would be no more of this carefree lifestyle. A few years later however, we decided to make a change....again. We had discovered a small town in the ranges behind the Coast where we took the family for regular camping holidays. The town is called Benabarra after the type of tree found there. We were tempted to make another 'final move', to the country this time, where we would enjoy family life on the farm. We both were hungry to have some meaning in our lives at this time and we agreed we should start going to Church. Neither of us had attended Church since we were youngsters. We sold our house near Brisbane. Little did I know at the time, how this move would impact all our lives. While I completed my contracts in Brisbane, we rented a house in Benabarra for Laura and the kids. I was commuting every few days between the two places while I completed business. While I was in Brisbane Laura met a man (as you do in the bush) who had 53 acres for sale. He drove her and our eldest daughter Leanne around the land in his four-wheel drive and they fell in love with the acreage.

I had almost finished my work and made my another rip to Benabarra a few days later, where I learned about the man and his land from Laura. The man, whose name is Michael, lived with his wife Laura on their farm outside of town. Michael was French by birth and Australian by choice. Their farm was called Galeed. It was near a place called Callum Ridge, which was the name of the Railway Siding which passed by the front of the property. She told me how Michael had shared the Gospel of Christ with them as he drove around the paddock.

He had stopped on a hill under a grove of trees, offered to pray with them and 'lead them to the Lord'. He had told Laura he was a born again Christian. I had ever heard the term before and had no idea what it meant. When I was introduced to Michael, in found him to be a very pleasant and helpful man.

Another thing that struck me over the following days was the change in my wife. She was even more bubbly than usual and keen to get along to Church as soon as possible. She told me one night as we lay talking in bed that she had felt different since Michael had prayed for her, in a way she couldn't explain. She said she was now saved. I stored these things in my heart for the time being.

I had to make my final work trip to Brisbane and it would keep me away for a week. By this time word had circulated that a Painter and Decorator was coming to town (thanks to Michael) and I had several jobs lined up around the district already. The morning I left I had to drag myself away from Laura and the children. I'd never felt so sad to be leaving them.

Chapter 44

I GREW UP in the Church of England and I would have been sprinkled with water there as a baby in a ceremony called Christening. I went to Sunday School in that Church. Laura did the same in the Baptist Church without the baby sprinkling. Being saved or born again were not terms I was familiar with, though my wife probably would have heard them when she was a child in the Baptist Church. Our own children were Christened as babies, because it was the thing to do. Even now I had no idea that the words born again and saved were Bible terms. I accepted my wife's description of Michael being born again, because I knew he attended the Anglican Church in Benabarra. I had no idea how or why anyone should be led to The Lord but if an Anglican said ithen it must be true. After all, I had seen an undeniable change in my wife who had assured me she was born again.

A week later I returned to Benabarra to find my wife on fire. Not literally you understand but certainly figuratively. She told me about a Church meeting she had attended and how exciting it had been. A Church meeting.....exciting? To me these words were strange bedfellows indeed. She asked me to bring my guitar to the next meeting and help the group sing 'choruses'. I agreed to go along to the meeting with her but added "That sort of thing is alright for women and kids but real men have important things to do". She smiled ever so sweetly at me, the way a pet lover might smile at a little puppy. We duly rolled up at the Church Hall in Nanango which was the central town of the diocese, where the meeting was being held by the young Minister.

When I walked in carrying my guitar case, the people present were genuinely happy to see me there. The meeting was almost under way when we arrived and they were just finishing their prayers.

That is to say they were standing in a circle where most were praying out loud. Everyone was praying at the same time, some of them in what seemed to be a foreign language. This for a Church of England boy was very strange indeed. Laura gave me a reassuring smile and squeezed my hand which did make me feel more at ease. 'This is the Anglican Church' I thought, 'So it must be alright'. I was handed a music book so I would be able to accompany the singers. Oh boy! Did they sing. They sang at the top of their voices with their hands in the air, while most of them including my wife, had tears streaming down their faces. Then I noticed at the back with her hands on another ladies head. The voice of the prayer was lost in the song but I saw the prayee fall to the floor where she stayed for quite a while. My eyes must have been popping out of my head by this time but I had a peace about what was happening around me.

Later she testified that she had been instantly healed of her sickness, by the laying on of hands and prayer. This signalled the start of more singing. I found the songs to be pretty special and written with feeling. The song book was called Hymns of Praise. Amazing Grace was next and I had never heard it sung with such a personal feeling of praise and thanksgiving before. Soon my attention was drawn to a small group where a man and his wife were praying for another woman.

While several others shouted something in another language, he with red face and spitting lips stood back and pointed his finger at the woman being prayed for. She started hissing like a snake, her eyes rolled back in her head and she too fell to the floor. She lay very still while others continued to pray for her. Everyone began loudly praising and thanking the Lord. Some praised Him in different languages. They were certainly a multi-lingual group of Christians. The Minister joined in the spiritual activities but he only used the English language spoken in the best Anglican tones.

More singing and praying followed with bodies steadily piling up on the floor until there were only a few of us left standing. The Minister finished this part of the meeting with prayer while Laura stood with her hand in mine. The ones who were still standing then gathered around the supper table. It was certainly hungry work. This was very different from any Church service I had ever attended but I didn't feel uncomfortable. As we munched on cake and sloshed our tea back, most of the floor dwellers joined us at the table. Every one of them had obviously benefited from the experience in some way. I beat a retreat to the veranda steps and lit a cigarette, whilst trying to digest this new experience. My wife was still inside. I could see her happily chatting with the others. All of this seemed totally logical to me. If the Church is plugged into an all-powerful God and switched on, then surely feeble humans would be affected in some observable way. Yes.... even the Anglican Church.

I noticed the Minister heading my way. I knew he was no fool from the way he had spoken earlier in the evening, so I waited to see what he had to say. He carried an open Bible in his hand. He joined me and said with a broad Anglican smile, "Hi Matthew, I'm Mark. This area including Benabarra, is my diocese". Yes, Matthew and Mark.

"G'day Mark. I'm pleased to meet you...er Father.."

He laughed, "Please call me Mark. I've heard a lot about you from Laura".

"Oh really?" I replied.

"Don't worry, it's all been good. Did you enjoy the night?"

"I enjoyed it very much," I said. Then, rather than having him think me a total dummy I added, "I was born in the Church of England you know."

I quickly changed the subject before he asked me which one.

"I loved the music. The songs were very good."

He ignored me with a smile and said, "The Lord has given me a passage of scripture for you Matthew."

"Has he. Thanks very much," I replied lamely.

"It's from the Gospel of John Chapter 14: verse 6", he said looking into my eyes.

He began to read from the Bible and as he did the words seemed to penetrate deeply into my heart. He said, 'I am the way, the truth and the life. No one comes to the Father but by me.'NKJV.

"Jesus spoke those words to many witnesses and they are recorded for our benefit in the Bible," he added. He turned and went back into the room with a wave of his hand. I've never forgotten that night or the scripture. The pure truth of the words hit me so hard and so completely, that my life was never going to be the same. A man would have to be a fool to speak the way Jesus did before witnesses and Jesus was no fool.

On the drive home that night we were very excited about the meeting but also about the beginning of our new life in the country. We started attending the Anglican Church on a regular basis and spent many happy hours with Michael and Laura discussing Christianity. Laura and I had considered ourselves Christians since as far back as we could remember. I know many others felt the same way. However, the more we studied the Scriptures the more we understood the meaning of the words 'born again'. My wife had indeed been born again and it showed. I was growing increasingly busy with work and we were nearly finished building our house on the land we bought from Michael. It was a modest place but we built it on a hill next to a copse of trees and added a veranda overlooking the valley. It was beautiful.

One day as I was renovating an empty house for a client in Benabarra I made a decision to become a born again Christian. I based my belief on what I had read in the Bible and the personal testimony of my wife's conversion. I knew enough to realise I was a sinner in need of salvation. Only the God of the Bible could provide a real salvation, so I sat on a paint tin and spoke to him. These days it is quite a cliché but I felt his presence and love flood my very being. I knew my life had changed for the better and for eternity. I was so happy! Why hadn't someone told me about this before? I'm 33yrs of age and this is the first time I've heard the truth about Jesus Christ.

Some friends of ours owned a farm in Kingaroy and they invited us along to a Bible study one evening. An elderly Bible Teacher named Mr Wilson who seemed to carry with him the wisdom of Solomon, was to bring us a lesson on Baptism. For a Church of England boy who had been sprinkled with water as a baby, his teaching was certainly an eye-opener. At the end of the lesson when he turned to me and asked if I had been Baptised, I had to say, "No Sir. I haven't."

"Matthew, If you believe you may be baptised," he said softly.

"I believe Jesus is exactly who he says he is in the Bible. The Son of God," I answered without hesitation.

Laura and I both made arrangements to be Baptised as soon as possible.

We very quickly came to the conclusion that the Word of God through the Gospel of Christ had to be taken to the world, starting in Benabarra. Every Saturday morning I took my guitar and Bible to the local Park and shared the Gospel with people in song and preaching. People listened and responded by giving their lives over to Jesus. Pretty soon we had a regular group meeting in the Park every Saturday. What were we to do now that Winter was around the corner? We must find a building in which to meet.

The Town hall was made available to us and we started to meet together on Sundays.

How would my wife and I minister to these folks, when we were only baby Christians ourselves? Out of the blue Michael and Laura financed us to commence a Diploma in Biblical Studies at Bible College. We began to lead the Lord's flock by teaching what we learned. The Church began to grow with the two of us as Pioneer Pastors, under the guidance of Mr Wilson, the Bible teacher we had met at our friends farm.

I have written a Diary of our Ministry during these early years. The following section is a compilation of this Diary and the recorded tapes of our Church Bible Studies. Names have been changed to protect the innocent but I hope the next few chapters portray the joy and freedom which permeated our group through the Grace of God. The year is 1983 and the town is Benabarra Queensland.

I stood in the morning sunshine outside the Town Hall, discussing the Bible with a young man named Daniel. He had listened to my sermon during the Sunday morning service from the safety of the back row. He was struggling to understand Jesus' words 'I am the way, the truth and the life and no one comes to the Father but by me'. NKJV.

Daniel said, "That's a weird thing for a person to say. It's hard to believe."

I agreed with him but replied, "It's only weird if that person is deluded or a liar. Jesus' actions and words proved he was neither."

"That's why I don't believe the Bible," he said. "It's full of crazy stuff."

I could sense he was feeling cornered and uncomfortable so I suggested a regular visit for an informal Bible study.

"Could you come to my house and do that?" he asked

His enthusiasm and thirst for knowledge was obvious.

"It would be my pleasure," I answered.

The following Wednesday evening was pencilled in as our first Bible study. Our study night rolled around and we duly set off to the young man's house. We drove along the driveway through the trees, guided by the porch light which glimmered through the winter darkness. It was a lovely old house set well back from the road in bushland. In the parking area at the front were parked three other cars. It looked as though we had a larger gathering than expected.

"This is going to be very exciting," said Laura with a smile.

As we walked to the door Daniel met us and we shook hands in greeting. Our breath hung misty in the night air as we introduced ourselves. He showed us through to a large kitchen/dining area where a group of people sat at a large wooden table. They were waiting for the new Preacher and his 'missus'. Daniel ushered us to our chairs and the introductions began.

"Ok everyone, this is Pastor Matthew and his wife Laura from the new Church I was telling you about. The folks around the table nodded in our direction. Those present were Daniel's parents Larry and Pauline, his younger sister Angela, the local Postman Nick and his wife Julia and the local Butcher Tom and his wife Jenny. I thanked Larry and Pauline for their hospitality and our evening began.

'So Matty," asked Larry. "How long have you and Laura lived in this town?'

"Only a couple of years Larry. We believe the Lord called us to start this Church."

"But aren't there Churches in this town already?" asked Nick.

I'm sure his wife Julia kicked him under the table at this juncture but she needn't have worried on my behalf.

"Yes there are Nick but we are different in that we believe in the authority of the Bible."

My wife gently kicked me under the table at this point. "Pastor Matthew means that we refer to the scriptures as the only basis for teaching in the Christian Church." Her soft words and sweet smile covered my churlishness as usual.

"How long have you and your family lived here Pauline?" My darling wife asked.

"Only a few months Laura. We made a tree change and moved away from the City."

I took the opportunity to dive into the conversation and steer it back on track.

"Do we all have our Bibles with us tonight?"

Bibles of all shapes and sizes appeared on the table. Some looked new while others looked quite old. Larry produced the biggest Bible, which he dropped on the table with a thump.

"This is our family Bible," he announced to all and sundry. As if to add more authority to the book he said, "It belonged to Pauline's sainted mother." His friends around the table nodded gravely in agreement.

Angela said, "Dad give us a break".

"Thank you Angela," said Pauline quietly.

I said, "Are we all Christians here tonight?"

Well, you could have heard a pin drop when I asked that question.

"I'm Church of England," said Larry. "The whole family is."

"I'll make up my own mind about that, thank you Dad," said Angela with a smile.

A disapproving look from her mother settled the issue temporarily.

Nick and Julia replied in unison, "We're Roman Catholics but not practising."

Tom said, "I'm an Anglican. I don't need any practice."

Jenny his wife said quietly, "I used to be a Baptist when I was young."

Daniel murmured, "Oh my. I think the Pastor wants to know if we are all adherents of the Christian faith, not what club we belong to."

"I think I am," said Tom. "What does being a Christian mean Pastor?"

"Ok," I said. "Let's start by reading some passages from the Christian's handbook. The Bible."

Everyone enjoyed seeking out the truth of their basis for assuming they were Christians.

"Basically it comes down to this," I said quietly. "If you were on trial for being a Christian would there be enough evidence to convict you."

"Ah," said Larry. "Now I get you. We must hear, understand and act on the Good News of the Gospel."

Jenny joined in saying, "We all must learn of and respond to, the salvation won on Calvary and freely offered by Jesus Christ. And we must do this personally."

"We must first recognise that we are sinners in need of forgiveness," added Angela.

"Folks, I've never heard it explained better," I said. "That's just brilliant."

I posed another question. "Now the next step is to ask ourselves whether we need to be born again in order to become a Christian."

The lively discussion lasted well into the night, with much fun but mostly much learning.

"Why haven't we been told this by our old Churches?" asked Daniel.

MY CALL TO THE MINISTRY IN THE MID 80'S

Chapter 45

THE BIBLE STUDY group joined the Church and they brought along their friends. The study group grew to such an extent we had to meet in the Hall on Wednesday nights. Many locals who called themselves nominal Christians joined our group. We were the talk of the town until folks understood what we were doing. We eventually started a Sunday School for the children of the town which was well attended. Ladies home groups were added for those whose home duties kept them from attending meetings. Through all of this excitement I still worked to support myself while we both ran the farm and finished the house. We were busy but happy.

Our children weren't happy. Their parents had changed into someone else almost overnight. We had been a normal couple who enjoyed partying and holidays, without a care in the world. I don't think we even took the time to explain to them that we were now a Christian family with different behaviour and life expectations. To their eternal credit they gathered themselves and to varying degrees shared the journey with us. I'm sure they had to fight because they were the 'crazy Christian's kids'. With the benefit of hindsight, we could have handled the situation a lot better.

Anyway, we continued to grow individually and as a Church. Laura and I finished our studies with Honours and our 'cred' around the district was established. I was invited to preach in other Churches and Conferences, while singing my own songs and accompanying myself on my trusty guitar. This entailed quite a lot of travelling. The leaders of several International denominations had contacted us with a view to joining their particular brand name. Consequently I didn't see much of the kids. It was during this period that Painting & Decorating work began to dry up. Probably because I was devoting less time and energy to this part of our lives.

I found work in Mt Isa which is a mining town in North West Queensland. We bought a house and established our business in the town, leaving Vanessa to look after the farm. Our aim was to return at a later date. How I expected the Benabarra Church group to continue in my absence, I don't know. Anyway it didn't survive, although the people who were involved in the group retained their beliefs and continued their Christian walk.

The First Epistle of John Chapter 1 verse 7 in the Bible says this; 'But if we walk in the light as He is in the light we have fellowship with one another and the blood of Jesus Christ His Son cleanses us from all sin.' NKJV. I realised very early on in my life as a Christian, the importance of these words when taken in context. The world since the rebellion of Adam and Eve, has laboured under the effects of both original and incurred sin. We learn from the Scriptures, that the blood of Christ which was shed for us on the cross at Calvary, enables the people groups of the world to have their sins forgiven. This is why the Bible urges Christians to preach the Gospel to all the nations. The importance of Evangelism is stressed throughout the Word of God.

We know from the book of Genesis in our Bible that sin and death came into God's world through the rebellion of Adam and Eve. Sickness is one of the curses of their sin which we carry around in our bodies. Until Adam and Eve rebelled against God, sin sickness and death were not a part of their lives.

From this we can safely infer that 'the blood of The Lord Jesus Christ cleanses us from all sickness', by faith in God's Word. Jesus says to us 'Only believe'. The power of these words can be applied to our lives in a literal sense. In the book of Revelation Chapter 12 and verse 11 we read that the Christians overcame Satan by the blood of the Lamb (Jesus Christ) and the word of their testimony (their daily speech) and they did not love their lives to the death. NKJV.

When our speech and prayers agree with the Word of God, the power we seek to overcome our circumstances can be released into our lives.

1 Corinthians 7:20 says this about becoming a Christian. 'Let each one remain in the same calling in which he was called'. NKJV. The Apostle Paul repeats this in verse 24. Basically what this means is, when you become a Christian don't forsake your present job, as long as it isn't some sort of illegal activity. You can be a much greater influence for Christ in your normal sphere of influence, than you can flitting about looking for another career. The Apostle Paul was quite adamant when he said, 'If a man doesn't work, then neither shall he eat'.If you are sure God has called you to the Ministry and called you away from your regular employment, you will be blessed in your efforts. Be sure of one thing. While every Christian is called to minister in different ways and at different times, not all are called to full-time Ministry.

Having said that, I will now proceed with my memoir. Both of these passages of Scripture had a great bearing on my personal call into the Ministry. In always felt that I shouldn't be a drain on the small pioneer Churches I Pastored. The apostle Paul with his expansive intellect and spiritual comprehension, saw fit to work at his trade of tent-maker as he ministered. I decided to follow his example and work at my trade. Amazingly enough, I did manage to make myself feel guilty while doing this, after all most young ministers like to think of themselves in a three-piece suit and shiny leather shoes. In large Churches of course, as senior Pastor, this may be a desirable mode of dress.

I remember Michael telling me I should keep working because I had been called as a Painting Contractor. I had a struggle accepting his advice initially, thinking I should be a full-time Pastor or Evangelist while wearing the appropriate clothing and projecting the correct image.

I believed then and even more now in the truth of the Scriptures regarding modern day miracles of healing and provision. A firm belief in the aforementioned two passages of Scripture, set me on the right course for the future. I was sure my calling was that of an Evangelist. I wanted everyone to know the Good News about Christ. Initially I didn't see myself as a Pastor or Teacher, even though I eventually grew into those roles by necessity. While in Mt Isa we became involved in street Evangelism and music, culminating in outreach trips to the Mission on Mornington Island in the Gulf of Carpentaria. This was to be our introduction to working with the Aboriginal people of North Queensland. To be continued... Maybe.

We seemed to be caught between two worlds. Our eldest son was born in our first house and we had a need to settle down. I had my own Contracting business by this time and I was doing well but the big wide world was always beckoning. It was only a few years later that we rented the house and left for Townsville in North Queensland where I specialised in hanging wallpaper for an Interior Decorating firm. While there our youngest daughter was born but Townsville wasn't big enough to hold us and we returned to Redcliffe. We sold our house and bought and sold some other properties without realising a pattern was developing.

In hindsight I wish someone had tried to talk some sense into our heads but I doubt we would have listened. We were on a mission to find life and live it. Our youngest son was born during this period, making our family complete.

We decided to make a tree change and headed for the little town of Benabarra on the hinterland ranges. We bought 53 acres of land and built a house where we thought we would spend the rest of our lives in country bliss. For several wonderful years that's exactly what we did but for some strange reason we sold our farm. By this stage of the proceedings it was the late 80's.

During the next 53years until this present time Laura and I have shared many exciting times and we still love each other dearly. However, I'm presently going through a period of rebellion for want of a better word, in as much as I'm getting tired of spending my life having to consider others. I've a need to do things that I have always wanted to do for myself, without regard for others. This is not to say I've stopped loving others but that I want to spend some time loving me, if you know what I mean. One of these desires of mine involves sailing back to England in my own yacht, or riding there cross country on a motorcycle. Either will do but I would prefer to do both if possible. Maybe one different journey each way. Success or failure isn't even important but the attempt is. This is not something that my dear wife wants or needs to do, so if I am to complete either or both of these journeys, it will be solo. I know she isn't happy about it but she says she will support me.

These feelings have caused an interruption to the writing of this book. I haven't yet described the married part of my Australian life between 1965 and 2018. That, as they say in the classics, is a story for another day. Presently I'm writing in my Log, whilst bobbing about in the Indian Ocean in my yacht.

As I reminisce, I feel an overwhelming sense of devastation and loneliness deep within me. I feel as though I have lived a lie, even wasted my life. I've led a full, exciting and productive life but I feel empty and unfulfilled. It's as though I've been following an all-purpose script, designed to guide a person through, if they have no script of their own to follow. I am now 70 years of age and though I've always been surrounded by those who love me and whom I love, I feel alone. I am alone.

I can't write any more for the time being. I must try to concentrate on what I'm doing or I could find myself in more trouble than I'm in at the moment. It is late 2018 and I'm making slow progress somewhere between the Maldives and the Seychelles in my 1979 built 37 footer. This is one tough sail-boat. The humidity is almost choking me and the heat is oppressive.

I know I'm fairly close to land because I see Gulls and there's the occasional mangrove branch floating by on the water. Yesterday evening I watched a loaded Container Ship pass by about 10 miles off my starboard bow just after dark. I must remain vigilant, I seem to be in a main trade route now. He must be headed to the Suez Canal. I'm disappointed I haven't been able to repair my radio yet but since seeing him I'm fairly sure I'm on the right course. I believe I'm sailing very slowly North-West towards the Gulf of Aden and The Suez Canal.

I had to jury-rig a mainsail, after losing part of the main mast in one of the many roll-overs I have experienced, since entering the Indian Ocean from Western Australia. It was during one of these brutal storms that I lost most of my electrics. I thought this journey of a lifetime would bring happiness but I feel as though I'm sinking deeper into depression every day. What on earth am I doing here? I must pull myself together, after all, isn't this the life I've dreamed about for fifty years? I've always thought myself totally suited to the life of a hermit and always comfortable with my own company. Now I'm not so sure. I miss the company of Laura and our family much more than I dare to admit to myself. My heart is aching.

I'm very tired now and my 6 hour watch periods punctuated by 2 hour sleep breaks which I have practised since the beginning of my voyage, are also playing tricks on my mind. I must stay alert in case another vessel collides with me. Large ships have a great deal of difficulty seeing small boats at sea, particularly at night. During my short periods of sleep I'm haunted by a dream in which I'm stuck alone in an empty prison cell. I'm separated from all of my loved ones and unable to live in either Australia or England. I awake in a sweat each time paralysed with fear until I realise where I am. My beautiful boat used to give me so much pleasure but is it now the prison of my dreams? It's becoming more and more difficult for me to differentiate between dreams and reality.

It is 60 days today since I sailed out of the Brisbane River and headed North. I stopped over in places like Mackay, Townsville, Cairns and Darwin, before heading West North-West into the wild blue yonder. Many people told me when I started this voyage that I was undergoing a mid-life crisis. I reckon right now I'm undergoing a life-threatening crisis. I feel lost....well I am lost. I'm lost at sea on a starless misty night but that's not what I mean. I feel the way I did when I underwent major cancer surgery in 2002 followed by a 10 year addiction to morphine. That sort of lost. Then I was comfortably numb, now I'm uncomfortably numb. What a mess. I wish the ocean would open up and swallow me. At least if that happened I would be with the Lord and I wouldn't have to put up with this confusion any more. I pick up my old guitar and sing 'How Great Thou Art'. I remember singing this hymn as a young lad, in the old stone Church in Etherley, England.

'The crew of a dive boat off Nanadhoo at Noonu Atoll in the Maldives came across a drifting yacht yesterday. Though still afloat it was severely damaged by what appeared to be a collision with a larger vessel. The Police are holding the craft and studying the Log pending further investigation. The Police Chief told this reporter that the owner of the yacht whose body wasn't found, must have been asleep when the collision occurred. He said the smaller boat wouldn't have been visible because of the murky weather the last couple of nights. He told me it wasn't the first time this had happened to a lone yachtsmen and it wouldn't be the last. Exhaustion eventually overtakes them, he said. The sailor's family has not yet been notified. He is thought to be an Englishman'

Sonia Baruza. ALT. Maldives.

Among the items found around the wrecked yacht, were these two poems enclosed in an envelope and folded inside an old tobacco tin. A young local boy found them and gave them to his mother as a present. They now hang on her bedroom wall.

A Letter From Australia.

Oh Britain my heart adores thee,
Britain so great, yet so wee,
It's a cliché to say it this way
but when I'm done wandering,
I'm coming home to stay,
But will you still know me
and will I know you,
the land of my birth.

When it's all added up
just what you are worth,
the influence and blessing you've been,
to each nation on earth.
You opened your doors and windows,
to all whom desired to enter.
Your ancient ones, like me,
will turn in our graves,

When they see on their quiet green land,
the colours, the creeds and the anger.
They trample and scheming they plan,
Don't cry for her Argentina,
As the Falklands come back to haunt you.
A nation of shopkeepers, maybe so
up alongside the North Sea flow
but we push back 'neath the Union Jack,
because the Oceans are our playground,

Oh Britain, land of Fergied fields and Macadammed road,
M.1.Concrete and Mole and Toad,
I am thine.

By Matthew Tyndale.

I Long To Run.

I long to run where the North Wind blows,
crashing, crushing, carving ice-flows,
Driving rain in cold confusion pelts,
Rocks hard, streaming in gales screaming,
await the unwary raider's carved prow,
who come to take a Northern lass,
not by hand and not for cash,
but to bear a child, a name, a town.
A farming lad to raise the whelp,
grown tall and strong, fair-haired and long.
The stocky local clans, shoulders wide,
banded muscles tempered in watered soils.
Let me be driven by the shrouded cliffs
where mist hides grumbling surfs,
that tumble on craggy beach,
before a stony cottage door.
Or mighty Abbey perched above,
where stone steps echo the tread,
and laboured breath of one Saint Ced.
I long to run where the North Wind blows.

By Matthew Tyndale.

CPSIA information can be obtained
at www.ICGtesting.com
Printed in the USA
BVHW081003140820
586401BV00001B/19